Praise for *In the Bleak Midwinter*

"Terrific action scenes . . . what really distinguishes *In the Bleak Midwinter,* however, is the author's skillful portrayal of her protagonist's inner conflict."
—*The Washington Post Book World*

"One of the most impressive 'first' crime novels I've read. A priest, a cop, a baby on the doorstep, and a lot of snow combined with suspenseful results for one great book." —Charlaine Harris, *New York Times* bestselling author of the Sookie Stackhouse series

"Atmospheric . . . A freshly conc   unit."
                                                                Book Review

Praise for

"Spencer-Fleming's second cozy-cum-thriller . . .   veting as her first . . . with eloquent exposition and natural dialogue, the precisely constructed plot moves effortlessly to its dramatic conclusion."
—*Publishers Weekly* (starred review)

"The plot is complicated, and the ethical issues are even thornier. Wisely, Spencer-Fleming treats them with the same delicacy she extends to Clare's forbidden love."
—*The New York Times Book Review*

Praise for *Out of the Deep I Cry*

"The third and most densely textured mystery in a series by Julia Spencer-Fleming brings new airs and graces to the traditional small-town mystery. . . . Yes, this is a very small town, but under Spencer-Fleming's grave and tender touch it becomes a world that you want to visit and hate to leave."
—*The New York Times Book Review*

"Triumphant . . . The author expertly portrays the power of grief, guilt, greed, and love, and their effect on good people in a story as chilling as the month of March in Millers Kill. A subtle sense of humor further enhances this poignant and provocative mystery." —*Publishers Weekly* (starred review)

"This is the author's best story yet . . . presented with the flair and polish of the finest artisan. . . . The ending is enough to make the hardest heart melt."
—*Chicago Sun-Times*

"This is a surefire winner. . . . This series, as intelligent as it is enthralling, just keeps getting better."   —*Booklist* (starred review)

"An absolute tour de force! Both a superb murder mystery and a gripping examination of the suffering of returning soldiers."
                                   —Louise Penny, *New York Times* bestselling author

A FOUNTAIN
FILLED WITH BLOOD

~

JULIA SPENCER-FLEMING

MINOTAUR BOOKS

A THOMAS DUNNE BOOK

NEW YORK

A THOMAS DUNNE BOOK FOR MINOTAUR BOOKS.
An imprint of St. Martin's Publishing Group.

A FOUNTAIN FILLED WITH BLOOD. Copyright © 2003 by Julia Spencer-Fleming. All rights reserved. Printed in the United States of America. For information, address St. Martin's Press, 175 Fifth Avenue, New York, N.Y. 10010.

www.thomasdunnebooks.com
www.minotaurbooks.com

ISBN 978-1-250-00782-7 (paperback)
ISBN 978-1-4299-0906-8 (e-book)

Originally published in the United States in April 2003 by Minotaur Books

St. Martin's Paperbacks edition (mass market edition): April 2004

First Minotaur Books trade paperback edition: July 2012

10 9 8 7 6 5 4 3 2 1

We will meet, but we will miss him
There will be his vacant chair
We will linger to caress him
While we breathe our evening prayer

—Henry J. Washburn and George F. Root

ACKNOWLEDGMENTS

I would like to first thank my husband, Ross Hugo-Vidal, without whom, literally, this book could not have been written. Thanks to my thoughtful readers, Roxanne Eflin, Mary Weyer, and my mother, Lois Fleming. Thanks to my perspicacious editor, Ruth Cavin, and my inestimable agent, Jimmy Vines. Thanks to everyone who helped me with the details, especially my father, John Fleming, who let me fly his helicopter; Rachael Burns Hunsinger, for information on PCBs in the Hudson River Valley; Lt. Col. Les Smith (USA, Ret.), who taught me about falling; and the staff and clergy of St. Luke's Cathedral, Portland, Maine, who continue to inspire me.

Finally, thanks to all the readers I met through e-mail or signings or at book group conference calls. This book exists because of you.

There is a fountain filled with blood drawn from Emmanuel's veins;
And sinners plunged beneath that flood lose all their guilty stains.
Lose all their guilty stains, lose all their guilty stains;
And sinners plunged beneath that flood lose all their guilty stains.

The dying thief rejoiced to see that fountain in his day;
And there have I, though vile as he, washed all my sins away.
Washed all my sins away, washed all my sins away;
And there have I, though vile as he, washed all my sins away.

Dear dying Lamb, Thy precious blood shall never lose its power
Till all the ransomed church of God be saved, to sin no more.
Be saved, to sin no more, be saved, to sin no more;
Till all ransomed church of God be saved, to sin no more.

E'er since, by faith, I was the stream Thy flowing wounds supply,
Redeeming love has been my theme, and shall be till I die.
And shall be till I die, and shall be till I die;
Redeeming love has been my theme, and shall be till I die.

Then in a nobler, sweeter song, I'll sing Thy power to save,
When this poor lisping, stammering tongue lies silent in the grave.
Lies silent in the grave, lies silent in the grave;
When this poor lisping, stammering tongue lies silent in the grave.

—WILLIAM COWPER, in *Conyer's Collections of Psalms and Hymns*

A FOUNTAIN
FILLED WITH BLOOD

CHAPTER ONE

The yahoos came by just after the dinner party broke up. A few young punks—three or four, picked out as streaks of white in the cab and bed of an unremarkable-looking pickup. Emil Dvorak was tucking a bottle of wine under his arm and reaching to shake his hosts' hands when he heard the horn haloowing down the Five Mile Road like a redneck hunting cry, and the truck flashed into view of the inn's floodlights.

"Faggots!" several voices screamed. "Burn in hell!" More obscene slurs were swallowed up in the night as the truck continued past. From their run in the back, the inn's dogs began barking in response, high-pitched and excited.

"Goddamn it," Ron Handler said.

"Did you see the license plate this time?" Stephen Obrowski asked.

His partner shook his head. "Too fast. Too dark."

"Has this happened before?" Emil shifted the bottle under his other arm. The inn's outdoor spotlight left him feeling suddenly exposed, his car brilliantly illuminated, his hosts' faces clearly visible, as his must have been. His hand, he noticed, was damp. "Have you reported it?"

"It started a couple of weeks ago," Steve said. "Probably kids let out of high school."

"Released from county jail, more likely," Ron said.

"We've told the police. The inn's on the random-patrol list now."

"Not that that helps," Ron said. "The cops have better things to do than catch gay-bashers out cruising for a good time. The only reason we got a few drive-bys in a patrol car is that the inn is bringing in the precious *turista* dollar."

"Tourism keeps Millers Kill afloat," Emil said, "but Chief Van Alstyne's a good man. He wouldn't tolerate that trash, no matter what business they were targeting."

"I better call the station and let them know we've been harassed again.

Thank God our guests have already retired." Ron squeezed Emil's upper arm. "Thanks for coming. I'm sorry the evening had to end on such a sour note." He disappeared behind the inn's ornate double door.

Steve peered up the road. "Are you going to be okay getting back home? I don't like the idea of you all alone on the road with those thugs out there."

Emil spread his arms. "Look at me. I'm a middle-aged guy driving a Chrysler with M.D. plates. What could be more mainstream?" He dropped his hand on Steve's shoulder and shook him slightly. "I'll be fine. Anyone comes after me, I'll break his head open with this fine Chardonnay."

"Don't you dare. That bottle's worth more than you on the open market."

Emil laughed as they made their good-nights. Tucking the bottle under the passenger seat of his Le Baron convertible, he considered putting the top back up. He sighed. He knew he was getting old when a couple of drunken kids yelling out of the darkness could make him this nervous. To hell with them. It wasn't worth a twenty-minute struggle with the roof or missing fresh air blowing around him on a hot June night.

The high-Victorian architecture of the inn dwindled behind him as he drove east on Five Mile Road. He turned right onto Route 121, two country lanes bordered on one side by Millers Kill, the river that gave the town its name, and by dairy farms and cornfields on the other. In the dark of the new moon, the maples and sycamores lining the sides of the road were simply shades of gray on black, so the round outline of his headlights, picking out the violent green of the summer leaves, made him think of scuba diving in the Caribbean, black blinkers around his peripheral vision, gloom and color ahead.

Twin blurs of red and white darted into view, and for a second his mind saw coral fish. He blinked, and they resolved themselves into rear lights. Backing into the road, slewing sidewise. Christ! He slammed on his brakes and instinctively jerked the wheel to the right, knowing a heartbeat too late that was wrong, wrong, wrong as the car sawed around in a swooping tail-forward circle and crunched to a stop with a jolt that whipsawed Dvorak's head from the steering wheel to his seat.

The smell of the Chardonnay was everywhere, sickening in its excess. Steve would kill him for breaking that bottle. His ears rang. He drew a deep breath and caught it, stopped by the ache in his chest. Contusion from the shoulder restraint. He touched the back of his neck. Probably cervical strain, as well. Behind him, some awful hip-hop nonsong thumped over a gaggle of voices. He turned off the engine. Better go see if anyone needed any medical attention before he took down the driver's insurance and sued him into next week. The idiot.

A door thumped shut at the same time he heard the hard flat *thwack* of shoes or boots hitting the macadam. Glass crunched. "Look what we got!" A young man's voice, taut with excitement. "We caught us a faggot!" Another thump, more crunching, several whoops almost drowning out the stifling beat of the bass. Dvorak's hand froze on the door handle. The idiot. He was the idiot. He lunged for his cell phone, had the power on, and actually hit a nine and a one before the blow hit across his forearm, tumbling the phone from his grasp and making him gasp from the flaring pain. A long arm reached down to scoop the phone off the passenger seat.

There were hands on his jacket, tugging him sideways, and he watched as the cell phone arced through the edge of his headlights into the thick young corn. "Queerbait! You like to suck dick? You like little boys?" He twisted against the hands, groping for his car keys, his heart beating twice as fast as the sullen song, thinking he could still get out of this, still get away, until one of them hit him in the temple hard; *supraorbital fracture*, the part of him that could never stop being a doctor thought as his vision grayed and the key ring jingled out of reach.

In front of him, the headlights illuminated a swath of achingly green corn, cut off from the shoulder of the road by a sagging fence of barbed wire twisted around rough posts. His door was yanked open, and he wanted to think of Paul, to think of his children, but the only thing in his head was how the fence looked like the one on the cover of *Time*, like the one Matthew Shepard died on, and he was going to die now, too, and it was going to hurt more than anything.

"C'mere, faggot," one of them said as he was dragged from his seat. And the pain began.

CHAPTER TWO

"T his stuff is going to kill us all!"

"Why are we having this meeting? This problem was supposed to have been resolved back in 'seventy-seven."

"I want to know if my grandchildren are safe!"

The mayor of Millers Kill squeezed the microphone base as if he could choke off the rising babel with one hand. "People, please. Please! Let's try to keep some sense of order here! I know it's hot and I know you're worried. Skiff and I will answer your questions the best we can. Meanwhile, sit down, raise your hand, and wait your turn." Jim Cameron glared at his constituents until the more excitable ones grudgingly lowered themselves back into their overly warm metal folding chairs.

The Reverend Clare Fergusson, priest of St. Alban's Episcopal Church, slid sideways an inch in her own chair. She had come to her first aldermen's meeting with the nursing director of the Millers Kill Infirmary, and though she was glad for the expert commentary, Paul Foubert was a good six four and close to three hundred pounds. Not only did he spread across his undersized chair onto hers but he also radiated heat. She pulled at her clerical collar in a useless attempt to loosen it. She was sitting next to a giant hot-water bottle on the last and stickiest night of June. In a meeting that had already gone on an hour longer than planned.

"Yes. The chair recognizes Everett Daniels."

A gangly, balding man stood up. "Back in 'seventy-six when they started making such a flap about PCBs, we were told we didn't have anything to worry about because we were upstream from the factories in Fort Edward and Hudson Falls where they used the stuff. Are you telling us it's now migrating up the Hudson and into Millers Kill?"

"They did find elevated levels of PCBs in our river, Everett. Obviously, water doesn't flow backward. But we are awful close to the core contamination sites, and our river joins up with the Hudson just a couple miles

5

from where we're sitting. The DEP folks don't know yet if the stuff is coming into the Kill from the wetlands or groundwater or what."

A woman's voice cracked through the air. "Why don't you tell the truth? The stuff is coming from that damn storage dump we allowed in the quarry back in nineteen seventy! And that new resort development is bringing up the chemical and letting it run straight downhill into town land!"

"Mrs. Van Alstyne, I asked that everyone raise a hand to be recognized!"

Clare jerked in her seat. The only Van Alstyne she knew in town was Russ Van Alstyne, the chief of police. His wife, Linda, was supposed to be gorgeous. Clare made a futile swipe at the damp pieces of hair that had fallen out of her twist and craned her neck for a better view.

A woman in her early seventies stood, sturdy as a fireplug and so short, her tightly permed white hair barely cleared the heads of the people sitting around her. Clare tried to see around the people sitting near the woman. She couldn't see anyone who could be Linda Van Alstyne.

"I was saying it back in 'seventy and I'll say it now: Allowing that PCB dump was a big mistake. They said it was airtight and leakproof and they waved a chunk of money in front of the town council until the aldermen rolled over and said yes. Then they put the blasted thing in the old shale quarry, even though a high school geology teacher, which you were at the time, Jim Cameron, could have told them shale was a highly permeable rock!" She turned her head to address her neighbors. "That means it leaks!"

"I protested against it, too, Mrs. Van Alstyne," the mayor said.

Clare's mental fog cleared away. That wasn't Russ's wife. "It's his mother," she said under her breath. Paul Foubert looked at her curiously. She felt her cheeks grow warmer.

"The state cleaned up that site in 'seventy-nine," Mayor Cameron continued. "Last tests show traces of PCB in the quarry, but they're at acceptable levels."

"Of course they are! The blasted stuff leaked away into the bedrock. Now along comes BWI Development and gives us the same song and dance, this time promising lots of money from the tourists and lots of jobs, and what does the Planning Board do? Roll over and hand 'em a permit to start plowing and blasting over fifty acres of Landry property. It's been three months they've been working, and suddenly we find PCBs in the Dewitt Elementary playground. This stuff causes cancer, and it's in our playground!"

"Can we just stop the hysterics and stick to the facts!" An angular blond woman stood near the front row. In contrast to the Wednesday-night casual dress of the rest of the crowd, her suit was so sharply cut, it looked bullet-proof. "Before we ever started construction, we had to get a permit from the state Department of Environmental Protection. It took them two years to grant it. Two years! They tested the quarry. They tested the water. They tested the damn trees, for all I know. The PCBs are at acceptable levels at the resort site. *Acceptable. Levels.* There may be more of the stuff in the river, but there's no reason to act as if my property is some sort of Love Canal!"

"Damn it, Peggy, will you just wait your turn!"

She rounded on the mayor. "I came here tonight because I was told there was a motion to suspend construction due to the so-called PCB crisis." She pointed toward the aldermen's table. "My property was certified by the DEP. I have provided you with their environmental-impact state-ments, which, if you bother to read them, clearly say the development is within parameters approved by New York State. I have also provided you with copies of our zoning approval and our construction permits. Which documents you, gentlemen, issued only six months ago!"

The mayor turned away from the microphone and leaned over the wide wooden table. The four aldermen shoved in closer to hear whatever it was he was saying. They were shuffling papers like blackjack dealers. Clare nudged Paul. "Who's the woman?" she whispered.

"Peggy Landry. She owns a huge chunk of land northwest of the town. She's been trying to develop it for years, but she never had the wherewithal to do anything more than plow a few roads in. The only money she made off it came from paintball groups and back-to-nature nuts. You know, people who scoff at amenities like toilets, showers, or cleared land for pitch-ing tents." He rolled his eyes. "She got a group out of Baltimore interested in the parcel a year or so ago. Before you came. They do spas, luxury resorts, that sort of thing. It was big news at the time because of the prospect of jobs for the town, of course. I didn't realize they had already—"

Jim Cameron straightened up. "Application papers of Landry Properties, Inc., and BWI Development, a limited partnership," he read from a sheaf of papers in his hand. "Okay, Peggy, the town isn't going to suspend your con-struction permits." Several in the crowd yelled angrily at this. Several others cheered. The mayor frowned. "Keep it down! Look, our lawyer tells us we don't have the authority to stop properly permitted projects unless the state rules they are, in fact, violating DEP standards."

"What about the possible release of more contaminants by the development?" Mrs. Van Alstyne asked. "How much of that poison is stored in the rock, waiting to be let out when they start blasting? Anything they let loose is going to wash straight down the mountain and into the town and the river!"

"Who's going to pay for the cleanup?" someone asked from the crowd. "Seems like the Landrys will be making a pretty penny and we'll be left holding the bill."

Jim Cameron held up his hands. "People, if we can't stick to the rules of order, I'm calling this whole meeting off!"

A man stood up next to Peggy Landry, who was glaring at Mrs. Van Alstyne with enough venom to have caused a lesser woman to collapse back into her seat. "Mr. Mayor? May I say a few words?"

The mayor looked pathetically grateful that someone was recognizing *Robert's Rules.* "Yes. The chair recognizes . . ."

"Bill Ingraham. BWI Development." Cameron gestured to him to continue. Ingraham was thickly set, of middle height and middle years, with the sunburnt skin of someone who spends a lot of time outdoors. He looked more like a plumbing contractor than the developer of a luxury spa to Clare's eye, but then, she had never really met any luxury-spa developers. "My partner and I—stand up, John, and let the folks here get a look at you." A smartly dressed corporate type stood, waved unenthusiastically, and vanished back into his seat. "John and I are here to create a new resort, the best cross between the old Adirondack mountain retreats and an up-to-the-minute health spa. We want to build this because we think it'll make us a whole lot of money." There was a snort of laughter, quickly stifled, from the crowd. "I also think it'll make your town a whole lot of money, because we see this as a destination resort, not a place to stay overnight while your visitor heads over to Saratoga during the day. This is gonna mean money spent in your town and jobs for people who live here, year-round jobs, because this is gonna be a year-round resort." There was a scattering of applause across the town hall. "John and I are putting our money where our mouth is in more ways than one. We're sponsoring the Fourth of July road race this year, and we've got plans for a ski meet at one of the local mountains this winter. Eventually, we want to support a special event in each of the four seasons." He rubbed his hands together theatrically. "Give those tourists a little incentive to get into town and loosen their purse strings."

There was even more laughter than there had been applause. Ingraham paused for a moment, then went on. "I like this area. Don't want to see it polluted any more than you do. And I'll be frank with you. Our budget for the Algonquin Waters Resort and Spa does not include the costs of coming into compliance with the DEP. We had a run-in with them once before, when we were cocontractors on a Georgia project that had PCB contamination. We're still paying folks to dig sludge down there. It was a total loss. Now, we bought into this project based on the work Peggy had already done with the permits. So here's how we're gonna handle it. If you all want to call in the state to retest our site because PCB levels have been rising several miles away, go ahead. But if the ruling goes against us, we're shutting down. In my experience, once the government gets its teeth into things, it doesn't let go until you've gotten a spot cleaner than it ever was originally. We don't have the time or money to spend the next ten years chasing down stray leaks."

"What?" Peggy Landry turned to Ingraham, clutching his arm. "You can't—" The rest of what she had to say was lost as she sat down, hauling him down with her.

"Huh. It'll certainly spoil her plans if the deal falls through," Paul said. He shook his head. "Being an Adirondack land baron just isn't what it used to be." Throughout the room, rule-abiding citizens waved their hands in the air and rule-ignoring ones called out questions.

Out of the corner of her eye, Clare caught the movement of the big double door swinging open. A tall man in a brown-and-tan uniform slipped through. He paused by the door, unobtrusive despite his size, and scanned the crowd. Clare quickly looked back at the front of the room, where a redhead in a nurse's jacket was talking about the health effects of PCBs. Clare had seen Russ Van Alstyne rarely, and mostly from a distance, since last December, when they had first struck up a friendship while unraveling the mystery surrounding an infant abandoned on the steps of St. Alban's. It had been so easy to talk and laugh and just be herself with him, without worrying about that man-woman thing, because, after all, he was married. Very married, as she had told her church secretary. It still smarted that she had been so completely unaware of her own emotions all the while. She had been Saul on the road to Damascus, oblivious until a moment's revelation struck her and she realized she had fallen for him but good. It was embarrassing, that's what it was. It was embarrassing and something she was going to *get over.*

When Clare glanced back at him, he was looking straight at her. Even from across the room, she could see the summer-sky blue of his eyes glinting beneath his glasses. Her face heated up as he continued to look at her, his thin lips quirking into something like a smile. She pasted a pleasant expression on her face and gave him a small wave. He glanced next to her, frowned, and then looked back at her. He pointed and mouthed something. What? She shrugged. He pointed again, more emphatically. She raised her eyebrows and jerked a thumb toward Paul Foubert, who was absorbed in whatever the nurse was saying. Russ nodded.

"I think Russ Van Alstyne wants to speak with you," she said.

"Hmm? The chief? Where? I didn't know he was at this meeting."

"He wasn't. Wednesday's his regular patrol night. He's just come in."

"You know his schedule?" Paul looked at her, bemused.

"I'm good with schedules. Natural gift. Go on."

Paul rose with a groan. "Probably one of the Alzheimer's patients wandered off again."

Clare resisted the urge to follow the nursing home director, although she was unable to keep herself from swiveling around to see what was happening. Russ looked serious. Grim. Washed-out beneath the fluorescent lights, despite his tan. He removed his steel-rimmed glasses when Paul reached him, then took hold of the larger man's shoulder, drawing him close. A thread of unease coiled through Clare's stomach, then tightened sickeningly as Paul abruptly twisted away from Russ and sagged against the wall.

By the time Russ caught her eye again, she was out of her chair and excusing herself as she made her way down the crowded aisle. He urgently jerked his head in a summons. Paul was leaning on the town-hall bulletin board, his face turned toward a pink paper announcing summer dump hours, his huge fists clenched and shaking.

"What is it?" she said quietly. "What's wrong?"

"Emil," Paul said. "Attacked."

She looked up at Russ. "I don't think I've met Emil before."

He put his glasses on. "Emil Dvorak. Our medical examiner." His thin lips flattened. "A friend of mine. He was found a while ago on Route One Twenty-one. Looks like his car hit something and went off the road." Russ pinched the bridge of his nose beneath his glasses. "He was attacked. Beaten bad. He's in the Glens Falls Hospital right now." He tilted his head toward Paul. "Emil is Paul's, um, friend."

"Dear God." Clare pressed her hand against Paul's shoulder, then moved closer, draping her other arm across his back. "Oh, Paul, I'm so sorry. I'm so sorry." She had known Paul lived with someone, but he had never mentioned anyone by name in their conversations at the nursing home. She looked at Russ. "We came to the meeting together. I'll take him to the hospital."

"I can get there. I'm okay," Paul said in a reedy voice, an oddly small sound coming from such a big man. Clare's heart ached. He straightened up and looked around as if he had never seen the town hall before.

"No. Clare's right. You shouldn't try to drive, Paul." Russ ran his hand through his shaggy brown hair. "I have to stop at the station." He looked down at Clare. "Can you find the Glens Falls Hospital?" She nodded. "Okay, I'll meet you there."

Russ held the door open for them as Clare steered Paul out of the meeting room. Despite the hot air rolling off the street below, she shivered as she caught Russ's last, whispered direction: "Hurry."

CHAPTER THREE

The whirling red lights of Russ's squad car made a strobe effect with the blazing blue ambulance lights as he pulled into the emergency bay at the Glens Falls Hospital. He parked in the spot marked RESERVED FOR PO-LICE and left the relative cool of his cruiser for the oppressive weight of an impending thunderstorm. He strode across the blacktop and was almost to the ER's doors when they hissed open and Clare tumbled out, hair flying away from her knot, her face drawn so that her high cheekbones and sharp nose stood out in stark relief. Her mouth opened when she saw him.

"It's you. Thank heavens." She grabbed the sleeve of his uniform and dragged him away from the doors. "It's bad. They're prepping Dr. Dvorak for a life flight to Albany."

"Jesum. They couldn't transfer him by ambulance?"

"No. Brain trauma. I couldn't understand half of what the doctor was saying to Paul, but from what I gathered, every minute counts. It was awful in there, Russ. They weren't going to let Paul go in the helicopter because he wasn't a spouse or a blood relative. What a stupid, bureaucratic waste of time. . . ." She pulled a hank of hair off her neck, twisted it viciously, and shoved it back into her knot. "Paul is just . . . well, you can imagine. Oh, I got so mad. I told them if he couldn't go in their helicopter I would rent one and fly him myself. Jackasses."

Russ grinned in spite of himself. "Can you afford to rent a helicopter?"

"No." She looked up at him and grinned back. "But I think they were so taken aback at the idea of the flying priest that it inspired them to come up with another solution. Turns out Paul and Emil have medical power of at-torney for each other, and we got a copy faxed over from the Washington County Hospital." She glanced back at the ER's doors. "I've got to go get the car. He's going to be ready to transport in just a minute, and I'm driving Paul. They land the helo at the West Glens Falls fire station's parking lot, and I haven't the faintest idea where it is. If I don't follow the ambulance,

I'll get lost for sure." She laid her hand on his forearm. "You will come, won't you?"

He had a bizarre urge to take her hand in both of his and kiss it. He squelched the notion, nodding instead. "Yeah. Absolutely. You get your car and I'll follow you." She flashed him another smile and jogged off toward the parking lot, her long black skirt flapping around her ankles. How the hell did she manage to be so damn pleasant and open and normal, when he felt like a seventeen-year-old around her? Ever since he had crossed that line last December, he had pretty much avoided her, on the theory that his feelings must be middle-aged idiocy and absence would make the heart grow indifferent. It hadn't worked that he could tell. Spotting her in the park, running into her at the IGA, or even driving past the rectory made his chest squeeze and the back of his throat ache. Maybe this would be better, to go on as friends, ignoring that other thing. Hell, maybe if he acted normal, he'd come to feel normal, too.

A blast of noise and movement swung his attention back to the entrance to the ER. Two EMTs, a doctor, and a nurse were moving a gurney in a carefully controlled frenzy through the bay, heading toward the open doors of the waiting ambulance. Between the bodies surrounding him, Russ could catch glimpses of Emil's face. He winced. Christ. "Careful! Keep those lines clear!" the doctor said, levering himself into the ambulance as the EMTs maneuvered Emil, strapped to a spine board, from the gurney to the ambulance bed. The nurse passed over the IV bag she was holding above her head and scrambled up into her seat.

The doors into the ER hissed open again and Paul emerged, accompanied by another nurse. On his face was the look Russ knew from Vietnam—the face of someone who has just seen his buddy blown away beside him. A mix of shock, fear, and terrible comprehension. "Paul!" he called out. The oversized man looked up. "Clare's gone to get her car. I'll follow you to the airport." Paul nodded, as if speech was too much of an effort right then.

One EMT had finished strapping Emil in and was jumping out of the back of the ambulance when Clare screeched in behind the wheel of her little white-and-red Shelby Cobra. She waved to Paul, who lumbered over and squeezed himself into the tiny passenger seat. The EMT slammed and sealed the door and dashed to the cab of the ambulance. It began moving before the cab door had swung shut.

Russ and the ambulance both kept their lights flashing all the way to the fire station. He couldn't shake the image of Emil's ground-meat face. They had never been more than professional friends—he had precious few real friends for someone who had come back to his hometown, Russ realized—but in the five years he had headed up the department, he had spent a lot of time with Emil Dvorak—in the ME's office, at the hospital, in courthouse hallways. He thought about the pathologist's razor-sharp wit, his orderly office, full of thick books and opera CDs, his addiction to Sunday-morning political debates. The damage to that fragile brain when Emil's skull had been pounded again and again—bile rose in Russ's throat, threatening to choke him. He followed the ambulance across the intersection and into the fire station's parking lot. Lights blazed from the station bays, burnishing the garaged fire trucks and emergency vehicles, glittering off the blaze-reflective strips on the life-flight helicopter, which was hunkered down in the middle of the asphalt. Several firefighters stood inside their bays, watching. He followed Clare's car to the farthest corner of the lot, where the firefighters' cars were parked.

The life-flight team—a paramedic, a nurse, and a pilot—jogged over to the ambulance to help the EMTs off-load Emil on his spine board. Clare leaped from her driver's seat and paused while Paul wriggled his way out of the passenger side. Russ joined them, a little apart from the medical team, which was carefully transferring Emil into the helicopter.

"Paul," he said, "I wanted to ask you—what was Emil doing tonight?" One of the nurses hoisted the IV high as they smoothly lifted the board into the belly of the chopper. "Do you know where he was? Who he was with?"

Paul kept his gaze fixed on the figure disappearing into the helicopter. He rubbed his hands up and down, up and down along the seam of his shorts. "He had dinner with some friends of ours. Stephen Obrowski and Ron Handler. At their bed-and-breakfast, the Stuyvesant Inn. He was going to come straight home. . . ." his voice trailed off.

"Okay. Thanks. I'll be talking with them tomorrow. We're going to get whoever did this." Russ knew that was cold comfort when measured against Emil's broken body in the helicopter. Paul looked at him, his eyes wide and red-rimmed.

"Paul," Clare said, "it's time. The pilot's going to warm up the engines now."

The pilot had been tying down straps by the door and didn't look as if he was headed for the cockpit, but Clare was the one who had flown these monsters in the army, not Russ, so he walked with them to the open door. Sure enough, the pilot disappeared, and a second later, he heard the unpleasant whine of turbines kicking in.

Paul stepped forward. Stopped. "The dogs," he said to Clare. "Did I ask you about taking care of the dogs?"

"You did." She rubbed his arm. "First thing tomorrow, I'll collect them and take them to the kennel. Don't worry about them."

"C'mon, sir," the paramedic said, jumping from the chopper. "Time to go." He held out a helmet to Paul and helped the big man strap it on correctly, then pointed out the stepping bar and straps where Paul could climb up into an empty jump seat. The IV bag trembled where it hung from a hook in the ceiling and the flight suit–clad nurse bent over Emil to adjust something.

Paul turned toward Clare, his brown hair and beard sticking out improbably from beneath the helmet. "Clare," he said too loudly, "I've never been one for religion, but Emil is Catholic . . . he was . . ."

Clare stepped close and spoke directly to his face, enabling Paul to see her lips moving, an aid to hearing inside the bulky helmet. "I'll pray for him," she said in a normal tone of voice. "I'll pray for both of you." She squeezed his hand. "Don't be afraid or embarrassed to reach out to God the Comforter if you feel the urge. You can always go back to being an agnostic after Emil is well. I won't tell on you."

"Sir, we have to go!" The EMT beckoned Paul urgently. Paul hoisted himself into the belly of the chopper as Clare and Russ backed away. Above them, the rotors began to circle slowly, then faster and faster, until the hard-edged chop of the blades challenged the turbines' whine. Clare stopped in front of the nose of the ambulance. The hair fallen from her knot danced in the updraft, strands the color of honey, caramel, and maple syrup. Russ was caught by the look on her face.

"You miss this, don't you?" he yelled over the noise. She shrugged, never taking her eyes from the helicopter. He could feel the vibrations through the soles of his shoes. Looking inside the cockpit, he saw the outline of the pilot, dimmed and warped behind the reflective smoke-colored Plexiglas. The beat of the rotors increased to a sound he still heard sometimes in nightmares. And then the skids left the ground, bumped, rose, hovering half a foot off the parking lot, and the chopper was away, its fat insect body rising smoothly and improbably into the darkness over Glens Falls.

They both looked up into the sky. A freshening wind sprang up, and from the mountains Russ could hear a distant rumble. "Is it safe for them to fly with a storm coming on?" he asked her.

"Mmm. They're headed south, in front of the leading edge. They'll stay ahead of it with no problem." Another gust sent a scrap of paper skittering across the asphalt. "Feels good, doesn't it?"

"I hate helicopters," he said.

She looked at him with surprise. Over her shoulder, there was a tapping from the ambulance windshield and the driver leaned out of his window. "Would you folks mind stepping out of the way? I've got to get back to the hospital. My shift's just starting."

Russ and Clare retreated to their parked cars. Russ waved as the ambulance pulled away.

"You hate helicopters, the machines, or you hate riding in them?" Clare asked, crossing her arms over her wilted black blouse.

"I don't know. Both, I guess. I had a bad experience in one." His brain caught up with his eyeballs. "Shit! I wanted to talk to the doctor! 'Scuse my French."

"I was listening while he spoke with Paul. I think I got the gist of things. Dr. Dvorak has a lot of fractured ribs, a fractured skull, internal bleeding. . . . It sounds like someone kicked the crap out of him." She glanced up at him. "Excuse my French. What happened to him? Why on earth would anyone try to murder the county's pathologist?"

He shook his head. "That may be it right there. He's been our medical examiner for ten years now. I don't think he was ever involved in a capital case, but I'm sure he's had a hand in sending lots of men to Comstock. Maybe he gave evidence against someone's brother or buddy. Maybe someone he put away has been released without managing to rehabilitate himself into a model citizen."

Clare glowered at him. "Don't start in with that. If we made more services available to support prisoners—" She huffed and waved her hands. "Never mind. That scenario seems a little far-fetched. I mean, suppose you were this guy, just released and slavering for vengeance?"

" 'Slavering'?"

She ignored him. "Would you go after the medical examiner who gave some of the evidence first? Or would you go after the prosecuting attorney, or the arresting officers, or even your own attorney first?"

"Well, you know how I feel about lawyers. I'd definitely go for them first." She whacked his arm. "No, I know. Point well taken. There's another possibility. His car was in an accident, not bad enough to cause his injuries, but enough to give everyone involved a good smack. Maybe the other driver went ballistic. Cut loose on him."

"Road rage run amok?"

"It happens."

She worried her lower lip. "Could it have been personal? Someone he knew?"

He nodded. "In most assaults and homicides, the victim and the perpetrator know each other. That's why I asked Paul about where Emil had been." He ran his hand through his hair. "I don't know. There are too many possibilities right now. I don't like that. The only thing we know for sure is that the vehicle he hit was red. We got some paint scraping on his left-front fender."

"We know he wasn't robbed."

He raised his eyebrows.

"One of the nurses gave Paul Dr. Dvorak's belongings—clothes and stuff. He had a very expensive watch and a wallet full of credit cards. Untouched."

"I almost wish he had been robbed. We're going to have some good prints off Emil's car, but they're not going to do us any good if whoever did this hasn't been arrested before." Thunder rumbled, closer and louder than before. He glanced up. Heavy clouds had moved in, their underbellies reflecting a faint sodium glow from the lights of Glens Falls. "Time to go. You can follow me back to Millers Kill if you need to."

She reached into the pocket of her skirt and pulled out her keys. "I need to." He watched her get into that ridiculous mosquito of a car. Another impractical sports car, and a convertible to boot. He shook his head. She had slipped, slid, and stuck in her old MG last winter, finally wrecking the thing trying to drive through a snowstorm on Tenant's Mountain. He had assumed that would have taught her to buy a sensible four-wheel-drive vehicle. He had assumed wrong.

As he climbed into his cruiser, it struck him that he didn't feel like a hormonal teenager anymore. He felt . . . pleasant. Friendly. He had enjoyed Clare's company without making an idiot of himself. He reached for the mike to let dispatch know his destination. He was going to work out this friendship thing after all.

CHAPTER FOUR

Thursday morning, Clare woke early with the sound of helicopter rotors in her mind. She ran through the tree-lined streets of her neighborhood as the sun was rising, looping east to return along Route 117, parallel to Riverside Park and the abandoned nineteenth-century mills. A short run on Thursdays, so she could shower and be ready for the 7:00 A.M. weekday service of Morning Prayer. It was one of her favorites: cheerful and intimate, with the same five or six faces showing up regularly. Since Memorial Day weekend a month back, the size of her Sunday-morning congregation had dropped like a stone through water. She was lucky if she saw thirty faces at the ten o'clock Eucharist. But she could rely on her Morning Prayer people, and no matter how much turmoil she brought with her, she always found her center in the orderly succession of prayers, psalms, and canticles.

Today, though, she was seized by the thought of Paul and Dr. Dvorak as she and her tiny congregation read the Second Song of Isaiah, the Quaerite Dominum. "'Let the wicked forsake their ways and the evil ones their thoughts; And let them turn to the Lord, and He will have compassion. . . .'" Paul's broken, lost expression. Dvorak's still form at the eye of a whirlwind of activity. "'For my thoughts are not your thoughts, nor your ways my ways, says the Lord.'" She tried to imagine what would lead someone to stomp an unoffending man half to death. It seemed infinitely more vicious, more personally hateful than that American classic, murder by cheap gun. "'So is my word that goes forth from my mouth; it will not return to me empty. . . .'" Sometime during her once-a-week visits to the Millers Kill infirmary, Paul had become her friend, one of the very few people in Millers Kill who didn't look at her and stop when they got to her collar. A man who spent his days caring for the weakest and most vulnerable members of society. His world had collapsed in the space of a few minutes because of—what? Careless malice? Cool calculation? An explosion of anger? "'But it will accomplish that which I have purposed, and prosper in that for which I sent it.'" She wanted to know. She wanted to know why. And who. Was it a monster? She didn't believe in monsters. She believed in redemption. But some days, it was awfully hard.

After the service, she checked the calendar. Two premarital counseling sessions today and another three next week. Whoever said Generation X was not interested in marriage hadn't been looking in the Adirondack region. And the MacPherson-Engals wedding rehearsal Friday evening. She underlined that. She left a note for Lois, the church secretary, asking her to contact the organist, and another for the sexton, reminding him to unlock the door by eight o'clock Saturday morning to give the florist time to arrange the wedding flowers. Then she dashed back to the rectory next door and changed into an outfit that compromised between the weather and her customary clerical uniform: a long, loose-fitting shift in black linen, with a collar attached by hand.

Outside, it was promising to be another ninety-degree day, but the storm last night had cleared the air. The light, dry breeze reminded Clare of the best sort of weather at her parents' home in southern Virginia. She had dropped the top of her convertible, and once she had taken care of Paul's dogs, she might have time for a little spin through the countryside before the first of her two counseling sessions that afternoon.

The first hitch in her plans came when she got to Emil and Paul's handsome old farmhouse. For some reason, she had pictured little dogs, Jack Russells or toy poodles perhaps. The pair that bounded out of the attached barn were big. Really big. Big, hairy, bouncing, barking black-and-white Bernese mountain dogs. She turned around and looked at the minuscule backseat, which would have been a snug fit for Jack Russells. She looked back at the dogs, which were excitedly tearing along the limits of an invisible fence. "Oh . . . shoot," she said.

The dogs were ecstatic at meeting her. As she crossed from the driveway onto the lawn, they leapt and wiggled against her, pawing at her ankle-length dress and frantically licking at her hands. "Not exactly standoffish, are you?" she said. They discovered her sandal-clad feet and immediately began licking her toes. "Stop!" she shrieked. "Sit!" They plunked down, looking up at her hopefully, their tails thumping hard against the grass. She fished for their collar tags among handfuls of silky hair. "Okay, Gal and . . . Bob?" The dogs thumped more energetically. "Who names a dog Bob?" She sighed. When he had mentioned the dogs while they were waiting in the emergency room, Paul had said their bowls and leashes were in the barn. "C'mon, then," she said. "Let's get your things. Then we'll try to fit you into my car."

She wound up squeezing Gal, who was the slightly smaller of the two, across the backseat, the dog's head out one side of the car and her tail out the other. Bob sat in the passenger seat, his dinner plate-size paws precariously balanced on the very edge of the smooth leather. Clare's trunk lid barely shut over leashes, bowls, fifty pounds of dog chow, and an assortment of squeaky toys the dogs had brought and dropped in her way while she was loading the car.

The second hitch came at the Clover Kennels. "I'm sorry, Reverend Fergusson," the plump, blond owner said. She vigorously scratched the dogs' heads. "All of our big dog runs are booked up through next week. It's the Fourth of July weekend, and lots of folks are traveling." She crouched, running Gal's floppy ears through her hands and kissing her nose. "And we can't fit these two into anything smaller. You wouldn't be able to move, would you, you sweet thing?" She looked up regretfully at Clare. "There are a couple kennels over to Saratoga, of course, but I'd call first before going over. It's going to be hard to find any spaces this weekend. Maybe some friends could watch them?"

And so Clare found herself taking her spin through the countryside with two hundred pounds of dog packed in the car. The only friends of Paul and Emil she knew of were the two Paul had mentioned last night, the owners of the Stuyvesant Inn. Maybe they would take the dogs off her hands. Bed-and-breakfasts were supposed to have cats or dogs hanging around.

The road to the inn ran along the river—what the early Dutch settlers had called a "kill"—through green shade and sunlight. Falling away from the water, it climbed westward through lush fields of tender-leaved corn and grazing pastures landscaped by Holsteins and Herefords, grass as trim and tight as a broadloom carpet, set off by lichen-mottled rocks and bouquets of thistles and wildflowers. The road rose and dipped, rose and dipped, until it came to a high spot and Clare saw the exuberantly painted inn, a well-maintained fantasy of Carpenter Gothic, with mauve and coral and aqua trimmings. Behind the inn, perennial beds and ornamental trees gave way to a meadow that rolled over the top of a hill and was surmounted by the first in a series of mountains, sea green and smoky in the morning sun. She pulled into the semicircular drive and was not surprised to see a Millers Kill police car already parked in the shade of one of the massive maples sheltering the dooryard.

She had barely pulled the key from the ignition when the dogs bounded out, Gal squashing Clare's shoulder as she squeezed herself from the narrow backseat and over the door. They snuffled around the cars, the trees, and the neatly edged bed of annuals before relieving themselves against an iron hitching post and the rear tire of the squad car. "Gal! Bob! Come!" They fell in behind her as she climbed up to the wide porch and rang the doorbell.

The mahogany door opened a moment later, revealing a gray-haired man with a face as pleasantly rumpled as an unmade bed. "Hello, can I— Why, Bob! And Gal! Hi there!" The dogs abandoned Clare to butt their heads against the man's knees. "Come in, come in," he said, trying to scratch the dogs' heads and offer his hand to Clare at the same time. "I'm Stephen Obrowski." He swung the door wider and stepped back into a wide hallway papered in velvet flock and furnished with chairs and tables that were so ugly, she knew they must be authentic Victoriana.

The dogs pushed past Obrowski, their toenails clicking on the polished wooden floor. "Thank you. I'm Clare Fergusson, the rector at St. Alban's Episcopal Church." She reflexively fingered the clerical collar attached to the neckline of her shift, then noticed that the linen dress now resembled mohair, with great quantities of white dog hair sticking out every which way.

"Please, come on back to the kitchen. We were just talking with Chief Van Alstyne about last night. Poor Emil. It's unbelievable. You read about these things, but when it's someone you know . . ."

Clare followed him down the long hallway, through an alcove formed by a spindle-banistered stairway, and into a kitchen that was mercifully not true to the period. Russ was standing next to a stainless-steel cooking island, polishing his glasses with a tissue. He looked up as they came in, eyes vague and out of focus. An attractive man in his mid-thirties was pouring coffee into chunky ceramic mugs. He had the look of a German skier—lean, tan, blond. She wouldn't be surprised if his name was Hans or Ulf. "This is Ronald Handler, chef extraordinaire. Ron, this is the Reverend Clare Fergusson. And I take it you two know each other?" he said, looking at Russ.

Russ replaced his glasses and tucked the tissue in his pocket. "Yup. What brings you out here, Reverend?"

Before she could open her mouth, the dogs muscled open the door and swarmed into the kitchen, tails whipping like rubber hoses, tongues hanging, mouths drooling. Ron Handler stepped to a curtained door tucked away to the left of a large commercial range. "Gal! Bob! Out!" He opened the door and the Berns galloped out into the sunshine.

"Bob?" Russ said.

"Coffee?" Handler offered, tilting the pot toward Clare.

"Please. So have you found anything new? Do you know what happened last night?"

Obrowski picked up his mug and blew across the steaming surface. "We were just telling the chief. We had a small dinner party last night—just us, Emil, Samuel Marx, and Rick Profitt. Samuel and Rick are staying with us. They're up from New York City."

Handler handed Clare a mug. "They own a travel agency. They send us a ton of business."

"We put it together very spontaneously, because it was a free night in what's otherwise a pretty busy season for us. I don't see how anyone who might have been intending to hurt Emil could have known about it."

Russ shifted his weight. "Your other guests, Marx and Profitt. Did they know Emil beforehand?"

"No," Obrowski said. "And they both retired before Emil left. They didn't even realize we had had a drive-by."

"Maybe Chief Van Alstyne thinks they shimmied down the drainpipe in the rear and went after Emil while we were distracted washing up," Ron said. "Like in one of those British murder mysteries on PBS."

Russ ignored this and continued looking at Obrowski. "Anyone else invited who didn't show? Did you tell any vendors, any delivery people?"

"No. No need. Ron can throw together a five-star meal out of whatever we have in stock." Stephen Obrowski swept his hand toward the chef, who bowed. "We had invited Paul, of course, and our other guest, Bill Ingraham, but they both had to attend the aldermen's meeting instead."

"Bill Ingraham?" Clare said. "The developer?"

"That's right. He's been staying with us at least once a month since this winter." Obrowski pointed at a mullioned window centered over a stainless-steel sink framing a view of the mountains. "The Landry property, where he's working, starts about a mile west of us. As a matter of fact, this house used to be the Landry mansion. The family made their fortune in logging and real estate speculation. Archibald Landry built his own railroad line into Adirondack Park to transport timber and holidaymakers, but the connecting lines that other developers were supposed to build never came through, so his track just petered out in the wilderness." Obrowski took a sip of coffee. "Then a son died in World War One. When the stock market collapsed, it took most of the family money with it. They sold this place in the thirties."

"So this guy Ingraham, he's the one who's building the new hotel?"

"Luxury spa," Obrowski corrected. "Very exciting. It's going to bring in lots of people, lots of money. Lots of traffic past our door."

"And he couldn't make it to your dinner last night."

"He was definitely at the meeting," Clare said. "There was quite a to-do about PCBs in the area maybe coming from the old quarry on the Landry property. He stood up and told everyone what a good thing the spa was going to be, but he said that he wouldn't be building it if the town called in the DEP for another go-round."

"You're kidding! That would be a disaster. Let's hope they don't jump the gun and call in the DEP prematurely. Lots of people are counting on that resort going forward."

"Not the least of whom is that Landry woman." Handler rolled his eyes.

"Oh, cut it out. She's not that bad."

"Joan Crawford on hormone-replacement therapy."

Russ snickered. Clare pressed her lips together, trying not to smile. "How about his partner?" she asked. "Did he stay here, too?"

Handler and Obrowski glanced at each other. "Well . . ." Obrowski said.

"He used to," Handler said.

Obrowski sighed. "They had a big blowup here at the end of May. The kind where Ron and I try to disappear into the woodwork for the duration. We haven't seen him since then."

Clare put her mug down. "But he was at the meeting last night. Mr. Ingraham introduced him."

"He did what?" Handler goggled at her.

"Wait. Wait." Obrowski laughed. "Slightly chunky guy with lots of slicked-back dark hair?"

"Yes, that's the one. John something."

"Opperman. John Opperman." Obrowski grinned at Handler. "She meant his business partner."

"We thought you were referring to the Queen of Tarts," Handler said.

"His girlfriend?"

"His boyfriend."

Russ started. "Ingraham's gay?"

Handler grinned, showing his pointed eyeteeth. "We're everywhere. Scary, isn't it?"

"Cut it out, Ron," Obrowski said.

Russ's cheeks grew pink beneath his tan. "Did Ingraham know Emil?"

"No, not to my knowledge. He hasn't been one for socializing," Obrowski said. "When he stays here, he spends most of his time meeting with subcontractors and tramping around the woods, plotting out the resort and directing what construction they've already started—cutting down trees, plowing roads, that sort of thing. Opperman, his business partner"—he tilted his head toward Clare—"handles the paperwork. He's been up frequently, too, but he stays at one of those concrete-cube chain hotels along the Northway."

"I keep telling you, Steve, if we put up some bad art and wall-to-wall carpeting, we could get that trade, too."

"Ron . . ."

"Maybe if you put in an ice machine down the hall?" Clare offered. Handler looked delighted.

Russ cleared his throat. "Okay, it's unlikely anyone knew Emil was going to be here last night. Which leaves the possibility we were discussing earlier."

Obrowski looked down into his coffee cup. Handler's dazzling smile disappeared, replaced by a wary look in his eyes.

"What?" Clare said. "What?"

"When we were walking Emil out, there was a drive-by." Stephen Obrowski's amiable voice turned hard. "A truck with a bunch of rednecks shouting a lot of homophobic crap. They've been by before a few times, but the worst that's happened so far is a few beer cans chucked on the lawn."

"And they continued east toward Route One Twenty-one?" Russ asked.

"We asked him if he wanted to wait. I was worried about him heading in the same direction as the pickup." Obrowski shook his head. "I wish to God I had insisted. If he had waited until the police arrived, we wouldn't be standing here having this conversation."

Clare looked at Russ.

"They called in a report right after," he said. "We had an officer up to Cossayuharie who came down to check things out. It was when he was headed back into town that he found Emil's car."

"You think it was a hate crime?" Clare put down her coffee mug. "Somebody beat him half to death because he's gay?"

"It's not like it hasn't happened before," Handler said.

"They might not have even known Emil was gay." Obrowski turned toward his partner. "He might have been attacked because he was leaving our inn. Have you thought about that?"

Russ held up his hands. "Let's not speculate too wildly here. We—and by 'we,' I mean law enforcement and the business community—want to be real careful not to start unsubstantiated rumors about a bunch of punks targeting gay-owned businesses. I also don't want to be telling one and all that that this was a gay-bashing episode."

Ron Handler looked outraged. "We're supposed to ignore the fact that we might be killed because of who we are? That our friends and customers might be in danger? That's—"

"That's not what I said." Russ took off his glasses and rubbed them against the front of his shirt, the steel edge clinking faintly when it tapped the badge over his breast pocket. "If you call something a hate crime, you glamorize it. You make assault or vandalism sound like a political statement, and political statements have a way of attracting imitators. I've seen it happen. There's big play in the newspaper about somebody painting a swastika on a bridge, and next thing you know, every asshole in the county with a can of spray paint and pretensions of grandeur is doing the same thing. 'Scuse my French."

"But that's different from what happened to Emil," Clare protested. "It may be vile, but painting a swastika isn't kicking someone into a bloody pulp."

"No, it's not. But right now, our only pieces of evidence are a scrape of red paint on Emil's car and the fact that a pickup truck drove by here a half an hour or so before he was attacked. We can't take those facts and label them a hate crime."

"You don't have to confirm that what happened to Emil Dvorak was definitely a hate crime," Clare said. "But you've got to warn the community that it might be repeated. That another gay man might be attacked. If people know that their friends and neighbors might be at risk, you have a better chance of preventing copycat crimes before they happen."

"Clare, you've got a real uplifting view of humanity, but let's not kid ourselves. If word gets around that someone in Millers Kill might be going after homosexuals, it's more likely to scare everyone away from associating with the potential victims. Let law enforcement take care of this quietly by finding these jerks and slinging their butts in jail. I promise you, that'll get the message across."

"The chief is right," Obrowski said. "Bad publicity, even for a good cause, can kill a business, especially one like ours, which relies on word of mouth."

"So we cower quietly in the closet and wait for the big bad police to save us? Until the next time it happens?" Handler flung his hands over his head and looked at Clare.

"Ron is right," Clare said. "I come from the South, and I can tell you that sitting quietly and not making a fuss didn't do diddly to stop black folks from being vandalized, assaulted, or even killed. It wasn't until those crimes were held up to the light of day that things changed."

"Oh, for God's sake," Russ said. "We're not talking about lynch mobs and Jim Crow laws. It's assault and battery, not a civil rights issue."

"Isn't it?" Handler said.

"What's a more basic right than the right not to be attacked because of who you are?" Clare said.

"Thank you, Reverend King," Russ said. He looked at Stephen. "Look, I've gotten all I need—" A torrent of barking, both deep and high-pitched, erupted from behind the kitchen door, cutting him off. "What the hell?" he said.

CHAPTER FIVE

"T he rat pack is back," Ron said. He held out a hand for Russ's empty mug and thrust it into the sink, twisting the tap on full force.

"We have five Pekingese," Stephen explained over the noise of dogs and running water. "They like to make their rounds in the morning. They were out back in the barn, herding hens. Now it's time for a mid-morning snack; then they all retire to the music room for a nap. They all share one big basket." He walked to the outside door.

Stephen's deliberate high-pitched cheerfulness was the adult version of a kid clapping his hands over his ears, humming, and saying, "I can't hear you!" Clare crossed her arms tightly and exhaled. Ron rolled his eyes and collected the three remaining mugs with a great deal of clattering. Russ opened his mouth, glanced at Clare, and snapped it shut.

"I ought to get going," he said. "Thank you both for your cooperation. I'll, uh, keep you updated."

Clare took a deep, calming breath. "I didn't even get a chance to tell you why I came," she said to Stephen, who was body-blocking the two enormous Berns at the doorway while what looked like a walking carpet swarmed into the kitchen. "I was hoping you two could keep Gal and Bob here at the inn while Paul is in Albany." It was awkward, talking about him as if he were away on a business trip, but she had a strong feeling Stephen didn't want to be reminded of why the dogs were temporary orphans. "The kennel is full up, and the owner said it wasn't likely I'd find—"

"I wish we could," Stephen said. "The Berns are lovely dogs. But having them and our five would be way too much."

"Too much hair, too much barking, and too much missing food," Ron added, taking a box of kibble off a shelf and shaking it into five tiny stainless-steel dog bowls squared against the wall.

"They're very well-behaved dogs," Stephen said, frowning at his partner. He took a firm hold on each Bern's collar and marched them toward the hall door, ignoring their whining and longing looks at the kibble. "I'm sure you won't have any difficulty finding someone to take them in. Or leave them at Paul and Emil's. Someone can drop by once a day with fresh food and water." Clare raised a finger and started to speak. "Not us, unfortunately," Stephen said quickly. "It is our high season, after all. But surely someone can."

No good deed ever goes unpunished. Her grandmother loved that saying. Clare mustered a smile and followed Stephen and the Berns through the front hall to the porch. "It was very nice to meet you, Reverend Fergusson," Ron called after her, emphasizing the *you*. Stephen released the dogs, who galloped to her car and scrabbled over the sides into their former places, leaving visible scratches on the paint.

"See?" Stephen said. "Good dogs."

The porch creaked under the weight of Russ's step. He paused beside her to shake Stephen's hand. "We'll keep an eye on your place," he said. "If you see anything that makes you itchy, anything at all, call nine-one-one."

Stephen nodded. "You can count on that." He took Clare's hand in both of his. "Come back and see us again, Reverend Fergusson. Bring the dogs for a visit."

Clare and Russ trudged down the porch steps in silence. When she reached her car door, she paused. Stephen Obrowski had disappeared into the inn. Russ had gone to the cruiser and was leaning against the driver's side, his hand resting on the open window. He fished into his pocket and pulled out sunglasses, which he clipped over his glasses. It gave him an aura of faceless authority, like every lawman in every movie since *Cool Hand Luke*, and even though they were only clip-ons and should have made him look like a middle-aged tourist, she started to get mad again. She opened her mouth to speak, but Russ beat her to it.

"Before you start in again on how wrong and insensitive I am, let me tell you that I know a place where you can board those two monsters." He flipped the shades up, as if they were little plastic-topped visors, and her incipient tirade turned into a laugh. He removed his glasses and looked at them. "Pretty sharp, huh?" He wiggled the shades. "Prescription bifocal sunglasses are not covered by my health plan. Got these at the Rexall. Six bucks."

"They look it." She glanced at the dogs, who were panting enthusiastically, tongues lolling. "All right, I'll bite. Where can I board these puppies? The county jail? Your house?"

"Sorry, no. Linda is not a pet person. We'll take 'em to my mother's place."

She looked at the dogs again. She hadn't seen much of Russ's mother at the town meeting, but she was willing to bet Gal and Bob outweighed her by at least seventy-five pounds. "Are you sure?" Bob shook his head and saliva sprayed over the windshield of the Shelby. "Wouldn't they do better in the care of some tall, hefty guy named Spud?"

"Trust me. Inside, my mom *is* a tall, hefty guy named Spud." He put his glasses on and flipped the shades down. "Follow me."

"This means I'm going to have to drive the speed limit, doesn't it?"

He grinned.

They drove back across the river and onto Old Route 100, turning away from Millers Kill and heading north into the mountains. The trees crowded in against the edges of the road, which swooped, twisted, and climbed steeply enough to make Clare's ears pop. It would be a great place for a long, hard run, cool in the shade of the trees and undisturbed by much traffic. Of course, if she were to twist her ankle, she'd have a long way to go for help. There wasn't even the occasional dirt drive or mailbox signaling human habitation. She was beginning to think Russ's mother must be either a hermit or a squirrel, but then the forest cover broke apart, and they were at an intersection that might have passed for a tiny town. Strung along the two-lane highway were several sagging Victorian cottages that escaped dilapidation through creative paintwork and an abundance of flower baskets. There was one road leading off to the left, squared by a two-pump gas station, a general store, an antique shop, and an art gallery.

Russ turned. The battered green sign read OLD SACANDAGA ROAD, and Clare wondered if any of the roads in northeastern New York State were new. Less than a hundred feet down the road, Russ turned right into what was either a very small dirt parking lot or a very wide grassy driveway. She pulled in beside his cruiser and got out.

"Good heavens," she said. "Someone shrank Tara!" They were parked next to a perfect Greek Revival mansion in miniature, deeply shaded by towering pines. Tiny second-story windows peeped from underneath a pediment upheld by square columns. More windows ran along the white clapboarded side of the house, each one framed with forest green shutters. "This looks like an oversized playhouse. Is this where you grew up?"

"Nah, my old house is a museum now." She rolled her eyes at him. "No, really!" He laughed. "The people who bought it from my mom sold it to an enterprising couple who turned it into a museum of Indian art. With a gift shop. Actually, the gift shop is bigger than the museum part."

A former school bus, now painted purple and topped with several large rubber rafts, rattled past. HUDSON RAFTING EXPEDITIONS, its hand-painted sign read. The dogs flailed their way out of Clare's car and went into high alert, racing around in circles and barking.

"Bob! Gal! No! Bad dogs!" Clare lunged after them, but they stopped at the sidewalk of their own accord. Across the street was another antique store and a small Presbyterian church that appeared to have been made out of river boulders. The town ended there, sheared off by a leafy-treed gorge. The Old Sacandaga Road crossed a bridge and disappeared into dense forest.

"That's the Hudson down there," Russ said, joining her. "Fast and shallow at this point. There're a lot of rafting companies putting in around here."

"Is it going to be safe for the dogs?"

"Sure." He pointed to the edge of the drive. "Behind those lilac bushes, there's a good strong chain-link fence. I helped Mom put it up myself. And if it turns out these two like chasing cars, she's got a nice fenced yard out back. Mom's used to taking in strays—of every sort. C'mon, I'll introduce you."

He walked toward a white-and-green carriage house set well back from the drive, then vanished between two pines. "Mom?" He reappeared. "She's not out back." He gestured to Clare. "Come on in." He stepped up to a green kitchen door set near the rear of the house and held it open. She climbed the steps, solid blocks of dense gray stone, and went in at his heels.

"Mom?"

Clare could hear a muffled voice from upstairs. "Is that you, sweetie? I'll be right down." The kitchen was cluttered with cooking utensils and shopping bags, and a basket of laundry sat atop a washing machine jammed in the corner. Signs demanding STOP THE DREDGING! jostled library books and stacks of papers on an oilcloth-covered table. An Amnesty International calendar was tacked to a door, and the ancient refrigerator was plastered with bumper stickers exhorting readers to work for peace, seek economic justice, and vote for Hillary Clinton.

"Mom's an old lefty peacenik," Russ explained. "A real tax-and-spend Democrat, just like you."

"I heard that." Russ's mother appeared in the doorway, looking even more like a fireplug this time in baggy red shorts and a red T-shirt. She reached up and tugged her son's ears, bringing his face down close enough to kiss. "Remember, my taxes pay your salary, sonny boy."

"Then I want a raise. Mom, this is Clare Fergusson. Clare, this is my mom."

Russ's mother had a firm, no-nonsense handshake. Clare wasn't surprised. "How do you do, Mrs. Van Alstyne."

"Call me Margy." She waved in the direction of Clare's collar. "Now, what's that? You a minister?"

"A priest. I'm the rector of St. Alban's Episcopal Church in Millers Kill."

"Well!" Margy Van Alstyne smiled, revealing teeth so uniform, they must have been dentures. "It's about time! A woman priest. Are there many of you?"

"Quite a few, actually. The Episcopal church started ordaining women in 1976. When I graduated from seminary last year, close to half my class were women."

"Don't that beat all! You always want to be a priest? You look to be a few good years out of high school, if you know what I mean."

"Mom . . ."

Clare suppressed a smile. "I just turned thirty-five. And no, my call came later, as it does for a lot of people. I was an army pilot before I went into the seminary."

"So you worked for the war industry but came to your senses!" She darted a glance at her son. "What rank were you?"

"I was a captain when I resigned."

"Ha!" Margy Van Alstyne's elbow caught Russ in the solar plexus. "She outranks you, son! Finally, a woman who can boss you around!"

"Every woman in my life bosses me around," he muttered, rubbing his stomach.

Clare started to laugh.

"You don't do crafts, do you? Make little things with yarn and twigs? Sew a lot?"

"No, ma'am. I don't know how to sew. I like to cook, though."

"Cooking's okay. I hate crafts. You can't walk into a person's house today without tripping over handwoven baskets and rag dolls covering up toilet paper or some such nonsense. I like you." She turned to her son. "I like her."

"I thought you would."

"So what are you doing here? You just come out to introduce me to this nice young lady? Or you after something?"

"I'm after something. Did you ever meet Emil Dvorak, our medical examiner?" Margy shook her head. "He's kind of a friend of mine. Last night, someone beat him up pretty bad. He was airlifted down to Albany."

"Good Lord." Margy pressed her fingers flat against her lips. "You catch who did it?"

"Not yet. I will." Russ replied. Margy nodded. "Anyway, his, um, roommate went down with him, and they left behind two dogs. Clare's helping them out by trying to find a place to board the beasts." He crossed to the door and opened it. Bob and Gal, lying in the shade of one of the pines, looked up. Their tails began thumping as Clare and Margy walked out.

"I hate to impose," Clare said. "When I told Paul I'd see to the dogs, I thought I'd simply have them boarded for a few days. But the kennel I spoke with said there's no room because of the holiday weekend." She couldn't keep a pleading look off her face. "I'd keep them at the rectory with me, but I have an unfenced yard on a fairly busy street. They'd have to be indoors unless I was there. And I keep weird hours."

"Well, don't they look sweet." Margy clapped her hands and the Berns rose, shook off pine needles and grass clippings, and trotted over. "Of course I'll have 'em here. What are their names?"

"Gal and Bob. They're Bernese mountain dogs."

The dogs snuffled at Margy's hands. "Bob? Who names a dog Bob?"

"That's what I thought. I've got their bowls and toys and a sack of food in my trunk."

"Russ can fetch those. Russell?"

"Yes, ma'am." He held out his hand to Clare. "Keys?"

"Oh, it's unlocked."

He shook his head. "Of course. Of course it is."

"He thinks I should be more careful about locking up the rectory and my car," Clare explained as Russ toted the fifty-pound sack of dog chow into the backyard.

"He's prob'ly right. He usually is about these things."

"I know. I guess I just feel that if someone is desperate enough to steal what I might have, he needs it more than I do anyway."

The dogs frisked around Russ, trying to snatch the toys out of his arms.

He flung them into the backyard, and Bob and Gal fell onto the rubber bones and squeaky ducks with abandon. He dusted off his hands and returned to the stone steps. "I'm on duty, Mom, so I'd better be heading back. I'll see you at the parade on Sunday. Got roped into driving the squad car again this year." He looked at Clare. "You want to follow me into town?"

His mother grabbed his ears again and kissed him. "Don't be a stranger, sweetie. And keep yourself safe! There're a lot of crazies out on a holiday weekend."

"Don't I know it. Bye, Mom. Thanks."

"Thank you so much for looking after the dogs, Mrs.—Margy. Please give me a call if you need me to sit them or take them for a while. I'm in the phone book." She extended her hand, only to be pulled off balance by Mrs. Van Alstyne's hug. "I don't shake hands," Margy said. "I like to give folks a squeeze." The old woman felt plump and sturdy and smelled of Elizabeth Arden's Blue Grass powder. "I'll have Russ bring you up here for dinner sometime soon. You can cook."

Clare laughed. "Okay, we'll do that."

As Clare slid behind the Shelby's steering wheel, Margy disappeared around the back. She could hear a cacophony of joyous barking. "Your mom's really something. Not quite what I expected."

Russ leaned against the door of his cruiser, facing her. "Mom's like the Spanish Inquisition in that old Monty Python skit."

"'Nobody expects the Spanish Inquisition!'" they both quoted. He laughed.

"I really am grateful to her. Now I can tell Paul the dogs are well taken care of."

"You gonna call him?"

"I'm not sure how to reach him. I gave him my number and asked him to call me. Of course, I haven't heard anything yet."

"Well, the hospital should update me on the situation at some point. I'll let you know what's happening."

"Why would the hospital . . ." He watched her as the answer came to her. "Oh. If Emil dies, it'll be a murder investigation." He jerked his chin in assent. She compressed her lips for a moment, and they both fell silent. Finally, she asked, "Do you have any leads?"

"Not any worth jack-all. We lifted prints but didn't get any matches. Paint flakes that are the most common red used by Chevrolet. Our best bet right now is finding a red Chevy vehicle that's recently gotten some damage. I've got Noble checking out all the area body shops and auto-parts stores this morning."

"That's it?"

"That's it. It's not like *Law & Order*—we don't always find the bad guy before the second commercial."

"Russ . . ." She paused. "What if Ron Handler was right? What if it is a hate crime?"

"I sure as hell hope it isn't." He sighed and pinched the bridge of his nose. "You know the real difference between an ordinary assault, if I can call it that, and a hate crime? The ordinary perpetrator is beating up on an individual. He's mad, he acts on his feelings, and then he's done with it. The perp attacking a victim because of the group he's in . . ." He sighed. "He might not stop until he's run out of people to hate."

CHAPTER SIX

O kay, so you won't forget that you're going to pick up the candles and bring them over to Mom and Dad's house."

"I thought I was supposed to take them to the church."

"No, Todd, you're driving Aunt Sue and Uncle Bill to the church, and you've got to be there no later than eleven-thirty! You've got to have those candles at Mom and Dad's in time for the florist to pick them up to take them to the church!"

"How come I can't just take them to the florist's and—" A rising screech cut him off. "Never mind. Never mind. I'll have the candles to Mom by seven o'clock."

"In the morning."

"Of course in the morning! You know, there wasn't nearly this much fuss when Tim got married. All I had to do was find a jacket and get there on time."

"That's because Tim's a man. I've been dreaming about this day ever since I was a little girl! Everything is going to be perfect. It's going to be a total fantasy come true."

"Yeah, well, that's what Princess Di thought."

"Todd! That's awful!" Her voice softened. "Someday you'll meet someone—you know, someone special—and you'll understand."

"Yeah? Well . . . maybe. Look, I gotta run. It's almost closing time, and the store's a mess."

"I love you, Oddball."

"I love you, too, Fish Face. I'll see you tomorrow."

"With the candles!"

"With the candles."

Todd MacPherson understood the power of fantasy. He had viewed every single one of the movies for sale or rent in his video store, and, just like when he was a kid, they still had the power to sweep him away into another world, where people were better-looking, danger was an aphrodisiac, and problems could be solved in a two-hour running time.

His own problems were more intractable. As he methodically reshelved the returns and straightened racks jumbled by the usual Friday-evening rush of renters, he considered where he was going after closing up shop. Supposing, that is, he didn't just crawl home and collapse in front of the tube. There was a little hole-in-the-wall bar in Hudson Falls, but he knew every guy who would be there on a Friday night, and he couldn't stomach the thought of the same complaints and conversations he had heard a hundred times before. There was a bigger, more open place in Saratoga, where he might see some new faces, but that meant a forty-minute drive each way, an awfully late night when he had to be bright-eyed and bushy-tailed the next morning for Trisha's wedding. And to be perfectly honest with himself, he had never yet come up lucky there. The guys who paired off there were lean and tan and knew how to wear sweaters tied around their shoulders, if they looked rich, or military gear, if they looked sexy. Todd's wardrobe consisted of jeans that bagged in the wrong way and T-shirts sporting old movie posters and film festival schedules.

He wiped a dusty copy of *The Green Berets* on his jeans and reshelved it in the John Wayne section. His best friend, Janine, had moved to New York City four years ago, after getting an associate's degree at Adirondack Community College. Now she was working as a gofer in Rockefeller Center, hanging lights for Off-Off-Broadway productions, and taking the occasional film class at NYU. Every weekend, she called and ordered him to get the hell out of Millers Kill and come share an apartment with her. They had both been teens from another planet in high school, completely unable to fit in with the kids around them. They'd been alternately tormented and ignored because if it. But now Janine had a whole circle of friends and was dating some aspiring playwright, while he was still a geek—a celibate geek.

He picked up a copy of *Truly Madly Deeply* off the floor and examined Alan Rickman's face. He thought he sort of resembled Alan Rickman, younger, of course, and with longer hair. Those snotty Saratoga summer boys just never got close enough to notice. He tossed the video in his hand. Maybe he wouldn't go out anywhere. Maybe he'd stay a little late and put together an Alan Rickman display on his film-festival shelf.

The bell over the door tinkled, and he heard blended voices, yelping laughter. Sounded like Nintendo customers, here to pick up a weekend's worth of bloody shoot-outs and pneumatically breasted women. That was the crux of his problem, the store. He had sunk so much time and money into it, and it was starting to do good business. Better than good. He had turned a profit the last two years. The loan officer at his bank loved him. How was he supposed to chuck it all on the chance that he might find something better in the city? What if he never found anything better? What if this was as good as it got?

"Hey, man, you got any Jujubes?"

Todd shelved *Truly Madly Deeply* under *T* and slid through the narrow aisle to the checkout counter. Two guys his own age lounged in front of the candy display, one of them leafing through this month's *Cinemagic* magazine. They wore low-slung, wide-legged jeans cropped at the shins and backward-facing baseball caps, which made them look, in Todd's opinion, like morons. "Didn't see any there?" He glanced at the rack. "Hang on—I got some more in the back. If you guys are checking anything out, Friday's our three-for-two special. Rent any two, get the third for free. Limit on one new release only."

The Jujube guy grinned. "Hell yes, we're checking something out." He swaggered toward Todd, leading with his pelvis, looking him up and down. It was an overt, exaggeratedly sexual gesture, which made the hair on the back of Todd's neck rise. He licked his upper lip and glanced at the other guy, who still leaned against the counter, flipping the magazine's pages, opening and closing the cover so that Patrick Stewart appeared and disappeared between flashes of the other guy's smirking face. Todd had been beaten up too many times in high school not to recognize what these guys wanted.

"We heard you got something special in the back room," Jujube guy said. He was close enough that Todd could feel the heat and excitement radiating off his body. "Some special movies."

Patrick Stewart appeared and disappeared, his face grave. Todd thought he might be saying that he should beam the hell out of this scene.

"Like those old gladiator flicks," the guy with the magazine said. "Except for grown-ups."

"So, whaddaya say?" Jujube guy reached both arms over his head and cracked his back. "Gonna show us some of that gay-bo porn? I always wondered how guys do guys."

"I'd rather see chicks on chicks myself," the other guy said.

"That ain't gay, asshole. You can see that in any porn flick. You're missin' the point."

Todd backed away slowly, keeping his trembling arms relaxed, forcing his face into an unalarmed expression. He thought he might throw up at any moment. "Sorry to disappoint you, but I don't carry any X-rated stock. There's a convenience store outside Fort Henry that rents videos; they have a small selection." If he could get to the back room, he could lock the door and call the cops. "Let me grab you those Jujubes and I can show you the address in the phone—" His words were choked off as an arm circled around his neck, clamping him tightly against an unseen chest. Oh, sweet God, there had been a third one in the store and he hadn't even realized. He flailed against the man behind him, kicking backward, clawing at his head.

"Ow! Help me with this pussy, you assholes!"

Jujube guy punched Todd in the stomach, and he lunched forward, retching. The man behind him let go of his neck, clenching his hair in a fist and twisting one arm behind his back. Todd cried out. His wrist was forced higher, wrenching every joint in his arm. Todd bowed forward, straining on tiptoe to loosen the grip that was forcing his muscles and tendons to their limits, but the fist in his hair held him tightly against his invisible tormentor as he vibrated between pain and pain. "I got money in my cash register," he said, his voice reedy and desperate. "Please, just take it. Take whatever you want and go. Please." The last word cracked.

Todd felt a hard tug as his hair was yanked upward once, twice. "You really got me there with some of those kicks, pussy," the unseen man behind him said. "Now I gotta hurt you bad."

"Hey, man, let's get the money. It's no fancy electronic safe system or nothing. He's probably got a wad of cash in there."

"Shut up," the man behind Todd said. "You know the deal. Nothin' gets taken."

"How's he gonna know?"

"No. Now put the goddamn magazine down and help me with this fag."

The last thing Todd thought, in the moment before all his thoughts were wiped away, was how businesslike they sounded. Like in *Pulp Fiction*. Nothing personal. Nothing personal. Nothing—

CHAPTER SEVEN

In her dream, Clare was floating in an inner tube on an emerald green pond. It was kind of like her special place in the woods near her parents' home, except the water was bathtub-warm and there was much more open sky above her, the light dazzling through her closed eyelids. The tube spun slowly, her hair and feet trailing through the water, and then a man surfaced at her side and she saw with delight that it was Russ Van Alstyne. He floated close, smiling, and then his hands were running along her body, warm and liquid as the water. She noticed that she was naked. How wonderful. A car alarm went off on the distant shore, but she ignored it, watching his face and his hands, flowing from relaxation into a sweet tension. The car alarm was louder, annoying her. She worried that it might be her car. She fought to focus on the tingling sensations in her body, but the shrill was too . . . damn . . . loud. She woke with a sideways lurch across her bed, the phone ringing on her nightstand, sunshine splashing over her tangled sheets.

"Good Lord," she said. She could feel her cheeks coloring. She took a deep breath and snagged the phone. "Hello?"

"Reverend Fergusson?" It sounded like a girl, trying not to cry.

"Yeah. I mean, yes, this is Clare Fergusson."

"It's me, Trisha MacPherson." MacPherson. As in MacPherson and Engels, the celebration of Holy Matrimony, twelve o'clock this afternoon. "I'm afraid . . . I'm afraid we're going to have to cancel the wedding." The girl's voice was choked with tears. Clare rubbed her eyes and tried to focus. Trisha's fiancé must have dumped her. During their three sessions of premarital counseling, Clare had thought he looked shifty. A little too eager to please. The weasel.

"Trisha, I'm so sorry." Clare sat up in bed, pulling herself away from the green, green pond and into the here and now. "I know it seems like the end of the world at this moment, but when someone breaks off an engagement, it's a realistic reflection that they're not ready to—"

"Nobody broke off the engagement!" Outrage tightened Trisha MacPherson's voice. "Kurt is here with me right now. It's my brother Todd. He was beaten up last night. He was hurt very . . ."

Trisha's voice was replaced by a young man's. "Reverend Fergusson?"

Clare was wide-awake now, the floating world drowned in cold shock. "Kurtis? What's up?"

"Trish's brother Todd was assaulted in his video store last night. His brother Tim went looking for him this morning when we couldn't raise him at home . . . found him unconscious and called an ambulance. We're all at the Glens Falls Hospital right now."

"How is he doing?"

"It's pretty bad. They're taking him in right now for a ruptured spleen. There may be kidney and liver damage, too."

Clare tilted her clock toward her. Eight-thirty. "I'll be there in forty-five minutes."

"Oh, thanks, Reverend. I know Trish's family aren't churchgoers, but I think they could use . . . we could all use some extra . . ." he foundered. "Thanks."

There are no agnostics in foxholes, she thought after hanging up, and I'm meeting a lot of folks in foxholes lately. She had to call the sexton and the organist to let them know the wedding was off, have someone at the church to help guests who wouldn't hear the news in time, tell the florist—oh, no, no wedding flowers meant someone on the floral committee would have to whip up a quick arrangement for Sunday. . . . Despite the whirl of practical details, she couldn't keep from wondering: Was it a terrible coincidence that Millers Kill had seen two violent attacks in the space of two days? Or was there some connection between Trisha's brother's assault and what had happened to Emil Dvorak?

◆ ◆ ◆

The surgery waiting room was full of anxious MacPhersons. The bride-to-be was curled up on a sofa in the corner, clutching her mother's hands. The groom rubbed the back of his fiancée's neck, while the father of the bride sat four-square and straight-backed, leafing through a two-year-old copy of *Field & Stream*. Half of the low artificial-leather chairs were occupied by people Clare had seen yesterday evening at the rehearsal. Some were watching a CNN anchor report on a possible pilots' strike; others were paging restlessly through magazines. The best man stood with his back to the wall-mounted television, talking into a cell phone in a low voice. Everyone looked up as Clare entered, then let out a collective breath of relief or disappointment.

Clare crossed to Trisha and her family, expressed her condolences, and sat down to listen to whatever they needed to say. She again heard from Kurt how Todd had been found unconscious in his store earlier that morning. Trish told Clare about her brother's errand to deliver candles. She heard about what a sweet, inoffensive, good boy he was from Mrs. MacPherson. Mr. MacPherson grunted something about a shotgun being better than insurance. She approached the brother who'd found Todd, a soft-spoken young man named Tim, who kept glancing worriedly at his obviously pregnant wife. Clare had to draw his story out in a backward spiral, first talking about canceling the caterer, then about speaking with the police at the scene, and finally about finding his brother's battered body. "I can't tell them," he said, looking at his parents and sister. "They only saw him prepped for surgery, cleaned up and covered by sheets." His eyes teared up. "But, oh God, I can't stop thinking about what he looked like."

After an hour or so, a doctor came in with a report from the surgical team. They had removed Todd's spleen. His liver was undamaged. There might be a problem with his kidney functions later on, but they would simply have to wait and see. They were closing up now and the surgeon would come in with more news soon. Yes, there was no question he would survive—he was young and healthy and should make a good recovery.

The atmosphere lightened after that, and when the door opened again, everyone looked up with expressions of bright expectation, but instead of a surgeon, they saw a cop. His short-sleeved uniform shirt was tucked into jeans, and he was wearing sneakers instead of shiny brown shoes. Clare guessed she was the only person in the room who knew he was normally off duty on Saturday morning. He caught sight of her and raised his eyebrows in surprise. "Mr. and Mrs. MacPherson? I'm Russ Van Alstyne, the chief of police."

Todd's parents stood up, Mrs. MacPherson clinging to her husband's arm. "You find the bastards who did this?" Mr. MacPherson asked. "It was a robbery, wasn't it? I told that boy he needed real protection. Cash business like that. Bound to attract attention."

"We don't know who assaulted your son yet, sir. We've taken prints, and hopefully that will lead us somewhere. One of my officers is interviewing neighboring business owners to find out if anyone saw anything." He looked around. "Is Tim MacPherson here? The one who found him?"

The brother stepped forward. "That's me, sir."

"You use a key to get into the store?"

"No, sir. The lights were off and the CLOSED sign was hanging on the door, but the door was unlocked. I told the officer who showed up after I called."

Russ nodded. "That's what he said. Just checking. Sometimes people remember more after they've had a chance to get over the initial shock." He took off his glasses and pinched the bridge of his nose. "It doesn't appear to have been a robbery. The till is full of cash and credit-card slips. It looks like whoever assaulted Todd either grabbed him outside before he had a chance to lock the door or did it inside the store and turned off the lights before leaving." He replaced his glasses. "We found a ring of keys hanging on a hook in the back of a shelf beneath the cash register."

"That's where Todd kept his keys," Trisha said. "I spoke with him on the phone maybe ten minutes before ten. He said something about cleaning up the mess in the store."

"I'm thinking if someone got to him while he was locking the door, they wouldn't have put his keys away in exactly the right place," Russ said. "I think whoever did this went into the store, maybe right at closing time, and I think they were looking for Todd." He ran his hand through his hair. "Do any of you know of anyone who might have wanted to hurt him?"

The MacPhersons looked at one another. Something moved between them, a message or a collective memory. "No," Tim said. "Not really."

"Not really?"

"Well . . ." Mrs. MacPherson hesitated. "Todd used to have trouble back when he was in school. He was one of those kids who attracts the attention of bullies. He got beaten up a few times. We reported—I reported every instance to the principal. Some kids got suspended as a result."

"For Chrissakes, Cathy, he finished school six years ago. Todd's a grown man now. Nobody's going to go after him because his Mommy got them suspended." Mr. MacPherson shook his wife's arm free. "Goddamn it, none of this would have happened if he had learned how to defend himself like I wanted. If you hadn't stopped me from teaching him how to fight—"

"Dad, Todd was never going to be like that." Tim's even voice sharpened to a hard point. "Give it a rest."

Russ glanced at Clare, then back at the family. "Is Todd gay?"

"No!" Mr. MacPherson said immediately.

There was another collective moment. Mrs. MacPherson glanced at her husband. "Yes," she said. Russ looked at Trisha and Tim. They both nodded.

Russ exhaled. "Okay. Thanks."

"Do you think that's it? That's the reason Todd was hurt? Because he's . . ." Mrs. MacPherson pressed her lips together in a tight line. Her eyes filled with tears.

"There was no theft, no vandalism. . . . Did Todd sell drugs? Smuggle cigarettes from Canada? Was he a heavy bettor?"

"No!" Mrs. MacPherson said. "Todd's not like that. He works incredibly hard at his store. He's doing a lot better than so many people his age."

Tim shifted and scratched the back of his neck. "He did, you know, smoke pot sometimes." He shrugged at his mother's expression. "Sorry, Mom, but he did."

"Smoking a few joints isn't what I had in mind." Russ's eyes flickered toward Clare, and she caught a glimpse of amusement before he looked back at the MacPhersons. "We're going to investigate every possible angle in order to find out who did this, then put them away for a good long time. Mrs. MacPherson, if you and your kids could give me a list of those boys who were expelled back when Todd was in school, I'd appreciate it."

He pulled out a small notebook and pen from his shirt pocket. Mrs. MacPherson pursed her lips thoughtfully. "Well, there was Andy Poccala." She looked at her other children as if for confirmation. Tim and Trisha nodded. Clare slipped away while Russ collected what information he could from the MacPhersons.

Mr. MacPherson was standing, his shoulders rolled forward in the posture of a usually erect man too tired to stand straight. He was staring with apparent fascination at a CNN reporter interviewing a movie star who was gushing with happiness over her new—and fifth—husband.

Clare drifted next to Mr. MacPherson and came to a parade rest, staring at the screen. "We are totally in love!" the improbably youthful actress was saying. "I'm so totally happy!" Clare waited.

"Your church," Mr. MacPherson said suddenly. "Do they do anything to help boys like Todd. Any programs?"

"Help him? How?"

"You know. When a boy is confused. Help him see that he can be a perfectly normal man. It's all conditioning; that's what I've read. You just have to help them make the right connections." He broke his gaze away from the television screen and looked at Clare. His eyes had a desperate quality to them. "I know he could stop being . . . *that way* if he just had some support. Like AA." He shot a bitter look at the rest of his family, who were clustered around Russ. "They're no help."

Clare took a moment before answering. "I have heard of those programs. Attempting to convert homosexuals to heterosexuality. St. Alban's—and the Episcopal church in general—doesn't do anything like that, no. And from what I understand, the groups that do have a very poor long-term success rate." She touched his sleeve lightly. "I do believe there's a much higher level of success in support groups that help parents come to grips with their kids' sexual orientations."

His eyes sparked, hot and hard. "He's just had the crap beaten out of him because of what he is. Why the hell should I accept that?"

"Because he's just had the crap beaten out of him for being what he is. If he could have changed himself, don't you think he would have?"

"I just want my kid to be normal. Is that so bad? They can fix anything in your head these days, between the drugs and the therapy. Why not fix this?"

"Mr. MacPherson," she said, "what sort of counseling or drug could make you turn from a heterosexual to a homosexual?"

He looked at her, and she could see that she hadn't reached him at all. She sighed and turned back to where Russ was finishing up with the other MacPhersons. He reached into his pocket and pulled out three business cards. "If you think of anything, even if you're not sure it has any relationship, even if you think we already know it, give us a call." He gestured toward the door. "I'm going to be back later, when Todd is awake. I'll interview him. If we're lucky, he'll be able to identify his attackers, and all the rest of this will be moot. I'll see you all then." He shook hands with Mrs. MacPherson and Tim. "Thanks for all your cooperation. Reverend Fergusson, can I see you outside for a moment?"

As soon as the door to the waiting room closed behind them, they turned to each other. "What are you doing here?" Russ said.

"Why didn't you tell them about Emil Dvorak?" Clare asked at the same time.

"I didn't—" he began as she said, "They were—" They both took a breath.

"Why don't you—" they both said.

Russ put his hands on her shoulders and gave her a small shake. "You first. Why are you here with Todd MacPherson's family? Do you know him?"

"I was supposed to marry his sister, Trisha MacPherson, and Kurt Engels this afternoon."

"Ouch. That's gotta be tough. Do they belong to your church?"

"No. I didn't know them before I did their premarital counseling. If you want to get married in Millers Kill in a beautiful old church, your choices are St. Alban's, First Presbyterian, or High Street Baptist. Dr. McFeely at First Presbyterian wants engaged couples to have some connection to his parish, and Reverend Inman wants to be assured they haven't been sleeping together before the ceremony. So. I do a pretty brisk business. My turn. Why didn't you tell them this is the second episode of gay-bashing in four days?"

"Because my thinking hasn't changed on this. I don't want to start rumors that someone is going around attacking gays, or gay-owned businesses."

"That is completely irresponsible! You can't possibly believe that this is a coincidence!" Her voice rose on the last word. He took her upper arm and dragged her a few steps down the hallway, away from the waiting room.

"I don't believe in coincidence. But starting a panic about who might or might not be next in line for a visit from the heterosexual hit men isn't going to serve any purpose other than to scare a lot of people and give the town a bad name."

"It could alert potential victims to take precautions. It could bring in more information to help you find the perps." He gave her a one-sided smile. She ignored it. "It could tell people to keep their eyes on gay-owned businesses for suspicious activities. If Todd MacPherson had known there was a chance he was going to be attacked because of his sexual orientation, there's a good chance we'd all be getting ready for a wedding right now, instead of waiting for him to get out of surgery." She tucked her hair behind her ears.

"One," he said, counting off on his fingers, "there wasn't any pattern of attacks until after MacPherson was beaten up. So there wasn't anything for him to know. Two, we've already briefed the *Post-Star* on Emil's attack. Our take was that an area doctor was rammed and mugged while he was out driving in his convertible. We asked for anyone with information on a red vehicle with new damage to the body to call us."

"That makes it sound like he was robbed. If people read the words *doctor* and *convertible,* ninety-nine percent of them are going to assume he was rich."

"Fine. I don't mind scaring rich people. They already take precautions against attack." He ticked off a third finger. "Three, like I said when we were at the inn, if word gets out that someone might be targeting gay-owned operations, it's likely to cost the owners business. Even if there are good-hearted neighbors around to keep watch, customers are going to stay away. It's my job to protect Millers Kill and Fort Henry and Cossayuharie. Some businesses make half their yearly income between Memorial and Labor Day. I'm not going to hurt them if I can help it."

She leaned against the smooth, cool wall. "Now you sound like the mayor in *Jaws.* Don't yell 'shark,' 'cause it'll hurt business."

"If I thought I could catch who's responsible for these attacks by closing down the town, I would. But singling out certain businesses or individuals and telling them they may be next won't do that."

"But you might prevent another person from being hurt!"

"Look, the take on MacPherson's attack is going to be that a small-business owner, closing up all alone, was assaulted. There's going to be a statement from me in the *Post-Star* urging all businesses to take extra precautions at closing time. The population around here doubles in the summer, and God knows what sort of lowlifes come floating in for the carny rides in Lake George and the fake rodeos in Lake Luzerne."

"Is that who you think is behind this? Some rednecks from out of town, up here for a little fresh mountain air and blood sports?"

He sighed. "It could be. The timing certainly suggests so." He pushed his hand through his hair, causing it to fall unevenly across his forehead. "If it is, it should be easier to spot the red vehicle. You can't just garage your car and drive another one when you're on vacation."

"Russ, I can understand your concern about singling out businesses as potential trouble spots. And I can understand you not wanting Millers Kill to be associated with this sort of vicious behavior. But if you don't let it be known that you believe gays are being targeted, you're keeping individuals from being able to protect themselves."

"I'm keeping them from being singled out. This is a small town, Clare. How many homosexuals do you think are out of the closet here? Every guy with a high voice and every woman with cropped hair and no makeup will suddenly be a source of speculation. Or worse, a potential target for any homophobe reading the paper who thinks, 'That's a good idea! I'm gonna get me a faggot!' " He leaned against the wall. "Let them stay safely hidden."

"That's bull."

He straightened up and looked at her, raising his eyebrows. *"What?"*

"You heard me. Bull. It's that sort of attitude that allows homophobia to flourish. 'They're different. They're not like us. We don't know any. Don't ask, don't tell.' " She pushed away from the wall and pulled her hair back in both hands, twisting it. "I saw the same sort of crap in the army. Force people to hide who and what they are and then act surprised that you've created a culture where it's okay to make fag jokes and harass people who act 'funny.' How do you convince Joe Six-Pack that being gay's not a fate worse than death when it is a fate worse than death if you're found out?"

"Clare, I'm trying to solve a pair of assault cases here. I'm sorry, but eradicating prejudice and stupidity are beyond the scope of my job. As is reforming the U.S. Army."

She exhaled. "I'm not asking you to do that. Sometimes I get a little . . . global when a problem gets under my skin." She glanced up at him. "I still think you're making a mistake."

"I respect your opinion. But this is a real short chain of command here. I'm the cop and you're the priest, and what I say goes. Period. I want you to promise me that you aren't going to run to the *Post-Star* or preach your next sermon on the possible connection between Emil and MacPherson."

She frowned and crossed her arms.

"Promise me—"

"All right. I promise. But I swear, if there's one more incident, I'm going to organize a Take Back the Night march and start it right at the front steps of the police station."

"Don't worry. If there's one more incident, the press is going to be all over this like a hog on slop, and then everybody will be weighing in with their opinion." He pushed away from the wall and began strolling toward the elevator doors at the end of the surgery unit. Clare fell into step beside him. "However," he added, "there's not going to be another incident if I can help it. Every man on the force, full- or part-time, is on duty this weekend."

"Is that because of these assaults, or because it's the Fourth?"

"Everyone's usually on duty for at least part of the Fourth. The road race tomorrow will suck up a lot of manpower. Then there are parties and barbecues. . . . I can guarantee you that before the fireworks go off, we'll have handled a dozen domestic fights, three car accidents, at least one kid doing something incredibly stupid with a bottle rocket, and somebody who's gotten drunk and fallen into the Kill." He stopped at the elevators. "You coming or staying?"

"I'm staying with the family until Todd's out of surgery."

He punched the down button. "Every one of my men is gonna be briefed on this and on the alert for anything suspicious. Not to mention looking for a red vehicle with impact damage."

The elevator chimed. The door opened and Russ entered, waving a half salute at Clare.

"Speaking of prejudice," she said.

"Huh?" He caught the edge of the door before it closed.

"How come there aren't any women on the police force?"

The last thing she saw of him were his eyes, rolling back in his head.

CHAPTER EIGHT

"Great day for a race, huh, Chief? Gosh, I love the Fourth of July."

Russ looked over at Kevin Flynn, who was standing with his hands on his hips beside their cruiser, eyeing the crowd of runners and spectators filling the park. Then he looked up, where heavy-bellied clouds dragged over the mountains and sailed low under a silvery gray sky. He reached through the window to retrieve his windbreaker. "At least we won't have to worry about sunstroke," he said.

A cluster of woman runners walked by him, evidently not worried about the day's unseasonably cool temperatures. They were wearing what looked like neon-colored body paint and shoes that must have cost more than his first car. "Whatever happened to running in baggy shorts and T-shirts?" he asked Kevin.

The juniormost officer was grinning at a trio of giggling girls. Russ pegged them as coeds who had been hiking on the Appalachian Trail, from their chunky boots and serious backpacks. "Huh?" he said without turning away from the girls.

"Never mind. Just wondering when Lycra became the national fabric." On the other hand, he thought, his attention riveted by one woman bending way over to retie her laces, there was something to be said for Lycra. He hadn't seen that much of Linda until after they were married.

The radio crackled inside the cruiser. "Fifteen fifty-seven, this is Dispatch." Harlene, their most experienced dispatcher, had volunteered to work this holiday, even though she would have had it off, due to rotation and seniority. He was grateful. No matter how crazy it got, nothing could flap Harlene.

Tearing his eyes away from the scenery, he leaned in and unhooked the mike. "Dispatch, this is fifteen fifty-seven."

"I wanted to let you know Noble's in position for traffic control by the bridge and Paul is at the intersection of Main and Canal. Kevin's going to stay with you in Riverside Park, right?"

"That's right. It looks like they'll be starting in about fifteen minutes. They're trying to get the runners in position."

"How's it looking?"

Another woman runner paused, frowning, and reached inside her sports bra to redistribute the load. It must have been one of those high-performance sports bras, because it had a lot to contain.

"Everything looks real good here," he said truthfully. "Hey, you heard the latest weather yet?"

"It's supposed to hold off raining until tonight," Harlene said. "I heard from the fire department. They're assuming the fireworks will go on as planned, nine o'clock or so. Whoops! Lyle's on the line; I gotta go. Dispatch out." The radio crackled off.

He replaced the mike. A gust of wind reminded him to shrug on the windbreaker he had been holding. The wind made the banner stretched across the entrance to the park billow like a spinnaker sail. MILLERS KILL THIRD ANNUAL INDEPENDENCE DAY 10K, it read; BWI Development logos were prominently displayed on each side. To call it "annual" was something of an exaggeration, since the first one had taken place five years ago. The event's organizers—a hardcore group of runners who also got up a trip to the New York Marathon every year—had had difficulties finding sponsors over the years. The last race, two years back, had been sponsored by an Adirondack dot-com company that went belly-up six months later. This year, they had latched onto BWI, which was splashing out a lot on the event: big booths piled with free oranges, bananas, and energy bars, fancy bottled water, T-shirts for volunteers and competitors.

Riverside Park was a broad swath of green undulating along a twisty stretch of the river between two now-abandoned mills. When serious construction had begun in the early nineteenth century, some entrepreneur had snatched up the land in the hopes of developing it at a great profit. Unfortunately for him, he had failed to account for the fact that the water-powered mills of the time needed long, straight riverbanks. The land escheated to the town for failure to pay taxes and had been a park ever since. Russ suspected the mill workers who had once picnicked here would have laughed themselves sick at the sight of their descendants crowding together for a chance to run six miles in a circle to get a T-shirt.

BWI had sent some of their construction workers to build a platform stand near the riverbank. The mayor, a few members of the running club, and a well-polished man in a pressed polo shirt and khakis, whom Russ pegged as Ingraham, were taking up the space now. Later on, it would be a stage for local bands to play on until the nine o'clock fireworks—if the rain held off. Russ looked up at the sky again. The wind pushing the storm clouds forward seemed to bring the mountains themselves closer, their color an intense green-blue, the texture of spreading leaf and spiky pine picked out in a way you never saw when the day was hot and sunny.

Kevin Flynn's voice broke into Russ's musing. "Hi, Reverend Fergusson. You running today?"

He looked over the roof of the cruiser. Clare, kitted out in baggy shorts and a ratty gray army T-shirt, was smiling bemusedly at Flynn. "Yes, I am, Officer Flynn. You have a sharp eye." She grinned at Russ. "You ought to get the chief to make you a detective."

"Nah," the oblivious Flynn said. "You have to have more than one year's experience."

"I'm surprised to see you here," Russ said. "It being a Sunday and all."

"I don't think my congregation—all thirty of them who turned up for this morning's Eucharist—will mind. I like to compete once in awhile, especially in the summer. It keeps me from slacking off on those mornings when it feels too hot to run." She shivered as another cool breeze gusted past them. "Not that that's a problem today."

Flynn hitched his belt up, setting his rig jingling. "Say, Reverend, did I see you driving a Shelby Cobra the other day? That's a way cool car."

Clare's face lighted up. "It is, isn't it? I bought it from a man who collects early muscle cars. It's a 'sixty-six, in great condition. Just needed a new carburetor and a little work on the electrical system." Her voice had taken on a faint southern drawl. "I always wanted me a Shelby."

Russ crossed his arms and leaned against the roof of the cruiser. "You should have gotten something heavy, with four-wheel drive. Something that can maneuver in the snow."

Clare and Flynn looked at him. "I'd rather have something I can maneuver on the road," Clare said.

"Yeah," Flynn said. "After all, you can always load some weight in the trunk and put on chains come wintertime. What are the specs?"

"Four hundred fifty-two liters and a V-eight. Let me tell you, that little honey can eat up the road."

"Oh, man, I bet. I've heard they can run at eighty without even opening up the throttle full. That I'd like to see."

"You're not suggesting Reverend Fergusson break the state speed limit, are you, Officer Flynn?"

Kevin looked abashed. "Um," he said.

"Don't pick on the boy, Russ. He has the right idea." She gave Kevin a gleaming smile. "Just because the only thing you think of is—"

"Safety."

She waved a hand in the air, dissipating his word like so much blown smoke. "I am a very safe driver. And you've never had me drive you any- where, so you can't say otherwise. Can you?"

"I've let you drive me crazy," he said. The second it was out of his mouth, he felt the tips of his ears go red. God! What an asinine thing to say!

Clare's cheeks pinked. Her throat moved as she swallowed, but she didn't say anything. His mind raced feverishly for something, anything, to throw out to break the silence, since he was pretty sure the earth wouldn't conveniently open up and swallow him whole.

"Have you heard from Paul Foubert?" he blurted.

She blinked. "No," she said. Then her face brightened. "No!" she re- peated, relief plain in her voice. "Nope, nope, haven't heard from him. How 'bout you?"

"Not since Friday. Emil's serious, but stable. He hasn't woken up yet, so we haven't been able to get any information from him." He felt steadier, although his ears were still burning. "We're still trying to track down the truck involved. Nothing yet. But we've got three county sheriff's depart- ments and the state police looking, so we've cast a pretty wide net. I'm hopeful."

A skinny teenager in a volunteer T-shirt paused while hurrying past them. "Hey, if you're racing today, better get over to the pen," he said to Clare. "They're starting now."

"Gotta go," she said, looking even more relieved. "Wish me luck."

"Break a leg!" Flynn said.

Clare and Russ both looked at him. "Kevin—" Russ began.

Clare cut him off. "Thank you, Officer Flynn," she said. "See you at the finish line." She loped off to join the throng of runners crowded into a rectangular starting area marked off by snapping Tyvek ribbon.

Russ reached beneath his glasses and pinched the bridge of his nose. He had missed the bullet on that one, for sure. "Kevin, I'm going to take a turn around the park and—" The shout of the spectators cut him off as the starting official in front whirled and lowered her flag and the runners surged forward, sprinting out of the park entrance and onto Mill Street. He leaned back into the cruiser and keyed the mike. "Dispatch, this is fifteen fifty-seven."

"Fifteen fifty-seven, I hear you."

"The runners have left the park. Remind the guys on the intersections that we're supposed to get an all clear from one of the race coordinators before letting traffic through again. I don't want to have any stragglers run over."

"Roger that, fifteen fifty-seven. I'll get right on it."

He hung up. "Kevin, I'm going to go show the flag. You stay with the cruiser." He figured as long as the three hiker chicks were hanging around, it would take a major civil emergency to get the young officer to leave his present post, but it didn't hurt to reiterate things where Kevin was concerned.

Russ strolled along the perimeter of the park, seeing and being seen, greeting people he knew by name, his eyes constantly scanning for the off note that would mean trouble. A bushy-bearded man who had been celebrating the Fourth a little too hard. A couple whose argument rose and then fell away as he walked by. A pair of bony-shouldered girls who carefully avoided meeting his gaze. Overall, though, it was an easygoing group. Real trouble would come later, after the runners had left and the bands moved in, after the darkness had fallen and the bottles came out from hiding, after the families packed up sleepy children and the remaining party hearties went looking for more fun. As much as he loved a sunny Fourth, he was thankful for the cool breeze and heavy clouds. The threatening skies would ensure that the crowd at the fireworks tonight would be smaller than usual. If they were rained out, he might even be able to pull a few officers and let them go home.

He checked his watch as he neared the bunting-draped platform. It had to be getting close to time for the first runners to make it back. When he had been in his prime—he didn't want to think how long ago that was—he could complete a ten-kilometer run in well under forty-five minutes. In army boots, too, none of this fancy pumped-up, triple-cushioned, shock-absorbing stuff they loaded onto sneakers these days. Of course, running in army boots probably explained the terrible shape his knees were in now.

"Chief! Over here!" His head swiveled in the direction of the voice. It was Mayor Jim Cameron, waving to him from the platform.

"What's up?"

"I want you to meet some people. Come on up here." Russ mounted the steps at one end of the platform while Jim Cameron went on. "Russ Van Alstyne here is the finest chief of police we've ever had. He came to us with over a quarter century's experience as a military policeman. We were lucky he wanted to come back home after he got tired of wandering the world. Russ, this is Bill Ingraham, who's developing the new resort, and this is John Opperman, Bill's partner."

You mean his *business* partner, Russ thought, remembering what Stephen Obrowski had said.

"How do you do, Mr. Opperman, Mr. Ingraham." The man in the polo shirt and khakis, who looked as if he had stepped out of a men's magazine, turned out to be Opperman. Ingraham, surprisingly, was dressed like one more ordinary Fourth of July spectator, wearing a ratty plaid shirt that his wife would never have let out of the house. Except, of course, Ingraham didn't have a wife. Russ squeezed the man's hand a little harder.

"Call me Bill," Ingraham said, reclaiming his hand. "How long have you been with the Millers Kill PD?"

"Five years now. My wife and I moved back here when I retired from the army." Dropping mention of Linda into a conversation was automatic for him when he was meeting a woman. Just one of those married-guy things. Now he was doing it with a glorified construction worker. Why? To make sure it was clear up front that he was straight? Damn it, he didn't need to prove anything. It was obvious to anyone that he wasn't gay. He realized belatedly that Opperman had asked about his wife.

"Hmm? No, she's not here. I'm on duty all day today, so Linda went to visit some friends." Of course, Ingraham didn't come across as gay, either. Neither did Emil Dvorak, now that he thought about it. He shook himself and forced his attention back to the conversation. Might as well do his bit for the town. "I'm sure Mayor Cameron has already said this, but thanks for sponsoring the race today. It's nice to have it back."

"It's good business to be a good neighbor," Opperman said, sounding like a man who had read too many business-advice books and taken them to heart.

"Right," Russ said. "Neither of you interested in running, though, I see."

"John wanted to, but I persuaded him to stick around and help me show you folks the human face behind BWI today." Ingraham grinned at Opperman. Russ thought the bean counter wasn't the best candidate to show the human face of anything. He exuded all the warmth of a wet mackerel. Ingraham went on: "John is Mr. Fitness in our organization. He plays pretend army in the woods in the summer, leads a touch-football team in the fall, heads up the basketball league all winter, and—what *do* you do in the spring, John?"

"Competitive rowing. Six-man shell."

"There you go. It tires me out just thinking about it. Now me, I agree with Robert Benchley. Whenever I feel the urge to exercise, I lie down until it passes. How 'bout you, Chief? Cops have to stay pretty fit, don't they?"

"Well, I'll tell you. At my last checkup, my doctor said, 'Congratulations, Chief, you have the body of a forty-eight-year-old.' I said, 'But I am forty-eight years old.' 'Well, there you are,' she said."

Ingraham and the mayor laughed. "Seriously," he continued, "there's not as much call for foot pursuit as you'd think from watching TV shows. And fortunately, the criminals around here tend to be in worse shape than I am."

"The crime-rate statistics I studied before we bid for the Landry property indicated very little other than small-scale property crimes and domestic violence," Opperman said. "One of the attractions for tourists is that this area is safe."

"That's true," Russ said. "And I aim to keep it that way."

Ingraham turned to his partner. "You do know the police are investigating a serious assault that took place Wednesday last, don't you? The victim had actually been at the inn where I'm staying right before he was attacked."

Mayor Jim Cameron leaped in, a reassuring look pasted on his face. "But that's very, very rare. And the doctor who was attacked was local. I don't think we've ever had any incidents involving tourists, have we, Chief?" He went on before Russ could respond. "I think it's the influence of our superlative setting. Surrounded by magnificent mountains, pristine lakes, and fish-filled rivers, who can fail to feel happier and more relaxed?"

Plenty of folks, Russ thought, but he kept his mouth shut.

Ingraham laughed. "You don't have to sell me, Jim. If I didn't believe this place would draw in visitors, I wouldn't have picked it for the new resort."

"It is a site with a lot of visual appeal," Opperman said. "I've flown in several potential investors, and I always swing through the mountains and over the surrounding countryside on those trips. Everyone comments about the extraordinary setting."

"So, you're definitely going ahead with the construction?" the mayor said.

"Well, like I said at the meeting, we will as long as we don't have any trouble from the DEP."

"Good," Cameron said. He looked as though he was about to say more, but instead, he closed his mouth and nodded.

Russ thought maybe a change of conversation would be in order. "You said you fly, Mr. Opperman?"

"We hire pilots as necessary, but I'm licensed for both our two-engine prop plane and the company helicopter."

"What type of helicopter?" Russ asked.

"Why?" Ingraham said. "You like to fly, Chief? John could take you up sometime. No problem."

"No, but thanks. I've got a . . . friend who used to fly, that's all."

The noise from the spectators in the park had surrounded them with a constant hum. Now Russ could hear yells and cheers. "They must be coming in," he said. "If you'll excuse me, I need to check on how the roads are clearing. Nice meeting you, gentlemen."

The coed hikers must have headed for greener pastures at some point, because Kevin Flynn was moping about the squad car, looking like a dog left too long outside a store. "Everything okay?" Flynn asked, raising his voice to be heard above the cheers of the crowd around the finish line. Runners were pounding through makeshifts chutes, drenched with sweat despite the cold weather, as a large digital clock displayed their times in tenths of a second.

"No problems yet," Russ said. He slid into the car, closed the door, and rolled up the window so he could hear Harlene over the noise outside. Flynn hopped in the other door. "Dispatch, this is fifteen fifty-seven."

"Fifteen fifty-seven, this is Dispatch."

"The runners are coming in. Make sure those intersections are getting opened up as soon as possible."

"Roger that."

"Any news?"

"It's been pretty quiet so far. There was a fight out to Lockland's Whispering Pines campground. Somebody pulled out their RV without disconnecting the water and sanitation lines, and Lockland decked the damnfool."

Kevin snickered. Russ shot him a look. "They get it all sorted out?" Russ asked.

"Yeah, Lyle convinced the RV guy not to press assault charges and Lockland not to press vandalism charges. Lyle said he hadn't smelled a stink like that since his brother's cesspool overflowed."

"Remind me not to complain about sweaty runners. Anything else?"

"We got a call from Bob Mongue over to the state troopers' headquarters. They've got a possible on your red Chevy."

Russ sat up straighter. "Yeah? Where?"

"The Burgoyne campground on Route Four, south of Whitehall. Big 'ninety-seven pickup with Pennsylvania plates. Good-sized crunch in the right rear."

"They run the plates?"

"They're doing it now. Sergeant Mongue'll call back when they've talked with the driver and checked his ID."

"Raise me as soon as you know anything, Harlene."

"Will do. I've got one more thing for you."

"Okay."

"Mrs. Bain called. Thought she saw a man poking around her house, trying to get in."

"Oh for—" He clenched the microphone and took a deep breath. "How long has it been since her son came for a visit?"

" 'Bout three months now."

"Okay. She's definitely due for a prowler. There's a copy of the last incident report in the files. Get that out and change the date, will you? That way, it'll be ready to go when she asks for it."

"Roger that. Dispatch out."

"Damn," he said, hanging up the mike. "If Bob Mongue collars those sons of bitches while I'm chasing down one of Mrs. Bain's imaginary prowlers, I'll never hear the end of it." He shook his head. "This is what a quarter century of police work gets you, Kevin. Keep it in mind."

◆ ◆ ◆

Of course, Mrs. Bain was very apologetic when they failed to flush out a burglar. The hardest part on one of her calls was getting away—she kept pressing lemonade and homemade brownies on them. Russ extricated himself and Flynn by promising to have the young officer bring over the incident report in person. They escaped into the squad car, clutching a paper bag of brownies.

"You're pretty good at that, Chief," Flynn said. "How do—"

The radio crackled. "Fifteen fifty-seven, this is Dispatch."

"Dispatch, this is fifteen fifty-seven. Come in."

"Multiple reports of a disturbance at Riverside Park. One caller described it as a riot."

Russ stared at the microphone in his hand. "A riot? Over what? Who took second place in the forty-and-over division?"

"Another caller described it as a rowdy demonstration. You better get over there. I've sent Noble and Mark, but you're closer."

A demonstration. The brownie in his stomach suddenly felt like a small lead brick. "We're rolling, Dispatch. Keep me informed."

"Will do. Dispatch out."

Kevin Flynn was almost beside himself with excitement. "A riot? Are we going to get out the riot gear?"

"No, we're not going to start lobbing gas grenades into a bunch of runners on the Fourth of July." He switched on the lights and siren, dreading what he suspected he might see when they got there. BWI . . . a large open space . . . plenty of people around . . . He knew he should have put the elements together before now.

They couldn't reach the park entrance in the cruiser. Despite blipping the siren to get people out of the way, it was too crowded. He parked and waded through the press of bodies, hauling people out of his way if they didn't move fast enough, Kevin bobbing along in his wake.

"Two! Four! Six! Eight! We don't want precipitate!"

All around him, spectators, picnickers, and runners were talking loudly and excitedly, pushing forward for a better view.

"A! B! C! D! Keep your lousy PCB!"

He could see the placards bouncing above the protesters' heads, seven or eight of them: BAN PCBS and NO DREDGING and WILL WORK FOR CANCER."

"In! Out! Up! Down! Don't contaminate our town!"

Sounded like the goddamned cheers were written by a preschool teacher. There was a scuffle on the platform, which was so jammed with people now that he couldn't make out what was going on yet. He spotted Noble Entwistle forcing his way through the crowd from the riverbank side of the park.

"Brown! Blue! Gray! Green! Keep our soil and water clean!"

The sounds of a loud argument came from the platform; then the banner with its prominently displayed BWI logos shivered, and both weighted poles holding it toppled over with a loud clang. Aldermen leaped from the back of the structure to escape the tangle of fabric. In the ensuing confusion, the demonstration's spokesperson thrust herself to the front edge of the small stage, bullhorn pointed toward the spectators. "Parents of Millers Kill! Do you want to risk your children's health to make a development company in Baltimore rich?"

Russ fought to keep from closing his eyes in denial. There it was, his worst fear, in the flesh.

The remaining people on the platform stood helpless, unwilling to tackle the protester, and who could blame them? A seventy-four-year-old woman's bones could break mighty easily.

He was within shouting distance now. "Mom!" he bellowed. "Get down from there!"

CHAPTER NINE

"G ood Lord," Clare said to no one in particular. Behind her, someone shoved forward, causing her to stumble and splash herself and the man in front of her with half the contents of her water bottle. The wet man turned and snarled at her. "I'm so sorry," Clare said. She plucked her sodden T-shirt away from her goose bump–prickled flesh. She cooled down fast after a run, and all she had wanted to do was collect her official time, get back to her car, and pull on the sweats she had stashed there. Now she was stuck in a gridlock of excited humanity, pinned between the placard-waving protestors in front of her and what seemed like half the population of Millers Kill behind.

"Mom, get down from there!" she heard Russ order.

Mrs. Van Alstyne lowered her megaphone. "You'll have to come and get me," she said. The crowd nearby roared with laughter, and Clare could see Russ's cheeks and ears turn pink.

"I know some of you think we're doomed to be exposed to PCBs because we're near Hudson Falls," Mrs. Van Alstyne said through her megaphone. "I know some of you think the jobs that'll come out of the new spa are worth a few extra chemicals in the groundwater."

The eager watchers behind Clare pushed her steadily forward toward the center knot of protestors. Around her, faces were amused, incredulous, angry. She could see one . . . two . . . three video cameras in the crowd, pointed at Margy Van Alstyne, the chief of police, the demonstrators. This thing was going to be better documented than a Rose Garden speech. A young woman slipped between spectators, thrust one flyer from a ream of photocopied papers into Clare's hand, and disappeared, working her way through the crowd. In the press of bodies around her, Clare had to hold the paper close to her face. STOP BWI DEVELOPMENT NOW! the heading screamed. On one side, it was a broadside against BWI; on the other, a gruesome list of the effects of PCB exposure. She tuned back in to Margy Van Alstyne's speech.

"PCBs are known to cause cancer! PCBs are known to increase aggression!" Clare could see Russ's head above the crowd as he made his way to the platform.

"Baltimore-based BWI stands to make millions from this development! Meanwhile, we get minimum-wage service-industry jobs and enough PCBs in the water to cause cancer in thirty percent of our population!"

"Any job's better'n no job!" someone shouted from the crowd.

"They're promising to pay eight dollars an hour," a woman yelled.

Bill Ingraham was moving purposefully toward Mrs. Van Alstyne. Russ vaulted onto the platform's edge and waved him off.

"Look around you at your friends and neighbors!" Margy Van Alstyne shouted. "One out of every four people you see could be dead from cancer within a decade. How many dollars an hour is that worth? No! Get your hands off me!"

Russ had wrapped his arms around his mother's waist and lifted her bodily off the platform. She waved her megaphone out of his reach. "I have a right to speak! I have First Amendment rights!"

Russ grunted from the effort of pulling her away from the platform's edge. "No permit," he managed to gasp out. His mother flailed and twisted, and he staggered back, sending the mayor and several top runners scrambling to get out of his way. Boos erupted from the crowd.

"Let her speak!"

"What're you afraid of?"

Russ put his mother down. "No permit for public demonstration," he said more firmly. "Disturbing the peace, resisting an officer, and possible battery. Cuff her, Officer Flynn."

"Me?" said Flynn.

Another protestor, the redheaded nurse Clare had seen at the town meeting, launched herself over the edge of the platform. Mrs. Van Alstyne tossed her the megaphone. "Ask yourself why the police and the mayor don't want us to speak to you," she shouted.

"Damn it, Laura, get down off there. Don't make me write you up again." Russ turned to drag her away from the impromptu podium. She danced out of reach.

"The government of this town is too blinded by the thought of the tax income from this development to look after your health," the nurse shouted. "But you can demand the DEP stop this spa! You can demand new testing of the Landry site! You can demand—oof!"

Russ picked her up with considerably less effort than it had taken to move his mother. Boos mixed with cheers. The central knot of protestors took up the chant again, reinforced by other voices chiming in. To Clare's right, someone called out, "Development means jobs! Development means jobs!" and the cry instantly spread into a ragged countercall. "Damn Commies," one beefy man in front of her said to another. "They think government control of property is so great, I say let's ship 'em off to North Korea."

Officer Entwhistle was trying to remove the protestors, or the people harassing them. It was impossible to tell. Despite her soggy clothes and her clammy skin, and despite her grandmother's voice warning her, *This isn't any of your business, miss,* Clare couldn't keep herself from trying to get closer. She edged sideways between individuals, couples, clumps of people, buffeted by excited voices.

"Folks? Folks? I'm Bill Ingraham, and I *am* BWI Development." Someone had rescued the microphone stand from beneath the fallen banner and set it up in front of Ingraham. "I said this at Wednesday night's town meeting and I'll say it again: If you folks don't want our resort in your community, we're outta here." He didn't look like the genial, controlled businessman he had been at the meeting. He looked like a construction boss who had just found out his crew was threatening to unionize. "Personally, and professionally, I think connecting your PCB problem with our development site is bad science and worse business."

"PCBs were stored on that site twenty-five years ago!" someone yelled from the crowd.

"Yeah, and then the storage canisters were removed by the government and the site was cleaned up. Look, folks, the feds and the state have both given the place the thumbs-up. Either you trust the government or you don't. But if you don't, why the hell would you want to call them in again?"

"He's right! Listen to the man!" another person yelled.

"I take pride in my resorts. I build 'em right and I try to be as environmentally sensitive as possible." The protestors jeered. "If you don't want us here, call in the DEP and we're gone. But don't send a bunch of scientifically illiterate witches after me!" He thrust the microphone into the stand with enough force to set it rocking, stalked to the rear of the platform, and leaped down, disappearing from view.

The babble of the crowd was deafening. Mayor Jim Cameron visibly wavered between snatching the microphone or running after Ingraham.

The urge to apologize to the developer must have won out, because he let himself down over the rear of the platform and also vanished.

Russ, who must have unloaded his mother on Officer Flynn, strode back to the front of the platform. He didn't bother with a microphone, simply cupped his hands around his mouth and shouted, "You people are demonstrating without a permit. You must disperse now. Anyone who fails to disperse peaceably will be arrested." The central knot of protestors promptly sat down and started singing "We Shall Overcome." Clare could see Russ's lips moving, but it didn't look like he was saying anything fit for public consumption.

She heard the siren of another police car. Time to get out of here. She had to keep her head down and use her elbows aggressively to wedge her way between bodies. Very few people seemed inclined to leave before the show was over.

"Certainly the most interesting thing to happen on the Fourth of July since that streaker in 'seventy-nine, don't you—"

"No proof that any of the stuff is coming from the development site."

"—with husbands supporting them and too much time on their—"

"Thank God somebody has enough guts to stand up to the Board of—"

"You said the same thing when they did the Million Mom March, and you were wrong then, too."

"He's not gonna be a problem after tonight, is he?"

Those words, accompanied by a little laugh, raised the hairs on the back of Clare's neck. She stopped dead, turning to see who had spoken. A pair of parents bore down on her, arms full of squirming children, and she was pushed out of the way. By the time they passed, the crowd had shifted around her again. She had no idea whose gravelly, gloating voice had made a simple sentence sound like a threat. That group of teenage boys? They looked too young. That man with his wife? Too old. She rubbed her forehead with the heel of her hand. She was losing it. The attacks, and now this public pandemonium, had tipped her over the edge. She continued working her way to the back of the crowd, holding fast to the thought of her car, a warm sweatshirt, and a peaceful ride back to her quiet rectory. Small-town rural parish indeed. She should have asked the bishop for combat pay before coming to Millers Kill.

◆ ◆ ◆

When Clare got home, the first thing she did was shower until her hot water ran out. She had never been so cold on a Fourth of July in her life. Then she wrapped herself tightly in a full-length terry-cloth robe identical to a monk's habit, complete with cowl. It had been a gift from her brother Brian, who over the years had also given her a clock in the shape of an Apache helicopter, a pair of army tap-dancing boots, and a recruiting poster featuring Michelangelo's God and the words I WANT YOU. She had just eased a half pound of linguine into a pot of boiling water in preparation for a carb fest when her phone rang.

"Clare? Russ. I need you to do me a favor."

His voice was strangely hushed. "Russ? Where are you?"

"At the Washington County Jail."

"What are you doing at the jail?" As soon as the words were out of her mouth, she realized how inane they sounded. "I mean, I thought you'd be back on patrol."

"It's my mother," he said, his voice as grim as she'd ever heard it. "I'm trying to get her out."

She decided not to mention that he had been the one to put his mom there in the first place. "Is there some sort of delay with the bail bondsman? Does she have to wait for a hearing or something?"

"I put up her damned bond myself. She won't accept it! She says she's a damned prisoner of conscience and she's not leaving until she gets to make a public appearance before a judge!" He was practically hissing at this point. "'Scuse my French," he added.

"Why are you whispering?" she said, involuntarily whispering, as well.

"I'm calling you from the booking room. There are about a dozen cops and guards here, and every one of 'em knows I arrested my own mother for disorderly conduct. You know what she kept calling me in front of the bondsman?" He dropped his voice further. "'Sweetie!' I'm never gonna live this down."

She bit the inside of her lip. When she knew she could speak without a trace of laughter in her voice, she said, "What do you need me to do?"

"Get the dogs."

"The dogs?"

"Those two beasts we left with Mom. She put them inside the house. Her hearing isn't until nine o'clock tomorrow morning, and she may not be processed and out until noon. They can't stay inside the whole time." He exhaled. "I'd go up there and let them out myself, but I'm on duty until midnight and things are already picking up. I need to get out of here and back on patrol."

She looked at her linguine, the tomatoes and garlic cloves lined up on her cutting board, the wineglass waiting to be filled. "You know I'm glad to help, but . . . getting into your mom's house . . . isn't this something a family member ought to do? Your sister? Your wife?"

"Janice took the kids to her in-laws for the weekend, and my brother-in-law is alone with forty cows. He wouldn't leave them unattended if God himself got on the phone and asked him over. And I can't ask Linda." The tone of his voice did not invite further questions.

"What about . . ." Her mind cast around for reasons why this was a bad idea. "But they can't run around here in my yard. They're big dogs; they need their exercise."

"Well, then, take them to the park and let them run off-leash."

"You can do that in the park?"

"Hell, yeah. The park's very animal-friendly. There used to be two big water troughs there for dogs and horses, until they were torn out in the eighties."

The only other objections she could think of were even more inane than the last one.

"Clare," he said. His voice went even lower. "Please."

She closed her eyes. "Of course. I'll do it. I'm on my way right now."

"Can you find her place again?"

"The U.S. Army trusted me to fly very expensive helicopters over large stretches of unmarked territory without getting lost. I think I can find Old Scanadaiga Road."

"Old Sacandaga Road."

"That, too. Is her house locked? How do I get in?"

"Yes, her house is locked." She could hear him restraining himself from commenting on her own habits. "The spare key is under the geranium pot farthest to the left on the front steps. Not the kitchen door, where you go in, but the front."

"Don't worry. I'll keep the dogs as long as necessary. Just tell your mom to give me a call when she's sprung"—she grinned at the noise he made—"and we'll take it from there."

"Thanks, Clare. I owe you one."

"Your debt is forgiven. Now go and do likewise."

He laughed. "Yes, Father Flanagan."

She hung up, thinking she liked making Russ laugh. It almost made up for the leaden way her body responded to the idea of getting dressed and going back out. Parishioners had invited her to three cookouts, two fireworks-watching ensembles, and on a trip to the Saratoga Performing Arts Center for the concert tonight. She had declined them all, knowing that after celebrating two Eucharists and running the 10K race, the only thing she would feel up to doing was collapsing in front of the television. She pulled the linguine off the burner. "'Once more unto the breach, dear friends,'" she said, heading back upstairs to change.

◆ ◆ ◆

Old Route 100 between Millers Kill and Margy Van Alstyne's house was far busier than it had been on Thursday. Clare passed minivans crowded with sticky children, tiny cars with kayaks teetering on top, and bass-thumping stereos on wheels, filled with wind-whipped hair of indeterminate origin. Along the heavily wooded stretch she had to slow to a stop to accommodate a truck that seemed, at first glance, to be picking up National Guardsmen on maneuvers. It wasn't until she got a closer look at the men straggling out of the forest that she saw the fluorescent orange and green splatters on their jackets and realized they were paintball players. Near the intersection of Route 100 and the Old Sacandaga Road, she saw no fewer than three buses headed back from rafting trips on the Hudson. She marveled that people would pay good money to get stuck, not to mention soaking wet, on a rubber raft on a day that had promised sixty-degree weather and rain.

The dogs, when she had found the key and unlocked the kitchen door, were as ecstatic to see her as they had been the last time. "Don't get used to this," she warned them. "I won't always be here to rescue you from being left alone. No, Bob! Down!" She let them have the run of the backyard while she slung the already seriously depleted bag of kibble into her tiny trunk. She made a metal note to stop at the IGA and buy another fifty pounds before returning the dogs to Margy. God knew when Paul Foubert would return from Albany.

Returning to the kitchen to get the dogs' bowls, she gave in to the temptation to take a peek at the front room. At first glance, it looked like a typical seventy-year-old lady's living room: braided rug on the floor, comfortable well-worn furniture from the fifties, a prominently positioned television with a *TV Guide* and glasses on top. But the books piled on the coffee table had titles like *Environmental Impact of Modern Manufacturing* and *The Consumers' Guide to the Waste Stream.* One wall was almost completely covered with framed photographs: small kids in ancient black and white who must have been Russ and his sister, modern color portraits of Janice's three little girls. Margy at a sit-in, Margy beneath a banner reading SEEDS OF PEACE, and, on a page from a 1970 *Time* magazine, Margy face-to-face with Nelson Rockefeller, thrusting a framed picture toward the governor. Both of them were yelling at each other.

The picture Margy was holding in the magazine photo was hanging just below. Clare unhooked it from its nail and held it up. It showed a tall, too-thin young man, tan and shirtless, hair bleached blond from the sun, set off against exotic palms in the background. He could have been a late-sixties surfer, if not for the dog tags and the fatigues, and the M16 slung over his shoulder. She ran a finger over the glass. She had never imagined him that young. She would have been six or seven when this picture was taken, learning to read Dick and Jane books while he slept in mud and fought off intestinal parasites and tried to keep from getting killed every day. Their difference in age, which had never meant anything to her before, suddenly yawned wide, a vast chasm filled with events he had lived through as an adult that were nothing but stories and history and vague childhood memories to her.

Margy Van Alstyne would probably love to tell her stories about Russ as a young man. She could come out for a visit and hear about his childhood, and what he was like in high school, and where he went while he was in the service. Maybe she could find out more about his wife. Her grandmother's voice broke in. *If you don't want to go to Atlanta, missy, you'd best not get on that train.* She took a deep breath. Or, she could mind her own business and leave the Van Alstynes alone. She rehung the photograph carefully in its spot, squaring it just so with its neighbors. Then she retreated to the kitchen before she could yield to temptation again.

The ride back to Millers Kill took even longer than the ride out, in part due to the heavy end-of-the-day traffic and in part due to the necessity of driving slowly when the car was filled to capacity with dogs. It didn't help that she felt irritated at her foray into Mrs. Van Alstyne's living room. She was asked to do a simple favor for someone who had helped her out immeasurably by taking the dogs in the first place, and she had used it as an excuse to moon over the woman's married son. It was just plain tacky, that's what it was.

Everyone in the seminary had heard of some priest who had crossed the line between compassion and passion and broken up a marriage or two in the process. Nine times out of ten, it was a parishioner who had been in counseling, or the church secretary. Well, most of her counseling these days was with young engaged couples, and Lois was certainly no threat to her virtue. If she just showed a little more self-control, she wouldn't have a problem.

There had been a time, when she was a lieutenant, that she had developed a terrific crush on an out-of-bounds man. He was a captain, directly above her in the chain of command, and if anything had happened between them, it could have meant both their jobs. Handling her feelings, she had discovered, meant never lingering over the thought of him, never daydreaming, never fantasizing. Eventually, her tour of duty finished, she left, and within a year she couldn't recall what it was that had gotten her so hot and bothered in the first place.

By the time she pulled into the rectory driveway, her little car shimmying from Gal and Bob's excited wriggling, she felt better. Self-discipline was something she knew how to do. As if in reward for her good thoughts, there was a message on her answering machine.

"Clare? Hi, it's Paul. I hope you can hear this okay, I'm using the pay phone in the lobby and the thing dates back to the Eisenhower administration. Great news! Emil has woken up and is responding to speech! He's having trouble talking, but the neurologist says that's normal at this point, that it doesn't mean anything. He recognized me, and his kids, and he managed to squeeze our hands a little. I feel so grateful, I can't tell you. I hope Bob and Gal are doing okay"—the dogs both barked sharply when they heard their names—"and that they're not wearing you out. I'll try to reach you again as soon as I know something new. Thanks again for everything, Clare."

"You see?" she said to the Berns. "Doing good is its own reward. Let's go make some dinner."

◆ ◆ ◆

Two plates of linguini later, stretched out on the sofa with a glass of Chianti, watching the Boston Pops Esplanade concert, Clare was beginning to think she ought to look into getting a dog. It was fun having someone to talk to in the kitchen, even if neither Gal nor Bob was a great conversationalist. And seeing them stretched out on the hardwood floor was deeply satisfying. It made her feel English. *The Vicar of Dibley* crossed with a James Herriot story. Maybe she could get herself one of those canvas coats, and a walking stick. She yawned.

Gal and Bob got up, shook themselves, and walked into the foyer.

"What is it? Do you two want to go out?"

At the word *out,* both dogs barked. Clare groaned. As she rolled off the sofa, they began to whine and pant, and by the time she joined them in the foyer, their nails were clicking madly on the wooden floor as they jostled each other to be first out the door.

She opened the door to the damp and cold and the dogs bounded out, ran straight to the edge of the sidewalk, turned to look at her, and began barking.

"Shhh! Shhh!" She wrestled on her sneakers and pulled a running shell with reflective stripes over her head. Where had she tossed those leashes? In the kitchen? When she finally stepped out onto the front porch, the Berns ran to her, leaping joyously and barking even louder. "Sssh! It's nine o'clock, for heaven's sake. This isn't the country! I've got neighbors." The dogs promptly sat, tails thumping, looking at her expectantly. "I get the feeling that, unlike me, you two didn't get enough exercise today. Am I right? C'mon, then, we can walk down to the park. If they haven't canceled because of the weather, we might even see some fireworks."

Each wrought-iron lamp along Church Street had its own halo, its light a soft glow in the mist. The usually strident sodium orange looked like gaslight, shading the red-white-and-blue bunting, flickering over the slick leaves rustling in nearby trees. The dogs had fallen silent as soon as Clare had led them out on the leashes, and she could hear far-off noises amplified in the developing fog. There were few people on the sidewalks at this hour. Clare would hear footsteps clicking and someone would emerge from the mist, smile or look startled, and then vanish behind her. It might have been unnerving if she had been alone, but walking behind two large and well-behaved dogs made it a genteel adventure, like strolling through Victorian London. She added Sherlock Holmes to her list of English images.

They crossed Main Street, turned down Mill, and continued toward Riverside Park. As they got closer, she could hear distant voices in a current of many conversations. A flicker of excitement made her smile. The fireworks must still be on. She picked up her pace, hurrying past shabby shops and mill offices whose brick facades were the color of old blood in the dark.

From the abandoned textile mill on its left to the decrepit pulping mill on its right, the park was set off from the street by almost half a mile of high iron-rail fencing. The central entrance, which had marked the start of the race this afternoon, had a wide ornate gate overtopped by a wrought-iron arch, the whole fixture a monument to the prosperity that had vanished from the area after World War II. It was that gate she was shooting for, but she had scarcely passed the textile mill when the first muffled thud sounded somewhere over the river and she saw a dazzle of green light. A chorus of oohs and aahs came from inside the park.

The trees grew close along the fence and the underbrush had been left to fend for itself, so it was hard to see. She couldn't even make out the next explosion, but in the fog-reflected light, she could see a faster way into the park: an unobtrusive door-size gate almost indistinguishable from the fence around it. A century before, it must have been the quick lunch-hour entrance for the mill workers.

She pulled the dogs up short, almost jerking herself off her feet in the process, and pushed against the gate. She was actually surprised when it opened. Bob and Gal didn't need any encouragement to desert the sidewalk. They plowed through the underbrush, sending whip-thin branches lashing back toward Clare, showering her with the collected damp off the leaves. When they emerged, Clare's sneakers were thoroughly soaked and her hair was clinging to her head in wet clumps.

Another explosion, a halogen-bright expanding sphere that collapsed into a rain of stars. It was still too thickly wooded for her to see clearly. "Come on, guys, this way," she said, heading toward the water. The next explosion was a series of green and pink shell bursts, accompanied a second later by a staccato of ear-popping bangs. She glanced down at Bob and Gal, but they were too busy covering every square inch of ground for scents to notice what was going on in the sky. Bob lurched toward a tree to leave his mark and Clare followed, her face still turned toward the sky. "Oh, look at that, I love that one," she said as a series of red, white, and blue lights fountained across the sky. The dogs tugged her farther, snuffling and peeing as they went. A swarm of yellow lights spread round and flat, creating shapes in the middle of a circle. "Is that a smiley face? It is! Good grief."

Gal whined.

Clare bent down and ruffled Gal's silky hair. "Don't like smiley faces? I can't say I blame you."

The dog didn't respond to Clare. She quivered, body tense, nose pointed toward the thicket of brush and trees dividing the park from the mill. Bob turned in exactly the same position. Both dogs whined.

"What is it, boy?" Clare scratched Bob's broad head. "Did you see a squirrel?"

The dogs pulled toward the thicket. "Is anybody there?" Clare asked, feeling foolish. Far away from the spectators at the water's edge, hidden in the shadow of the three-story mill wall, the long stretch of vegetation was probably the perfect spot for necking. She didn't want the dogs to flush out some poor pair of half-naked teenagers.

Gal growled, stopped, then barked once. Bob stopped beside her, growling. The hairs on the back of Clare's neck rose, and she involuntarily looked behind her. "Who's there?" she asked, infusing her voice with every ounce of authority she could muster.

The mist lit up as whirls of green and pink spun overhead. There was an explosive sound from the fireworks, but nothing except rustling leaves ahead. She knew she ought to just go. Take the dogs to the waterside and watch the end of the display. She could easily find someone with a cell phone and call the police if she honestly thought something was not right. She should go.

She tugged the leashes up to move the dogs toward the thicket. "Come on," she said quietly. As they drew closer, Gal began whimpering again. The dogs slowed, too well trained to refuse but clearly reluctant. Two yards away, they both dropped to their bellies, whining.

Despite the cool dampness on her face and her wet hair, Clare felt hot prickles down her arms and along her back. She blinked, light-headed for a second, and realized she had been breathing too fast and too shallow. She opened her mouth and took a deep, shuddering breath that didn't do anything to stop her heart from skittering inside her chest.

She tugged the leashes again, but the dogs had reached their limit. They whined, then whined even more fretfully when she stepped past them to part the branches of a bittersweet-entwined sumac to peer inside. Nothing. She made herself step through the undergrowth and brush, pushing through something with tiny twigs and clumps of berries that tapped against her cheeks and fingers. Nothing. She stubbed her sneaker-shod toe against something hard and swallowed a scream before she heard the clanking sound and felt a pipe rolling beneath her foot. She had stumbled across the graveyard of an old plumbing system. She squatted down and waved through the darkness until her knuckles hit something—smooth marble or polished granite. The shape of it under her hands made her think of a sarcophagus. She thrust the morbid idea from her mind. Rectangular, rounded edges—a basin? Her fingers slipped through something wet clinging to the cool stone interior. She gasped and jerked her hand away, lurching to her feet. Then she realized what she had found. One of the old watering troughs Russ had mentioned. It smelled of old water and decayed leaves and the iron tang of rust. The dogs keened behind her, and in a split second her fear flashed into irritation. "What is it?" she snapped. "If there's some drowned cat in here, I'm going to be—"

Overhead, a white explosion cascaded into yellow and purple, and blue spheres filled the sky. A crash of explosions battered the air. She could see the watering trough now, bone-pale, long as a child's coffin, mottled by the leaves' shadows. And there, finally, was the reason for the dogs' whimpering. Clare saw the fireworks reflecting in thick black blood, winking along the edges of torn flesh, illuminating dull, flat eyes.

Over the cacophony of the fireworks' finale, she heard a wavering, high-pitched moan, rising and rising until she cried out, her voice choking, and she realized it was her. She was making the terrible noise as the cloudbursts of light exploded overhead, revealing and concealing the puffy, battered thing that had once been Bill Ingraham.

CHAPTER TEN

The crime scene was lighted like a carnival midway by the time Russ arrived. Two tall tungsten lamps flooded the ground and trees with a white glare, turning every shadow into a razor-edged anti-leaf and non-branch. The red lights of two squad cars circled monotonously next to what the Millers Kill PD referred to as "the meat wagon"—the squat mortuary transport used when there was no hope the ambulance would be useful. From behind a taut yellow tape, a dozen or more flashlights bobbed aimlessly as their owners, packing blankets and coolers, crowded in to get a glimpse of something much more exciting than fireworks. White, red, and yellow reflected off the lowering mist until the night itself glowed and Russ thought he could see individual drops of water suspended in midair.

Mark Durkee, who had been bumped up the seniority ladder when they'd hired Kevin Flynn, was working the crowd, notebook out, presumably taking names and statements. Russ ducked under the tape and waved at Lyle MacAuley. "Hey," Russ said. "You set him on that?" He gestured with his head toward Durkee.

"He thought of it on his own. He read up on spotting perps who return to the scene and on this new technique of taking pictures of the spectators before running them off. It gets the possible witnesses on film, so we can match 'em up with their statements. He whipped out one of those little disposable cameras and went to it. He's got a lot on the ball."

"Yeah," Russ said. "Let's hope he doesn't take it to someplace where they pay better."

Lyle snorted. His unofficial status as detective had finally been rewarded with a promotion at the spring town meeting, after four years of Russ lobbying the Board of Aldermen to create a detective position. He couldn't get that approved, but they had eventually given in to his argument that Lyle would leave if his experience wasn't recognized. So now Lyle was deputy chief, on a force with eight full-time officers and four part-timers. The only way he could make sense of it was to conclude the aldermen felt they were getting their money's worth if they got two jobs filled with one paycheck.

Sergeant Morin, one of the state police technicians, was opening his portable lab box and pulling out his elaborate camera equipment. "Has he been in yet?" Russ asked.

"He and I searched the area adjacent to the body. Nothing turned up. People were swarming up from the riverbank, so I made getting the tape up a priority."

Russ nodded. "Good call. Let's go see this guy, shall we?" He pulled on the latex gloves he had removed from his squad car.

"He was done right here and then laid out in this thing," Lyle said, holding a wet sumac branch out of the way. "There's a hell of a lot of blood—on the ground, on the basin, in the water."

Russ stepped carefully in Lyle's footsteps. When they reached the crumpled form in the watering trough, he sucked in against his teeth. "Jeez. You're not kidding." He squatted down slowly so as not to catch his clothing on any vegetation. "That must have been a garrote. I don't think a knife could do that."

"That was my take. It'll make it harder if it is. No cut pattern to match to a knife. Just wash off a length of wire and roll it back on the spool. Whose gonna know?"

Russ stood again. The metallic smell of blood was strong enough to make his eyes water. "Yeah, but to use it, you have to be in close. Real close. Whoever did this must have been splattered with blood." He looked at Lyle. "Anyone see anything?"

"Nothin' yet. But it couldn't have happened too long before he was found. A lot of that's still wet."

"I'll wait for Emil's opinion, but I have to—" Russ stopped, feeling foolish. "I mean, not Emil Dvorak . . ."

"Dr. Scheeler is acting as our ME. He's the pathologist on loan from Glens Falls Hospital."

"Until Emil gets back."

"Right. Until he gets back." Lyle smiled a little.

"Hey, guys," Sergeant Morin called through the foliage. "I need you to clear out for a few so's I can get my shots." Russ and Lyle retraced their steps slowly and deliberately, disturbing the plants as little as possible. "Thanks," Morin said, disappearing into the leaves.

"Okay. Who found him?"

Lyle ran a hand over his bristly gray crew cut and nodded at a cluster of three trees, past the yellow tape, almost out of reach of the tungsten lights. "They did."

He could see a woman, her face a pale oval, sitting at the base of a maple tree, squeezed in between two enormous black-and-white dogs. "You're kidding me," he said.

"Nope. It's your priest all right."

"She's not *my* priest," he said over his shoulder, striding toward Clare.

She looked up as he approached her. Her eyes were red-rimmed and puffy, her skin was starkly pale, and her dark blonde hair hung lankly over her shoulders. She had an arm wrapped around one of the huge Berns, her fingers buried in its thick fur. He stopped several feet away because he didn't trust himself to get any closer without touching her. He squatted to be at eye level. "Are you okay?" he asked.

She nodded. "Yes," she said, as if trying out a new voice. "I'm—whatever happened, it was all over by the time I got there."

"Can you tell me about it?"

She nodded again. Took a deep breath. "I walked the dogs down here to see the fireworks. I was coming along that way"—she pointed toward the east side of Mill Street—"when I saw the fireworks were starting. There was a gate, a little gate, just past the corner of the mill, and I pushed on it to get through faster, because I wanted to see the fireworks, and they had started, and then Gal caught the scent. They both started whining and growling, and I thought it was—I don't know, I don't know what I thought it was, but I went to see what was scaring them." She clamped a hand over her mouth. Her eyes flooded with tears. "It was so . . . I keep thinking of this gruesome old hymn we used to sing at my grandmother's church." She tilted her head against the tree. "'There is a fountain filled with blood drawn from Emmanuel's veins,'" she sang, her voice a shaky thread. "'And sinners plunged beneath that flood lose all their guilty stains. . . . The dying thief rejoiced to see that fountain in his day; and there have I, though vile as he, washed all my sins away.'"

One of the dogs whined and butted her with its head. She clutched at its hair, scrubbing her eyes with her other hand. "It used to scare me when I was a little kid."

"I don't blame you." His hand twitched toward her, then stopped.

"It was that developer, Bill Ingraham, you know. I could tell, even with . . ."

"Yeah. I saw. Tell me about the gate. It was open?"

She took another deep breath. "Yes. It surprised me at the time, because it obviously isn't used regularly. There wasn't any path leading from it into the park."

He glanced in the direction she had indicated. "Did you see anything as you came through the bushes there?"

"No. But I was mostly just trying to keep the branches from smacking me in the face. There wasn't anyone there, if that's what you mean." She frowned, and he relaxed somewhat, seeing reason replace her sheer emotional reaction. "The dogs would have reacted if whoever did that had gone the way we came in. The smell of blood made them very nervous, and he must have been—" her face wavered for a moment, but she went on: "He must have had a lot of blood on his clothing."

"That's what we think, yeah. Did you see anything around the body? Anything that looked disturbed, out of place?"

"Oh, God, I don't know. There could have been signs hanging in the trees and I wouldn't have seen them." She turned her face into one of the dog's necks for a moment. "I probably messed up the area some. I remember thinking not to touch anything, but I kind of fell backward and . . . I was in a hurry to get away." Her expression changed again, and he realized she was ashamed. "I didn't even think of saying a prayer. All I thought of was getting my sorry self out of there. I didn't stop running until I found someone with a phone, and even after she called it in, I didn't want to go anywhere near . . . him."

"Good," he said firmly. "We don't want you standing around praying at a crime scene. You did exactly the right thing. You got out, you reported it, and you helped us get here fast so we have a better chance of finding the bad guy."

"Oh." She looked down.

"When you were walking over here, did you pass anyone on the street? Anyone who seemed out of the ordinary maybe?"

"Anyone dripping gore like Banquo's ghost? No." She immediately waved her hand. "Sorry. I don't mean to be flip. I passed a few people on Church and Main, but after I turned onto Mill Street, I didn't see anything, not a person; not a car."

"Okay, thanks." He stood up, his knees complaining mightily. "You stay right here. I need to talk with Lyle and the crime-scene tech, and then we'll see about getting you home."

"How's your mother?" she asked suddenly. "Did you ever get her out?"

"Safe and sound in the woman's wing of the Washington County jail," he said, "so I can rule her out as a suspect."

"Russ! That's a terrible thing to say about your own—" She let go of the dogs and stood abruptly, glancing around. "At the protest this afternoon. I heard something." She looked up at him. "It was right after you had ordered the demonstrators to disperse. I was trying to leave, and as I was making my way through the crowd, I heard someone say, 'He's not gonna be a problem after tonight, is he?'"

"Uh-huh. Look, it's common to put all sorts of ominous meanings into ordinary things when a murder—"

"Don't make me sound like I'm a few chimes short of a clock. This voice was creepy. Threatening. It made me stop where I stood to try to see who had said it."

He held up his hands. "Okay. I'm not saying you didn't hear something. But even if you did, it's not going to be of any use to us." Lyle was walking toward them, gesturing questioningly with his arms. "There must have been two hundred people in the park at that time. Maybe more. Whoever did this could have walked right past you, me, the mayor, and Officer Entwhistle, and there wouldn't be any way of knowing it."

Lyle ambled up between them. "What's up?" He bent over and scratched Bob's head and was rewarded by a tail thump. "Doc Scheeler's here, and Morin's waiting with his Baggies to catch anything good. Thought you might like to sit in."

"Yeah, I do. Reverend Fergusson didn't see anything."

"But I heard something," she said.

Lyle raised his bushy gray eyebrows. "You did? Great."

Russ shook his head. "Don't get all excited. She heard someone with a threatening voice say, 'He's not gonna be a problem after tonight' at the demonstration this afternoon. After the race."

"Oh." Lyle turned to Clare. "I'm sure it sounded scary, but it really doesn't tell us anything."

"If it *was* the man who killed Bill Ingraham, it tells us this wasn't some case of gay cruising gone horribly wrong. This was planned out in advance." Clare folded her arms, her posture challenging them to prove her wrong.

Lyle and Russ looked at each other. "Ingraham was gay?" Lyle asked. Russ nodded. "Well, that puts a different spin on things."

"A bad pickup was the first thing that popped into my head," Russ said to him. "Although I think Payson's Park and out by the old cemetery are the only places we've chased off guys cruising before." He frowned and swung back to Clare. "How do you know about cruising?"

"Oh, for heaven's sake, Russ, I didn't spend my entire adult life locked in a seminary. When I was teaching at Fort Rucker, there was a strip where men would cruise for anonymous sex. With other men. There was a murder there, too—a young man from town. Two privates on leave picked him up and then beat him to death." She looked from him to Lyle and back again. "But if I heard someone talking about murdering Ingraham this afternoon—"

"Reverend, you probably heard someone talking about his blister, not planning a murder," Lyle said. "That park was filled with the whole crowd from the race and a lot of folks who were going to stay on for the bands and fireworks. The chances the perpetrator was hanging around making threats within earshot are slim to none."

"You mean it's unheard of for someone intending murder to follow his victim around? Keep an eye on him? Scout out the best place to do it?"

Lyle looked at Russ and shrugged. "She's got a point."

Russ pinched the bridge of his nose. "She always has a point, trust me. Maybe we are looking at a premeditated murder."

"Which would mean it's tied in with the two other assaults," Clare interjected.

"Which would mean no such thing," Russ said, speaking more loudly. "We don't have any indication the attacks on Emil Dvorak and Todd MacPherson were planned. In fact, they seem to be pretty clearly crimes of opportunity. Which would argue that *if* this murder is connected to the previous assaults, it's more likely to have happened spontaneously as part of a pickup."

"Why would Bill Ingraham come to a cold, wet park for sex?" she asked. "He's staying in a comfortable inn run by hosts who wouldn't blink no matter what guy he brought home with him."

"Why do guys get trussed up in leather and let someone walk all over them with spike heels? I don't know! That's how they get their jollies!"

Lyle broke in: "This is getting real interesting, but if you want to see what Doc Scheeler finds, we'd better get over there now. I get a feeling the body could be bagged and slabbed before you two finish up."

Russ sighed. He grasped Clare's upper arms and gave her an imperceptible shake. "I don't want you walking back to the rectory alone," he said. "You understand? Stay here and I'll get someone to take you home."

"Yes, I understand," she said, a tinge of exasperation coloring her voice: "Believe me, I don't have any desire to go wandering off by my lonesome in the dark. Even with these two tagging along." She glanced down at the Berns, who had risen when Clare had and now stood leaning their broad heads against her blotchy sweatpants.

"Okay." He released her and strode toward the center of activity, Lyle matching his steps.

"You really think this might be unrelated to the previous assaults?" Lyle asked, pausing before the bushes to put his latex gloves back on.

"No." Russ tried to tug his gloves on too quickly and got his fingers stuck. He wiggled them partway off and eased them on more carefully. "I don't believe in coincidences. I think he was targeted. What I want to know is how." He held an armful of wet spiny-leafed branches out of the way. He and Lyle stepped into the now partially cleared opening where Sergeant Morin and Dr. Scheeler crouched over the body in the trough.

Scheeler glanced up and nodded at Lyle. "Deputy MacAuley. And you must be . . ."

"Russ Van Alstyne. Chief of police. Whaddya have there?"

The medical examiner gestured with a long probe. "By the temperature, I'm going to say he died within the last two hours. There's not enough water in here to change his lividity much. You don't see this very often." He delicately traced along what used to be Bill Ingraham's neck. "Cut right through almost to the spine. He must have bled out almost instantly."

"We were thinking a garrote."

"Yes, I think you may be right. I'll need to examine the edges under the microscope, of course, but it doesn't have the shape characteristic of a knife cut." The dead man's hands were already encased in opaque Baggies to preserve possible unseen skin samples trapped under the fingernails. Scheeler slid a probe under one of the plastic-wrapped hands and lifted it slightly. "He had no lacerations or defensive marks here. You'd expect to see those if someone had been coming at him with a knife." He removed the probe and lightly touched several places on the face. "And see here, and here, where the bruises are? I can't be sure until I can examine the bone underneath, but I think he was beaten after he was dead."

"After?" Lyle said.

"The bruises are flat, hardly diffuse at all. There's been no swelling. Swelling happens fairly quickly to tissue while it's alive, but it slows down markedly postmortem. I suspect he was killed quickly and then beaten."

"Uncontrolled rage?" Lyle asked, raising his thick eyebrows at Russ.

"Or he wanted it to look like the other beatings," Russ said. "It was a he, wasn't it? It takes a hell of a lot of upper-body strength to pull a wire through someone's throat."

"Absolutely. I suppose a particularly muscular woman might have been able to accomplish the feat, but I'd lay my money on an adult male. And the wire or fishing line he used must have either been wrapped around something sturdy he could hold on to or—"

"He wore gloves," Lyle said, completing the thought. "That's something I'd like to find."

"If the glove fits, you must convict," Russ misquoted. "Can you confirm it was done here, Doc?"

"Oh, yes." Dr. Scheeler pointed to the edge of the trough, where blood was congealing to the consistency of skim on a pudding. "There's no doubt in my mind that he was alive when he walked in here. Once he's in the lab, I may be able to see some markings that will tell me if he was coerced or not," he added, forestalling Russ's next question. The doctor unfolded himself from his crouch and stood, snapping his gloves off and pocketing them. "I'm done with the in situ examination. I should have the preliminary report to you within twenty-four hours. Toxicology will take longer—the state lab has been backed up."

Russ peeled his gloves off and shook the medical examiner's hand. "Thanks for getting out here so promptly."

"It's good to work with you. I'm just sorry it had to be under these circumstances. I know Emil Dvorak well. He's a fine pathologist. Damned shame."

They exited the small copse, and Russ waved the mortuary boys over to do their job. "We need to extend the tape all along here," he said to Lyle, his arm swinging wide. "I want this line of brush gone over from the little gate down to the riverbank as soon as it's daylight. He left one way or the other, dripping blood, maybe shucking gloves. There's got to be something." He caught sight of Clare, still sitting beneath a tree with the dogs. "And I need to figure out how to get Reverend Fergusson home."

"What's going on with you two?" Lyle asked, his voice neutral.

"Whaddya mean 'what's going on'? Nothing. I'm a happily married man."

"So was I," Lyle said. "Until I wasn't anymore."

Russ's reply was cut off by a gleeful crow from Sergeant Morin, who emerged from the thicket ahead of the two mortuary attendants. "Take a look at what was under the body," he said loudly. A damp and bloodstained piece of paper dangled between Morin's latex-covered fingers. The tungsten lights seared the paper, popping the black lettering off the page so that even from several feet away, Russ could see the boldfaced heading: STOP BWI DEVELOPMENT NOW!

CHAPTER ELEVEN

R uss closed his eyes for a moment, but the overly illuminated image of the bloody paper was there, too. "Okay," he said, "bag it. Maybe we'll luck out and there will be usable prints."

Lyle sidled closer. "Your mom *is* still in the county lockup, right?" When Russ rounded on him, teeth bared, the deputy chief held up both hands in mock surrender. "Just kidding! Just kidding!"

Russ grunted. "*You* are. Whoever thinks it next won't be. Christ, this is all I need—someone thinking I have a personal stake in the outcome of a murder investigation."

"Oh, come on. In the first place, who's gonna believe one of your mom's tree-hugging friends slit Ingraham's throat? And it's not as if you've coddled them. Trust me, slinging your own mother's butt in jail showed the world you are an incorruptible cop."

Russ looked at him. "Thank you, Officer Friday. Now, let's wrap up this scene and get the gawkers out of here." He shaded his eyes against the glare of the lights and squinted toward the dwindling crowd. "Looks like Durkee has finished taking names. Get him to run the tape down to the water." He looked at his watch. "Glens Falls Dispatch is taking our calls right now. I'm going to get them to buzz Davies and McCrea at home to let them know to come straight here when their shifts start tomorrow morning. I want you here, too."

"That'll put me on—"

"Overtime. I know, I know. Be here anyway."

The slither of tires on grass and the bounce of a new set of lights made him look away. The Channel 6 news van was pulling up, just in time to get the story taped for the eleven o'clock broadcast. He shook his head. Dealing with the press was his second-least-favorite part of the job, surpassed only by presenting the department's budget to the Board of Aldermen.

A pretty young blonde who looked more like a kindergarten teacher than a reporter slipped out of the van, followed by a gorilla of a camera-man loaded down with what must have been sixty pounds of equipment. They conferred for a minute. From the way their arms were moving, they were figuring out what he was going to shoot. Then the gorilla caught sight of Russ and Lyle and pointed at them. The reporter ducked under the tape and advanced on their position, trailed by her cameraman.

"You want me to deal with 'em?" Lyle asked. There were only two types of cops who liked talking to the press: ambitious politicians or frus-trated performers. Lyle, who once told Russ he had wanted to be Buffalo Bob when he grew up, fell in the latter group. He could spin out a "No com-ment" into a twenty-minute story without ever letting on it was all puffed air.

"Naw, I'll handle it. Just button this place up fast, okay? I want to be out of here before Channel Thirteen decides this is newsworthy enough to send over a van, too." If it were a single news outfit here tonight, he would only have to appear on TV once. After the initial photo op at the crime scene, he could usually get away with commenting to reporters over the phone.

Lyle waved an acknowledgment as he headed off to collect Durkee. The reporter pulled up in front of him and stuck out her hand. "Sheena Bevin, WTYY News. You're Chief Van Alstyne?" Her voice was that peculiar combination of melodious and strident that all television reporters seemed to have.

He started back toward the police line. "Yep."

She smoothed her white shirt and tugged on something clipped under her navy windbreaker. It was a microphone in a holster, which she un-spooled and extended toward him. Behind and to the left of her shoulder, the camera light blazed on. "Chief, the report we got was that there was a possible homicide here tonight. What can you tell us? Who's the victim?"

He stopped next to the yellow tape, which was shivering in a barely per-ceptible wind. He hoped to hell the rain would hold off. Trying to search the stretch of brush in the dark was going to be impossible; finding anything in a downpour in the morning would only be marginally less so. "We're not releasing the name of the victim until we've been able to notify any rela-tives."

"So it was a homicide?" Her shining blond hair seemed to gleam in interest.

He held up his hands. "Let me put what information I can give you in the proper order. At approximately nine-thirty tonight, we received a call that one of the spectators at the fireworks here had found a body. Deputy Chief MacAuley and Officer Durkee responded. Upon arriving at the scene, they secured the area and sent for Sergeant Morin, a state police forensics technician, and Dr. Scheeler, our temporary medical examiner. The victim was a middle-aged white male who was killed within an hour or so of the start of the fireworks. We are actively pursuing leads, and if anyone in the vicinity saw anything suspicious, we ask that they report it to the Millers Kill Police Department."

"How was the victim killed?"

"I can't release that at this time."

"Do you have any significant evidence? Any suspects?"

"Dr. Scheeler believes there may be some excellent forensic evidence once he's had a chance to examine the body." The doctor hadn't actually said that, but in Russ's experience, all pathologists were sure they'd find something if they looked hard enough. "We have no suspects at the moment."

"Thank you, Chief." The camera light went out and she said, "Thanks a lot," in a more natural voice. "We want to get some establishing shots and some reactions from the witnesses. Do you mind?"

It was a pro forma question, since he didn't have the authority to stop the press, but he appreciated the courtesy. "Just make sure you don't cross the line. We're still securing the scene."

"Will do. Matt, let's go." There was a clunk of metal hitting metal as the gorilla shouldered his camera and followed her.

Russ ducked under the tape and jogged to his cruiser, popping open the door to reach the radio. He watched the mortuary assistants leaving the thicket. The bag boys—Lyle's name for them—picked their way through the brush, careful not to dislodge the contents of their pallet. The mound of shiny black plastic suddenly made Russ think of the fat blood sausages his grandmother Campbell used to urge on him. The image made his stomach churn. The Channel 6 cameraman was following the body's progress from the brush to the back of the van.

Russ gave his instructions to one of the Glens Falls dispatchers who handled Millers Kill 911 calls between 10:00 P.M. and 6:00 A.M. Sheena Bevin was working her way through the remaining spectators, asking questions, occasionally pulling out the little microphone. He finished up with the Glens Falls dispatcher and headed over to help Lyle and Durkee finish up.

He was a good fifteen yards away from the scene, twist-tying tape to a flexible plastic pole, when a flash of light in the corner of his eye made him look up, just in time to see the camera trained on Clare. Even from that distance, he could see her body language had changed from shocked and horrified to . . . well, righteous indignation was probably the right description, seeing as she was a priest. Their conversation in the hospital corridor outside the waiting room resurrected itself: Clare, arms akimbo, swearing to march on the police station if there was one more attack. "Oh," he said. "Oh no. No, no, no." The Reverend Clare Fergusson on a crusade was likely to say anything.

He dropped the tape and strode toward the small cluster of trees where Clare, now gesturing widely, was making her point. God, why hadn't he put duct tape over her mouth and locked her in the squad car when he'd had the chance? He kept himself from breaking into a jog, but double-timed his steps until he was close enough to hear, "lack of respect for common humanity and basic civil rights—"

"Clare!" he said. Clare and the reporter both jerked their heads in his direction. He propped what he hoped looked like a smile on his face and tried again in a less threatening tone of voice. "Reverend Fergusson? I hope I don't have to remind you that giving out some information could jeopardize this investigation."

"How?" she asked.

He sucked in air between gritted teeth, but before he could reply, Bevin and the cameraman had pivoted toward him. "Chief Van Alstyne, we've heard that tonight's murder victim and the victims of the two assaults in Millers Kill this past week were all gay men. Can you comment on this?"

"No," he growled.

"Are the police investigating this as a hate crime? Are you linking it to the other assaults?"

"We pursue any murder to the fullest extent of our resources, whether you label it a hate crime or not. I'm of the opinion every murder is a hate crime, and I'm not going to treat one differently from another because of who the victim was."

"So tonight's victim was gay?"

He wanted to strangle Bevin. No, he wanted to strangle Clare. The camera light pinned him like an interrogation lamp.

"I can't comment on the victim until we've notified the next of kin."

"How about the assault victims?"

"Look, I'm not going to comment on this. I'm not going to out anyone on the eleven o'clock news."

"Would you advise area residents who might be homosexual to take extra precautions?"

"Whoever did this tonight is on the loose until we bring him in. I'd advise *all* area residents to take extra precautions. Now, I need to wrap things up and make sure Reverend Fergusson gets home." He smiled at Clare in a way that conveyed she might arrive in several pieces. "So we'll have to cut this short."

Bevin slid a finger along her throat in exactly the same line that the garrote had taken when it cut through Ingraham's neck. The cameraman killed the light. "We know that the dead man is the president of BWI Development," the reporter said, "and we'll sit on his identity tonight. But I'll give you fair warning that we're going to run it on the five-thirty show tomorrow. This is going to be a big story."

He waited until Bevin and the gorilla had decamped before taking Clare's elbow. "You," he said, his voice barely audible. "In the car. Now."

"What about the dogs?"

"In the back." He steered her toward the squad car. "I'm going to sign out with MacAuley and Durkee." He reached through the window on the driver's side to unlock the back doors. "Then you and I are going to have a little talk."

Things were winding down. Dr. Scheeler was gone, the mortuary van was pulling out, and the Channel 6 news team was loading their equipment. Durkee was bent over the electrical cords running from his car to the lamps. All but a few hard-core spectators had drifted away.

"Make sure you clear out the last of those," he said to Lyle, jerking his thumb at the remaining handful of gawkers. One of the tungsten lights blinked out, and the thicket was suddenly half-dark, heavy with mist and shadows. The pole clattered as Durkee telescoped it down. "I'm taking Reverend Fergusson home."

"Hey, you've had a long day," Lyle said, folding his arms across his chest. "Why don't you head on home and let me take care of her? I want to go back to the station anyway, to get my report down."

"Do you know what she did? She told that reporter it was Ingraham. *And* she told her he was gay. *And* that the other guys were gay. It's gonna be all over the news that Millers Kill is running rampant with hate crimes. God! I could . . ." He wasn't sure *what* he could do.

"Let me handle it, then. Give yourself a chance to calm down."

"Oh no. I want to tell her exactly how bad she's screwed us. When I get done, she's not going to pick up her newspaper at the front door without running it past me first." He exhaled.

Lyle opened his mouth and then shut it again. "Okay. I'll see you tomorrow, then."

"Yeah. G'night." He stalked back to his squad car, got in, buckled up, turned on the ignition, and threw the car into reverse without saying a word. He looked over his shoulder, ignoring the woman in the passenger seat, and discovered two hairy heads blocking his rear view. "Down!" he said. The dogs whined briefly and then lowered themselves, paws pitter-pattering on the cruiser's vinyl upholstery as they arranged themselves on the backseat. He rolled backward between two trees, turned around, and drove slowly over the grass to the park entrance. He nosed through the gates, looked both ways, then bumped the car over the curb onto Mill Street.

"Well?" Clare said. "Say something!"

"You broke your promise to me."

"I did not!"

"Yes, you did. You stood right in front of me and promised you wouldn't talk to the press about this."

"That was when there were only two attacks. For God's sake, Russ, a man has been murdered! That's more important than some exercise in spin control."

He turned on her at that. "Damn it! Do you really think that's what I'm worried about? Bad press?" He snapped his attention back to the road. "You insult me." She glanced at him and then looked down. "You think my job is about solving crimes?" he continued. "It isn't. Solving a crime means I've already failed. My job is preventing crimes. And you and Sheena, Queen of the Reporters, have just made that more difficult."

"By telling the truth?"

"Your version of the truth."

"Oh, come off it. If you mean to tell me you still don't think these attacks are connected, I will laugh in your face. I swear I will. It's time to speak out, Russ. It's *past* time."

He swung the cruiser onto Main Street. "Fine! Preach against prejudice. Start a voter initiative to change the state's constitution. Get up a gay-pride parade and march it down Main Street. I don't care so long as you have a permit. But don't compromise my investigation and start a panic because you've decided the three cases are connected!"

"I don't need your permission to help people! And I don't need your permission to speak out against hatefulness! If you had warned the press Saturday that someone was going around beating up gay men, maybe Bill Ingraham wouldn't have been caught in the bushes with his pants down!"

The light at Main and Church turned red and he slammed on his brakes, throwing them both against their shoulder harnesses. The dogs barked and scrabbled against the seat for purchase. He twisted so he could look at her head-on. Her hazel eyes were glittering in the light from the dashboard and he could see patchy red spots high on her cheeks.

"Is that what you think? Is that what you really think?" His rage, which had been feeding on each exchange like a fire consuming logs, died out. She opened her mouth, closed it again, and compressed her lips. Her eyes shifted away from his. "It is," he said, a part of him surprised at how much the realization hurt. "You think I'm responsible for Ingraham's death."

"No. I said he *might* have acted differently if . . . if he had been aware . . ." She sounded strange as she tried to backpedal. It wasn't like her.

The light turned green, and he faced forward, his eyes fixed on the road. They traveled the length of Church Street in silence. He turned onto Elm and drove up the rectory drive, then put the car into park.

"Russ," she said, "I didn't mean it like that. Please."

He popped the locks and got out. He released the grateful dogs, who tumbled over themselves exiting the back seat.

"Russ . . ."

He looked at her over the cruiser's roof, thought about tossing off some line about cops always having critics, then found he couldn't. He didn't have the energy to playact with her. He shook his head. "Never mind. It's been a long day. Just . . . never mind."

Clare stood at the edge of the drive, looking at him, twisting the bottom of her sweatshirt. The dogs were already nosing at the front door, whining to be let in. He got back into the cruiser and started it up.

"I didn't mean to hurt you," she blurted out. "Russ, please. I'm sorry. . . ."

He waved a hand in acknowledgment as he pulled out of the drive. He could see her face as he drove down the street, a white oval in the darkness. The image stayed with him for a long time.

CHAPTER TWELVE

W hen Clare opened her front door the next morning to let Bob and Gal out, the air was clear, the grass and leaves were sparkling in the sunlight, and she felt rotten. Guilty. Lower than a worm's belly, as Grandmother Fergusson would have said. She leaned against one of the columns on the front porch, her hands thrust in the pockets of her seersucker robe, and tried to take some pleasure in the sight of two happy dogs sniffing out every corner of a perfect morning. But all she could envision was Russ's face, changing from anger to pain as she fumbled and missed her one chance to take back her hurtful words.

Well, she had gotten what she wanted. She had taken a stand against homophobic violence and had raised the red flag against hate crimes. And all it had taken was eviscerating her best friend.

She walked barefoot down the steps and across the lawn to the newspaper box to retrieve Monday's *Post-Star*. She took the paper back to the porch and sat on the steps, but she couldn't bring herself to open it. She didn't want to deal with murder, protests, arrests, real estate developments, and PCBs. Since when is Russ Van Alstyne my best friend? she wondered. It's not like we go out bowling together or anything. Still, it rang true. She groaned and beat herself over the head a few times with the newspaper. It didn't make her feel any better. She dropped it in her lap and bent forward, burying her face in her hands.

"God," she said, "I believe you brought me here to Millers Kill for a reason. But so far, I mostly seem to be screwing up my own life. Please help me out here. I need to know what it is I'm supposed to be doing."

Somewhere beyond the open double doors, the phone rang.

Clare raised her eyebrows and rose from her seat on the porch steps. In her experience, God didn't respond to prayer with a phone call outlining His thoughts and expectations, but she was willing to keep an open mind.

She tossed the newspaper on the sofa and went into the kitchen to pick up the phone.

"Hello, Reverend Fergusson? This is Peggy Landry."

Clare couldn't have been more surprised if it *had* been the Almighty. "Ms. Landry," she said. "Um . . . how can I help you?"

"We haven't met, but I believe you know my niece. Diana Berry? She's getting married July Thirty-first."

The whirl of speculation snapped firmly into place. Diana Berry and her fiancé, Cary—what? Wall? Ward? Wood, that was it. She remembered wondering how anyone could name a child Cary Wood. Diana had been in twice, once in February to reserve the church and once in April with her fiancé in tow for the first of the mandatory three counseling sessions. She had mentioned that her family was from the area.

"Yes, of course. I've met Diana and Cary. Although I haven't seen either of them for quite some time." In fact, the pair needed to get back in touch with her about the rest of their counseling if they wanted to tie the knot in her church.

"Diana lives in the city"—by this, Clare presumed she meant New York—"and her mother, my sister, lives over in Syracuse, so I'm helping out with organizing on this end. I've been running myself ragged lately with business, and I'm really falling behind on this wedding thing. But! Things have happened this weekend, and that's why I'm calling you."

Clare thought for a moment that Peggy was referring to Bill Ingraham's death. She blinked. No. The jaunty tone, the brisk speech—Peggy Landry had no idea that the man who was developing her property had been bloodily murdered the night before. Good Lord. She clapped her hand over her mouth. Should she say something, or just let the woman rattle on?

"We always have a family get-together over the Fourth of July, and this year a bunch of people decided to stay on for a few days. I thought, What a perfect time to get all the last wedding details pinned down! So I was wondering if Diana and the florist and I could drop by the church sometime today to work on the floral design."

"The floral design," Clare echoed.

"Yes, well, evidently you can't just order up flowers in vases and have someone set them here and there anymore. Nowadays, the florist wants to design the site, so we need to get her in to take a look."

Clare weighed her options. Monday was her day off. Also Mr. Hadley's day off, since the sexton worked all weekend, cleaning up before and after the services. She wouldn't be able to pass the buck by having him open the church for Landry and company. She would have to be there herself. Talk with Peggy Landry. Find out more about Bill Ingraham.

"Of course, Ms. Landry. I'd be happy to meet you at the church and let you all in. When's a good time for you?"

They agreed on ten o'clock. Clare decided not to use her two hours lead time to go running—she still felt yesterday's race in the slight stiffness in her thighs—but instead dressed quickly and put in a call to Robert Corlew's office. Corlew was a member of St. Alban's vestry. He was also a prosperous local builder, whose work ran to small developments with names like Olde Mill Town Homes and the occasional strip mall. Clare figured he might have some information on Ingraham and the Landry property, seeing as how he was in the same business. He hadn't arrived at his office yet, but she left him a message.

She let herself consider her sudden interest in Ingraham's background while she was scrambling eggs and brewing coffee. After all, if she had been right last night when she cut Russ down, his murder was more or less random, the result of being the wrong man in the wrong place. Her time would be better spent organizing that march Russ had suggested. But as soon as Peggy Landry had identified herself, Clare had felt a powerful impulse to take a closer look at Ingraham. What had Russ said to her last night? "Your version of the truth"? *There's 'I'm right' and there's 'you're right' and there's 'what's right',* her grandmother Fergusson had always said. *You can't have but one of them. Which one will it be?* The only way she was ever going to be able to face Russ again was if she let go of "I'm right" and went looking for "what's right."

◆ ◆ ◆

The great Gothic doors of St. Alban's, polished by the sun and framed by masses of summer flowers, seemed preferable as a spot for getting married, rather than the cool and shadowed interior of the church. Of course, Clare thought as she unlocked the doors, the florist couldn't charge for the design if that were the case. She had just emerged from the sacristy, where the light switches were, when she heard the clatter of sandals on the tiled floor of the nave.

"Hello? Anybody home?"

"Over here," Clare called.

Diana Berry resembled her aunt—angular, tanned, no-nonsense. Her fair hair was long and loose, where Peggy Landry's was cropped close to her head, not a strand out of place. But Clare could envision her at her aunt's age, a tough businesswoman or one of those relentlessly efficient wife-mother-volunteer types who ran their communities. Or both. She and Peggy were dressed much as Clare was—sleeveless blouses and chinos or jeans. The woman accompanying them was obviously the florist, an Asian woman of perhaps forty, whose thick, bobbed hair swung along her jawline as she glanced around and then approached the altar.

"Fabulous space," she said.

"Thanks," Clare replied.

"Reverend Clare!" Diana said. "It's great to see you again. Thanks for letting us in on such short notice. This is Lin-bai Tang, our floral designer, and my aunt, Peggy Landry."

Clare shook hands all around.

"What is it," Tang asked, her eyes taking in the ornate woodwork, "mid-nineteenth century?"

"Started in 1857, completed just after the end of the Civil War."

"Wonderful. I adore Gothic churches. Come here, Diana, let's start at the altar rail. I see faux-medieval swags with flowers that look as if they've been gathered on the riverbank by the Lady of Shallot. . . ." She whipped out a notebook and a measuring tape.

"Wow," Clare said. "She's good. I don't know what her flowers look like, but she's good."

"She's the hottest floral designer in Saratoga. We were lucky to get her at the height of the season. My brother-in-law's dropping a fortune on this thing. For the amount he's spending, the bride and groom ought to give him a money-back guarantee."

"Where's the reception?"

"At the Stuyvesant Inn. Do you know it?"

Clare blinked. "I do, yes."

"Of course, we think of it as Grandfather's house. It used to be ours before my grandmother sold it. Enormous old place, impossible to keep up."

Clare got the distinct feeling Ms. Landry wouldn't mind trying, though. "The inn's lovely," she said. "How nice for you that it's available for a family celebration."

"Well, it's been a pain to try and handle the latest owners, I can tell you." Landry sat down in a pew, tipped the kneeler into position with one sandal-shod foot, and propped her feet up on the red velvet surface. "Fussy little pair. All these rules we have to work around. 'No drinks in the parlor. No high heels in the music room.' They're trying to make it a historically correct tomb. They've been running it as an inn for a year, and I can't imagine how they're managing to stay in business."

Clare sat down sideways in the pew in front of Landry's, crossing her arms over the smooth, age-darkened wood. Ron Handler's unflattering description of Peggy Landry suddenly made sense. Why hadn't he and Stephen mentioned that Landry's niece was one of their clients?

"It's a shame you couldn't have seen it in its heyday, when my grandfather was alive. It had real elegance then, and comfort, and dash. I still have quite a few family pieces at my own house." She stretched a well-toned arm along the back of the pew. "If I ever manage to get the place back in the family, I'll have a head start on furnishing it properly."

Clare, who had been trying to fit Emil Dvorak, the Stuyvesant Inn, Peggy Landry, and Bill Ingraham into some sort of logical picture, snapped back to attentiveness. "You're hoping to own the inn someday? But the new innkeepers just bought it a year or so ago, from what I understand."

Landry snorted. "That pair are the third owners in the last decade. So far, the Landry house has proved too expensive for a summer home and too distant to be a retreat from New York City. I'm not particularly confident that it'll be any more manageable as an inn." She snorted. "I suppose the fact that I still refer to it as 'the Landry house' gives my feelings away. Up till now, I've never had the wherewithal to make it more than a pipe dream."

"You must be delighted about the new spa being built," Clare said, keeping her voice as casual as possible.

"Delighted? Yes, I suppose you could say that. It makes it sound as if it's a piece of good fortune that happened by chance, though." She crossed her arms over her chest, crinkling the smooth white cotton of her blouse. "I've worked like a dog for three years putting this thing together. Not to mention all the time before, keeping my ear to the ground, building up my capital, forgoing the income I could have made if I had done what everyone said and put a campground or a couple of rustic cabins at the site." She smiled in a satisfied way. "I knew the potential that was there. I knew that land could be used for something much, much bigger. I played my hand out, and now I've got the pot, metaphorically speaking."

"You must be worried about the protests and all. I mean, if the resort doesn't go forward . . ."

"Won't happen. I guarantee it. The protesters are just a bunch of tree-huggers blowing smoke. They have no real political clout."

What if the head of the development company is dead? Clare thought. She absolutely did not want to be the one to break that piece of news to Peggy Landry. She cast about for an innocuous response. "Um . . . I confess I don't know how it works, but what if the state looks at the site again because of this new pollution problem?"

"We've gotten an absolutely clean bill of health in all the site surveys up to now. I don't expect that will change."

Landry sounded utterly sure of her statement. Clare raised her eyebrows. "Aren't you worried that an inquiry, or recertification or whatever, would bring the development to a halt for however long the DEP was poking around? I thought Mr. Ingraham"—the name recalled the image of what she had seen in the scrub at Riverside Park, and her breath caught for a moment before she could go on—"said he would withdraw from the project if they even got involved."

"John Opperman and I agree that's unnecessary. We have a perfectly legal right to proceed full speed with the development, which means the bulk of the work would be done before the DEP finished with its initial evaluations here in Millers Kill. The workers are supposed to be on site today. We need to pick up the pace in order to get all the outside work done before winter." She looked distracted for a moment and reached for her purse. "In fact, I need to speak with John." She retrieved a cell phone. "If you don't mind, Reverend Fergusson?"

Amusement won out over amazement at the sheer brass of being asked to remove herself from a pew in her own church so that Landry could use it as an office. Clare slid out of the pew and wandered to the back of the church, where the great double doors were open to a warm breeze, the smell of roses, and the faint sound of children playing in the gazebo across the street. It seemed strange to be planning for winter at the delicious peak of summer. It also seemed strange to think of death in the middle of such a cornucopia of life. She thought of the old words from the graveside committal service, which she had always disliked for their fatalistic view: "In the midst of life we are in death."

Behind her, Diana Berry and Lin-bai Tang had descended to the center aisle, exclaiming over the possibilities of sprays and ribbons and candelabra. Tang's measuring tape snapped briskly as they made their plans. If the rest of the celebration was anything on the scale of the flowers, this *would* be the wedding of the century. Peggy Landry's brother-in-law was either rolling in it or about to go broke. She wondered how much

Landry had sunk into the development. Would she be ruined if the deal didn't come off? What about the construction workers and everyone else employed by the project? She shook her head. Anything she might think was sheer speculation at this point. Maybe Ingraham's partner would simply carry on without him. Of course, that begged the question of whether the construction at the location of the old quarry was indeed responsible for the rise in PCB levels.

She was suddenly struck by a thought. What if someone who wanted to stop the project knew that Peggy Landry and Ingraham's partner were planning to proceed full steam ahead? Would the death of the president of BWI slow things down? Long enough for the DEP to address the environmental concerns and halt the development for a retesting of the site? She reached up to her hair and twirled her ponytail into a bun, thinking furiously. She wished she had paid closer attention to the business end of her parents' small aviation company. She might know more about what happens when a company's principal owner dies.

"Reverend Clare? Is everything all right?" Diana Berry's voice broke her concentration. Clare let her impromptu bun fall back into a ponytail and dropped her hands. "You look a little upset," Diana continued.

"No, I'm fine. Just thinking." The florist was standing next to the young woman, tucking the measuring tape back into her purse. Clare glanced toward Peggy Landry, who nodded and raised her hand, then said something into her cell phone. "All set?" Clare said. "Did you get everything you need?"

"Yes, thank you," Lin-bai Tang said. "It'll be a real pleasure working in your space."

Peggy Landry finished up with her call and replaced the phone in her purse. She rose and joined them. "Sorry, everyone. Business before pleasure."

Diana grinned. "Business *is* your pleasure, Aunt Peggy. I'm amazed I could tear you away today."

"I have to run," the florist announced, looking at her watch. "Diana, I'll write up the plan and fax a copy to you and to your mother, along with the estimates." She held out her hand to Clare. "Thank you again for letting us in on such short notice, Reverend Fergusson. Bye, all!" With a final swing of her heavy hair, she was gone.

Clare unclipped her key ring from a belt loop. "Are you two all set?" she asked.

"I am," Diana said. "Next stop for me is the mall near Glens Falls. I'm checking out tablecloths and napkins for the reception."

"Doesn't the Stuyvesant Inn supply the linens?" Clare asked.

"Oh, of course. But you know how it is with a hotel or caterers. You can get any color you want, so long as it's white. I'm going to have pale floral undercloths with a filmy overcloth caught up around the rim of the table with tiny clips of flowers. And solid napkins picking up one of the floral colors. Doesn't it sound stunning?"

Clare thought it sounded criminally extravagant, but she held her tongue. "Mmm," she said.

"Aunt Peggy, is Mal going to be able to pick you up?" Diana continued. "I don't mind running you, but we'll be all day trying to fit everything in."

Her aunt pointed to her purse. "I called him. He's on his way. He just got out of bed. You know Mal."

Diana gave a look that said that she knew Mal very well. "All right. I'm off. But look, I've got my phone, so if he bails out on you for whatever reason, call me." She shook hands with Clare. "Thanks again, Reverend Clare. I'm so glad I picked your church for the most important day of my life."

She was through the door and halfway down the walk when Clare remembered, calling after her, "I need to see you two for more counseling sessions!" Diana waved in acknowledgment but did not pause. Clare sighed.

"Do engaged couples still have to do counseling?" Landry said. "I thought that went the way of ladies wearing hats in church. It's not like they haven't already done everything already."

Clare was reminded of her mother's response when her brother Brian had said the same thing during his girlfriend's first visit: *You haven't done it in my house.*

"If the Episcopal church is going to put its official stamp of approval on a couple, it wants to be satisfied the pair knows what they're doing. Priests can refuse to marry a couple who seem unready for the responsibilities of marriage."

"Really? Does that ever happen?"

Clare shook her head. "Not much. What's more common is that the priest might schedule more premarital counseling, or direct the couple to other professionals who can deal with the problem areas—a sex therapist, a financial planner, what have you. It's weird, really, when you think about it. An engaged couple will spend months picking out menus and flowers and clothes, but only three hours sitting down and talking about what happens after they make a lifetime commitment."

Landry smiled cynically. "Well, it's hardly a lifetime commitment anymore, is it?"

"It should be," Clare said. The words made her think about Russ, and she felt a sting. Enough about marriage. She wanted to know more about Bill Ingraham. She shoved her hands into her pockets and encountered her key ring. "Look, Peggy, if you have to wait awhile for your ride, why don't you come over to the rectory? It's just next door."

Landry slid her purse strap over her shoulder, her long, thin fingers caressing the leather. "My nephew is supposed to pick me up. Mal is nothing if not unreliable, but he did say he was getting into the car as soon as he hung up, so I ought to stay here. If he doesn't find me where he expects, he's likely to get distracted, and then I won't see him again until Tuesday morning."

"Does he live in Millers Kill?"

Landry let out a short laugh. "He doesn't live anywhere right now. No, that's not entirely true. He's staying at my house until either he can get his act together or I lose all patience and throw him out."

"Did he lose his job? Or is it that he just doesn't know what he wants to do with his life?"

"I think he knows what he wants to do. He's just having trouble living a life of wealth and leisure without any visible means of support."

Clare grinned. "Yes, I've heard that can be tricky. Are you sure I can't get you to—"

"My God, I can't believe it. He's broken his land speed record." Landry gripped Clare's arm and tugged her through St. Alban's great double doors. Stepping into the sunshine from the thick stone interior was like being released from an ancient prison, going from dimness into light, from cool to warm, from stillness to life. Clare couldn't help closing her eyes and lifting her face to the sun for a moment before turning to secure the antiquated iron lock. She could hear Landry striding across the lawn toward the parking lot on the opposite side of Elm Street. Clare dropped the keys back into her pocket and trotted toward the lot, where Landry was standing beside a Volvo sedan.

"Don't worry, I won't keep you all day," Landry was saying to the driver. She turned to Clare. "Thanks, Reverend Fergusson. Look, about Diana and Cary's counseling. I'm throwing a party for them out at my place this Friday.

Seven-thirty. Come an hour early and I promise I'll lock the happy couple in the den with you and let you go at it." Her gaze flicked over Clare's outfit. "We'll be dressing. Oh, let me introduce you to my nephew. Mal, come out of there and say hi."

The young man who reluctantly got out from behind the steering wheel could have stepped just as reluctantly from the pages of a glossy magazine. He was beautiful, in the full-lipped, thin-bodied, blank-eyed way of models. His shining hair fell in an artless tousle that could only have come from frequent and expensive attention, and his five o'clock shadow was more of a statement of style than a missed shave.

"Malcolm, this is Clare Fergusson. She'll be officiating at Diana's wedding. Clare, Malcolm Wintour."

Upon closer viewing, Clare could see he wasn't quite as young as she had thought. Telltale lines framed his eyes, which were extremely dilated. It looked as if this exotic hothouse specimen had taken some sort of pepper-upper before breaking that land speed record. "How do you do," she said, shaking his hand. His grip was stronger than she would have guessed from his fashionably wasted frame. He dropped his gaze and mumbled like a shy adolescent. It sounded like "Pleasameetcha."

"I'm afraid we have to get going. Come along, Mal, lots of stops to make before I can turn you free." Malcolm got back behind the wheel and leaned over to unlock the passenger door for his aunt.

Clare bit the inside of her lip in frustration. She had spent all her time talking about weddings and the development, and now Peggy was leaving and she didn't know a thing more about Bill Ingraham than she had sitting on her front porch. Weddings. The development. *The development.*

"Peggy, I'd love to visit the site and see where the new spa is going to be."

Landry paused in the act of sliding into the passenger seat. "What?"

"The development. I'd like to drive out and see the development. There's been so much talk about it, pro and con, I'd really like to get out there, see what it's all about, get a feel for what sort of jobs are going to be created. So I can convey that to my congregation." She flushed a little at that instant fabrication. Now she would have to write a sermon about the development to keep herself honest.

Landry frowned again. "It's pretty much a bunch of rough-plowed roads, holes in the ground, and big piles of dirt, Reverend Fergusson. I don't think you'd get much from it at this stage."

"Please?" She copied her mother's wheedling voice, like sugar syrup over crushed ice. "It'd mean so much to me."

Landry gestured with her hands, half in puzzlement, half in surrender. "Okay. Sure. When?"

"Today? It's my day off, and I don't have anything scheduled. You did say they were working today."

Landry checked her slim watch. "It'll take me at least another three hours to hit the tent rental, the craft store, and the lighting place. Then I need lunch. . . . Shall we say three o'clock? That should give me enough time."

"Three o'clock it is."

"Do you need directions?"

"No, no," Clare said. "I'll just follow the road until I hit the dirt pile."

CHAPTER THIRTEEN

The road leading up to the future Algonquin Spa was dirt and gravel, narrow, marked by switchbacks every quarter mile as it made its way up the mountain. It put Clare in mind of a hunting-camp road, so when she reached the end, she had to blink three times in order to reconcile what she had been envisioning with what was actually before her.

An area the size of two football fields had been denuded of trees, terraced into four levels, and scraped flat to the yellow-orange soil. Several openings had been cut into the trees surrounding the building site, all but their first few feet hidden from view by the dense forest. She could see pallets of lumber covered in clear plastic tarps and barrels of steel rebars, waiting for the start of construction. Dump trucks, excavators, bulldozers, and a half dozen other machines she couldn't name dotted the site like dinosaurs grazing, but the only engine she could hear running was the Shelby's, purring quietly after its chug up the mountain. Nothing was moving. In fact, the place seemed unpopulated, with the exception of a few hard-hatted men clumped in front of a long trailer. There was an uneven line of pickups, interspersed with a token car or two, to her left. She pulled in next to a Ford truck with a toolbox in the bed and a gun rack in the window. Probably not a lot of Sierra Club members here, she thought as she got out of her car. The sense of openness and clear sky was dazzling after the tunnel of trees that was the road. It smelled good, earth and oil and the wet odor of new concrete, like the small airfields around her parents' place. It had heated up since morning, but despite the strength of the sun beating the soil into powder-cake dryness, there was enough of a cooling breeze from the surrounding woods to make it comfortable. Clare pocketed her keys and walked over to the trailer.

The cluster of men loosened a little as she approached. There were five or six of them, in dirt-stiffened jeans and well-worn T-shirts featuring NASCAR racing, a plumbing company advertisement, and the Desiderata.

One man wore an illustrated catalog of sexual positions on his chest. She decided, all things considering, to address the Desiderata guy.

"Hi, there. I'm supposed to meet Peggy Landry at three. Can you tell me where to find her?"

"Dunno," the man said. "She was here for about five minutes and then took off again."

"You ain't here with Leo Waxman, are you?" the NASCAR-shirted man asked. "From the state geologist's office?"

"Nope," she said, "I'm just here to get an eyeful of the site. Peggy told me I could have the three-dollar tour."

The one with the educational shirt grinned at her, revealing that while he may have known all about sex, he had a way to go with dental hygiene. "Well, we've all been taken off duty for now, so I can show you around, baby. You wanna see my big machine?"

The big guy in the plumbing shirt whacked him. "Shut up, Charlie." He looked at Clare. "You a friend of Ms. Landry's, ma'am?"

Clare smiled beatifically and gave them what she thought of as her *Touched by an Angel* look. "I'm her priest," she said, stretching the truth. "Reverend Clare Fergusson of St. Alban's Church."

The leer vanished off the face of Mr. Sexual Positions, and his eyes darted around frantically, evidently looking for a rock to crawl under. The big guy whacked him again, grinning. "Ha! Ya mook!" He nodded to Clare. "Pleased to meet you, Reverend. I'm Ray Yardhaas. Like Charlie here said, we were called off duty 'bout an hour ago, after Ms. Landry had gone. We're just waiting to hear if we're going to work again today or if we can go home. I'm afraid if you came out to see the big dig, you're out of luck."

"Actually, I was interested in seeing the grounds," she said. "Not that I don't have enough of the kid in me to enjoy great big construction machines." She glanced at the long trailer, which could only have been the field office. "Just this morning, Peggy told me work would be going on as usual. How come you all were pulled off the job?"

"They don't tell us why, ma'am." The big man sounded more amused than offended. "Something's up, though. Ms. Landry no sooner gets here than she gets a call and takes off; then the geologist shows up to meet with Opperman, but he ain't—isn't—here; then we get a call from him, telling us to lay off until he gets back to us. Last time I saw so much telephoning back and forth on a job, the bank had pulled the financing. Sure hope that's not what's happening here."

"I'm betting that one of the guys who didn't show up today's called in a fake bomb threat, so's we can all take off," said the Desiderata guy. "We should have gotten a vacation day anyway, since the Fourth was on Sunday."

"Knock it off," Ray said. "You're getting paid to hang around and tell lies about fish, ain'tcha? If he closes down the site, we can all go home on full pay. Better than the mooks who never showed up today."

Clare had a pretty good idea of what it was that had caused the flurry of telephoning and the work stoppage. "Is Bill Ingraham usually here while you're working?"

Ray thumbed at the trailer. "Right in there. He's a hands-on kind of boss, Bill is. Hasn't been in today, though."

The guy in the sexual positions T-shirt sniggered. "Maybe he's found some cute young—"

"Cut it," Ray said, spearing the other man with a look. When he spoke again to Clare, he raised his voice slightly so everyone could hear. "Bill's a good guy. He knows the building trade from the ground up and he always treats us fair. His personal life's his own business." He glanced at Mr. Sexual Positions. "Me, I kinda wonder about guys who spend a lot of time thinking about it, you know?"

The other men hooted. Within seconds, Ray's target was the eye of a hurricane of jokes about his own proclivities. They were moving past men and getting to sheep when Ray cupped a hand beneath Clare's elbow and drew her a few feet away.

"Sorry you had to hear that, ma'am. These guys, they're not used to having"—he looked as if he were struggling between the words *lady* and *priest*—"to watch their language."

Clare compressed her lips to keep from grinning. "Thank you, Ray. I appreciate your concern. So, what about the tour I was promised? I'm guessing I'm not supposed to clamber about all on my own. Can you spare me a few minutes to show me around?"

Ray frowned, looked back at the trailer, then at Clare. "I don't know, ma'am," he said finally. "Without an okay from one of the bosses—they've been keeping a tight watch on this place since the tree-huggers started kicking about PCBs and all that. Not that I think you're here to cause trouble," he added quickly.

She wasn't as sure as Ray was. "What do you think about the PCB talk? Do you have any worries, working here day in and day out?"

He shook his head. "I think it's a load of bull puckies. Bunch of hysterical women who don't know anything about construction and who'd like to make it a federal offense to cut down a tree. I'm here, moving dirt and sucking dust five days a week, and I'm as healthy as a horse." He jerked his head in the direction of the other men. "And those guys were already brain-damaged."

Clare grinned. "So there's no danger to me if I look around, right?"

Ray looked unhappy. "Well, no, but I still think you need to wait until Ms. Landry is here herself. Why don't you come back tomorrow? I'm sure everything will be back up to speed then. You'll get a better idea of what we're doing, anyway."

"Ah, but today's my day off," she said, taking a few casual steps farther away from the trailer. "C'mon, Ray. Help me out." She looked up at him, radiating sincerity and innocence. "It's not my fault Peggy didn't make our date. I'm here, just like she said, and this may be my only chance to see this place before the buildings go up. Show me around." She waved her arm to indicate the whole site and followed her own gesture toward the nearest hole in the ground.

"Oh, for heaven's sake—ma'am! Reverend!"

"What's this going to be? Is this the main building?" She strode briskly around the edge of a rectangular excavation, trying to think of an intelligent question to ask. What do you think you're going to find here? was the only one that came to mind. Russ's voice, his face last night, seemed fixed in her consciousness. "Your version of the truth," he had said. Maybe he was right. Maybe she wanted him to be right.

"Look," Ray said, catching up with her. He gave an exasperated sigh, which she ignored. "Okay, I'll show you around. But the rules say you gotta have a hard hat. So just stay there, okay? Just stay there while I get you one."

"Absolutely. Anything you say."

He dashed back to the trailer, banged inside, and emerged a few seconds later with an orange hard hat, which she dutifully strapped on. It made her hotter, but it wasn't as bad as walking around a tarmac in a flight helmet, so she couldn't complain. Then, true to his word, Ray showed her the site.

It wasn't much to see, a bunch of half-finished foundations and trenches laid with pipes. Ray pointed out where the main lodge was going to be, the guest wings and the health club. She tried to envision the lawns and gardens as Ray described the layout, but it was hard to see anything except the raw gash in the forest. Ray was very fond of numbers, so she heard about the tons of cement, the gallons of sewage, the meters of piping, the square footage of the buildings. She listened and made appropriate comments, all the time waiting for something that would reveal more of Bill Ingraham to her, trying not to analyze the impulse that had made her jump on Peggy Landry for this chance to see the man's last work in this world. Thinking too hard about her impulses always made them seem a little stupid. Better just to trust in her unconscious—or whoever it was directing her inner voice—and go with the flow.

Ray was going on about the inflow and the outflow to the whirlpools when she realized she hadn't seen something she would have expected. "Where's the pool?" she said. "I mean, they're not just going to have hot tubs, are they? On a day like today, you'd really want to be outside, soaking up the sun."

Ray pointed toward one of the openings cut into the forest. "That way." They went up the earthen ramp linking one terrace to the next and walked out of the heat and into the coolness of the trees. "The pool for this place is something else. Bill designed it around the quarry. You come here as a guest in the summer, you're going to feel like you're back at the ole swimming hole"—he grinned at her—"except the ole swimming hole didn't have a bar." The road, two ruts of bald dirt sunk between overgrown grass and delicately stemmed wildflowers, curved and headed slightly downhill. "Best thing about it is, we're killing two birds with one stone. Right now, the quarry's set up as our cement works; plus, we're getting all our stone for the paving and the walls out of it. So we're digging out the pool just by working there. When we don't need it anymore, we cement in the bottom, tile it, and there you go, just like the real thing, only better."

"Wasn't Mr. Ingraham"—she caught herself—"isn't he worried about the PCBs? I assume this is the same quarry that was used for storage back in the seventies."

The road opened up to a breathtaking view. They were at the upper end of the quarry, to one side of a curving cliff of pale rock that fell dramatically to the working quarry below. It sloped as it reached the lowest point and was riddled with ledges and dotted everywhere with stubbornly surviving plants. A narrow crevasse split the cliff, and Clare was delighted to see a thin waterfall pouring out of it, splashing over the scree and filling a wide, dark pool. "Water from the cleft," she said, grinning at Ray. "Very biblical. Is that going to flow into the swimming pool?"

"Naw. That stream comes from up the mountain, and it's too unreliable. When we started, it was gushing so fierce, you wouldn't want to go near it, but by the end of July, it'll just be a damp spot. Besides, there's no way to guarantee the quality of the water. We're gonna build a catch basin and channel it off the property. Put a screening wall of natural stone in front of it, so the guests can still see the water falling. It'll be real pretty."

Below, in the work pit, a rock crusher and a cement mixer squatted amid a tumble of rocks and enough bags of sand and chalk to stop a flood. The road Ray and Clare were standing on wound down in a curve to an earthen staging ground plowed out between the quarry and the trees. Three dump trucks, idle now, sat on the dirt, flanked by an excavator and someone's Jeep. She took off her helmet to let the breeze cool her head. Ray was right: It would be pretty. If you didn't worry about carcinogenic chemicals floating around with you, that is.

"Hey, there's Leo Waxman," Ray said, pointing. Clare squinted. She could make out a man approaching the natural pool across a field of scree. Wearing shorts and a backpack, he looked like a hiker. "Leo! Hey!" Ray headed down the steeply angled road in long strides Clare had to hop to keep up with. "Sorry," Ray said, "you were asking about the PCB stuff, right? This place was cleaned out in the eighties by the feds. Leo Waxman here, he's from the state geologist's office. He's been over this place two, three times now for the certifications. It's clean. I'd take my grandkids here for a swim"—he grinned at her again—"except once the place is built, I won't be able to afford to get through the gate."

The peculiar flat tang of rock dust rose to meet her as they neared the quarry floor. "Hey! Leo!" Ray yelled again. The man in shorts stopped, reversed himself, and began picking his way down a rubble-strewn trail toward the machinery.

Leo Waxman was surprisingly young, with a goatee and ponytail that made him look more like a grad student than a state employee. He wiped his hands on his rumpled, sweat-stained shirt, hitched his backpack more comfortably on his shoulders, and reached for Ray's hand. "Hiya, Ray, What are you doing down here?"

"Showing this lady around. Leo, this is Reverend Clare, um . . ."

"Fergusson," Clare supplied.

"Leonard Waxman," he said, shaking her hand. He glanced back up the curving road, as if to see if any other tourists would be emerging from the woods.

"Peggy Landry kindly said I could see the place. Since she's not here, Ray volunteered to be my escort." She raised her eyebrows at Waxman's backpack. "I hear you're the state geologist for this project. Are you here for business or pleasure?"

He shifted the backpack again. Clare could hear things clanking inside. "Business. Getting soil and water samples."

"Again?" Ray asked. "Jeez, how many tests does it take to satisfy the government?"

Waxman smiled briefly. "You know how it goes. Ours not to reason why, ours but to do and die. I get paid whether I think it's necessary or not."

"I thought the testing was all done and the site had been cleared," Clare said. "I was under the impression that the protests in town were to try to persuade the aldermen to get the state to take another look, not that the certification process wasn't complete."

Waxman blinked. "Well, yes, you're right. I'm doing ongoing monitoring—because of the local concerns. Actually, John Opperman asked me to do the testing. To be prepared if the case reopens." He looked at her warily. "You aren't with the Clean Water Action group, are you?"

"Me? Nope. I'm with the Episcopal church." She opened her hands. "I'm just curious. I only moved to Millers Kill last November, so I don't really have a good grasp of what the issues are."

Waxman's closed-off expression eased, and he hitched the backpack off his shoulders and set it on the ground. "It's pretty straightforward. From the early fifties to the mid-seventies, General Electric made PCB-filled capacitors at their Hudson Falls and Fort Edward plants. The waste-water from cleaning the capacitors went into the Hudson and settled into the sediment, where it sits, waiting for the state, the EPA, and the Fish and Wildlife folks to figure out whether to let it lie and degrade or dredge it up in the hopes of getting it out."

Clare waved a hand at the mountainside. "This is pretty far away from the Hudson."

"Not as far as you might think. The river originates in these mountains. Adirondack aquifers feed the Hudson and—this is why the folks in your town are up in arms—Millers Kill." He pointed to the rock cliff rising in front of them. "By the late sixties, the companies producing capacitors and the companies in charge of cleaning 'em up and disposing of them realized they had a problem on their hands. The usual technique—rinsing them—produced contaminated wastewater, which, when you released it into the environment, made a kind of toxic sludge. They were trying out different containment techniques, and one of the companies involved with solid-waste disposal came up with the idea of soaking the water into cellulose-filled containers—sort of like a giant sponge—and then capping them off and putting them someplace high and dry. Peggy Landry's dad struck a deal with them to use this quarry as a storage site. Landry and the town split the profits. Of course, they didn't really have the technology back then to safeguard adequately against seepage." He wiped his hands on his shirt again. "That particular company went belly-up in 'seventy-four, G.E. stopped making the capacitors in 'seventy-seven, and the state cleaned this place up in 'seventy-nine."

"So you don't think the rise in PCBs in the town has anything to do with the digging going on here?" Clare said.

He shook his head. "Nope. No way."

"How about the water coming from that crevasse? Does that go into the aquifer?"

"Yeah, it does. But that's from a stream that originates way up. That gorge it runs through knifes right down the mountain. It's never been used for storage or anything. Too inaccessible."

"So where do you think the pollution's coming from, then?"

"There was a fresh contamination site discovered in 'ninety-one," he said, "if *fresh* is the right word to use. An abandoned mill that had been used by G.E. Tons of sediment, seepage into the rock and groundwater—very high percentage of the stuff. Some of it was almost pure PCB. This area has had some heavy winters and rainy summers since then, which causes the contaminated sediment and water to travel through the aquifers in ways it didn't before. The PCB contamination in Millers Kill is coming from the Allen Mill site." He nodded in a satisfied way.

"You sound pretty sure of yourself," Clare said.

"I am."

Ray laughed. "See why I'm not worried, Reverend?"

Waxman hoisted his backpack. "I was just about to take my Jeep back up. Why don't I give you two a ride? It's an awful steep road."

"You done already?" Ray looked impressed. "You just got here a little while ago."

Waxman popped the back gate of the Jeep and lifted his backpack inside. "You're just used to the rate your guys work at, Ray. Fifteen minutes, coffee break, another fifteen minutes, cigarette break . . ."

Ray let out his short, explosive laugh. Waxman opened the passenger door and gestured for Clare to get in. She squeezed past the flipped-down front seat and climbed into the back, pushing aside crumpled shirts and shorts, empty soda cans, back issues of *Science* magazine, and an oily box containing unidentifiable engine parts. "Sorry about the mess," Waxman said. Ray got in the front, the Jeep sagging to one side beneath his weight. Waxman hopped in and slammed the door. The Jeep's ignition sounded as if it needed new spark plugs, and from the sound of the exhaust, a new muffler, as well. As Clare peered into the box, they lurched, and the Jeep began chugging up the hill.

"This is a bear to climb." Waxman spoke loudly over the noises coming from the Jeep. "They're going to have to regrade it if they expect to have regular traffic here."

"Bill's plan is to have a bunch of those little golf carts," Ray said just as loudly. "People will be able to drive themselves all around the complex if they want to."

Clare leaned forward. "How have you found working with Bill?" she asked Waxman.

There was no reply. For a moment, she thought she hadn't been speaking loudly enough, but then Waxman said, "I don't know him very well. Peggy, the landowner, is the person I deal with usually. And sometimes John Opperman. He's responsible for the permits."

A pothole jarred the Jeep, flinging Clare back into her seat. She jabbed at her hair, which was falling out of its twist in earnest now. She wasn't going to get many insights from Waxman, evidently. "Are you used to large developments like this?" she shouted toward the front seat. "Or is this the first big project you've worked on?"

"This is the first I've soloed on," Waxman yelled back. "I assisted on several surveys while I was getting my doctorate."

Which couldn't have been all that long ago, Clare thought. Everything about Waxman screamed graduate school poverty. He was probably still living off peanut butter sandwiches and Ramen noodles. The Jeep bumped hard again and let out an alarming rattle. "It must be gratifying, working for the state. I can't imagine there are a lot of teaching jobs out there."

"You got that right." Waxman twisted the wheel and downshifted. "State and federal agencies hire a lot more geologists than universities do. Private's really the way to go, though. You get a berth with an oil company, and you're set for life, man."

The Jeep heaved over the top of the hill and Waxman shifted into park. The sudden drop in noise level left Clare's ears ringing. "Are you two headed back, or what?"

Ray turned around in his seat. "Anything else you'd like to see, ma'am?"

So far, the only thing she had gotten from this venture was a coating of dust and a couple of mosquito bites. She didn't have any more of a feel for Bill Ingraham's life than she'd had when she started out that morning. "What else is there?" she said, stalling.

"Well, up that way is going to be the waste-reclamation plant and the power plant," Ray said, pointing to where the rutted track led up and out of sight between the trees. But there's nothing there now but a dump. It's a pretty-enough walk, if you like that sort of thing." The tone of his voice revealed that he hoped she didn't. "You can get real close to that gorge Leo was talking about. See it from above. Along this way." He gestured back toward the way they had walked. "We've cleared land for a garage for those golf carts I was telling you about. There's a helipad farther along the—"

"Whoa. Did you say helipad?"

"Yeah, but it's only temporary. For bringing in cargo that's too delicate to hump over the road, and for the VIPs to fly in and out. When construction finishes up, it'll be converted to a tennis court."

"I want to see the helipad." Something in her voice must have been different, because Ray and Waxman looked at each other. Ray shrugged.

"Okay," Waxman said. "The helipad it is."

CHAPTER FOURTEEN

W e have to backtrack to the central complex and get on the other road
there," Waxman said.

The road leading back to the main site had been a pleasant walk but was
a terrible ride. They lurched through the trees into the blinding sunlight of
the construction area, then bounced along a beaten dirt track running along
the uppermost terrace and plunged back into the forest. The Jeep jumped
and jolted, until Clare thought she would suffer permanent kidney damage.
The sample bottles in Waxman's backpack clinked together violently.

"You okay back there?" Waxman shouted.

"Just great!" she said, grabbing the seat to avoid her head smashing into
the roof.

"We're going to pave all this over before they start rolling out those golf
carts," Ray explained loudly.

"That's g—ouch!"

"Sorry," Waxman shouted. "Rock. Here we are." The tree-shrouded road
opened into more brilliant July sunshine. Waxman stopped the Jeep. Ray
hopped out, flipping his seat forward and extending a hand to Clare.

She staggered out of the backseat, feeling a sudden kinship with airsick
passengers she had seen over the years. Her gratitude at touching the ground
must have been the same as theirs. She took a deep breath.

The air was heavy with the smell of pine, warm asphalt, and oil. "Oh
my," she said. "I was expecting a little touchdown space. This is . . . professional." The clearing was the size of a house lot, squared off and leveled. It
had been fitted out with four pole-mounted lights in each corner for night
landings, with a remote refueling tank parked next to a prefab shed, which
she guessed held tools, compressors, and other maintenance requirements.
Smack in the middle of the clearing was a tennis court–size asphalt square
painted with directional markings that glowed whitely in the sun. Taking
pride of place was—

"There it is," Ray said. "It's a helicopter. You seen one, you seen 'em all, if you ask me."

"It's a Bell Four Twenty-seven." She prowled around the edges of the pad, taking it in from all angles. "A real classic. You can configure it in a half dozen ways. Very versatile. Like here, they've opted for a cargo door and boom." The cargo door was shut, but the boom, a pair of struts holding a cigar-shaped winch pod, was still rigged with a net, which puddled on the tarmac like abandoned rigging from a long-ago sailing ship. Just the sight of it made her long to be up and away.

Out of the corner of her eye, she saw Waxman and Ray exchange glances. Waxman tugged his baseball cap farther down over his eyes. "Are you a big, um, helicopter buff?"

"I was a pilot in the army," she said. "And my folks have a small aviation company." She ducked under the tail boom and peeked into the cabin window. There were two comfortable seats backed against the partial bulkhead separating the cockpit from the cabin, with a curtain of wide webbing to protect traveling VIPs from shifting cargo in the rear. She moved up a step to look into the cockpit and rested her hand on the handle of the pilot's door. It turned in her grip. It was unlocked! She hissed in excitement and twisted the door open.

"Oh, hey, Reverend!" Ray protested, but she had already hiked herself over the lip into the cockpit.

"Hello there," she said. She dropped into the seat. The controls were neat and streamlined, much simpler than the bulky instrument displays she had been used to. Must be the new digital systems. She hadn't ever flown a 427, but she had logged a lot of hours in its military version, the Kiowa.

"Reverend! You shouldn't be in there!" Ray's voice came from behind her, through the open cargo door.

"I just want a peek at the cockpit," she said. "Then I'll get right out, I promise."

"Reverend!"

The windscreen was huge, much larger than the ones she had seen in the army. The view from the air would be fantastic. She tapped at the key snug in the ignition, then looked at the fuel gauge. It was reading half-full.

The old ache to fly rose in her chest. She knew exactly what it would feel like to bring these panels to life and begin the preflight check, each movement as much of a ritual as those she used when consecrating the Host during the Eucharist. She could imagine the moment when the rumble and whine grew muffled, her headset connecting her to a world that turned and centered on the machine. The fierce vibrations through metal and bone, her eyes and hands moving over the instruments, and then, at that moment when she lifted away from earth, frustrated gravity pressing her into her seat as she broke its grip and soared into the sky.

She suddenly thought of a verse from Matthew: "Lay down all you have and follow me." She smiled one-sidedly. God certainly shouldn't have any complaints in that department. She had given up all this, every lovely leaping moment, to follow Him to Millers Kill, and for what? A congregation that was largely nonexistent in the summer and a man she shouldn't try to be friends with. She let her head drop back until it almost touched the edge of the passenger seat behind her. A man whose feelings she had unexpectedly lacerated with her big mouth and her insistence that she had a monopoly on truth. The only truth was that a man was dead. And two men had been beaten. And she had no business with any of it.

Make whole that which is broken. Her head came up again. She wrapped her hands around the steering yoke. What was that? Was that a verse from Scripture? Along with the words came a memory of Paul Foubert's face in the flashing emergency lights. Todd MacPherson's brother in the waiting room, holding back tears. Russ's expression when she blindsided him in his patrol car. Make whole that which is broken. "Is that it?" she said. "Is that for me? Does this come from You, or am I just remembering something? Are You there, or am I talking to myself?"

Of course, there wasn't any answer. Just the rising heat in the cockpit and the familiar comfort of the pilot's chair. But it wasn't familiar. This was someone else's ship, and she didn't belong here. She suddenly felt stifled by the small enclosure. She kicked open the door and jumped out, nearly landing on Ray Yardhaas.

His big, broad face was crinkled with worry. "I don't think you should have done that, Reverend."

She laid her hand on his arm. "I know. I shouldn't have. I'm sorry, Ray." She turned, shut the door, and twisted the handle, sealing it tight. "Let's head back, shall we?"

Waxman was looking at her with a peculiar expression. *Remember, wherever you go, you're an ambassador for the United States,* her grandmother used to tell her. As an ambassador for the Episcopal church, she was evidently working without a portfolio. "I like to bless flying vehicles," she said in an attempt to reassure him that she really was a priest and not an incipient thief. "Want me to do your Jeep?"

His face twitched with the strain of not showing what he thought of that offer. He shook his head. "Um, I'm headed back now, if you want a ride."

She didn't, particularly, but Ray was already opening the door for her. She stifled a resigned sigh and climbed back into the battered vehicle. "So why does BWI keep a fully equipped heliport out here? That costs a lot to maintain."

Ray grunted as he took his seat. "The way I heard it, they install one of these at every one of their project sites. Most of their resorts are in pretty hard-to-reach places. That's Opperman's strategy: buy up good land before the roads get put in and everyone and his brother catch on to it. I guess it's not worth their time to drive to a local airport."

Waxman shifted, reversed, and they shot forward onto the rutted road. "Plus, there are a lot of advantages to having a helicopter when you're in the planning stages of a major project. Mapping, surveying, bringing in the first crews fast . . ."

They went over a rock and everyone levitated for a moment. "Ooof!" Clare clutched at her seat. "Do they have a full-time pilot?"

"John Opperman flies it," Waxman shouted over the grinding noise of the Jeep's clutch. "He's the one who needs the flexibility, because he's traveling between here and Baltimore so frequently as well as to other developments."

"He's the bagman," Ray yelled, grinning.

They lurched into a rut that almost overturned the Jeep and then they were out again on the dirt track at the upper edge of the main site. Waxman roared down the earthen ramps and came to a neat halt beside the collection of pickups and old cars that constituted the crew's parking lot.

"I have to get to the lab with this stuff," Waxman said as Ray clambered out and tipped the seat for Clare. "Nice to meet you, Reverend. Ray, I'll see you around." He barely waited for Clare's sneaker to clear the door before throwing the Jeep into gear and disappearing down the forest road.

"That's a man in a hurry," Clare said, waving some of the Jeep's dust cloud away from her face.

"Yeah, well . . . From what I've seen, when Mr. Opperman says, 'Hop,' Leo Waxman asks, 'How high?' Remember how he was talking about all those good-paying jobs with private companies? I think he's hoping BWI will take him on permanently."

Clare handed Ray her hard hat and brushed dust off her shirtfront. "I may be naïve about how these things work, but doesn't that create a conflict of interest?"

Ray smiled, stacking her hard hat on top of his. "It kind of seems like it would, doesn't it?" He tucked the hats under his arm and turned toward the office trailer. The crew had abandoned their vigil in front of the steps and had retreated to a pair of wooden picnic tables under the fringe of trees behind the trailer. Clare could see a couple of coolers on the tables.

"I'm afraid there's nothing else to see, Reverend. Sorry Ms. Landry hasn't shown up. You can use the phone in the office to give her a call, if you want."

She shook her head. "No, I don't have the number for her cell phone." Her mind churned furiously. Her last chance to find out anything about Bill Ingraham was about to come and go. *Aw right, ladies, it's time to fly or die.* Msgt. Ashley "Hardball" Wright used to say that during her survival training. Male or female, he had called all his trainees "ladies," unless he was calling them something much worse. She tended to recall his aphorisms in situations her grandmother would never have found herself in—like pumping Ray Yardhaas for information about a man he didn't know was dead.

"I want to ask you something." She shaded her eyes from the sun's glare when she looked up at him. "You seem to think highly of Bill Ingraham. Does the rest of the crew feel the same way?"

Ray shifted the stacked hard hats from one arm to the other. "Pretty much, I guess. There's always a few who see management as the bad guy. But the new guys on the crew are making fourteen bucks an hour, and the senior guys are making up to twenty, so most of 'em don't have a problem with the boss taking his profit. I figure, you want everybody to earn the same, go to Cuba."

"Actually, I was thinking more about his . . . personal life." She wiped a trickle of sweat off her forehead with the heel of her hand. "Does anyone have a problem with Mr. Ingraham, um, being, you know . . . gay?"

Ray frowned. "Why?"

"Well, because sometimes straight men don't relate well to—"

"No, I mean why do you want to know? You're not one of those preachers who go around telling folks God hates queers, are you?"

She recoiled. "Good Lord, no!" She wiped her hands against her jeans reflexively. "That's a . . . sick perversion of God's work. No. Just the opposite. I'm trying to get a handle on who might be propagandizing that kind of hate around here. I don't know if you've kept up with the news, but there have been two assaults in Millers Kill recently. Two decent men beaten half to death because they're gay." She caught herself. "At least that's the most likely explanation for the attacks. I want to understand where that rabid homophobia comes from, do what I can, as a priest, to stop it." The image of Bill Ingraham's savaged body came to her, causing her words to get stuck momentarily in her throat. Too little too late, she thought, and took a deep breath. "I can't exactly waltz into the nearest pool hall and say, 'Hey, guys, what do you really think of homosexuals? And be honest now!'"

Ray snorted.

She tilted her head toward the picnic tables at the edge of the construction area. The guy in the Desiderata T-shirt had opened one of the coolers and was passing out cans. It looked like it was Miller time. "Here you are, a bunch of manly men doing manly construction work, and your boss is a homosexual. An out-of-the-closet gay man. How do your coworkers feel about that? Have there been any problems?"

"You think maybe some of the crew could have been involved in those beatings?"

"You tell me. You're the one who knows them."

Ray looked over at the men sprawling in the shade and then glanced at Clare. "You're not running back to Ms. Landry with any of this, are you?"

"No."

"Or some kind of reporter?"

"I've told you the truth, Ray. I'm the rector of St. Alban's Episcopal Church."

He crossed his arms, obscuring the plumbing company ad on his chest. "I guess the reaction's been mixed. I don't think it really makes any difference to most of the guys, although you hear a whole lot more pansy jokes than at the last job I worked. Most guys figure what you do in your private life is your own business, and so long as nobody prances through playing the Sugar Plum Fairy, they don't say much."

"I hear you saying 'most' of the guys. What about the rest of them?"

Surprisingly, Ray grinned. "We got one Gen Xer, I guess you'd call him, thinks it's totally cool to be working for someone like Bill. Of course, Carter's got both ears pierced and these weird tattoos around his biceps."

"So not only is he out of the mainstream but he's got enough self-confidence to wear earrings on the job. Is there anyone else on the opposite end? Maybe some older guys? Or somebody who has to spend all his time proving what a jock he is?"

Ray's smile faded away. "There are a few who just can't seem to let it alone. Like Charlie back there. They always gotta have some snotty remark about Bill and his 'lifestyle.'" Ray made quotation marks with his forefingers. "You work on a construction site, you expect to hear some pretty raw stuff. And the guys like to rib you. If I had a dime for every 'dumb Dutchman' joke I've heard, I could retire to Florida right now. But there's a difference between making queer jokes to be funny and garbage-mouthing someone personally."

Clare, who had endured way too many sexist jokes during her years in the army, thought the difference might not be all that apparent to the person who was the butt of the joke. But she knew what Ray was trying to convey. The former was the casual cruelty of ignorance, like the major who had been truly baffled when she took offense at his endless string of dirty jokes. The latter was viciousness, designed to fence someone off from the group with a line as subtle as barbed wire. She thought of the *Hustler* babes she used to find taped up in her cockpit. "Yeah," she said, "I know what you mean." She swiped away another trickle of sweat. "So who is it doing the trash-talking? And does it stop at talk?"

Ray squinted up at the sky, frowning in thought. "Well, there's Charlie; you met him. Matt Beale and Toby, they have a pair of potty mouths on 'em, but they're both so lazy, I can't imagine either of 'em working up the sweat to beat on somebody. Elliott McKinley, him I can see doing it, but not on his own. He's like a dog that slinks around on the edges of a pack, whining. He wouldn't dare come out to bite until another, bigger dog had done it first. Gus Rathmann is the sort who could definitely do it. You should hear the way he talks about his wife. I've never met her, but I'll bet good money he's beating up on her."

"Could he be the big dog that this McKinley would follow?"

"Nah. Gus can't stand Elliott. The thing I'm wondering is, Would he risk it?"

"Gus or Elliott?"

"Gus. He's on probation. I don't know what for. But I've heard him turn down offers to go out for a beer after work. I got the impression he was trying to keep straight for his probation officer."

"Either of these guys here today?"

Ray looked at her, alarmed. "These are not people you ought to be hanging around with, Reverend."

"I know. But are they here?"

Ray sighed. "Gus Rathmann was here this morning. He took off when we were told to stand down until further notice. Which wasn't unusual— half the guys left after Opperman called."

"Did Elliott leave, too?"

"He had to. Whitey Dukuys was leaving, and he's Elliott's ride."

"Are they roommates or something?"

"Nah. Elliott's truck broke last week and he's been bumming rides with Whitey ever since."

Clare blinked. "His truck?"

"Yeah. Whitey lives out in Glens Falls, and he drives right past where Elliott—"

"What kind of truck? What color?"

Ray looked at her as if the heat and the bouncing Jeep ride had scrambled her brains. "I don't know. Let me think. It's a Chevy two-ton. Red. Why?"

CHAPTER FIFTEEN

The first thing Russ saw when he turned into the construction site was Clare's car. He was following Opperman and Peggy Landry, who were undoubtedly a hell of a lot more comfortable in Landry's well-sprung Volvo sedan than he was in a five-year-old cruiser that needed new shocks bad. He hadn't been real gung ho on the idea of the two of them alone in their car, able to coordinate their stories, but since they had both shown up promptly at the station when asked and were about to open their office for a voluntary search, he was willing to extend himself a little.

Then he saw her car.

What is it with her and tiny red cars? More important, why was he stumbling over her every time he made a move on these cases? Next thing he knew, he was going to start seeing her in the urinal when he went to take a leak.

He rolled in beside Landry's sedan and threw his cruiser into park. He sucked in a lungful of air-conditioned air. The hell with it. He was here for background on Ingraham. Clare had nothing to do with it, or with him, or with this case.

Except, of course, that she had found Ingraham's body. For a moment, he allowed himself to think of her sitting on the damp ground, barricaded behind those two dogs. Then he snorted. She was about as weak and vulnerable as a Sherman tank. And about as subtle. He turned off the engine and stepped into the midafternoon heat.

Bill Ingraham's business partners were waiting for him. John Opperman, who looked like the kind of guy who took his suit and tie off only to shower, seemed awkward and out of place standing in dust and scrub grass, framed by construction machinery. Landry could have stepped off the cover of one of his wife's Martha Stewart books. Although, as Linda liked to point out, Martha ran her own billion-dollar empire. He suspected he ought to keep that in mind when dealing with Peggy Landry.

"The site office is this way, Chief Van Alstyne," Opperman said. "Though as I told you at the station, I doubt there will be much of use to you there. It's used strictly for work—I don't know of Bill ever mingling his private and professional life."

Russ followed the pair up a slight incline to a trailer set up on a concrete foundation at the edge of the work site. Several men sprang up from picnic tables set in the shade behind the trailer. Opperman stopped and pointed at them.

"Go home," he said. "You're off for the rest of the day. You'll get a call about tomorrow."

"Do we get full pay today?" one man shouted.

"Yes, yes, you'll get your full eight hours today." Opperman turned to Landry and gave her a look as if to say, See what I have to put up with? "Right in here, Chief," he said over his shoulder, mounting the trailer steps and opening the door. He disappeared inside, and Russ could hear him speaking to someone in the office. With a sense of inevitability, Russ shouldered through the narrow aluminum door and saw exactly whom he expected, Clare Fergusson. She was seated beside a metal desk with a fake wood top, and her eyebrows tried to climb off her forehead and hide in her hair when she caught sight of him. Opperman was talking with a heavily muscled man in his fifties. The man, who had the easy stance of a crew chief who knew what he was worth, folded his arms and nodded toward Peggy Landry.

"Yes, sir, I understand. But Reverend Fergusson was invited here by Ms. Landry," he said.

Landry stepped forward. "He's right. I'm so sorry, Clare, but this afternoon has turned out to be"—she shot a glance at her surviving business partner—"the worst-possible time to show you around. Let me walk you out and we'll reschedule."

Russ intended to ignore Her Holiness, but he couldn't help it. "You know her?"

Landry frowned, probably at the irritated tone in his voice. "Reverend Fergusson is marrying my niece Diana in August. Well . . . not marrying. Officiating. You know what I mean." She braced her hand on the Con-Tact-paper wood and gestured to Clare. "This really isn't a good time, Clare."

Clare opened her mouth and closed it again. She rose from the folding chair she had been sitting in and obediently followed Landry toward the door, giving Russ as wide a berth as possible in a single-width trailer crowded with tables and chairs.

She paused at the exit, framed by a stack of soda cans in cartons and a flimsy-looking water cooler. "I'd like a chance to talk with you at some point, Chief Van Alstyne," she said in a fakely chirpy voice. Russ grunted noncommittally, and Landry practically dragged the priest onto the steps. Opperman swung the door shut behind the two women. "Ray, we're shut down for the rest of the day. Peggy or I will give you a call to let you know when we're starting up again." Ray nodded and headed for the door. "And Ray?" Opperman kept his hand over the doorknob, denying access for a fraction of a second. "Don't let an unauthorized person onto the site unless one of us is here. Ever." He smiled. "Insurance, you know."

"It's your site, Mr. Opperman," Ray said, shrugging. He let himself out.

"Okay," Opperman said, clasping his hands in front of him. "What is it you'd like to see?"

Russ looked around at the suddenly empty office. A large drafting table with an elaborate CAD setup occupied one end of the trailer. A messy desk flanked by filing drawers and a fax machine filled the other end. In between were folding tables layered with rolled blueprints, manila envelopes, and torn-open FedEx packages. "Like the Supreme Court justice said, 'I'll know it when I see it.'" He pointed to the desk. "Was that Ingraham's?"

"Yes." Opperman dragged aside two folding chairs and pulled out a sturdy metal chair upholstered in vinyl. "Bill wasn't one for show. Function—that's what he wanted." He pressed his lips together for a moment, then let out a cross between a snort and a smile. "He had this old chair for as long as I knew him. I was ribbing him about it once, telling him he should get something more ergonomic. He said it performed perfectly—it kept his ass off the floor. Anything else was just bells and whistles." He looked out the small window set horizontally beside the desk.

"Was he like that about his construction projects? Did he build just enough to function?"

"God no. When it came to BWI Developments, he was a true perfectionist." He waved at the cramped interior of the trailer. "He always spent as much time as possible at or near a site. Got to know the contractors, the subcontractors, the workers. I swear, he probably knew the name of the quarryman who chiseled the marble for the bathroom floors. And God help him if those tiles were anything less than top-quality."

"And what's your role in BWI? Did you work for Ingraham?"

"Not *for* him. I'm his partner. Bill handled the physical plant, and he did so beautifully. I handle everything else: land acquisition, limited partnerships, permits, financing, insurance." Opperman smiled faintly. "Which is why, unlike Bill's, my office fits inside a laptop." His smile faded. "I don't know what I'm going to do now that he's gone."

"Will this project have to fold? Or will you be able to replace Ingraham?"

Opperman gave him a sharp look. "I don't think I'll be able to *replace* Bill. If I can find a sufficiently skilled construction manager, we can proceed. I hope we can. It would be a damned shame if his final project were left unfinished."

"What happens to BWI if you do have to abandon the project?"

Opperman rubbed his knuckles against the bottom of his chin. "It's going to be tough. We're insured for any catastrophe that might cancel the project. But our reputation will take a hit. Then again, our reputation will take a hit just because Bill's gone. He was the driving force behind BWI. He was the reason people invested in our projects."

"What about Peggy Landry? How would she fare if you had to cancel?"

"Peggy? She's one smart businesswoman. Part of our deal was primary partners' insurance and a pay-or-play clause." Russ's blank look must have given him away. Opperman laughed. "I won't bore you with the legal details. The end result is, she's a beneficiary of our partners' insurance policy. And if the Algonquin Spa doesn't get built, she still receives rental on her land for five years. Or until she finds another developer."

"She gets a payout from insurance? Insurance on Ingraham?"

"That's correct."

"How about you?"

"The death benefit for either Bill or myself goes directly into the business. That's the purpose of having partners' or principals' insurance—to cover the business losses when one of the key players dies." He sat down in his late partner's chair and spread his hands. "To be blunt, if you're looking for a financial motive for either Peggy or myself to have . . . have"—he looked away, then back at Russ—"butchered a man we respected, you're going to come up blank. We both relied on Bill."

Russ leaned back, catching the edge of a long folding table under his thigh. It felt too insubstantial to sit on. He folded his arms across his chest instead. "Seems to me you'll do okay. She gets a big insurance payoff and money for her property, and you get sole control over the business. It's not public, right? So all the profits go back to whoever owns it."

"In the first place, I can show you projected net and gross earnings of the future Algonquin Spa for the next ten years. Peggy Landry stands to make considerably more money if the project goes through. To address your second point, yes, I am the sole surviving partner of our privately held company. But not for long." Opperman pushed himself out of Ingraham's chair. "Despite the fact that we do very upper-end, high-margin projects, this is still fundamentally a construction company. And I don't do construction. I can quote you the cost of bricks and the provisions of our contract with the bricklayers' union and the amortization rates of the equipment needed to haul them here, but I couldn't lay one brick on top of another to save my life. I'm a lawyer. And if I'm not going to become a retired lawyer, I need to find another partner who can step into Bill's shoes." He leaned over and turned on the desk computer. "I understand why you need to pursue this line of inquiry." He tapped in a name and password. "I just hope you aren't letting whatever scum took Bill's life slip away while you're digging through our old files." He stepped back from the desk. "It's all yours. Hard copies and correspondence are in the filing cabinet. There's no diary. As far as I know, Bill kept his schedule on his computer and in his Palm Pilot."

Russ made a mental note to ask Lyle MacAuley if he had found a Palm Pilot after searching Ingraham's room at the inn. He looked at Opperman. "Thank you. And I can assure you that Bill Ingraham's killer isn't going anywhere. We'll find him."

Which was bold talk, since the initial autopsy and the early-morning search of the crime scene hadn't given them anything new. Ingraham had had a meal and some booze a couple of hours before his death. He hadn't engaged in any sexual activity—or at least none that left any traces on him. MacAuley's and Durkee's search of the grounds down to the river had turned up several cotton threads that might be helpful to the state prosecutor, *if* they ever found a viable suspect and *if* they could find a matching article of clothing belonging to him.

"If you don't need us to be here, I'm going to have Peggy take me into town to retrieve my car." He handed Russ a business card. "Here's the number for my cell phone. "I'll be heading back here afterward to close up, so we can talk again if you need to."

"Okay," Russ said. "That's fine by me." He had originally planned to question Landry and Opperman while he was going through the files, but one look at the office had told him he would need several hours just to get a grasp on what he was reading. "I understand you frequently travel back and forth for your business, Mr. Opperman."

"That's correct."

"I'd appreciate it if you'd stay in the tricounty area for the immediate future. I want to be sure I can reach you if anything comes up."

Opperman didn't even blink. "Of course." He thrust his hand at Russ, who shook it perfunctorily. "I'll leave you to your investigative chore, then. Contact me as soon as you have any questions." Then he was gone, the door swinging shut behind him with a dull aluminum clank.

◆ ◆ ◆

Three hours later, Opperman still hadn't come back. Which probably wasn't a loss, as Russ had been wading through the history of the project and still didn't have any information he could use to hook a line of questioning to. If there was a money trail leading to something that stank, he sure as hell couldn't find it. He could stand in line for one of the state's forensic accountants—a description that conjured up an image of a guy with a scalpel and eyeshades–but their backlog of work was so huge, he'd probably be retired before they could fit this case in.

He stood and stretched, cracking his back. God, that felt good. People thought you were getting old when you couldn't run around the way you used to. But the really depressing thing about middle age was not being able to sit as long as you used to. He checked his watch. Seven o'clock. He had called Linda an hour ago to tell her not to hold dinner, and she had gotten ticked off and told him if he couldn't manage to get home to spend some time with her, she might as well eat out with her friend Meg. Now his stomach growled. He needed to eat something, even if only leftovers. And his brain was fried. No matter what else he read tonight, he wasn't going to absorb it. He turned off the computer and the desk lamp, walked to the door, stumbling slightly as he shook feeling back into his legs, and let himself out.

The long shadows cast by the setting sun softened the hard angles of the construction site and turned the tangled northwoods pines into a hazy dark cloud. He cracked his back again and strode down to his cruiser, the sole remaining occupant of the parking lot. There was something tan beneath his windshield wiper. He sighed and slid it free.

It was a program, one of those things they handed out in churches. Beneath an etching of St. Alban's Church, it read "Holy Eucharist—the

Sixteenth Sunday of Pentecost." There was a list beneath the heading, presumably stuff they did during the sixteenth Sunday of whatever: the greeting, Sanctus Spiritus, a Bible reading. He flipped it over.

The message was in bold black letters, written with a felt-tip pen in the wide margin of the program. "Please call me. It's urgent. Clare." She had drawn a long scraggly arrow, which pointed to an underlined sentence from one of the Bible readings: *"He is near that justifieth me, who will contend with me? Let us stand together; who is mine adversary? Let him come near to me."*

"Gosh, Marty, it's a secret code," he said. "Let's go to the old abandoned mine and see what's up!" He stuffed the program into his pocket and got into the car. He felt like the Pillsbury doughboy being slid into the oven. He turned the cruiser on and cranked the air conditioning, sticking his face in front of the blast from the vent. She had some nerve, he'd grant her that. It wouldn't get him to make a side trip out to her place, but he had to admire her willingness to come right back to him, even after last night. The car interior had cooled enough for him to sit back in his seat without sticking to it. He shifted into gear and headed down the shadow-dark road through the forest. Unless, of course, it wasn't bravery, and she was just oblivious to what she had said. No, she knew. She had probably been wallowing in it all day, dying to make an apology. The dirt road turned onto pavement in a crunch of gravel. Sooner or later, he would get in touch with her. Let her say she was sorry, accept it in good grace. But he sure didn't need any distractions while he was working a homicide, not to mention the two assaults. He swung onto River Road, heading into town. Besides, he didn't want to give the impression that he put too much weight in what she said. He knew damn well he wouldn't have given a rat's ass if any other person in that park had accused him of lying down on the job. In fact, the only opinions that mattered to him were those of the men on his force. And his wife, of course, who cheerfully acknowledged she knew next to nothing about police work and therefore kept out of it.

Traffic was light on Main Street, but he had to stop and go for the pedestrians jaywalking left and right as they went from art gallery to antique store to ice-cream shop—or SHOPPE, as the fake-old sign proclaimed. When he was a kid, the upper end of Main Street had had real stores, like Woolworth and Bilt-Rite Shoes and Biretti's, which his mom had always referred to as "the Eye-talian bakery." Then, while he had been traveling from post to post, building his career in the military police, one by one the old stores closed, victims of the Aviation Mall and the shopping centers that sprang up on Route 9. In the late eighties, while he had been looking at the world through the bottom of a bottle, the Board of Aldermen had gotten a major grant for downtown revitalization. Now the street was full of folks again, at least in the summer. You could buy pastries and etchings of Fort Ticonderoga and fancy clothes just right for a garden party in Saratoga during the racing season. What you couldn't buy was a razor or a pair of shoes or a cheap sandwich.

He turned onto Church Street, where the shops were older, considerably less glamorous, and the pedestrian traffic a lot lighter. The thought of Biretti's put him in mind of his mother. He hadn't even called her to see if she had gotten home all right. His sister Janet had reached him that morning at the station, and she had given him an earful before letting him know she would be picking Mom up at the courthouse. He tightened his grip on the steering wheel and scowled, causing the man who was in the crosswalk in front of the cruiser to sprint across to the other side. All he was trying to do was his job, as best as he knew how, and every woman in his life was dumping on him for it.

He swung around the small park at the end of Church Street and drove onto Elm. The rectory was dark, but a few of the stained-glass windows of St. Alban's Church were glowing, the ones farthest from the door. He frowned. He didn't think there were any services on Monday.

He parked the cruiser in Clare's drive and walked back down the sidewalk to St. Alban's entrance on Church Street. He decided not to think about the fact that he knew the Episcopal church's worship schedule, even though the last time he had attended any religious services regularly was back in junior high. And then only because he had had a crush on a girl in the Methodist Youth Group.

He pushed against one of the great wooden doors and it swung open silently. He stepped through the narthex into the body of the church and paused to let his eyes become accustomed to the dimness. The sky outside was still orange and red, but the twilight glow couldn't pierce the stained-glass windows that punctuated the stone walls. There wasn't a single electric light on anywhere. He walked forward in a few more steps, hesitant about trespassing in the middle of a service. But there was no one sitting in the rows of pews. His eyes followed them, rank on rank, to the front of the church. Past the gilt and mahogany altar rail, past the plain rectangular table draped in embroidered linens, past the choir's gleaming pews and Gothic arches was Clare. White-robed, on the steps leading up to an ornately decorated high altar, where a mass of candles provided all the light in the world. Her back was to him, her head bent over what he guessed was a book.

"Be present, O merciful God, and protect us through the hours of this night, so that we who are wearied by the changes of this life may rest in your eternal changelessness; through Jesus Christ our Lord, Amen."

Her voice wasn't pitched to carry, but whoever had shaped the space had known what he was doing. In the cool silence of the empty church, Russ could hear her as well as if he were standing next to her.

"Keep watch, dear Lord, over those who work, or watch, or weep this night, and give your angels charge over those who sleep. Tend the sick, Lord Christ; give rest to the weary, bless the dying, soothe the suffering, pity the afflicted, shield the joyous, and all for your love's sake."

He walked up the center aisle quietly, as the place seemed to demand, although not trying to hide his presence. He wondered if she really believed in angels swooping around, watching over people, or if that was just the company line.

She started singing in a clear alto voice: "Lord, you now have set your servant free, to go in peace as you have promised; for these eyes of mine have seen the Savior, whom you have prepared for all the world to see. . . ." It wasn't a song exactly, more like a chant, rising and falling from one line to the next, even though there wasn't any rhyme and only scant rhythm. She dropped back into speech to conclude, "Guide us waking, O Lord, and guard us sleeping; that awake we may watch with Christ, and asleep we may rest in peace. The almighty and merciful Lord, Father, Son, and Holy Spirit"—he could see the movements of her arm as she crossed herself— "bless us and keep us."

He joined in on her "Amen." It seemed like the polite thing to do. She stilled for a moment, then pivoted. She squinted. Facing the candles as she had been, the rest of the church must have looked pitch-black.

"It's me," he said, stepping up to the first cloth-covered altar.

"Russ?" She sounded as if this were the last place on the planet she would expect to find him. "What are you doing here? I mean"—she glided down the steps from the high altar, her robes lending a sober grace to her usually athletic movements—"I would have thought you'd be at the station."

"I'm not on call," he said. "I wasn't actually scheduled for duty today." He shrugged. "But you know. Murder knows no overtime, or something like that."

"But didn't they call you on the radio? Earlier today, at the construction site, I found out—well, I wanted to tell you in person, so I left you that note, but then after I got home, I figured it was irresponsible to wait, so I called the station and spoke to Officer MacAuley—that is, Deputy Chief—"

"I know who he is, Clare. Get to the point."

She grinned. "The man who owned the red truck. I told him I knew who he was."

CHAPTER SIXTEEN

I t was faster to call the station from Clare's office than to retrace his steps and use the radio in his car. She had shown him to her desk and then excused herself to change out of her vestments. He was talking to Lyle MacAuley when she slipped quietly back into the office.

"We ran the registration, and sure enough, it's a 'ninety-four Chevy pickup, registered to one Elliott McKinley. He's got a few arrests on his sheet: one obstructing, a couple drunk and disorderlies, never anything that went anywhere. He pled out to everything. Eric remembered him from, his last arrest, which was about two years back. He thinks this guy is a hanger-on. He was one of half a dozen guys: Eric and Noble and Nathan Bougeron—you remember Bougeron, right?"

Russ did. He was one of the several promising young officers who had headed south to the state troopers' barracks in Loudonville during the five years Russ had been chief of the department. He'd worry that there was something wrong with his style of management, except every one of them had cited the same reason for leaving: better pay and more chances for advancement.

"Anyway, they broke up a fight outside the Dew Drop Inn. McKinley got picked up for obstructing, along with everyone else. But get this—he was there with Arnie Rider, who was the one who had started the fight."

"Hold on. Is this the same Arnie Rider—"

"Who's doing twenty years in Comstock for stabbing Chhouk, that Cambodian immigrant, yep. Get this. The Dew Drop brawl was a week before the stabbing. According to McKinley's sheet, he was brought in and questioned about the Chhouk murder, but he didn't turn anything useful."

"Do you have McKinley?"

"Not yet. Eric and I went over in civvies right after Reverend Fergusson called. He lives in a rooming house on Raceway Street, down past the mills. No truck in sight, and there's no parking provided by the landlord, so he would have had to keep it on the street. It must be stashed somewhere. He wasn't home, and the landlord didn't know when he'd be in. Eric's there now on stakeout, waiting for him to show up."

"I'll bet whoever is holding that truck is up to his eyeballs in it."

"I'll take that bet."

"Can we ID any known associates?"

"The rest of the crew who was picked up two years ago at the Dew Drop. I did a quick look at their rap sheets, but none of 'em look particularly promising. I didn't want to start picking people up for questioning and scare off McKinley. Especially since there've got to be others involved."

"No, you did good, Lyle. This is exactly the way I would have set it up. As long as we don't shake the bushes too much, he'll come home. And then we grab him. I want to be ready to move fast on any names he turns. If we need to, we'll call up a few of the part-timers to cover patrol."

"You know that'll involve—"

"Overtime, yeah. I'm sure the Board of Aldermen will eventually have my—" Russ glanced over his shoulder, remembering Clare in the nick of time. She had settled into one of two leather chairs placed in front of the empty fireplace. "My feet to the fire. You can reach me at St. Alban's if anything happens in the next few minutes. Then I'll cruise over to the station before going home."

"When are you going to get a cell phone like the rest of the world? Docs get 'em. Vets get 'em. Even Lithuanians and Letts get 'em."

"Don't quit your day job, Lyle. Bye."

He hung up the phone and spun around. "Yes!" He pumped one arm like a hockey fan witnessing a beautiful slap shot. "Looks like your Elliott McKinley may be one of our boys. A few years back, he hung around with a bad guy named Arnie Rider. Arnie had some wrong strong views about racial purity in the United States, which he expressed by getting into fights with Cambodian and Vietnamese refugees in the area. Eventually, he got carried away and stabbed a young man named Chhouk." The name made him think of the kid's mother, a tiny woman who knew maybe ten words of English and who had keened incessantly, a high-pitched, barely audible wail, when she identified her son's body. He shook his head. "They put him away for manslaughter, but I thought it should have been murder one. Who picks a fight while carrying a bowie knife in his jacket unless he's itching to use it?"

Clare pulled her legs up so she was sitting tailor-style in the chair. "Are you saying McKinley is attracted to extremists? He's a kind of hate-crime groupie?"

"Well, we don't know enough yet to take it that far. But it certainly drops a few more pieces in place." He strode to the bookcase-covered wall opposite her desk, then to the sagging love seat, then back to the desk, too charged up to sit. "You say the foreman at the spa site told you McKinley has problems with his boss being gay. Maybe he gets together with some of his buddies who were left behind when Rider took the long trip out of town. They piss and moan about gays, just like they used to about Asians, until somebody gets the great idea to go out cruising and get themselves a homosexual."

"Emil Dvorak."

"And they take McKinley's truck." He paused at the bookcase, standing in front of a clock shaped like an Apache helicopter. Its rotors were ticking the seconds away. "Okay, we don't have confirmation yet that it was McKinley's truck. I'm just speculating."

"No, no, I see what you're driving at." She leaned forward in her chair, her cheeks slightly flushed. "You're thinking they were working themselves up to attack Bill Ingraham."

"Maybe. Emil's attack seems the most like sheer opportunism. Maybe they were driving by the Stuyvesant Inn, hoping to catch Ingraham himself, not knowing he was at the town meeting."

"But then they succeed at that one. They don't get caught. That eggs them on to the next attack."

"MacPherson. Which strikes me as being more carefully planned out than when they went after Emil. Like they had set on a definite target."

"So what about Bill Ingraham? Was he targeted? Was he what they were working up to with the other two assaults? Or did one of them just get . . . carried away?"

"I don't know," he admitted. "We're way out in cloud cuckooland here. Once we bring in McKinley, I expect the missing information will fall into place extremely quickly. These sons of scumbuckets fall apart under questioning. I've seen it before. He'll give up his own mother to knock a few years off his sentence. It'll just be a matter of rounding 'em up." He threw himself backward onto the lumpy love seat. "And thank God for it, too. Between this case and my own mother disturbing the peace in the park, I'm about tapped out. And then there're the news stories. If I don't have ten messages from the mayor and the Board of Aldermen waiting for me on my answering machine, I'll eat my hat."

She pulled a long strand of hair between her fingers and fiddled with it. "Look, I need to apologize for running my mouth off last night in the park. Sometimes I have this tendency to speak before I've had a chance to think everything out."

He laughed. "No kidding? I never would have guessed that about you!"

"Cut it out! I'm trying to say I'm sorry here."

He waved a hand, erasing her words from the air. "Don't beat yourself up. We were both tired and had had too much to do on a very long day. I should have thought about what you had just been through before I snapped your head off. You weren't saying anything I wasn't already telling myself." He was surprised, as he said it, to find it was true.

"That's part of why I feel so bad," she said, leaning forward again, her elbows on her knees. "I know how personally you take your responsibilities to this town. For me to accuse you of lying down on the job was just . . . jabbing you in your weak spot."

He was still trying to figure out where that little confession had come from. "You know, I was still ticked off at you when I came over here. I didn't even quite know I *was* coming over here until I pulled into your driveway." He leaned against the back of the love seat, crossing his arms over his chest. "You just said what lots of other folks would have said in the same situation. I gotta ask myself why it bothered me so much when *you* said it." He watched as she pulled her knees up until her sneaker-shod feet were resting on the chair seat. "I guess I'm afraid that, deep down, all my reasons for not issuing a general warning or going to the press with the gay-bashing idea are because of . . . who the victims were. Because I don't, you know, feel comfortable around gay guys."

She let her knees drop back down and crisscrossed her legs again. "But Dr. Dvorak was—is—a friend of yours. That doesn't make any sense."

"We were friends at work. I knew who he was and what he was, but it never impinged on our relationship. He never talked about Paul, just like I never talked about my wife. The fact that he was gay was like having a friend at work who's Jewish, or vegetarian. You know about it, but you don't have to think about it, because what you do together never intersects with that other part of the person's life." He looked away, focusing on the framed and matted aeronautical sectional charts covering the wall next to Clare's desk. "But then all of a sudden, there's this reality—that my friend sleeps with a big bearded guy. And hangs out with the prissy innkeeper and his limp-wristed boyfriend."

"Ron Handler is *not* limp-wristed."

"He's very obviously gay. Which made me uncomfortable. Then I meet Bill Ingraham, who I knew was gay but who never gave off a single clue, which made me even more uncomfortable."

"Why do you think that is?"

His mouth quirked in a half smile. Her voice had the tone of a professional counselor now. He glanced back at her. He didn't know how she managed to concentrate, listening until it seemed as active as speaking, but her focus on his words made him feel as if he could say anything and it would be okay.

"I'm a straight guy? Someone who spent twenty-five years in the army? As you yourself said, it's not exactly a hotbed of tolerance for sexual diversity." He snorted. "Furthermore, I was military police. And with cops, God forbid you ever touch another guy in any way except a slug in the arm."

"You don't strike me as someone who indulges in groupthink."

"What's that mean?"

"You don't base your decisions about what you'll believe and who you'll be on what the people around you think."

"No, no, I'm not saying the army made me prejudiced against gays. But I don't feel comfortable when some guy is rubbing my nose in it."

"Bill Ingraham didn't rub anyone's nose in it."

He twitched in his seat. "I know. Which makes me worry that maybe I am prejudiced against gays. Maybe Emil Dvorak is like my trophy friend, somebody I can point to in order to prove what a cool, open-minded guy I am. And maybe somewhere inside me this . . . dislike, distrust, distaste of homosexuality influenced my decisions about notifying the press and warning the town." He looked down at his hands. "Maybe all that stuff I thought I believed about businesses and outing people and copycat hate crimes was just a smoke screen, hiding what was really inside me."

"Russ."

He looked up at her.

"If you have enough self-awareness and insight to ask yourself these questions, I believe you've already proven that you didn't act out of some deeply buried homophobia." She opened her hands. "I've never known you not to confront your thoughts and feelings head-on." Her cheeks flushed again, and he wondered if she was thinking about last Christmas Eve, the two of them in this office, him holding her tightly in his arms. He felt the tips of his ears getting hot. She smiled a little. "You are a very congruent personality, to throw out some jargon. Who you are on the outside is the same as who you are on the inside." She folded her hands in her lap. "I thought you were wrong when you decided not to notify the press about the pattern of gay-bashing. I still think you were wrong."

He opened his mouth. She held up one hand. "But despite my disagreement with your decision, I believe—I *absolutely* believe—that your motives and reasons were exactly as you stated them and that you were acting in the best interest of everyone involved." She grinned suddenly. "And you can bet if I thought you were snarking around, I would have called you on it then and there."

"Huh. You didn't know how I felt about gays then."

"Oh please. I was there at the Stuyvesant Inn, remember? I saw you with Stephen and Ron. You were like a cat in a roomful of rocking chairs, as my grandmother Fergusson would have said."

"I was?"

"Yes." She twirled the single strand of hair around her finger and attempted to poke it into her twist. "In all honesty, I have to say there was a lot right with your decision, too. Especially if McKinley and whoever else were working their way up to attacking Bill Ingraham. You very well may have prevented those other things you were worried about—having a sort of witch-hunt for suspected homosexuals going on in the name of protecting them. You put a lot more thought into your approach than I did when I spoke with whats-her-name, that reporter—"

"Sheena."

"Was that her name? Good Lord. What were her parents thinking of?" She paused for a moment before getting back on track. "My point is, you think about things before acting. And the way you think is well reasoned, informed by your experience and your morals. So stop worrying that you're subconsciously in cahoots with creeps like McKinley."

He crossed his hands behind his head and worked his shoulders into a more comfortable position against the love seat's uneven back. "You know, it's true. Confession really is good for the soul." At that moment, his stomach rumbled loudly.

"Hungry?" she asked, pinching back a grin.

"Starved. You don't—" He stopped himself before asking her if she had something to eat at home. He could barely justify being here with her in her office after hours. He'd come here on police business. He had found out what he needed to know. He had no call to invite himself into this woman's house for a meal. Better his own abandoned kitchen and an intact marriage than a three-course dinner followed by divorce. He heaved himself out of the love seat. "You don't have a bathroom around here, do you?"

"Down the hallway, right before you get to the parish hall."

After he had used the facilities and washed up, he wandered back down the narrow hallway that ran from the huge parish hall past Clare's office, the church office, and something labeled "the Chapter Room" and then dog-legged into the church. This time, the lights were on. Clare was at the high altar again, putting out the candles with a four-foot-long brass snuffer. As it died, each candle sent a ribbon of smoke streaming up toward the gloomy reaches above, veiling the elaborately carved wooden reredos mounted on the wall behind the altar. The air was full of the smell of smoke and bees-wax and stone.

"So, nobody came to the service tonight?" he asked, stepping hard on the floor so as not to startle her.

"Hmm? No, I hadn't scheduled Evening Prayer. I just wanted to read the office of Compline for myself. I could have done it at home, but every once in a while I like to come here without it being a job requirement." She finished the snuffing and swung the gently curved brass pole over her shoulder. "I'm discovering that I have to work at making this my place of worship, and not just my place of employment." She descended the steps from the high altar and slid the end of the candle snuffer into its wooden stand near the wall. "Sometimes, when I'm leading the whole congregation in the Eucharist, I find myself thinking about what I have to do next—whether I remembered to tell the crucifer to stand up before the final hymn, and if I'll able to get Mrs. so-and-so to volunteer to lead the white-elephant sale. I didn't expect that when I became a priest."

"Huh. I never thought about it like that. I imagined someone could easily get burned-out doing the social-work part of the job. I guess I always figured priests and ministers kind of entered another world when they did their"—he stopped himself again, this time before saying "mumbo jumbo"—"worshiping thing." Lame.

She dug into her chinos and pulled out a jangle of keys. "I wish. Maybe there's something to be said for religions that engage in ecstatic rituals."

He wasn't sure what that was—it sounded sort of sexual. He figured it was better not to ask.

"As for me, I get charged up by the social-work side of it, as you aptly put it. I love counseling and visiting and helping people. Ah, here it is." She dangled the key ring from an old-fashioned long key that looked as if it had been cast a century ago. "Main doors. No, for me, it's the sacramental side I have difficulty with." She headed off down the center aisle. He fell into step beside her. "I wish I could be more like some of the students I knew at the seminary. You could just see the Holy Spirit working through them. Like it came out of their eyes. Makes me feel like a 'sounding brass, or a tinkling cymbal.'"

He wasn't sure what that meant either, but he could guess it wasn't someone with spirits shining from their eyes.

She swung one of the great double doors open. "Get the lights, will you? There, on the right." The air outside was warm and flower-sweet. She tugged the door into place and locked it.

"I'm glad to see you lock something," he said.

She looked up at him as she pocketed the keys. There was just enough twilight to see the prim expression on her face. "The church," she said, "does not belong to me."

"I'll walk you back to your place before I go."

"The rectory is the first house on this street. It's all of fifty yards down the sidewalk."

"Yeah, well, I also parked my cruiser in your driveway."

"Ah. Okay, then."

They walked in silence to the rectory. He opened his cruiser door, and she stopped on her lawn, halfway to the front porch. "Good night, then," he said. "Thanks for letting me use your office. And you did right, letting Lyle know right away about McKinley."

She shrugged. "I just hope you don't find he's loaned his truck to his aged mother and has been spending his nights working at the food pantry."

"I don't think there's much chance of that." He leaned on the door frame a moment, instead of sliding directly into the car.

She looked down at her sneakers. "So." She looked up at him, her face faintly etched by the light from the corner lamppost. "Am I forgiven?"

"What, for speaking your mind?"

He saw the flash of her grin. "No, I can't honestly say I've ever repented speaking my mind. I meant for how I did it. Hurting your feelings."

He was going to say his feelings didn't matter one way or another, that you take a hit and you keep on going, but he realized he would sound like an outtake from a Knute Rockne biopic. "Yes," he said. "Yes, you are."

A flash again in the darkness as she smiled. She turned toward the porch.

"Hey, Clare," he said. She turned back toward him. "You know that Holy Spirit thing?"

"Yeah?"

"I think you've got a little shine, too."

CHAPTER SEVENTEEN

Russ was parked behind number 2 Causeway Street when Elliott McKinley finally made it home. Russ's squad car was strategically wedged between the sagging two-car garage moldering at the rear of the lot and the rooming house Dumpster behind it. No one had emptied the Dumpster in a long time. He tried rolling his windows up to keep the smell to a bearable level, but as the sun rose and the morning heated up, he began to feel like a hunk of grizzled beef in a slow cooker. He wound up opening his door and praying for an upwind breeze.

He had been there since their shift change at 6:00 A.M. The neighborhood had been emptying out when he arrived, since even those who had had Monday as a holiday were back to work today. He had listened as the Chevy Camaros and the ten-year-old Skylarks and the occasional tiny import fired up and headed off for the first shift at the G.E. plant in Hudson Falls, or the software-packaging plant in Fort Henry, or to construction sites and auto-repair shops. Causeway Street was a neighborhood that worked in shifts, round the clock. At 4:00 P.M., all the bartenders and waitresses and bouncers would be off to the honky-tonks or the fake rodeos that lined the roads up to Lake George, or to hushed white-linen restaurants that had been serving the summering rich since Teddy Roosevelt's administration. Finally, at 10:00 or 11:00 P.M., the cleaning women and the night clerks would leave, returning too sleepy-eyed in the morning to give much thought to a few cop cars passing them in the streets.

Russ, Noble Entwhistle, and Eric McCrea had taken over from Lyle and Mark. Eric and Noble were in an unmarked car parked a few doors down from the rooming house. Eric made a radio check religiously every fifteen minutes, reporting that nothing had happened in the last quarter of an hour. That, the bluebottle buzz of flies feasting at the Dumpster, and the occasional shriek of children in danger of toppling rickety swing sets were the only company Russ had.

At 9:45, his radio buzzed. He reached for the mike, wondering why no one had invented a noiseless air conditioner that you could run while still hearing what was going on outside the car. "Yeah, Eric, I'm here."

"So's our boy."

Russ sat up straight. "What's happening?"

"A burgundy Ford Taurus wagon just dropped him off. A guy and a girl are in the front seat."

"Call in the plates and tell Harlene I want a unit on them."

"Already did."

"You guys get any better at this, I'm going to have to retire. What's he doing?"

"He's just entered the front door. He didn't check his mailbox."

"Has the postman been by?"

"Nope. Either he doesn't care what he gets or he was home yesterday in time to get the mail."

"Somebody must have reached him in the afternoon to let him know that the BWI construction site's closed today."

"Okay, I think he's had enough time to get to his room. Noble and I are gonna go in."

"Be careful." This was the thing Russ liked least about his job: sitting and waiting while his men stood on the wrong side of a door, behind which lay—what? A resigned perp who went without comment, or a nutcase with an arsenal? He held himself motionless, listening, waiting.

There was a noise from inside the rooming house, the sound of confusion, an indistinct shout. Then the back door banged open, and he got his first look at Elliott McKinley, skinny, with the thick, ropy arms of someone who breaks his back for a living. McKinley bounded down the four back steps in one stride and jackrabbited to the fence marking the end of the lot.

Russ tumbled from his seat, yanking his weapon from its holster as soon as he was clear. "Stop! Police!" he shouted, taking two steps forward to be clearly seen and dropping into a marksman's stance. McKinley didn't spare him a glance. He vaulted the waist-high fence, a ramshackle collection of wire and lathing, and tore off under the neighbor's laundry-heavy clothesline.

Russ spat out a curse as he jammed the gun back into its holster and heaved himself over the fence, which wobbled alarmingly under his hands. He was too old for this crap. He plowed through the laundry, board-stiff jeans and towels whacking him in the face. Behind him, he could hear Eric and Noble clattering down the rooming house's back steps. "Get the car," he screamed. "Go around the next street!"

He pounded down the short driveway to the sidewalk and spotted McKinley to his left: he was running like an Olympic contender toward the intersection. Russ didn't waste breath on a warning, just tore off after him, his hard footfalls slapping on the asphalt. Sneakers. Should have worn sneakers, he thought, and God, please don't let me have a heart attack, and then, What the hell is he doing? as McKinley abruptly veered off the road between two houses and disappeared.

Russ streaked after him, pulling hard with his elbows tucked to keep his pace up, his heart bludgeoning his chest. It was a beaten-down path that ran between the houses, vanishing into a row of dense bushes. He would have slowed down, but he could hear the thudding of McKinley's feet up ahead, so he plunged through the shrubbery at top speed, only to rebound violently against a chain-link fence.

"God! Damn!" Russ said, clapping his hand to his stinging face and reeling backward. He blinked tears from his eye. He ran down a dusty rut between the fence and the bushes until he spotted a place a few yards down where the chain link had been pried away from a support bar. He pulled the sharp-edged fencing away and squeezed himself through.

On the other side was a wide swath of overly long grass tipping gently downward into the featureless end wall of the old Kilmer Mill. Russ pushed himself into a trot, loping down the lawn toward the old brick pile below. There was no sign of McKinley. He stopped at the corner of the building and leaned against the cool brick while he clawed at the two-way radio on his belt.

He sucked in air. "Fifteen oh three? This is Van Alstyne."

Instantly, the radio crackled on. "Jesus, Chief! Where the hell are you?"

"I'm inside the Kilmer Mill grounds. On, um"—he pictured the town map in his head—"the western end."

"How did you wind up there?"

"Shortcut. Listen, there's no way you can get to where I am in the car. I think he's run into the mill, but I'm not sure how stoppered up he is in there. The other end flanks the park. I don't know of any way to get through, but there's the big gate on Mill Street, and I suppose he could go into the Kill. You two put a call in for the boat to patrol the river. I want you to block off the Mill Street entrance. I'm going in."

"Not a good idea, Chief."

He wasn't wild about it himself. "The kids in this neighborhood have had fifty years to discover hidey-holes on and off this property. If somebody's not right on his tail, he could vanish."

"We've already turned around. We can be there in five minutes."

"That leaves the street unguarded. Call in some more backup, whoever's available. But don't leave that street clear for him to beat a retreat to. You got me?"

"I got you. Don't like it, but I got you. Fifteen oh three out."

Russ pushed himself away from the wall and scanned the grass around him. He wasn't great as a tracker—his hunting technique in the fall consisted more of ambling around and drinking coffee from a Thermos than actively looking for any deer—but even he could see a few faint indentations in the grass. Lush and green, it would be springing back into place within minutes. McKinley did go this way, then. He walked along the side of the mill, casting back and forth, trying to spot some indication that McKinley had broken for the river. Then he saw it, bolted into the red brick—a rusting fire ladder running from a large third-floor window to five feet above the overgrown grass. It was a pre–World War II relic, from the days when the mill had employed a quarter of the town and occupational safety meant a straight three-story climb to the ground, if you could reach one of the windows before smoke or flames overcame you.

He jogged over to the ladder, reached up, and tugged on it with both hands. It creaked, but there was no shifting or shower of brick dust. He wrapped his hands around the lowest rung, chinned himself up, and pulled his legs to his chest, curling forward until his head was pointing toward the ground and he could get his knees over the iron bar. He balanced there for a moment, waiting to see if his two hundred pounds would shake the ladder, but the old bolts held true—for the moment anyway.

He climbed without looking down. The faded brick wall was punctuated by small granite-edged windows at the first- and second-story levels, oddly placed rectangles just big enough to let in some light and air. None of them were close enough to grab hold of if the rungs beneath his feet gave way or if the bricks holding the ladder's bolts crumbled. He breathed evenly and looked up. The window above the iron ladder was wide open.

He had to go headfirst through the window, a horribly vulnerable position, which made him feel like a hunting trophy mounted on a wall. He wiggled forward and flipped himself gracelessly onto his feet, thudding loudly enough to cause him to freeze in a crouch below the window. He breathed through his mouth, noiselessly, as if that would make a difference.

He was on a sturdy wooden platform encircling a vast area below. Railed and banistered, it had two steep staircases descending to the work space. What light there was came from windows hidden from his view beneath the walkway. There was machinery down there, behemoths of black iron, and a forest of chains and block and tackle hanging from runners in the ceiling.

A noise from below froze him in place. A scrabbling sound. And a clank. Too loud for an animal. He closed his eyes for a moment, straining to hear. The air stirred with the scent of iron and dry rot and mouse droppings. He listened harder and dropped to his knees and then to his belly on the walkway floor. He crawled forward to the opening between the railings that signaled the nearest stairway.

It was steep, like the gangway on a ship, built to occupy the least amount of productive space. The workroom floor was cleared for several feet around the final step. Descending would make him a sitting duck vulnerable to potential gunfire. He scanned the rest of the platform. The only other way down he could see was another staircase, equally open, at the end opposite him. He thought he could make out doorways there, too, but he had no doubt that McKinley had headed down to get out. Which meant he would have to go down, as well.

He suddenly thought, for the first time in years, of an argument he had had with a lunatic second lieutenant while squatting in the brush below a heavily fortified hill. He couldn't recall the hill's number. All the hills in 'Nam had had numbers, never names. They were supposed to take the damn thing, and he had been telling the FNG that it was idiocy to charge upward through the open into enemy fire. "It's not idiocy," the lieutenant had said. "It's our job."

He reminded himself that he had picked this job over running a security firm in Phoenix. He wiggled himself around, slid his legs over the edge, found the first step with his foot, and took it, hands loose on the railings, barking his shins as he scrambled down the ladderlike steps—one, two, three, four—and then there was a loud crack and his foot gave way, the step splintering beneath him as he plunged, then caught himself on the railings with a dislocating jerk to his shoulders. He was spread open like a wishbone, one leg dangling in space and the other stretched painfully behind him. A swirling cloud of dry rot made him cough. He hauled against the railings and tried to gain a footing on the step below, feeling a gun sighting on him as if it were a pointer pressed against his spine, trailing up to the back of his head. He flopped between the steps, hair prickling and the cold sweat of fear under his uniform shirt, and heard another noise from somewhere among the silent machines below. He remembered now that the second lieutenant hadn't lived very long. He let go of the railings, sagging still deeper through the broken stair tread, braced his hands atop the step in front of him, and pushed forward, just as he had done at the window outside, levering himself up, freeing the leg that had been trapped against the lower step. He didn't stop to think. He let both legs hang through the stair, gripped the step he had been braced on, dropped his torso and shoulders through the last of the splintery remains, and let go.

He fell far enough to regret his impulsiveness, but he had been taught how to land from a fall when he was young, and his body remembered the lessons, even if, thirty years later, he lacked the natural bounce that had once enabled him to jump up and keep running. He didn't spring up from the wooden floor where he had crumpled and rolled, but he did manage to keep rolling toward the nearest loom and tuck himself under its shadowed side.

"Elliott McKinley!" he yelled. "Police! Lay down your weapon and come out into the open with your hands raised!" The effort of shouting made his ribs hurt. Now he heard the clear sound of footsteps thudding, but he couldn't orient himself enough to discover the direction the sound was coming from. He rolled away from the loom, staggered to his knees, and rose cautiously, easing the Glock out again. Nothing in sight but rows and ranks of antiquated machinery and chains and block and tackle that would never be used again. He walked forward lightly, rolling from his heels to the balls of his feet, trying to make as little noise as possible. He heard another scuffle and a clank—ahead of him. They had to be close to the river by now.

"McKinley!" He crouched again, making himself less of a target. "We've got squad cars sealing off the other entrances to the mill, and a boat on the water to pick up anyone who goes in. You understand me? You're not getting out of here. Come on out and we'll wrap this up and nobody gets hurt."

Nothing. He stood up. There was a clank and a rattle, and he turned just in time to see an iron hook and a chain as thick as his wrist swinging straight at him, slithering through its pulley, sounding like the creak of the gates of hell opening. He lunged to the side, missing the hook, but the chain lashed across his shoulder and arm, hurtling his gun out of reach, knocking him off balance. He bounced off the nearest loom, staggered, then scrambled backward out of the way as the last of the chain tore through the pulley and fell over the iron machines and the wooden floor in a shattering clang that left him half-deaf. He looked around frantically for his gun, for McKinley, for another sign of movement among the chains and ropes hanging like malignant seaweed from the rafters. He caught a flash out of the corner of his eye. McKinley broke cover and bolted toward the far door, his head bobbing above the machinery in a weird, disembodied way.

Russ took off after him, any aches and pains wiped out for the moment in a surge of anger and adrenaline. He ran like a linebacker through an offensive field, dodging this way and that, trying to keep away from the machines. He could see the top of the door fling open, reached it on McKinley's heels, and made a flying tackle. He hit McKinley square across his midsection and they both went down, skidding and twisting across the wooden floor. The younger man struggled, lashing out ineffectually with his hands and feet, but Russ had at least thirty pounds and several inches on him. He rolled McKinley beneath him, facedown, and straddled him, his elbow pressing hard into the nape of McKinley's neck while he yanked at the pair of lightweight handcuffs snapped to his belt.

McKinley bucked, trying to throw him off. "Lie still or I'll smash your head into this floor, you little scum sucker," Russ roared. He hauled the young man's wrists together and cuffed him, then sat straddling his still-flailing legs. He patted his waist, grateful to feel the radio still clipped to his belt. He didn't relish the idea of wrestling McKinley out of the mill unaided. He keyed the mike. "Eric? Noble?"

"Chief? What's up? Where are you?"

"In the mill. First floor. I've got McKinley, but I could use some help moving him."

"I sent Mark to get the keys from the town offices." Russ knew the town kept copies of keys to all the abandoned mills, in case the police or the volunteer fire department needed them. "He just got here. We'll be right in."

"Bring Mark on in, too. We'll need two people for McKinley here. And I"—he pushed the bridge of his glasses against his face—"I think I'm going to need a little help finding my gun."

CHAPTER EIGHTEEN

He wants a lawyer." Lyle MacAuley reached across a litter of mugs and crumpled napkins and grabbed the coffeepot.

"Of course he wants a lawyer. They all want lawyers. It comes from watching too much television." Russ started to take a mug, winced, and shifted it to his left hand.

"You oughtta get that looked at."

"I'm a little banged up, that's all. I'll look like an Oriental rug in a couple of days, but I'll live. Who's he called?"

The deputy chief grinned. "Geoffrey Burns."

Russ choked on his coffee. "That asshole? Since when does he pick up work from a bottom-feeder like McKinley?"

"I guess there aren't enough car wrecks in the summer to keep him busy."

Russ put his mug on the dispatcher's desk and painstakingly poured the coffee wrong-handed.

"Careful with that," Lyle warned. "You leave a spill on Harlene's desk and she'll eat you for lunch." Their senior dispatcher was taking two days off after working on the Fourth.

Russ scooped McKinley's paperwork off the desk. "I'm going to talk to him."

"Chief, he's asked for his lawyer."

"I'm not going to question him. I'm going to *talk* to him." He grinned at Lyle's expression. "Don't worry. I won't violate his rights any. I just want to give him an idea of what he's facing."

The Millers Kill police station had been built in the days when suspects were booked at the desk and interrogated—without much thought at all to constitutional rights—in the holding cells below. Now the old cell block held an evidence locker and munitions lockup, and suspects in custody were questioned in a spacious, if windowless, room that had been carved out of two interior offices. Russ buzzed himself in and nodded to Noble

Entwhistle, who was propping up the wall while keeping an eye on Elliott McKinley.

McKinley was seated at a rectangular steel table. His hands had been uncuffed, but his ankles were in restraints attached to his chair. The table and its six chairs were bolted to the floor. McKinley looked up from a close examination of his knuckles. "Can I get a smoke?" he said.

"Maybe later," Russ said, throwing the paperwork down and easing himself into one of the chairs. His knees were beginning to ache, a deep, throbbing pain that would only intensify as the day wore on.

"I heard there's no smoking at the county jail no more."

"That's right. It's a smoke-free zone. The county doesn't want anybody contracting lung cancer on its watch."

"Oh, man." McKinley's hands twitched. His face was lined and leathery, the prematurely old face of someone who had been hitting the booze and the cigarettes since he was a boy. Despite his full-tilt attempt to avoid capture, he didn't look defiant. Merely resigned to another turn in what was probably a lifelong string of bad luck.

"So I hear you've asked for Geoff Burns," Russ said. "How'd you get his name?"

"Friend of mine. Burns repped him for a drunk-driving charge. Got him off, and he took a payment plan from my buddy, too, 'cause he didn't have all of his fee up front." McKinley knit his brows. "How come you want to know?"

"I was just wondering. I know Geoff. He and his wife have what you might call a general practice. You know, divorces, sue somebody for a dog bite, an occasional DUI. I would have thought you'd want more of a criminal specialist. Facing a murder charge." He didn't feel at this point he had to let McKinley in on the fact that the state usually supplied a capital defender when prosecutors went for the death penalty.

McKinley's face drained of all color. "What?" he squeaked. He looked wildly toward Noble, who was still stolidly planted against the wall. "They didn't say nothing about murder! They said assault!"

Russ glanced down at the sheets of paper in front of him. "Oh, yeah, that, too. Two assaults. One of those'll probably be a felony assault, since it was committed while you were robbing the video store."

"We did not!"

Yes. Russ felt an electric pulse surge through his body. He forced his hands and face to remain relaxed, his eyes on the paper in front of him. "Resisting arrest, assaulting an officer of the law, breaking and entering—that would be the mill. There's a warrant out on you for failure to report to your parole officer. You've also got three unpaid speeding tickets, you owe back child support to DHS in the amount of fifteen thousand dollars"—he titch-titched at this—"and we're charging you with capital murder in the death of Bill Ingraham." He looked up at McKinley, his voice calm and matter-of-fact. "And if you've been working under the table to avoid that child support, you may be in trouble with the IRS."

McKinley tried to stand up but could only manage to list drunkenly across the table because of the leg restraints. "I didn't have nothing to do with no murder! I never laid a hand on Bill Ingraham!"

Russ leaned back in his chair. "I really can't discuss it with you, Elliott. Seeing as how you've got a call in to your lawyer." He took off his glasses and polished them on the front of his shirt. "Geoffrey Burns. I think he did a breaking and entering once. That guy who was stealing drugs from the local pharmacies. You remember that case, Officer Entwhistle?"

"Fuck the lawyer!" McKinley's color had come back now. His face was blotched with red and purple. "I didn't kill Bill Ingraham! I never went near him!"

Russ glanced up at him. "Well, that's what I had figured originally. 'Cause when we picked you up in the Chhouk case, we only wanted you for a witness. To tell the truth, I never figured you for the kind of guy who would do the deed himself. Just that you had some rowdy friends."

"That's right! That's exactly right!"

"But when we come to pick you up to ask you about these assaults, you take off. Then you try to kill me by dropping that chain on me. And when we finally get you in to talk, first thing you do is call a lawyer."

"Chris said to! Chris said if anything happened, I should call a lawyer and let him handle it."

Even Noble shifted at that. Russ carefully replaced his glasses, not looking at McKinley. "Yeah? Well, Chris's not here, is he? You are. And you're the one sitting in the hot seat. So to speak." He glanced at Noble.

"Actually, it's a gurney now, Chief," Noble said. "Lethal injection."

"That's right." Russ turned to McKinley, who had collapsed back onto his chair. "You're a good friend, Elliott. I knew that when you wouldn't give up any information on the Chhouk case. But it takes one hell of a friend to be willing to go to the death house in Clinton."

"It's called the UCP now, Chief. The Unit for Condemned Prisoners."

"Thanks, Officer Entwhistle. I guess my head's still stuck in the sixties, when they used to send 'em to Sing Sing to fry."

McKinley made a sound deep in his throat.

"Hmm? I'm sorry, did you say something, Elliott?"

"You guys," he whispered, then coughed and spoke more loudly. "You guys are just messing with my head. To get me to talk."

"You've already expressed to Officer Entwhistle and Deputy Chief MacAuley that you decline to make a statement without representation. Isn't that right? I don't want you to talk with us. That might be violating your rights, Elliott. I'm sure Geoff Burns will be able to give you real good advice. I think he got the pharmacy burglar off."

"Two years, plus two probation," Noble said.

"Thank you, Officer Entwhistle."

McKinley leaned forward. "Chris Dessaint," he said hoarsely.

Russ leaned forward as well, opening his hands over the papers on the table. "Elliott," he said, his voice very quiet, "if you want to tell us your side of the story, it's got to be on the record. 'Cause I'm not going to waste my time chasing down another suspect if your statement is useless when it comes time to go to court. Now, if you're willing to put it on tape after being readvised of your right to have attorney's counsel, I sure would like to hear what you have to say."

Elliott peered into his face. "I still get to talk with my lawyer?"

"Yes, you do."

"Okay, then."

Russ rose, unlocked the door, and strode down the hall to grab a tape recorder from the squad room. He spotted Lyle. "Run the name Chris Dessaint. Anything we've got."

"What's up?"

"Elliott's giving us a statement."

Lyle's response was lost as Russ reentered the interrogation room. He turned on the machine, read McKinley his rights again, and had him state he understood and was voluntarily making his statement without the presence of his lawyer.

"Okay, Elliott, I don't want to put any words in your mouth. Why don't you tell me how you and Chris got into whomping on gay guys. Start at the beginning."

Russ expected to hear about Emil Dvorak, so he was surprised when McKinley said, "We went up to Lake George to party. Me and Chris and our friend Nathan. Then we decided to go barhopping. Anyway, we were outside some place—I think maybe it was the Blue Lagoon, or the Blue Parrot, something like that—and we went out back to smoke a joint. This guy comes out. You know, perfect teeth, nice clothes. He starts talking, and right away I know he's a fag." He frowned. "The guy starts hitting on us, wanting to know if we want to party with some of his buddies, bragging that they got some good stuff. Man, it was like, you know, all day long I gotta take orders from some rich fag, and now here I am on my own time, having to listen to the same bullshit. And Chris, he's a real good-looking dude, always has girls falling all over him, and I'm thinking, This queer's hitting on Chris! Anyway, I can see Chris is thinking just the same as I am. So we tell this guy off and punch him around."

"Nathan, too?"

"Naw, he just kept bleating about getting out of there. Like the fag's buddies were going to come out and take us on. Anyway, it felt good. You know, like we were standing up for our right not to have all that fag stuff shoved in our faces. We didn't really talk about it until almost a week later, when Chris asked me if I'd like to do it again."

"Find someone to rumble with?"

"Yeah. 'Go on a queer-hunt' was how he said it. Then he said there might even be a few bucks in it for us."

Russ blinked. "How so? You were going to find someone loaded and roll him first?"

"No, Chris had a friend. Someone who felt like we did, about the fags getting way too pushy and out of control. His friend couldn't get out and do anything about it, but he wanted to bankroll us. To make a statement."

Russ felt as if he had gotten on the Northway to Albany and had suddenly looked around and seen Kansas instead. He inhaled and exhaled slowly. "Chris's friend—you ever meet him?"

"Nope. Just Chris did. He lived up to his word, though. We got the money, and some bonuses, too."

The way he said the word *bonuses* was a tip-off. "Drugs?" Russ asked.

"Yeah. Chris handed it out—ecstasy, meth."

"Did Chris work with you? Had he ever met your boss?"

"Nah. He works at the Shape warehouse, doing inventory. You know, punching in the numbers on a handheld."

"How do you know him?"

"We went to school together."

Russ nodded. "Okay. So Chris said you could get paid for finding a gay guy and beating him up. Then what?"

"Chris said we needed to find someone else to help us. That we needed three all together."

"Your friend Nathan was out, I take it."

"Oh yeah. Anyway, I knew this guy Jason Colvin, from when I hung around with Arnie Rider. I thought Jason might be game. So I talked with him, and he was down with it, so we were ready to go."

"What happened next?"

"Chris told us about the fags running the inn on Route One Thirty-one, down a ways from where I work. He thought that would be a good place to find somebody. He told us he would let us know when. We made a couple drive-bys on nights when we had been partying, just jerking them a little. And then Chris gave me a call that Wednesday and told us we were on for that night."

"He picked that night particularly?"

"Yeah, which I thought was kinda weird, since we all had to be at work the next day."

"What did you do?"

"We got together in the woods first, partied a little. Chris passed out some meth, so Jase and I were feeling pretty pumped. Then we drove by, and we saw a bunch of guys out in front. One of 'em was getting into this Chrysler convertible—you know, your typical old rich dude car. So we went down to Route One Twenty-one and pulled off to the side, figuring he had to come that way and we'd be able to see him in time. I was at the wheel, 'cause it was my truck, and Jase and Chris were keeping watch. We all were smoking a little more. My idea was to force the guy off the road, but Jason yelled that the lights were coming and it was too late to get all the way back on the road. I was backing up, so he wound up hitting my truck, which really burned me. I put a lot of money and time into that truck."

Russ's throat tightened. He nodded for McKinley to go on.

"So we did him. It felt kind of righteous." He stopped. "Man, can I have a cigarette?"

"Officer Entwhistle, bring Elliott a pack and an ashtray." Noble unlocked the interrogation room and disappeared around the corner.

"You know," McKinley said in a confiding tone, "I probably wouldn't have done all this stuff if I hadn't been high while I was doing it. Chris was handing out shit like it was candy. He was calling the shots. I was, like, just along for the ride."

"Yeah."

Noble reappeared and handed Russ a pack of Marlboros and a disposable aluminum ashtray. Russ slid them across the table to McKinley and fished in his pocket for his dad's Zippo, circa 1945 and still working great.

"You smoke?" McKinley asked, proffering the pack.

"Not anymore. But I always carry this lighter. Comes in handy." He lighted McKinley's cigarette and clicked the Zippo closed, running his thumb over his father's initials, which were engraved on the case. A tiny reminder linking him to a world where beating men half to death wasn't part of anyone's recreation. "Go on. You were saying you did the man in the convertible. Did you know who he was?"

"Nah. But Chris said he knew he was gay, because there wasn't anybody but queers staying at the inn that week."

"Did Chris tell you that Bill Ingraham lived at that inn when he was in town?"

McKinley sucked hard on his cigarette, his eyebrows wrinkling together. "No, he didn't. Ingraham was there? No shit?"

"You didn't know?"

"How the hell would I know? It wasn't like we socialized."

"Okay. What happened next?"

"Chris said I probably ought to keep my truck out of sight until I could fix it. I got a cousin who does his own bodywork out of his barn over to Fort Henry. I parked it in there. Haven't had a chance to straighten out the fender yet."

"Who came up with the idea to hit the video store owner?"

"That was Jason," he said quickly. "Jason had known him in school and knew he was queer. He said it would be easy, 'cause we would know right where he would be. Chris said he'd check it out, and then that Friday we all got together. His friend had said okay, but we couldn't rob the place. And we were supposed to wear gloves so we wouldn't leave any fingerprints around."

Russ thought of the prints they had left on Emil Dvorak's Chrysler. "Did you?"

McKinley made a face. "Hell no. It was a video store, for Chrissakes. There would be, like, hundreds of fingerprints all over the place. And there we'd be, walking in with rubber gloves on. Might as well come in and announce, 'Call the cops,' right? That's when I knew his friend with the money was an amateur." He glanced at Russ. "Not that I'm, like, a professional. I'm not."

"It's just your hobby," Russ said.

"Hey, man, do you like queers? Do you like 'em shaking their booty everywhere, demanding their rights to make out in public and wear dresses? It's sick. It's a sick thing. I probably wouldn't have done it if I hadn't been so stoned all the time on Chris's shit, but I just done what a lot of people would if they weren't afraid."

Russ looked down at the table. His hands seemed relaxed, except for the white pressure points under his nails. He reminded himself that wiping the floor with McKinley was simply not an option. Stay calm. Control, he told himself.

"So you hit Todd MacPherson's video store."

"Yeah. But we didn't rob it!"

"You just gave MacPherson a lesson in straight pride."

McKinley looked confused. "Huh?"

"Never mind. What did you do afterward?"

"We went back to Chris's place. He gave us some poppers and then Jase and I each got five hundred bucks."

"You three talk about your next hit?"

"A little. Jase thought we ought to go down to Saratoga. But Chris said to cool it, that he'd let us know. 'Cause why do it for free when we could get paid?"

"Weren't you curious about who was bankrolling Chris?"

"Hell yeah. But he wouldn't say nothing. Chris is way big into all that fake militia, need-to-know stuff, like he was the general and we were the grunts. Screw it. I figured Chris was probably taking his cut off the top, but why should I complain?"

"Did Chris make any suggestions as to a target? Say anything that made you think he knew something you didn't?"

"Nah. He was mostly talking about getting out and buying some new gear with his money. He likes camping and all that healthful shit. Vitamins."

"But he also deals?"

"Chris? Not normally. He smokes, but everyone smokes. He mostly stays away from the other stuff. He does steroids sometimes, 'cause he lifts weights."

"Okay. What did you do after the meeting at Chris's place?"

"Are you kidding? It was the weekend and I had five hundred bucks. I took off. Just got back this morning."

"Have you seen the other two since Friday night?"

"Nope. Chris already had plans for the weekend, and Jase wanted to hole up with his new girlfriend."

"Where did you go?"

"Lake George. Around. I crashed with friends, mostly."

"You have any of that money left?"

McKinley laughed.

The door clicked open. Lyle MacAuley stuck his head in. "Burns is here. He wants to see his client."

Russ slid sideways out of the bolted-down seat. "Elliot, I want you to give Officer Entwhistle a detailed account of where you were and who you saw this weekend. I mean a minute-by-minute account. This is going to establish your alibi, so I don't imagine your lawyer will object."

Actually, he figured Burns would be screaming his head off in five minutes. He just didn't plan to be around to listen to it. He ducked through the narrow back corridor that was their supply closet and emerged by the squad room. He stuck his head in. There were voices raised by the reception desk, but he didn't see Lyle anywhere. He slunk toward Dispatch and stuck his head in. "Lyle?" he whispered.

Lyle appeared in the doorway. "What are you doing? Why are you whispering?"

Russ tilted his head toward the sound of expensive shoes marching down the hall to the interrogation room. Lyle's bushy gray eyebrows rose in comprehension. He thrust a manila folder into Russ's hand.

"Chris Dessaint. Twenty-five. He's been up on D and D, disturbing the peace, assault—a few fistfights. Small-scale stuff. He's got a juvie record, but it'll take some time to get that unsealed. Nothing to indicate he's suddenly likely to step up to the big time."

"Got a current address?"

"It's in there. His next of kin's listed as Alvine Harpswell; you'll remember her."

He did. Alvine had been in on numerous domestic charges, both as batterer and victim, and the speed with which she ran through her partners was astounding, considering her less-than-stellar looks. Lyle went on. "There's a bunch of Dessaints living in Cossayuharie and in Warren County. I figure he's related to them."

There was a rising noise from the direction of the interrogation room. Lyle jerked his thumb toward the front doors. "Paul's waiting in a black-and-white, and Dave's out on patrol. You better hightail it out of here before Geoff Burns gets hold of you."

Russ nodded, tucked the folder under his arm, and hobbled down the front steps and out the door as fast as his swollen knees would let him.

There was no problem finding Chris Dessaint's trailer in Lyon's Gate Mobile Home Estates. There was also no problem gaining access; taking a cue from McKinley's flight, Russ and Paul went through the tiny front door to make the arrest while Dave stood out back, weapon drawn. There was no problem with a resisting suspect. There was no suspect. The place had been cleaned out. Dessaint was gone.

CHAPTER NINETEEN

C lare wasn't surprised when the office phone started ringing promptly at nine o'clock. She was kneeling atop her desk, struggling to open the window. She knew it could be done, because Mr. Hadley, the sexton, had taken down the forties-era storm windows and hung screens in their place. When she had asked about an air-conditioning unit, he looked at her as if she had suggested installing a hot tub in the bathroom. "Waste of money," he said. "Won't get so hot an open window and a fan can't handle it."

And she had to admit he had been right, up until last week. The June temperatures had been balmy, and she had simply cranked open the narrow casements at the bottom of her diamond-paned windows for a little fresh air. But after the dismal Fourth, July had moved in like Sherman through Georgia. This morning, walking from the rectory to the church, she had already felt the heat rising from the pavement under her feet. Her sunny office would be an oven if she couldn't get some cross ventilation.

Unfortunately, the rise in heat and humidity seemed to have caused the window to swell. Knees sliding on loose papers, Clare braced her hands under the sash and heaved. Nothing.

Her speakerphone buzzed. "Reverend?" Lois, the church secretary, hadn't looked hot this morning. Lois never looked hot, or frazzled, or unkempt. Somehow, she managed to have two fans blowing vigorously in the main office without stirring a single strand of her perfectly cut bob. "It's Robert Corlew on the phone."

Corlew had taken over as the head of St. Alban's vestry since the beginning of the year, after former president Vaughn Fowler had . . . permanently resigned. When replacing him, the vestry had decided Corlew should use the more traditional title of warden, perhaps to encourage the idea of stewardship, rather than Fowler's approach, which had been more like Alexander Haig in crisis mode.

Clare grunted, trying the sash again. "What's he want? And can we get Mr. Hadley in to pry this darned window up?"

"Maybe Mr. Corlew could do it for you. He sounds as if he's ready to rip a window right out of its frame."

Clare sank back onto her calves. "He read the newspaper."

"He read the newspaper." After the Monday-night broadcast that outed, as it were, Bill Ingraham, the *Post-Star* had taken the story and run with it. Yesterday, they had a piece on Ingraham's death and the effect it might have on the Algonquin Spa development. Today, the Wednesday *Post-Star* featured a prominently placed story linking Ingraham's murder and the Dvorak and MacPherson beatings, including comments from leaders of gay organizations. Clare's name, and St. Alban's, had also been mentioned in both the Tuesday edition and today's. Lois had already cut out the articles for the church scrapbook. "It makes such an interesting change from all those community news stories about the Saint Martha's Group tea and white-elephant sales," she had said.

Clare clambered down from her desk. "Put him through," she said with all the enthusiasm of an early Christian asking to meet the lions.

"Try not to sound so eager and upbeat," Lois said before she clicked off and Robert Corlew came on the line.

"Reverend Clare?"

"Good morning, Robert. How nice to hear from you. I don't think I've seen you in church more than once since Memorial Day. I've missed you." She grinned to herself. Maybe she could land a preemptive strike and take the field before he recovered.

"Ah. Well, you know how it is—summertime, grandkids visiting, houseguests, sailing. And business is nonstop." She could hear him collecting himself. "I'm calling about the article in the paper today."

"Yes, I saw that. It mentions St. Alban's. Did you notice? We're really starting to get our name out."

"That's what I mean. I don't think we want to 'get our name out' in a story about gay guys who get killed while cruising for anonymous sex!"

Clare leaned back in her old-fashioned office chair. It let out a satisfying snap. "Are we talking about the same article? The one that describes how a doctor and a video-store owner were assaulted and then a highly respected businessman was killed?"

"In the bushes in the park, yes, that article. I can read between the lines as well as the next man. Gay man plus dark, secluded area in a park means one thing." His voice dropped into a confidential tone. "Look, I can understand. You happened to be there; your name got into the paper as a result. What's done is done. What I'm thinking of now is damage control. I want to make sure you aren't getting involved, that's all."

"'Involved'?" Clare's resolve to treat Robert Corlew with teasing good humor was cracking under the strain of his conversation. "Can you expand on that?"

"Reverend Clare, we can't afford to have St. Alban's name linked to any more . . . scandals. Not after last December. I've seen how you can get with these little pet projects of yours. The unwed teenage mothers. Those old drunks. Right? Let's all get on the same page with this. Homosexuals getting attacked while cruising is unfortunate, of course, but it doesn't have anything to do with us. I'm sure I'm speaking for the whole vestry when I say we sincerely don't want to see you in the news again unless it's the annual 'What Is the Meaning of Easter?' story."

Clare felt the phone go slippery in her grasp and realized she had been squeezing it too tightly. "So this means you don't think I should ride down Main Street buck naked, calling for all lesbian, gay, and transgendered people to join us in an interfaith service at St. Alban's?"

There was a heavy pause. "That's a joke, right?"

"Robert, are you deliberately trying to be offensive, or is it just accidental? My 'little pet projects'? Do you really believe it has nothing to do with us? Since when does hatred and prejudice breaking out in our own community not concern us?"

Over the line, she could hear him groan. "I knew it. I told Terry Wright. I said you were probably chomping at the bit to save the gays."

"You were talking about me with Terry Wright?" Terence Wright, senior vice president in the corporate loan department of AllBanc, was another vestry member. "Who else?"

"A few phone calls were made between members of the vestry. The situation was discussed. Some concerns were expressed."

The passive voice was used. Clare rolled her eyes. "I'm curious. Was Sterling Sumner included in these discussions?"

"I didn't happen to speak with him."

"Ha."

"What do you mean, 'ha'?"

"I mean, ha, he's the only gay member of the vestry."

"Sterling is not gay! He's just artistic!"

"Oh, for heaven's sake, Robert. Do you think he wears that scarf year-round because he's cold?"

The developer, who was a good twenty-five years her senior and probably did think the flamboyant Sumner had an 'artistic' temperament, sputtered over the phone.

"Look," she went on, "I had been concerned about the issues raised by the assaults on Dr. Dvorak and Todd MacPherson. But to tell the truth, I've been so swept away by events that I hadn't been thinking about anything in any coherent fashion. Now I will."

Corlew started to speak, but she steamed forward. "We'll have a meeting. We haven't gotten the whole vestry together since May. We'll talk about what it means to live in a community where homophobia rises to the point of violent hate crimes and what we, as Christians, ought to do about it."

"There's no way you're going to get everybody together at the church in July. Lacey Marshall and Sterling are both ensconced in their camps at Lake George, and I can guarantee you they won't leave before September. Norm Madsen is off on one of those Elderhostel trips, picking up old pottery shards in Greece."

"You and Terry are in town, aren't you?"

"We hardly comprise the whole vestry. And Terry's actually on vacation from the bank this week. I was going to take him sailing—"

"Okay, let's do that. Where is it you sail?"

"What? Where? Lake George, of course. But—"

"Great. Let's all meet at the lake and have our discussion there. We can do it before you and Terry go out, at either Mrs. Marshall's or Sumner's summer house, or—how big is your boat?"

"Forty-two feet. Are you proposing a floating vestry meeting?"

"Sure! That way, no one has to be dragged away from their summer fun."

There was a dead silence for a moment. Then he said, "That's a joke, right?"

"No, the transgendered liberation parade was a joke. This is a proposal. The alternative is that we drag everybody in here for a nice long un-air-conditioned meeting. I don't want to discuss this over the phone, one person at a time. We'll never get anywhere. And the issue needs addressing now, not in September. When were you going to meet Terry?"

"Friday," he said.

"Great! Friday would work well for me. I've got home visits in the morning and then the noontime Eucharist, but I'm free the rest of the afternoon. Look, I'm going to pass you back to Lois. You let her know where and when to meet at your boat, and she'll notify everyone else. I'm glad you called and brought this up, Robert. This will really help clarify where we, as a church, stand."

"Reverend Clare . . ." She could hear grinding noises from the other end.

"Yes, Robert?"

There were some more noises. Finally, he managed to say, "I'll see you on Friday."

"See you then. Bye." She pressed the transfer button before he could reply. She was getting a handle on the different personalities on her vestry. Robert Corlew was a well-intentioned bully, a man who knew he was right in most everything he held an opinion on and who didn't hesitate to wield his big voice and brusque manner like a blunt instrument. She thought of Msgt. Ashley "Hardball" Wright, her survival school instructor at Egeland Air Force Base. He had been big on turning other people's weapons against them. *You spot someone hunting for you with a gun, you remember: That's not his gun. That's your gun.*

She punched the main office button. "Lois? Mr. Corlew is holding. We're having an impromptu vestry meeting on his boat Friday. You get the time and place to meet and notify everyone who isn't out of the country. He may want to wiggle out of it. Don't let him put you off."

"As if," the secretary said. Clare hung up and looked at the window in front of her desk with an expression of smug satisfaction. Now. If she could deal with one old fossil stuck in his tracks, she could surely deal with another.

◆ ◆ ◆

That afternoon was her weekly hospital visit, but she would have gone anyway, to look in on Todd MacPherson. She sat and visited a while with Mr. Ellis, who was in for his second hip replacement, and with Mrs. Johnson, who was getting a biopsy after she had started bleeding from her uterus. The seventy-year-old already had diabetes, a pacemaker, and high blood pressure, and her surgeon, a sympathetic woman Clare's age, was cheerfully upbeat in front of her patient and considerably more cautious when speaking to Clare. The unvarnished truth about Mrs. Johnson's chances put Clare in a somber mood as she entered Todd MacPherson's private room.

She had expected to see family—and there was, his sister Trish—and perhaps someone from the police department—there wasn't—but she was surprised to see two men whose expensive clothing firmly stamped them as not from Millers Kill, as well as a photographer carrying fifty pounds of cameras and light meters around his neck.

Trish, sitting in a corner chair, noticed her first and waved her in.

"I don't want to interrupt," Clare said, hesitating.

"No, it's all right," Trish said. "Todd, you remember Reverend Clare. She's going to marry Kurtis and me. She came and stayed with us while you were in surgery Saturday."

Todd, lying propped up on a stack of pillows, was a patchwork of bruises, but already he radiated more energy than Clare would have expected. One of the benefits of being twenty-four, she guessed, "Hi, Reverend Clare," he said.

"I just wanted to pop in and see how you were doing," she said, taking his proffered hand. "You gave your family quite a scare there."

"It gave me quite a scare, too."

One of the well-dressed men, a fair-skinned blond who had been staring at Clare, snapped his fingers. "Clare Fergusson," he said.

She looked at him, surprised. "Yes."

"You're the one who found Bill Ingraham's body," he said.

"Oh, that was just—"

"Nils Bensen," he said, extending his hand and grasping hers. "This is my colleague Adam Coppela." Coppela was also blond, although from the coloring of his skin and eyebrows, this was more a monumental act of will than anything to do with his genetic heritage.

"They're from the Adirondack Pride team," Todd said, beaming as much as his battered face would allow. "I'm going to be on the cover of their next magazine."

"That's right," Bensen said. "Todd here illustrates the terrible trap of simply conforming to the strictures of the straight establishment."

Coppela clapped a thick-fingered hand on Todd's shoulder. "The kid tries to fly under the radar, giving no offense—"

"A promising young businessman, paying his taxes—"

"And what happens? Wham!" Coppela smacked his fist into his palm. Clare and Trish both started. "He gets the crap pounded out of him because he's queer. You can hide, but you can't run."

"I'm going to speak at the next regional meeting," Todd said.

"You're going to be our star," Bensen said, smiling down at Todd like a coach looking at his first-round draft choice. He glanced up at Clare. "Since the story broke, we've already gotten triple our usual volume of calls asking about donating."

"Ah," she said. "That's wonderful."

"Maybe we can do an interview with you as a sidebar to Todd's article," Bensen said. He framed a headline in the air. "The church's official representative speaks out against homophobia."

Clare raised her hands. "I'm not the church's official representative. I'm not even sure I'm St. Alban's official representative. If you want a statement, I suggest you contact the diocesan office in Albany."

"Yeah, but that's not as sexy as a young hip priest with—" Bensen broke off, his eyes thoughtful. "You aren't a lesbian, by any chance?"

"No!" she said, and immediately regretted denying it so fervently. "What I mean is, my sex life is private." Bensen looked very interested. She felt her cheeks getting pink. "That is, if I had a sex life. Which I don't. I'm practicing celibacy."

"You any good at it?" Coppela asked.

"I hate to interrupt this fascinating conversation, but I need to ask Mr. MacPherson to spend a little time with Ms. Nguyen from the district attorney's office." Clare spun around and discovered she had been right to expect the police to be here. Chief Van Alstyne was standing in the doorway, eyebrows raised. He looked at Todd. "She's going to show you some photos for possible IDs." He speared the Adirondack Pride pair with a look and gestured toward the door. Clare waited until they had cleared the room before she left, passing a petite woman lugging photo albums on the way.

She waited outside the door, hoping to catch him when they were done. She was surprised when he emerged alone only a few minutes later. "Did he make an identification that quickly?" she asked.

He shook his head. "No, I just made the introductions. We don't handle the actual viewing. Someone from the DA's office who doesn't know who we've tapped shows the pictures. That way, the guy's lawyer can't get the ID thrown out because maybe a cop breathed a little too hard when the victim pointed to the right one."

"Do you have the Elliott guy from the construction job?"

He looked up and down the hall, as if someone might be listening in. Except for an elderly man shuffling along with his IV bag on a pole, they were alone. "Yeah." He shifted his shoulder and winced. "He's in custody.

He gave up the two guys he says did the jobs with him. One's a loser named Colvin; we're trying to track him down through his girlfriend. The other's more interesting." He cupped her elbow in his hand and led her farther away from MacPherson's door. "According to McKinley, the ringleader was a guy named Chris Dessaint. He's a guy with a job and a short list, the kind of arrests that happen when you're young and stupid and get drunk Saturday nights. He and McKinley were up to Lake George a couple of weeks ago and they beat up some gay tourist."

Clare winced. Suddenly, she felt a lot more sympathy for the Adirondack Pride team.

"Then Chris comes back to McKinley and—get this—says there's money in beating up gays."

"What? But Dr. Dvorak wasn't robbed."

"Not that kind of money. Payroll. Someone was passing along money and drugs in exchange for assaults on homosexuals."

"You're kidding. That's weird." She looked up at him. "You think there's some sort of supremacy group going on? A militia?"

"I've never heard of them paying a bunch of losers to front them. They usually manage to recruit their own losers."

The door to MacPherson's room swung open. Ms. Nguyen stepped into the hall. "He's done," she said, passing them on her way to the elevator. "You can question him now."

"Be right there," Russ said. He looked at Clare. "This stays between you and me, right? Even if you get outraged by the injustice of life, et cetera."

She crossed her heart. "Even if." He glanced toward the door and she suddenly wanted, more than anything, to keep him there for a few minutes longer. Just because talking with him was easier than talking with anyone else. "Have you seen your mother? I took the dogs back. She seemed pretty cheerful about the arrest and all."

"Not yet. I'm going over there Friday to do some work on the porch. Or at least that's the excuse. Mostly, I'm going over for dinner and the game. Linda's redecorating the living room this weekend, and I need to be out of the way Friday. I can't stand tripping over ladders and breathing paint fumes."

"Your living room? Was that the room with the comfy chairs?" Clare had been to his house last winter—once. "But it was so pretty. I liked it."

"Me, too."

Trish MacPherson stuck her head out the door. "Chief? Are you—"

"I'm coming," he said. He paused before entering the room, his hand on the edge of the door. He looked at Clare. "Hey."

"Hmm?"

"*Are* you any good at that celibacy thing?"

CHAPTER TWENTY

The first thing that struck Lawrence Robinson was the quarreling of crows. A quarrel of crows—wasn't that what they were called? "Hey, Donna," he called back to his wife, who was methodically tramping up the steep trail behind him. "What's the collective noun for crows?"

She stopped beside him, breathing hard, and pushed her auburn hair out of her eyes. He handed her his water bottle. Two week's hiking in the Adirondacks had been his idea for their summer break from Cornell, and he was grateful she was being such a good sport about it. Alternating camp nights with bed-and-breakfast stays had been her idea. It meant they never got very far into the wilderness, but the promise of a good mattress and a shower every other night kept Donna gamely walking forward.

She swallowed the tepid water and rubbed her hands dry on her T-shirt. She squinted into the trees. The raucous cries of the birds increased in volume, and then a wide-winged black shape rocketed through the forest cover, breaking the air over their heads and diving down, swooping through the cleared space of the trail. It skimmed overhead, so close that Lawrence could have jumped up and caught a tail feather, and then disappeared over the next rise, like a supernatural messenger from an Edgar Allan Poe tale.

His wife, who taught biology to premed students and was not the sort for fanciful imagery, said, "The collective noun for ravens, you mean? That was a raven. Crows are much smaller." She eased her pack off her shoulders with a grunt. "They're making God's own racket down there, aren't they?"

Lawrence jerked his attention away from the raven's flight path. After twenty-eight years of marriage, he could take a hint. They had left the bed-and-breakfast in Millers Kill over four hours ago, and Donna was ready for a break. He unbuckled and dropped his backpack: The ravens couldn't be seen, but they certainly could be heard, guttural cries and sharp knocking calls that sounded as if they were demanding, "Talk! Talk!"

Donna fished a granola bar out of her waist pack. "Probably fighting over a carcass."

"Yeah? Cool! You think there might be bones? Some bones would be a great prop for my class next semester on ritual and imagery in premodern societies."

Donna stuffed the rest of the bar into her mouth. "I fawt you were gon' have 'em paint rocks," she said around a mouthful of oats. She rolled her eyes at him and swallowed. "Okay, let's go have a look. It's probably just a raccoon. I can't imagine too many premodern societies worshiped raccoons." She struck out toward the sounds. He followed after, occasionally slowing himself on a tree trunk as the angle of the mountainside increased. She was a good sport, his wife.

This part of their hike was through mature forest, tall trees and little underbrush, thick dark humus composted from decades of fallen leaves quieting their steps. The day was hot and heavy, even here underneath the shade of the forest cover, and no breezes stirred the crowns of the beeches and maples. The ravens' screams sounded unnaturally loud in the stillness.

"Whoa! Honey!" Below him, Donna scrambled back, her legs kicking against the downward slant of the forest floor.

"What? Are you okay?" He let go of the trunk he had been clasping and jogged down the slope sideways until he could reach her.

"It's a drop-off. Not terribly high, but it startled me." She pointed to where the rich earth of the forest floor crumbled into air. Lawrence leaned against the pebbled trunk of an old black-cherry tree whose roots thrust through soil and rock into the air. "Be careful, honey," Donna said.

He could see the striated rock beneath him, a gash in the mountainside maybe ten or twelve feet high. Below them was a brook, brown and speck-led as a trout, running between two narrow banks of shaggy grass, the closer side growing right up to the rock, the farther side petering out into the deeply shaded hardwood forest.

At the water's edge, a small tent was staked out next to a stand of paper birch gleaming in the midday sun like fragile polished bones. The flapping, quarreling ravens nearly obscured its dun-colored fabric, perching on the aluminum ridgepole, strutting on the ground, plucking at the window flaps. "You're not going to believe this." Lawrence glanced back at Donna. "It looks like *The Birds* down there. I think someone's in trouble."

To her credit, Donna didn't think twice. "How can we get down?"

He took in the lay of the land. "This drop narrows down to just a couple feet if we follow it west a few more yards. We can jump from there."

"West?"

"Go left."

They trotted as fast as they could along the gash in the mountainside until they reached the area Lawrence had spotted from above. Donna jumped first and was splashing through the shin-deep water of the brook before he had eased himself over the rocky ledge. "Shoo! Shoo!" she yelled, windmilling her arms as she charged the ravens. With a chorus of croaks and calls, they lifted into the air in a dark whirlwind and settled in the stand of birch trees. Their shiny black bodies tipped the thin branches down, and they looked so much like a caricature of vultures that Lawrence would have laughed if it hadn't been so damn creepy.

"Honey . . ." Donna's voice was uncharacteristically hesitant. "I smell something."

The tent, the narrow one-person kind ideal for long hiking trips, was zipped up tightly. But Donna was right. As he got closer, he could smell it, too, sickly sweet. He wrinkled his nose. They looked at each other. "I've got my cell phone in my backpack," she said. "We could . . ."

Lawrence shook his head. "We can't just leave." A few feet in front of the tent, ashy stones enclosed a scorched circle. He bent over and placed his palm on top of the crumbled charcoal. "It's cold."

Donna took a deep breath. "Okay, then. Let's open it up and see." Before he could say anything or stop her, she unsnapped the flap covering the zipper and unzipped the front of the tent.

"Oh, my God!" They both recoiled—Donna turning her head, eyes watering; Lawrence covering his mouth and nose with one hand. The smell from the confines of the overheated tent was like the worst-ever rotten egg. Inside, in the dim, dun-colored light, he could see—

"Mmmmmph!" Donna spun away and retched.

The only dead people Lawrence had ever seen were his own parents, antiseptically clean and laid out in satin-lined coffins. They had been made up, their sunken cheeks padded and rosy, looking bizarrely as if they had fallen asleep while dressed for church. They bore no resemblance to the smoothly bloated body in the tent, but Lawrence knew he was looking at death, the real thing, without any prettying up or euphemisms.

"We should—" he started to say, and then he watched, horrified, as a single greenfly buzzed through the overheated air, entered the tent, and settled delicately on the dead man's open eye.

Lawrence grabbed his wife's arm and hauled her away, their stumbling steps turning into a run, and they splashed across the brook and clawed themselves up over the low rock ledge.

Running through the forest toward the trail, Donna's hand clutched tightly in his, he remembered the collective nouns he had been searching for earlier: A conspiracy of ravens. A murder of crows.

◆ ◆ ◆

Lights in the darkness. Heat radiating off the tarmac. The inescapable *thwap-thwap-thwap* of rotors and the dust devils rising in the downdraft. Russ folded his arms across his chest, aware of the damp fabric clinging to his skin and the hopelessly sweaty patches under his arms. Last Wednesday night, he had been watching one of these damned machines take off, and now here he was this Wednesday night, only a week later, watching and waiting as the chopper eased down and its skids touched the sticky black asphalt of the landing pad at the Glens Falls Airport.

Only this time, he didn't have Clare's exhilaration to distract him. Instead, it was Kevin Flynn and Mark Durkee leaping out in a display of youth and machismo, followed more slowly by Lyle MacAuley and Dr. Scheeler, who, Russ was pleased to notice, eyed the slowing rotors above his head and walked bent nearly in half until he was well beyond their range.

"You should have come, Chief! It was great!"

Russ sighed and fixed Flynn with a baleful glare. "I keep telling you, Kevin, we don't describe felonies as 'great.'"

"The helicopter ride! That's what was great. You ever been on a helicopter?"

"Yes, I have." Russ turned to Lyle and Dr. Scheeler. "Well?"

"He was carrying a driver's license and cards that ID'd him as Chris Dessaint. Looked sort of like the picture on the license. Kind of hard to tell," Lyle said.

"Two days sealed in a hot tent will do that to you," Dr. Scheeler commented. His sardonic tone reminded Russ of Emil Dvorak. Maybe it was a pathologist thing.

"Wait till you hear what we brought back with us," MacAuley said. From around the corner of the nearest hangar, Russ could see the meat wagon pulling up to the now-quiet chopper. "Kevin, Mark," MacAuley yelled at the pair, "you two collect the evidence bags and meet us at the cars." The two younger officers ambled back the way they had come, dancing out of the way of the two mortuary attendants, who were sliding a shiny black body bag out of the belly of the beast.

Don't go there.

He turned on his heel, forcing Lyle and Dr. Scheeler to accelerate to keep up with him. "Why don't you two fill me in on the whole picture?" he said. "From the beginning." He knew he should have been there that afternoon. He wouldn't have needed a hand-holding briefing from Lyle and the medical examiner if he had just been able to get into the chopper and go with the rest of them. Lyle frowned at him from under his bushy gray eyebrows but didn't comment on his abrupt departure. They headed toward the squad cars, which were parked behind a chainlink fence near the North Country Aviation hangar. "We were able to put down a half mile or so from the scene. The two Cornell professors who found the body showed us where it was. Kind of an out-of-the-way spot. If there hadn't been a bunch of birds attracting their attention, he could have been there for a lot longer."

"You get statements from them?"

"Yeah. They didn't have much that was helpful. They were shook up pretty bad, as you can imagine."

Yeah, he could imagine it.

"We offered to fly them back," Lyle went on, "but they decided to walk out. I've got contact numbers for them if you want to talk with them yourself."

"What was the scene?"

"Looks like Dessaint hiked in and pitched camp. I'm guessing he knew what he was doing. His equipment was top-of-the-line, but a few years old, well used. He was ready to travel light. A single-man tent, a bedroll, a couple changes of underwear. But he had a lot of food with him—that fancy dehydrated crap—and two bottles of purification tabs for water."

"He was going to disappear into the mountains?"

"It wouldn't be the first time."

MacAuley was right. Any number of people had hiked into the Adirondack State Park and disappeared, intentionally or not. An experienced camper with enough food and water could stay out of sight a long time in the summer. Dessaint might have hoped to lie low until things cooled down. Or hike west to Route 30, the narrow road running more or less north through the million-acre park, and from there hitch and hike his way over the Canadian border. The Adirondacks were a wilderness, but a wilderness with small towns, camps, and settlements.

"Any money on him?"

"A little over three hundred bucks."

Russ snorted. "That's not much to start a new life with. Even with the Canadian exchange rate."

MacAuley shrugged. "He had maybe another four, five thousand in drugs—meth and coke, and enough OxyContin to fill one of those economy-sized vitamin bottles."

They reached the chain-link fence. The shadows from the hangar swallowed them as they went through the gate into the parking lot. Russ unlocked his car and opened the door, spilling light onto the gritty asphalt below their feet. "So what was the cause of death, Doctor?"

"Obviously I don't have either a toxicology screen or an autopsy to go by. But I feel safe in giving you a first opinion that he shuffled off this mortal coil due to an overdose." Scheeler beeped his car with his remote key. Russ could hear a dull thunk as the doors unlocked. "Based on the fact that he had a needle in his arm and his works spread out on the tent floor next to him. I'm guessing—and it's just a guess, mind you—that he gave himself a highball."

Russ leaned against the top of the squad car. Out of sight of the helicopter, he felt more relaxed, more thoughtful. "That doesn't jibe with what his weasely little friend McKinley told me. He described Dessaint as a sort of fitness buff. Hardly the kind of guy to shoot up heroin and injectable cocaine."

"Yeah," MacAuley said, "but according to McKinley, Dessaint was the one handing out the goodies as well as the cash after they'd had a party."

Russ frowned. "Were there any signs he was a regular user?"

"I didn't see any tracks on his arms," Dr. Scheeler said. "That doesn't mean he wasn't an occasional user."

"Wait till you see the real jackpot item, though," MacAuley added. "Remember I told you that it was a flock of birds that brought the Cornell folks down for a look-see? Well, most of 'em got scared off when all of us arrived and started working the site. But there were five or six of them, big buggers, that kept hopping around and pecking at one spot nearby, underneath a tree. So I went to take a look at it, and it'd been dug up recently and smoothed over. It was shaped like a drop pit. You know, for—"

"I camp, Lyle. I know what a drop pit is. But birds aren't going to be pecking at someone's latrine."

"That's what I thought. So we dug it up. Guess what we found."

"Jimmy Hoffa."

MacAuley crossed his arms and leaned back. Russ had an idea what he was going to say, but he wanted to give him his moment. Lyle loved a little drama. "No, really, I don't know," Russ said. "What?"

"Clothes. They had been rinsed out, but there were still visible bloodstains on 'em. And a tear in the sleeve that looks like a match to those threads we found at the scene."

Russ looked at Scheeler. "Could they be what Ingraham's killer was wearing?"

The medical examiner spread his hands. "Could be. I didn't want to examine them at the site, for fear of losing possible hairs, fibers, or skin flakes. The blood traces we could see were very faint, which would certainly be the case if the killer went into the river after he garroted Mr. Ingraham. Most of the blood would wash away in the cold water, but not all." He clasped his hands together like a man savoring the prospect of a good meal. "I think going over those clothes with a microvacuum and some Luminol will be very informative. First thing I'll do is type the remaining blood, of course. If I were a betting man, I'd put money down that it'll match Bill Ingraham's."

Russ reached under his glasses and pinched the bridge of his nose. "So it looks good that Dessaint is our killer."

"Yep," MacAuley said.

"And that he conveniently offed himself while sampling his wares."

"Yep."

"We can pretty much look forward to marking this one closed."

"Yep."

"Except"—Russ looked at MacAuley over the tops of his glasses— "we still have McKinley's story about Dessaint's mystery contact, handing off drugs and money in exchange for beating up on a few selected targets."

"Maybe he was making that up for the benefit of his audience. Dessaint, I mean. Covering himself in advance by putting the blame on some evil overlord. He might have guessed that McKinley or Colvin would turn him in within five minutes of getting picked up."

"I considered that. Problem is, his actions are consistent with McKinley's story. Neither Emil Dvorak nor Todd MacPherson was robbed. And that video store had a lot of walking-around money in it."

MacAuley plucked at his uniform shirt in a hopeless attempt to air it out. "Maybe he was a freak. Maybe he really did believe he was destined to wipe out homosexuals or something. Maybe he's got a bunch of pamphlets tucked away in his apartment, with his manifesto and a call to arms on 'em. We haven't cataloged near everything yet."

Dr. Scheeler interrupted. "Gentlemen, you're getting well out of my area of expertise. I'm going to bid you good night. Chief Van Alstyne, I'll have my report to you as soon as possible."

"Thanks, Doc. And thanks for being available to go to the scene on such short notice. We're usually not this busy."

The medical examiner's teeth shone whitely in the darkness. "That's okay. My patients never complain." His car door thunked behind him and he backed out of his parking spot. Russ could hear Faith Hill on the radio, wailing away about breathing as the doctor drove away.

He turned back toward MacAuley. "I want to keep Noble tracking down anyone who knew Chris Dessaint. I want to know the people he ran with, what he liked to do, and whether or not he might have played McKinley and Colvin. First thing in the morning, we're going back to his trailer and taking apart everything we didn't touch the first time. Maybe we'll find something that'll let us close this case."

"You don't sound very hopeful."

Russ sighed. He took off his glasses and tried to find a clean, dry spot on his shirt to polish them. "We still have that APB out on Jason Colvin?"

"Yeah."

"We need to update it. Let everyone know the suspect we're looking for may already be dead."

CHAPTER TWENTY-ONE

It was fifteen minutes after they left Robert Corlew's boat slip in the marina that Clare finally understood, really understood, why someone would voluntarily live through winter after brutal winter in the north country. They had motored out past the docks, the mainsail billowing, until they passed some unmarked point and Corlew turned the boat away from the wind, swung out the boom, and told her and Terry Wright to run up the jib. The forty-two-foot boat surged forward like a thoroughbred let out at the Saratoga racetrack. Clare stood clutching the mast with one hand, half-sheltered from the brilliant sunlight by the red-and-white curve of the jib sail, as the boat surged and rose repeatedly beneath the soft soles of her old Keds. Ahead of her, the long lake stretched out forever. Its water, a forbidding slab of black in the winter, was dancing blue now, a thousand sparks of spray and sunlight flashing all around her. And at the shoreline, the mountains rose up out of the water, smoky blue and alpine green. It was like living in a fairy tale. She half-expected to see a white-towered castle rearing out of the forest.

"I think Story Land amusement park is over there somewhere." Terry Wright waved in the direction of the opposite shore, where a little town emerged from the forest in a clutter of bright-roofed houses that ran down to the water's edge. The rotund banker eased himself down until he was sitting on the deck, his feet braced against the low lip running beneath the rail line. Clare followed suit.

"I was just thinking it looked as if there ought to be a castle here somewhere."

"There are. Fort Ticonderoga, at the head of the lake, at the point where it meets with Lake Champlain. And behind us, Fort William Henry. Fought over by the French and the Indians, the British, and the colonists. This place was called 'the key to the continent' in the eighteenth century. There's been a lot of blood spilled into these waters at one time or another." He smiled, his round cheeks sunburned underneath his enormous mustache. "That's not, by the way, a hint that there will be today."

Clare laughed. "Fair enough." She leaned back on her elbows, closing her eyes and letting the sun sink into her bones. "Hard to imagine wars here at the moment. It seems like heaven to me."

"There was a war over heaven, too, wasn't there? And now look. The place is overrun with tourists, just like Lake George. Of course, heaven isn't closed between October and May. I hope not anyway." He laughed. Terry's infectious laugh gave him a reputation as a comic because it made listeners join in even if what he said wasn't particularly funny.

"What are you two nattering on about up there?" Mrs. Marshall's voice cut through the rush of the water and the wind. "Come down here and join us. Robert's breaking out the drinks."

Clare followed Terry along the edge of the deck and dropped beside him onto a well-padded bench in the boat's cockpit. Mrs. Marshall and Sterling Sumner were occupying the opposite bench, Sterling holding the wheel steady with one hand. His ever-present scarf, in deference to the eighty-degree weather, was of jaunty striped silk rather than wool, and one long end fluttered in the breeze.

As she bounced into place, Robert Corlew leaned out of the hatch, his wide shoulders nearly filling the space. The developer had unusually thick hair that sprang with suspicious abruptness from his forehead. Clare had thought today might be the day when she would finally be able to verify that it was a rug, but Corlew had a captain's cap jammed firmly onto his head, hiding everything underneath. He handed two tall glasses up to Mrs. Marshall. "Lacey, gin and tonics for you and Sterling." He turned his attention to the other bench. "Reverend Clare, Terry, what's your poison?"

"Beer," said Terry. "If I don't keep working on it, this belly will disappear." He laughed again.

"Same here," Clare said. Corlew ducked out of sight and reappeared a moment later with two bottles, ice-cold and dripping. Clare handed Terry Wright his bottle and tilted hers back, drinking down a third of the beer at one go. "Boy, this sun sure makes you thirsty," she said, lowering the bottle.

Mrs. Marshall was staring at her with exactly the same expression Grandmother Fergusson used the time she caught Clare in a burping contest with her cousins. Too late, Clare noticed the pair of glasses Corlew was holding in his other hand. Silently, he handed one to Terry, who proceeded to pour his beer. Corlew proffered the other glass to her.

"Unless you'd rather . . ." *Swill it down like that*, Clare thought, finishing the sentence for him. She smiled weakly and accepted the glass, then dutifully poured and handed her bottle back to Corlew.

I'm thirty-five years old, she reminded herself. I'm these people's spiritual adviser. I'm not going to be intimidated by the fact that they're all old enough to be my parents. She glanced at Mrs. Marshall. Or grandparents.

Robert climbed back out of the hatch with his own beer, *in a glass*, and slipped behind the large wheel to sit on the transom locker at the very stern of the boat. "Cheers, everyone," he said, and raised his glass.

"Cheers," they all replied.

Clare twisted in her seat to look back at the shoreline slipping past them. A boardwalk jutted into the water, crammed with arcades, T-shirt shops, and rickety stands selling Italian sausages and fried dough. A redheaded man, bearded and bespectacled, was trying to keep a pair of skinny kids from falling off the edge of the pier. The children, holding clouds of cotton candy bigger than their heads, waved energetically at the boat. Clare waved to them and turned back toward her companions, inexplicably buoyed up again. It was too beautiful a day to feel bad, and the thought gave her another epiphany. The long, hard winter had given her an appreciation for the summer that she had never had before. The sun, the clear blue sky, the green and growing things were blessings that she enumerated day by day, because they would be gone in a twinkling, in a heartbeat. Winter was the default here, with summer a brief and glorious escape. She felt that this ought to provide her with some solid spiritual insight, but all she could think was that she now understood why no one was attending the Sunday services.

"You're looking particularly thoughtful, Ms. Fergusson." Mrs. Marshall, silver-haired and elegant, could never bring herself to address Clare either by her first name or as Reverend Fergusson. Clare couldn't blame her for the latter—she herself had grown up hearing that the word *reverend* was an adjective, not a title. Her grandmother Fergusson would no more have addressed a priest as Reverend than she would have attended services without a hat. Of course, Grandmother Fergusson's priests had all been male. Father was not a title that Clare would choose. She supposed she would have to either get her doctorate in divinity or rise to a post in the Episcopal hierarchy in order to get a proper gender-free title. Bishop Fergusson . . .

"Isn't this the point where you say, 'I'm sure you're all wondering why I brought you here'?" Sterling Sumner said. The word Clare usually applied to Sterling, in the deepest recesses of her mind, was *disagreeable*. In vestry meetings, the architect was impatient and prone to dismiss the opinions of others as uninformed. Today, his face was pinched into an expression that suggested irritable bowel syndrome.

Robert Corlew broke in before she could answer him. "I think we all know what we're here to talk about. Let me try to frame the issue. We've had some very unfortunate episodes of violence this summer around Millers Kill."

Clare opened her mouth to point out that a bloody murder was a bit more than an unfortunate episode, but then she thought better of it and shut it again.

"It appears that there may be a connection between the attacks and the victims' lifestyles. In other words, all the men involved were homosexuals. Reverend Clare made a statement to the press, expressing her opinions. I'm sure you all saw it. Now, if I understand what she's told me, she wants St. Alban's to get involved in some way." He sat back down on the transom chest so abruptly, Clare was startled. She had expected him to start in on what he wanted to see happen.

Everyone looked at Clare.

She could feel things slipping out of control, her own waspish reaction ready to burst forth, her impatience with having to deal with these people.

Not *these* people. *My* people, came the thought. Her thought? She wasn't sure. But she knew what she had to do. She put her glass into one of the cup holders molded into the side of the bench.

"I'd like us to start with a prayer," she said. Corlew looked surprised, then nodded. She watched each of them as they gathered into themselves. Mrs. Marshall folded her hands neatly beneath her chin. Sterling ducked his head and covered his face with one splayed-fingered hand. Corlew, still standing at the wheel, tilted his head back, a practical position that left his eyes half-lidded but still able to see. Terry Wright laced his fingers together easily and rested them in his lap, head bowed. For a moment, she wished she could bring them together, hold hands, and pray, but they were all Episcopalians, after all, and holding hands was not the way things were done. It would only make them uncomfortable.

"Lord God," she said, "if there's one thing we know about You, it's that You love boats. You chose fishermen to be Your companions, and You walked to them across the water to quell their fear and doubts. Be with our company in this boat, Lord, and help us to remember that, quarreling and disputatious as we might be, we are all Your apostles. In Jesus' name. Amen."

Everyone repeated the amen, and there was a moment when they all looked up and around them at the taut sails and the sun and the fast-slapping water racing past their hull.

"My thought is this," Clare said. "I believe we have an obligation to speak out against hate crimes. I believe that we can't, in conscience, stand aside and witness attacks like these happening and not come forward and say, 'This is wrong.'"

"But there's no doubt that it's wrong," Terry Wright said in his mild, reasonable voice. "It was obvious from the papers that the attacks were horrific and that the police are going after the culprits with everything they've got. What more could *we* do?"

"It's not as if the news of Ingraham's murder was followed by editorials ripping up gays for their lifestyle choice," Corlew said. "I can personally attest to the fact that not one person I've met over the course of the past week has said anything along the lines of 'Good, they've got it coming to 'em.'"

"My position is very simple. I don't want to see St. Alban's name dragged through the mud again," Sterling Sumner said. "After last winter's debacle, I say we need to keep our heads down and our noses clean. Where is all this going to lead? People associating our name with crime and homosexuality. That'll be bringing new recruits in by the busload. You do remember that we wanted you to increase membership, don't you?"

"There are three new families attending St. Alban's since I became rector," she said.

He sniffed. "That's a start. . . ."

"I haven't been here a year yet!"

"Calm down, Reverend Clare. No one is questioning your ability to get the job done. Get up on top of the bench, will you?" Corlew turned the wheel slightly and released the jib several inches. The boat responded by keeling starboard, away from the wind, and Clare and Terry stepped up on the padded seat and sat on the outer edge of the cockpit, leaning against the yaw of the boat.

"Sterling's raised a valid point," Mrs. Marshall said, taking a small sip from her gin and tonic. "How do you answer it, Ms. Fergusson?"

"I don't think anyone would mistake our concern for victims of crime as an association with crime, any more than our mentoring program for teen mothers is a stamp of approval for girls getting pregnant."

"Another idea of which I did not approve," Sterling said.

Clare ignored that. "And as for people shunning us because of our known association with homosexuals"—here she wiggled her eyebrows, because she sounded ridiculously like Joseph McCarthy—"I say we don't want new members who would think like that. We want people who will admire us for taking a stand and who will say, 'Yes, that's Christianity; that's how I want to live it and that's the church I want to belong to.'"

"So what is it you envision us doing, dear?"

Clare bit back a smile. She thought Mrs. Marshall's endearment was a slip of the tongue, but it was a sweet one. She had to confess that it didn't throw her so much when the eighty-year-old lady treated her as a girl instead of a leader. It was the men she had to whip into shape.

"Nothing aggressive or in-your-face. But noticeable. Something that makes us and our support of our neighbors visible."

"How about a one-eighth-page block ad in the *Post-Star*?" Sumner said.

She looked directly at him. "Sterling, what would you do if you wanted to tell your community that all people, regardless of their sexual orientation, were accepted and valued?"

"Huh." Sumner jerked one end of his scarf. "The truth is, not all people are accepted and valued. Whether it's because of their so-called sexual orientation or just because they're unlettered idiots." Mrs. Marshall murmured a reproving sound. "I can't help it, Lacey," Sumner said. "It goes against my grain. These men running around, doing whatever they want to, with no sense of discretion—"

"I rather think that's the point," Mrs. Marshall said. She laid a hand over Sumner's arm. "That people can live their lives without having to fear that a slip of the tongue or being seen in the wrong place at the wrong time will make them pariahs."

She knows. That was Clare's first thought, and she realized there was something very old here between these two friends, old and buried, but not forgotten. She felt suddenly ashamed that she had been trying to maneuver Sumner into a corner.

Corlew looked at Terry Wright, discomfort and determination chasing each other on his face. "We're not trying to make anyone a pariah. We're simply looking out for our own." Clare opened her mouth and he shot a hand up, waving the words away. "No, no, sorry, I didn't mean that the way it sounded."

"I think, gentlemen and ladies, that Clare is right." As always, Terry's voice was easy, jovial—the dealmaker making a deal. "I think we could have easily sidestepped the whole issue, but now that our, ah, energetic young priest has brought it up, we're not going to get away without some show of support. If for no other reason than if we don't, we'll feel like a bunch of bigots."

Sumner made a noise.

"So we might as well come to an agreement on how we're going to stand up and be counted. Clare?"

"I was thinking of a march from St. Alban's to the town hall and—"

"No. No marches." Corlew slugged back some of his beer. "The down-town merchant's association would kill us."

"He's right," Terry said.

"Maybe we could have a fund-raiser?" Mrs. Marshall suggested. "A dinner dance. It's short notice, but we could probably get together a com-mittee and be able to present it by mid-September."

Clare shook her head. "I think that's too removed in time from what's happening now. Besides, a dinner dance is private by definition. We need something public. How about a rally in Riverside Park?"

"You mean like that damned antidevelopment group?" Corlew's skin took on an alarming purple shade. "Those tree-huggers? Those backward, head-in-the-sand—"

"Well," Clare said, "not exactly like them, no. I was thinking we would get a permit, for one. . . ."

"I don't think a rally is a good idea," Mrs. Marshall said. "After all, they rather depend on a large crowd for their effectiveness, don't they? Other-wise, all you have is a handful of malcontents talking to one another."

"A candlelight vigil," Sumner said.

They all looked at him. "What?" Clare said.

"What are we? A church. What do people think of when they think of a church? Quiet, hymns, candles. You want to draw attention to the church's stance. Is this going to happen by marching through crowds of tourists in the middle of the day? No, it is not. You want contrast. People, at night. Light and darkness. Some music—not that dreadful guitar-strumming

'Michael, Row the Boat Ashore' protest stuff. Something that works as a counterpoint—a solo voice or a single wind instrument."

They all looked at him.

"You're thinking of this in terms of a military campaign. Think of it as a design problem. You have a message that may be uncomfortable or unpleasant to some. You have to create the appeal, the comfort."

"Sterling," Clare said. "I think you must be a remarkable architect."

He snorted. "Mostly retired now. I do teach a bit, though, at Skidmore and down in Albany. One thing I tell my students is that there is *always* a solution to a design problem."

"Sounds good to me," Corlew said. "As long as you keep it nice and peaceful."

"And don't block any storefronts!" Terry added.

"In front of town hall," Clare said. "Peaceful. And tasteful."

The four vestry members and their priest looked at one another in wary agreement, as if not trusting the fragile accord to bear the weight of anything more enthusiastic.

"Maybe getting known as a more liberal parish won't be so bad," Corlew said.

"We can hardly get a rep as a more conservative group," Terry said. "I think the last parish census showed the average age of our congregants was fifty-six. It's not like we've been bringing new blood into St. Alban's with what we've been doing."

"Didn't someone say that insanity is doing the same thing over and over and expecting new results?" Clare said.

"That holds true until you start thinking about having children, dear," Mrs. Marshall said.

"Or playing the stock market," Terry added.

There was another pause. Clare could hear the quick *thwap-thwap-thwapping* of the sail as it lost the wind. "I'm going to tack," Corlew said. He hauled in the jib and released the boom. Clare and Terry dropped down into the bench and ducked as the boat turned and the boom sliced through the air over their heads. "Reverend Clare, can you get up there and tie off the boom?" he asked. "Terry, take the wheel. I'm going below for a sec."

She scrambled over the hatch and secured the boom in its new position. The wind had lessened from its earlier slipstream rush and now the boat sailed up the lake like a determined woman through a crowded fairground, sweeping past the people and the glittering carny amusements, making her way steadily up the midway, headed for the open air.

She stood mastside for a few minutes, feeling the easy motion of the boat through her feet, hearing Corlew clumping around in the cabin below and the square clinking of ice in glasses.

"Reverend Clare, you want another one?" Corlew twisted backward to see her from the hatch.

She slid down to the rail deck and walked to the cockpit. "I'd better not. I've got to drive. And tonight's that party at Peggy Landry's."

"Is that Margaret Landry? I used to know her mother," Mrs. Marshall said. "How did you come to meet her? I don't believe any of the Landrys have attended St. Alban's since old Mr. Landry died, and that was before the war. World War Two," she added.

Clare sat on the edge of the cockpit and braced her feet against the seat cushion. "Her niece Diana is getting married at St. Alban's next month. She and her fiancé have been putting off their premarital counseling sessions, and when I pushed Diana on it, Peggy asked me to come to her house and sit down with them before this party. I guess she figured she owed me a dinner if I drove out there for counseling. I have to confess I'm not wild about attending. Standing around making small talk with a bunch of New Yorkers. Plus, I'll have to wear heels. I hate wearing heels." She waggled one sneaker-shod foot.

"I hope we're getting a good donation for the use of the church," Terry said. He reached past Clare's legs and accepted a new beer from Corlew. "We're becoming awfully popular with the wedding crowd. Maybe we ought to institute a series of fees. You know, one rate if you have some family connection, another if you're a total stranger. It's not as if their pledges are supporting our expenses."

"Peggy ought to be good for a hefty chunk of change, after what she got in that deal with BWI." Corlew emerged from the hatch with his own drink and took the wheel from Terry. "Word is, that spa is going to put her into the big leagues. I didn't think she was ever going to be able to unload that white elephant, to tell you the truth. I know someone out of Albany who looked pretty seriously at trying a vacation condo community there, but it never went through."

"Why not?" Clare asked.

"Who knows? It's a tough site. Environmental impact, the old PCB issue, and it's remote. People want to vacation where they can reach things, not where they have to drive half an hour to get a burger and a movie. Peggy needed an outfit like BWI, with deep pockets and a long-term plan. They're going to need to pump a hell of a lot of money into that place for the first few years."

"You mean to build the place? Or to keep it running?"

"To build clientele," Terry said. "It usually takes several years for any resort or vacation-oriented property to have enough name recognition to start making money, instead of spending it. Even when there's an established attraction nearby, like a good ski resort or"—he waved a hand, encompassing the water and mountains around them—"a lake. When the bank structures a loan for a resort-related development, we figure in a minimum of three years before we can expect any profit."

"So BWI isn't just going to build the place and put in the staff. They have to keep it afloat for the next several years?"

"That's why BWI is the perfect partner for Peggy," Corlew said. "They don't wait for visitors to discover nearby attractions. *They* are the attraction. I'd love to know how a small-time player like Peggy got their attention."

Sumner cleared his throat. "I understand that Landry's nephew was a particular friend of the late Bill Ingraham."

"What?"

"Get out!"

"Where on earth did you hear that?"

He affected a pained expression. "I normally avoid gossip at all costs, but still, one hears things." He leaned forward, and everyone else leaned in, as well. "I understand that the boy is what might have been called a gold digger by an earlier generation. What I heard is that he latched onto Bill Ingraham as his sugar daddy. At some point during their friendship, the boy introduced Ingraham to Peggy and she, evidently, put on the full-court press. Next thing you know, good-bye, white elephant, hello, Algonquin Spa."

Clare sat back up. "But I heard Ingraham broke up with his boyfriend months ago."

Sumner flipped his hand, as if to say, Life's like that. "In the matchup between youth and wealth, only the wealth stays the same. The youth has to be replaced periodically."

Corlew took a drink. "So the nephew is the missing piece." Terry snickered at his pun, and both men began sniggering.

Sterling tilted his head toward Mrs. Marshall. "You see why I rarely gossip."

Clare slung one leg back over the edge of the seat and propped her foot against the rail deck. Mal Wintour. What was it Peggy had said? "He's just having trouble living a life of wealth and leisure without any visible means of support." Even if she did have to wear high heels, she was suddenly looking forward to the party tonight.

CHAPTER TWENTY-TWO

"Marriage is meant to be for life," Clare said, taking a kir royale from one of the caterer's staff. "It gives ordinary people like you and me a chance to emulate Christ, to offer ourselves up for another person, to truly put another's happiness first."

The men and women clustered around her looked alternately interested, amused, and put off. Diana's fiancé shook his head. "See? She just puts a whole new spin on it for me." He gulped at his martini. "You should all take counseling from Reverend Clare. Keep you from screwing up so much."

"Or screwing so much," one corkscrew-curled young woman said to the man beside her. He was so tan and sun-bleached blond that his teeth appeared to be lighted from inside when he flashed a smile.

"Chelli!" The other woman, dangerously thin, with long nails that owed nothing to nature, frowned at her friend.

When Diana and Cary brought Clare into the enormous living room and announced her as their priest, she had immediately gathered a clump of interested listeners. She put it down to the curiosity value of her calling and gender, rather than a sudden desire for a conversion experience by anybody in the crowd, which looked as if it had been assumed bodily from the set of *Sex and the City* and set down in this three-story tumble of wood and windows clinging to the side of a mountain. Cary Wood—the name still made her shake her head—had dropped several interesting details about the counseling session they had just completed in the quiet home office next to the family room. "So we were talking about self-sacrifice and sticking it out, and tell them what you said about divorce, Reverend Clare!"

Clare flexed her feet inside her high-heeled sandals and thanked God for the thick carpet covering the floors. If she was trapped here, at least she wasn't in shoe hell. She smiled at Cary. It was possible she had impressed upon him some essential wisdom he was going to need a few years down the road, but she suspected she was being asked for this tidbit again because of its thrilling break with current thinking. "I said that if marriage made two people one flesh, then divorce was like an animal gnawing its leg off to escape a trap before it dies. It should only be considered as the very last resort."

"That sounds like me when I split from Annalise," the bronzed sun god said. "Except she was the animal chewing on my leg."

The perfect-fingernailed woman laughed. "You mean the only reason you can consider divorce is if you're threatened with death? That sounds extreme."

Clare sipped her drink. It was cool, tingly, and perfectly currant-flavored. "Not necessarily a literal death. Sometimes, a marriage can mean the death of your soul. The death of who you are. Or think of the traditional grounds for divorce or annulment: infertility, the death of your future, insanity—the death of the mind that made the vow—adultery."

"Death if you get found out!" Chelli's corkscrew curls bobbed as she laughed.

"What gets me, and no offense, Reverend Clare"—by this statement Clare understood that what the very tan man was going to say would offend her—"is how priests who have no experience with sex and marriage get off on telling the rest of us how to stay married."

"My mother says that a doctor doesn't have to have cancer in order to know how to cure it," Chelli said.

"Yeah, I've heard that one before," Clare said. "I think it's better to think of your priest as an investment adviser. Let's say you're going to invest everything you have, and commit all your future earnings as well, in the hopes that you're going to get a terrific return. Do you want to consult someone already deep into the market? Someone who may have opinions and self-interest based on his own experiences? Or do you want to hire an independent adviser, someone who has followed the market and read up on its history and all the different investment schemes? Someone with no vested interest in the outcome, other than to make sure you put your money where it will do you the most good?"

"Huh. I never thought of it like that." The sun god stuck out his hand. "I'm Dennys, by the way. With a *y*."

"Hello, Dennys with a Y."

"And I'm Gayle. Also with a *y*."

Clare took her hand gingerly. Those nails were scary. She wondered if she should figure out some way to spell her name with a *y*. Clayr?

"So tell me." Dennys dropped his voice and the two women leaned in to hear him. "What's it like? Being celibate? I mean, I can't imagine it."

"I bet you can't." Chelli giggled.

"I think you may be making a common mistake and confusing *celibate*, which also means not married, and *chaste*, which means . . . well, not having sex. Episcopal priests don't take vows of celibacy. Lots and lots of priests are married and have kids."

"You're not married," Gayle said.

"No, I'm not. How did you know?"

"No ring," she said, pointing to Clare's unadorned left hand. Clare was impressed. She knew women checked out men's hands, but other women's? It was a good thing she had been out of the singles scene for so many years. She'd have been eaten alive.

"Well, the church traditionally teaches that sex should be reserved for marriage. There's been a lot of talk in the General Convention lately about redefining that to a mutually committed, loving relationship. I think . . ." she paused. "I believe that a priest has an obligation to be a model for her or his parish. To try to live very much in the open, in the way Christ wants us to live."

"So no sex? Until you're married? At all?" Dennys was clearly intrigued by the idea. She hoped he wasn't the type of guy who got off on the idea of an unobtainable woman. Now that marriage didn't stop people fooling around, it must be hard to find any really challenging conquests.

"That's right," she said, and as she said it, an image from her dream appeared in her head, the floating warmth, the hands, Russ rising out of the water. She could feel her cheeks heating up.

"She's blushing!" Chelli said.

Clare smiled and hoped she looked composed. It was only a dream, for heaven's sake. "I'm afraid you've caught me out. We priests are used to asking the personal questions, not answering them. Oops! There's Peggy. If you'll excuse me, I want to say hello to our hostess. Nice meeting you all." She sidestepped quickly behind a waiter circulating a tray of chicken satay and made her escape through the crowd, headed for the open doorway through which Peggy could, possibly, have gone. *If you don't have to engage the enemy,* Msgt. Wright's voice echoed in her head, *don't stand there like an idiot, waiting to get shot. Retreat!* There were times, she realized, when being a priest was a distinct disadvantage, and one of them was at a big boozy party where you were hoping to hear some hot gossip about the hostess's nephew and his ex-lover.

The room she entered was smaller and cozier, with plump love seats and squishy chairs, instead of the sleek modular stuff in the living room. It had bookcases on its walls, mostly filled with photos and important-looking pieces of pottery. Clare decided this room must be called the library. Peggy Landry wasn't one of the seven or eight people crowding the available seating, but Clare did spot Peggy's nephew, Malcolm Wintour. He was even more beautiful this evening than he had been when she met him Monday morning, relaxed and younger-looking, with his honey-blond hair falling to either side of his face in perfect glossy wings. For a moment, she could feel the shade of her sister, Grace, beside her. Grace, who had always loved beautiful boys, sighing and saying, *What a shame he's gay.* . . .

The drinks waiter passed by and she deposited her empty glass and snagged a new one. She strode up to where Malcolm was standing and talking with two other guests, one a young woman whose fashion statement was "My clothes all shrank in the wash," and the other a man a few years older than Clare, perhaps, with close-cropped hair graying at his temples.

"Malcolm? Hi, it's nice to see you again. Wonderful party." Malcolm smiled vaguely, his expression the one people get when they can't recall an acquaintance. She smiled at his two companions. "Hi, I'm Clare Fergusson." She deliberately left off her title. She was wearing an outfit that reminded her of something she had seen on the quizmaster of *The Weakest Link*: severely cut silk pants and a long matching jacket with a dozen small fabric buttons marching up to a stiff high collar. She had modeled it for Lois, who'd said she looked like a cross between a Jesuit and a dominatrix. Maybe the people in this room hadn't heard Diana and Cary's introduction. Let them figure out if she was a religious or a disciplinarian.

"Hi," the young woman said, taking Clare's hand limply. Clare paused for a beat, but the girl evidently wasn't going to pick up the cue and introduce herself.

"Hugh Parteger," the man said, shaking her hand in turn. Surprisingly, he had a British accent.

"You don't spell that with a *y*, do you?"

"Not a one." He smiled, which gave him dimples on either cheek. *Cute*, Grace's shade advised.

"I'm trying to think . . . are you the florist?" Malcolm's voice was slightly off, as if it were coming from someplace other than his own throat. She looked at him more closely. He had evidently had a few too many kir royales. Or something.

She took a sip from her own drink. "Nope. I like flowers as much as the next woman, but I can't tell a dahlia from a daisy."

"Or a lupine from a lobelia?" Hugh Parteger said.

"Or a carnation from a chrysanthemum."

"You're obviously not into floral sects," he said.

She almost spit out a mouthful of kir royale laughing. Malcolm and the nameless girl just looked puzzled. She shook her head. "Mr. Parteger, I don't discuss what I do in my garden bed with anyone."

"It's nothing to be ashamed of," he said. "For most women, it's just a matter of finding the right tool."

She took another drink, enjoying herself immensely. The girl was murmuring something to Malcolm, who was looking around the room. "Yes, but it's such a tedious process, finding one that fits and works really well. Better just stick to hand weeding. Fewer complications that way."

"Ah, so you're a master gardener."

She actually giggled. How mortifying. She took a long swallow from her drink. "As Voltaire said, we must cultivate our garden."

"I believe he also said, 'Once, a philosopher, twice, a pervert.'"

"Hey, you two. Later." They had not only lost Malcolm and the girl; they had driven them away. With a pang, Clare watched them drift toward the door. This was not the way to untangle the relationship between Malcolm and his late business partner.

"Ah, did I put a foot wrong?" Hugh Parteger waved over the waiter, who had reappeared in the doorway with a trayful of fresh drinks. "Were you after speaking with Malcolm? Because I have to tell you, you're not his type."

She laughed again. "So I understand. No, I just wanted to talk with him at some point. And offer my condolences, I guess."

Hugh reached for her now-empty glass and put it on the waiter's tray alongside his own. He handed her another drink before taking one, as well.

"Condolences?"

"I had heard that he was . . . that he had been particularly close to Bill Ingraham, the developer. He died this weekend."

"I read he was knocked off."

Again, she almost choked on a mouthful of champagne and currant liqueur. "'Knocked off'?"

"Rubbed out. Done away with. Whacked. Fed to the fishes. Stop me if I'm using clichés."

She couldn't help laughing again, although it was horrible, too, with the sight of Ingraham's mutilated corpse still in her mind.

"No, really. The gossip mills in Saratoga are blaming it on the mob."

"In Millers Kill? What mob?"

"I don't know. You don't have a lot of Russian émigrés around, do you?"

"I believe I'm the last person to emigrate here, and I'm from southern Virginia."

"I thought I detected more of a drawl than usual. How did you wind up in this remote and desolate place?"

"It's not—" She stopped herself. His dimples were showing again. "I came for a job," she said. "How about you? You sound like you're a lot farther away from home than I am."

"Protecting my interests. I work for a venture-capital firm in New York that's made some investments in Saratoga. It gives me an excuse to come up during the racing season and hang about, sponging off people." He waved a hand, indicating the house around him. "Peggy had been extolling the beauties of her hometown, and it was the perfect opportunity to pump her for information about BWI Development, so here I am. Not a houseguest, thank God. I'm billeted at a bed-and-breakfast in town."

Several questions crowded into her head at once, all of them jostling for attention. She grabbed the first one she could articulate. "Why 'thank God'?"

"Peggy—look, she's not your best friend or anything, is she? Your cousin?"

Clare shook her head.

"Well, I find a little bit of Peggy goes a long way. She's a bit too ruthlessly organized and peppy. She'll probably have the houseguests up at five for a brisk scenic hike. Plus, she's been hitting me up about getting Malcolm a job at my firm, if you can believe that. Do you know him well?"

"We've only just met."

"Peggy is amazingly sharp, but Malcolm couldn't find his arse with both hands. I shudder to think what he could do if he actually had to take responsibility for something."

"I heard he was the one who got Peggy and Bill Ingraham together for this Algonquin Waters Spa development."

"Oh, he's good at the social thing, no doubt about that. Which is probably why Peggy has him down for my job. There's a lot of circulating and schmoozing you have to do. There's also a lot of researching and interviewing and digging into company books. I suspect the last book Malcolm cracked was *The Home-Brew Guide to Making Your Own Methamphetamines.*"

She clapped one hand over her eyes. "You're dropping a hint here. . . . I'm getting a clue as to what you think of him."

He laughed. "Oh, God, I forgot to ask. You're not a reporter, are you?"

She opened her eyes. "Nope. As a matter of fact, I'm pretty well known for my ability to keep things confidential." She sipped her drink. "But I am interested in the development. It's been a real source of controversy here in town."

"So I hear."

"Why are you trying to pump Peggy Landry for—"

"No, believe me, the last thing I want to do is pump Peggy."

She giggled again—no!—and clapped a hand over her mouth. "For information about BWI," she said firmly.

"We've been thinking about sinking some money into it. After the Internet bubble burst, the partners have become interested in more traditional investments. And there's not much that's more traditional than buying land and sticking buildings on it."

"Are you going to go through with the investment? Now that Bill Ingraham is dead?"

"I don't think that's the problem. He did a terrific job, and he had a real feel for what people wanted on these luxury resorts. But he can be replaced. Maybe not by one larger-than-life guy like himself, but by an architect, a construction boss, and a marketing designer. The problem is"—he moved closer and dropped his voice—"as near as I can tell, BWI is standing on a mountain of debt. Any investment we, or others, make is just going to go into the hopper."

In her sandals, she was exactly Hugh's height. It made her feel like they were swapping secrets. "What's going to happen now? Are they going to go under?"

He shook his head. "Not if they can carry off this resort. This one's funded by private backers, not by the banks. Oppenheimer has gotten smarter."

"Opperman. Oppenheimer invented the atomic bomb."

"Okay. The one that didn't invent the atomic bomb is now trying to put together consortiums of investors, rather than doing their financing through banks. Makes it a lot easier to sidestep those nasty time payments."

"What about insurance on Bill Ingraham?"

"What do you mean?"

Clare finished off her drink. "There would have been insurance on Bill Ingraham, right? As a partner? My folks run a small aviation business, and I know my dad has insurance that goes directly into the company if he dies."

"Oh, yeah, I'm sure Ingraham had insurance." Hugh frowned in thought. "Actually, that's a good question. I wonder how much it was?" He drained his glass and refocused on her. "But even if he was insured for a couple million, it wouldn't be a drop in the bucket against their debt load."

She worried her lower lip. "Something's not making sense here."

"I'll say. They keep sending in the drinks tray, but we haven't seen any of the hors d'oeuvres. C'mon, someone less hardy than ourselves has fled to find food and we can nab the window seat."

He slid his hand beneath her elbow and steered her toward a window seat tucked behind a large desk angling out from a corner of the room. She collapsed onto the well-stuffed cushion and slipped off her sandals. "Oh, yes. That feels good." Hugh flagged down the waiter. "No, I shouldn't. I think I've had enough all ready. Eventually, I have to drive home."

"You can ride with me," he said, lifting two glasses from the tray.

"You're not going to be in any state to drive, either, if you keep going like that."

"I know." He grinned. Those dimples really were awfully cute. "I'm getting a lift from the Spoffards. They're staying at the same B and B. She's preggers, so she's the designated driver. They already have a minivan, in anticipation of the blessed event, so there'll be plenty of room for you. You won't even have to sit on my lap. Unless you want to."

This man was flirting with her. Good God. When was the last time anyone had flirted with her? She instantly thought of the race on the Fourth of July, Russ saying, "I've let you drive me crazy," his voice suddenly husky, like a boy's voice changing between one word and the next. The thought of it, here in Peggy Landry's library, made a shiver run up her spine. That wasn't flirting. That was something much more dangerous. She blinked ferociously and took the glass from Hugh, gulping a mouthful.

"The Fourth of July race," she said. "That's what I was thinking of. When I said it didn't make sense."

Hugh sat down next to her. "How so?"

"There was an antidevelopment protest. There have been PCBs found in the groundwater in town, and some folks are blaming the construction work. There's a movement, I guess you'd call it, to get the DEP to take another look at the site. Bill Ingraham stood up and told the whole town that if they called in the state, he'd abandon the project. Said it wasn't worth the trouble." She turned toward Hugh, drawing one leg up onto the cushion. "Why would he say that if BWI needed this development to go through so badly?"

"Bluffing maybe? Perhaps he didn't know as much about the financial state of the company as he should have. Or maybe he was getting sick and tired of it all and was looking to retire anyway."

She sipped her drink, thinking of the possibilities. Her thoughts were all loose and slippery, hard to grasp and connect. But that was okay. Tomorrow, when she was stone-cold sober, she would be able to see a pattern. She was confident of it. Bill Ingraham. The resort. The debt. Malcolm Wintour.

"And how does Malcolm fit into all this?" She wasn't sure she had actually said the words out loud until Hugh answered her.

"Malcolm? I don't think he's going to have any influence on whether BWI goes under or not."

"No, I mean . . ." She wasn't quite sure what she meant at this point. "He and Bill Ingraham were an item, weren't they? Is there any way that Malcolm could have benefited from Ingraham's death?"

"You mean other than the fulfillment of every dumped person's fantasy that the dumper will drop dead? I don't think so."

"Maybe he inherited a stake in the company. Or maybe he was the beneficiary of another life-insurance policy."

Hugh grinned. "Are you suggesting that Malcolm bumped his ex-boyfriend off? Like some film noir tart?"

Clare swallowed another mouthful of kir royale. "You seem to know him some. Would you say he's incapable of it?"

Hugh crossed his arms and looked up to the ceiling. "No . . . not incapable of it. I can imagine him being a vindictive little weasel. Although it's hard to picture him doing anything that might muss his Brioni pants." He looked back at her. "Problem is, I can't imagine him doing anything without there being a direct benefit to Malcolm. And I very much doubt Bill Ingraham's death benefited him in any way."

"If he inherited—"

"Look, I didn't know Ingraham personally, but I've certainly heard tell of him over the years. And from what I understand, Bill liked—do you know those tycoon sorts who have a new surgically enhanced blonde on their arms every year? The man keeps getting older, but the girls stay the same age, until he's ninety-seven years old and marrying Pamela Anderson?"

Clare nodded.

"Well, Bill was like that. Only difference was in the gender."

"I see. So Malcolm was less like his true love and more like the flavor of the month."

"Flavor of the year, I would think. They must have been together for a while, because the initial contracts were signed on this spa deal over twelve months ago."

"So what about Malcolm? Someone described him to me as a gold digger. Was Ingraham just the latest in a string of sugar daddies?"

"That, I don't know. First I ever heard of him was in connection to Ingraham, after I'd gotten to know Peggy. That's just been in the past year." He leaned toward her, very serious now. "I do want to emphasize that none of my knowledge about Bill or Malcolm was obtained inside a gay bar, that I have never been inside a gay bar, and have no intentions so to do."

"Are you dropping me a little hint here? You're straight?" She grinned. "You know what they say about men who protest too much."

"I'm quite comfortable with my own sexuality, thank you. It's just that I realized I usually don't spend most of my conversation driveling on about shirt-lifters with a woman I'm trying to chat up."

"I just love those British expressions."

"All American women do. That's why I volunteered for the New York office. I'm really hopeless with women at home. Only in the New World do I stand a chance."

She laughed loudly.

"Reverend Clare! There you are! I've been looking for you. I have some people I want you to meet." Peggy Landry stalked through the library, making her way to the window seat. "Hello, Hugh."

"Reverend?" Hugh looked at her goggle-eyed.

"Oh, don't tell me you didn't get introduced. Hugh, this is the Reverend Clare Fergusson; she's the priest at our local church, St. Alban's. Reverend Clare, this is Hugh Parteger, vice president of Barkley and Eaton Capital."

"You're a priest? An Anglican priest?"

Clare nodded, smiling weakly. "I told you I wasn't a reporter."

"What on earth did you two find to talk about? Never mind. Reverend

Clare, I have a nice couple for you to meet. Cary's great-uncle and -aunt. They've just returned from a lengthy trip to the Holy Land, and I know you'll love hearing all about it."

"Ah." She tried to shore up her face into a cheerful and interested expression. From the dubious look Hugh was giving her, she doubted she was being successful.

"And Hugh," Peggy continued, "circulate, will you? I'm counting on you to find some single ladies and charm the socks off them. And don't sneak away later. I want to talk with you about a date for this financing proposal. John Opperman's flying to Baltimore tomorrow afternoon, and he won't be back until Tuesday. Now, off you go. *Unmarried* women only, please."

She flipped her hands up, indicating both of them were to rise and go forth to entertain her guests. Clare thought, all in all, that Hugh was getting the better job. Oh, well. At least here the elderly couple couldn't subject her to a slide show.

"Later for you, Vicar," Hugh said under his breath as they entered the wide living room. "I think you owe me a bit of an explanation." He peeled off in the direction of the nearest herd of young women.

"What was that all about?" Peggy asked, steering Clare toward the corner of the room. "Oh, look, here are the Woods, all set up on the table."

Clare's heart sank at the sight of a couple in their seventies, sitting on either side of an open laptop.

"You must be the minister Peggy's been telling us about," the sweet little old lady said. "Pull up a chair! We're all ready for our Powerpoint slide show!"

CHAPTER TWENTY-THREE

Clare found being half in the bag did not improve a slide show on the Holy Land. For one thing, the stupefying boredom of it was lulling her to sleep. And when she wasn't fighting to keep her chin from dropping to her chest, she couldn't help darting glances at the party beyond the small circle of chairs around the table occupied by Mr. and Mrs. Wood and herself. The wide French doors at the end of the room had been thrown open and couples were dancing outside on the deck. People she hadn't seen before kept appearing and disappearing at the head of the stairs, girls in fluttery dresses, their legs bare, young men in slouchy pants and open-collared shirts. Over the music, she could hear bursts of laughter drifting from the library. It was like the sort of bad dream where you show up at work, not knowing at all what to do and having to fake competence, while all around you your coworkers are having an orgy.

"And in this series of pictures, Cyrus really got up close to show the fantastic detailing in these mosaics. Honey, can you center that picture better? As I said to Betty—she was with us at this church—you can just feel the love and devotion in every tile. Oh, look, this is where they were making repairs. Cyrus, did you get a good look inside that grout bucket?"

God, Clare prayed, if you love me, help me.

"Uncle Cyrus! Aunt Helen! We're going to take some pictures." They looked up to meet Cary's cheerful face.

Angels walk among us, unawares. Clare gave him a smile of such undisguised pleasure, he started. "Reverend Clare? Would you like to be in the pictures, too?"

"Actually," she said, "I really need to escape to the bathroom." She rose to her feet. "I'll catch you all later." At the wedding, she added silently. She strode off as fast as she could manage in her high heels, crossing to the opposite end of the living room and entering the dining room. It was filled with people circling around a large table, forking up tidbits from chafing dishes and trailing phyllo crumbs behind them. "Bathroom?" Clare asked a woman who was about to bite into a miniature quiche.

"In the hallway to the kitchen," she said, gesturing to a doorway thronged with guests. As Clare watched, the caterer pushed her way through, wedging openings with her elbows to get her platter into the dining room. "But there's been a steady stream of customers. You're going to have a wait."

Clare made a face. "There must be some other ones," she said.

"There's one in the pool house, outside. You leave through the main door and go around the—"

"Anything closer?"

The woman sighed. "Well. It's supposed to be off-limits except for the houseguests, but there's one on the top floor. That's where the guest rooms are. Probably one on the floor above us, too, but I haven't been up there. Those are the family bedrooms." She cast a glance around, as if she were giving away a state secret. "Head back to the foyer in front of the main door. There'll be a door to your left. It opens onto a little stairway that runs up to the bedrooms. The bathroom is in the middle of the hall; you can't miss it. But you didn't hear about it from me."

"My lips are sealed," Clare said, "and my bladder thanks you."

She found the door in the foyer without difficulty and climbed up to the third floor, where the guest bathroom was, as promised, easy to find and unoccupied.

It was when she was washing her hands that the thought hit her. The family bedrooms. Which meant Malcolm's bedroom. One floor below her. Staring unseeing into the bathroom mirror, she could just picture herself finding the correspondence between Ingraham and his lover. An incriminating letter promising a fortune to the younger man. Or maybe an insurance policy. Another lover. Or an offer of part ownership interest in the firm. The possibilities bubbled up in her head like champagne, popping excitedly in a currant-flavored cloud. Malcolm, the mastermind behind the attacks. She would expose him, even though it countered her theory about the reasons behind the beatings. Russ would see she was big enough to embrace the truth, whatever it was. Ron and Stephen and all the other business owners would be so pleased. Russ would be happy. Paul would find peace. Russ would be proud of her. She pictured her vestry congratulating her for finally generating some positive publicity. She pictured Russ's face when she handed over the evidence that would put Malcolm away. She toweled off and left the bathroom, heading straight for the stairs.

The second floor was dark and hushed, thickly carpeted like the floors above and below. The hallway ran the length of the house, and the flood-light outside, on the house's facade, provided plenty of illumination for her to see where she was going.

The first door was open, and it led into a bedroom that glowed pale and gauzy in the ambient light. Clare knew without going any farther that this was Peggy's room. She cautiously made her way over to a door set in the wall at the end of the room, but poking her head inside revealed the muffled interior of a walk-in closet, instead of the next bedroom.

The second bedroom was much darker, its heavy curtains drawn against the outside. But it smelled strongly of Diana's perfume and Gary's cologne. She crossed the floor toward where she suspected another closet, intending to turn on the light inside it for a discreet look-see. She promptly tripped over an open suitcase. She went down hard, bouncing off the floor with a loud thud and an involuntary "oof" as the air was knocked out of her. Only the plush carpeting saved her from scraping her knee. She scrambled to her feet and stood motionless for a long moment, listening for the sound of steps on the stairs and an inquiring voice. What was she going to say if she got caught up here? Her mind drew a blank. No helpful advice from Msgt. Wright. No words of wisdom from her grandmother. She was on her own.

She made her way back to the door, skirting the suitcase by sweeping her foot in front of her like a blind man's cane. Her heart rate was up, and she breathed slowly and deeply to try to calm herself as she walked down the hall and then entered the last bedroom.

The curtains were drawn back and the windows were open, which allowed the faint light and sounds from the party below to float up to the wooden beams of the angled high ceiling. Clare could see the four-poster dominating the room, the dressers against the walls, the two doors, one ajar, leading to another walk-in closet, and the other closed. She crossed the floor and pushed the door open, revealing a tiny bathroom. She took the nearest pair of curtains and drew them tightly shut before reaching into the inside of the closet and sliding her hand along the wall. When she found the light switch, she flicked it on, quickly shutting the door until only a crack of light spilled into the room. Then, confident she would be able to see and thus avoid any more unexpected trips, she circled the bed and drew the other set of curtains shut. She went back to the closet and pushed the door wide open, eager to see what she could find.

In the closet was a fortune in Italian wools and enough polished shoe leather to stock a boutique. There might be something hiding under one of the sweater boxes that marched along the upper shelf, but there were probably more fruitful hiding places to try first. She turned back to the room.

The dresser between the closet and the bathroom held an antique mirror and a brushed-steel CD player the size of her first Kenner Close-and-Play record player. A row of CD jewel boxes stood trapped between bronze bookends. A flat leather box, when opened, revealed earrings and bracelets and cuff links, all of them gleaming with the luster only pricey jewelry had. There was nothing else cluttering up the top of the dresser. Either Malcolm was innately tidy or Peggy Landry employed a hardworking maid. She opened the top two drawers and decided it was Malcolm after all, not hired help. She couldn't imagine a maid arranging rolled socks and folded underwear with such precision. She slid her hands underneath the clothes and then worked her way through the lower two drawers, searching with her fingertips between silky cottons and feathery cashmere and finding nothing except more confirmation that Malcolm had champagne taste and caviar dreams, or however the slogan went.

She closed the drawers tightly and went on to her next search area. What she had thought was a second dresser, placed between the two windows, turned out to be a square mahogany writing desk. She drew out the spindly-legged chair that had been shoved beneath it and sat down. The surface held a cell phone, a cube calendar, and a few pieces of junk mail. She leaned over to check the wire wastebasket and saw that it was empty. So he didn't believe in the purloined letter theory of hiding things in plain sight. She opened the top left-hand drawer. Old bills, ripped open and restuffed into their envelopes. Second notices. Third notices. She shuffled through them. A whole series of demands from a car-loan agency, leading to an official-looking notice of repossession.

The second drawer held several fat paperbacks. Airplane reading. Evidently, Malcolm was a fan of Clive Cussler and Danielle Steel. She riffled through their pages, just to be sure, but the only things that fell out were old ticket stubs for flights to D.C., Chicago, and Houston.

The third drawer was heavy with telephone books, none of which had anything inside or in between them except white and yellow pages. She shut the drawer in disgust, then started on the right-hand side. There was a stack of mismatched stationery, evidence that Malcolm liked to steal hotel writing paper, but nothing indicating a more serious crime. The second drawer was full of junk—paper clips and matchbooks and half-used pads of Post-it notes, the kind of things that accumulate in your pockets and car but seem too potentially useful to throw away.

The last drawer held magazines that—whoops! She shoved the drawer back in. She did not want to look at those magazines. She especially did not want to look through those magazines to see what might have been stashed between the pages. Idiot, she thought. Maybe that's the point. Like a woman hiding her jewelry in a box of tampons. She nodded. That made sense. Reopening the drawer, she compromised by pinching each magazine by the staples and shaking it vigorously. Nothing, not even one of those annoying inserts selling perfume or subscriptions. On second thought, it was probably illegal to send stuff like this through the U.S. mail, so why would they need subscriptions? She returned the magazines to the drawer, trying not to look too long at the covers.

She stood up, light-headed, and shoved the chair back into place, staggering slightly as her heels caught in the deep carpet. For the first time, she considered that she might not be in the best-possible shape for the task she had undertaken. She tried to recall exactly how many kir royales she had taken off those circulating trays. Four? Five? Oh, well. Nothing for it but to soldier on. That, she could do. What next?

The bedside stand. It had a single shallow drawer, filled with photographs, a passport, and a well-thumbed guide to restaurants. She pawed through the photos, looking for anything that might show Malcolm with Ingraham, but they were all old—pictures of women with pin curls, wearing floral dresses, and men in shirtsleeves, fly-fishing.

There was a shelf below the drawer, holding more paperbacks—a row of Dungeons and Dragons novelizations. Yuck. She dropped to her knees and then to her belly, stretching out to check under the bed. Under the side closest to her, there was nothing, not even a dust bunny. Under the other side, however, visible as a series of black rectangles, were several suitcases or narrow boxes. They looked promising.

She clambered back up on her high-heeled sandals and circled around the foot of the bed again. She was balanced on two knees and one palm, her hand wrapped around an unseen handle, tugging the heavy suitcase out from under the four-poster, when she heard the faint noise of feet on the stairs. And voices.

She shoved the suitcase back into place and shot to her feet. Where to hide? Where to hide, where to hide, where to hide? She slapped off the light in the closet and stood stock-still, shaking, flushed, her skin hot and prickling, clenching her fists so tightly that her close-clipped nails dug into her palms. Think. Thinkthinkthink. Under the bed? Too obvious. In the closet? There was nothing to hide behind except Malcolm's suits. All it would take would be a light on in the room and someone to cast one glance inside to notice her legs taking up the space between his jackets and the shoe rack.

The hall light came on. She could hear a mutter of voices, indistinct, male, coming closer. She darted a glance behind her and realized the curtains were still closed. She leaped to one window, jerked the fabric apart, and then ran to the next, almost stumbling over the little chair in front of the desk.

No footsteps now because of the plush thickness of the carpet, just the sound of a voice complaining and another answering shortly. The bathroom was her only hope. She bounded in, shutting the door behind her. It had been shut when she came into the room, hadn't it? She couldn't remember. Light from the open window picked out a pedestal sink, a toilet, and a shower stall. She suddenly thought of the crowd around the bathroom downstairs. If she were Malcolm and had to pee, would she wait in line next to the dining room when she had a private John upstairs? Her throat closed and for a second she heard a roaring in her ears.

You're a pilot, damn it, "Hardball" Wright snarled in her ear. *You know what they call pilots who panic? Dead!* She drew in her breath, a quick, sharp gasp, and ruthlessly shoved everything except the problem out of her mind. She could hide behind the shower curtain. There was almost no chance he was going to shower, not with someone else accompanying him. Unless, of course, he was planning on a little private party for two.

She could hear the voices, louder now, and then there was a gleam of light beneath the edge of the bathroom door. Her choice was made for her. Slipping out of her heels and clutching them in one hand, she edged her way behind the shower curtain and into the cubicle, gritting her teeth at the quiet rustle and clank of the hooks on the curtain rod.

"I don't understand how you can be so calm," a male voice said, muffled slightly by the bathroom door.

"Chill out," Malcolm said, and suddenly Dave Matthews was singing "Forty-One," intense and seductive, pure high notes and a wicked bass coming from that suitcase-size CD player. How can his books be so lousy and his music so good? she wondered inanely, and then she heard Malcolm say, "I have to take a leak. Hang on."

She willed herself into immobility as the door swung open and the bathroom light clicked on. She couldn't help it—she squeezed her eyes tightly shut, like a child, as if not seeing would make her invisible, too. Her heart was tripping so fast, it was difficult to keep her breathing slow and steady. She fought the urge to hold her breath, knowing that if she did so, she would eventually make even more noise letting it out.

The toilet seat clunked up and Malcolm went about his business, peeing for what seemed like a half hour—did he have the bladder of a racehorse?—before zipping up, a noise like a small guillotine, and flushing. The water racketing down the porcelain bowl gave her enough cover to take a deep, lung-popping breath of air. Then the water was running in the small sink, and she opened her eyes, looking in horror at the half-dissolved bar of soap on the chrome caddy hanging over the showerhead. *Please*, she thought, *please, please, please* . . . Then she heard the sweet sound of a liquid-soap dispenser squirting and knew she had dodged the bullet on that one. When he twisted off the water and reached for the hand towel, she could actually see the tips of his fingers at the edge of the shower curtain as he grabbed the towel and then hung it up again. He clicked off the light and pulled the door behind him, so that it swung nearly—but not quite—closed.

She wanted to sag against the back of the shower and slide bonelessly to the floor. She realized she had been clutching her shoes so tightly, her hands ached. She took a deep, slow breath in an effort to settle her heart and unstring her muscles. All she had to do was remain still, quiet, and hidden, and eventually Malcolm and the other man would leave to rejoin the party.

Unless this is his new boyfriend and they've come up here to have sex. She tried out the idea. There was simply no way she was going to huddle unseen, like a rabbit, and eavesdrop on that. If it sounded like they were getting intimate, she would have to reveal herself and say—what? That she had come upstairs to use the bathroom? And had happened to walk all the way down the hall to the room farthest from the stairs to find one? Even if she had the excuse of being completely potted, that sounded lame.

The noise of the men's voices brought her attention back to the room beyond the bathroom. She wasn't hearing murmured sweet nothings. In fact, from the sound of it, she didn't have to worry about any tryst, unless they were a couple who used arguing as a substitute for foreplay.

"All I'm saying is, I didn't sign up for anything like this." She could hear the second man more clearly now that the bathroom door was slightly open. He sounded vaguely familiar, although she couldn't place a name or face to the voice. Maybe another party guest?

"Anything like what?" Malcolm spoke like someone who was very annoyed and trying not to show it.

"For God's sake! The man is dead!"

Clare dropped any speculation about lying her way out of the bathroom. The man's last statement stabbed through her, fixing all her attention to their words.

"So he's dead. So what? He went cruising in a park in a town where two queers had already been beaten up. He got what he was asking for."

The other man's voice was barely a whisper. "You don't—he wasn't—that can't be all there is to it!"

"Do you have any evidence otherwise?"

"No, of course not. I don't want any evidence otherwise. I just want your assurances that I'm not going to get picked up by the police and questioned about anything."

In the pause between the CD's tracks, there was a faint creaking sound, as if one of them had sat on the bed. "Well, if you are questioned, you won't have anything to tell them, will you?"

"How can you say that? I'm up to my ass in alligators on this thing! I feel like I'm being set up as the fall guy precisely because I don't know— Jesus Christ! What the hell is that?" The man's voice had shot up the scale.

"What's the matter? You've never seen one of these? It's a Lugar Five-fifty. Wicked, huh?" Over the sound of the music, she heard the click of the chamber being drawn back, but she couldn't tell if a round had gone in.

"I'm not looking for trouble," the other man said. His voice was thready and light.

"Hey, I know you're not. You're a team player. What? You think I brought this out to threaten you? No way, man. I wanted to show you what else is in here."

Clare oh so slowly and oh so carefully laid her sandals on the shower floor. She could be out of the shower, throw open the door, and tackle Malcolm in under three seconds, she estimated. She would have to hope Malcolm was a talker, and that he would play with the other man a little before actually shooting him. That would give her time to make her move. Like a pilot reading instrument gauges, she noted that her heart rate had actually slowed down and her limbs were more relaxed at the prospect of hurling herself on a loaded gun. That probably said something terrible about her priorities and fitness for the priesthood, but she couldn't figure out what at the moment.

"Holy shit. Is that what I think it is?"

"What, you never tried any when you were at school?"

"That's got to be worth thousands. What are you doing with a stash like that?"

"I'm an independent businessman now. It's funny. My cousin Diana thinks I'm a hopeless slacker. But really, I'm just as much old Eustace Landry's descendant as she is. There must be some sort of entrepreneur gene, don't you think? Unfortunately, I can't open my books and let the family admire how well I'm doing."

"Does your aunt know?"

"Leave my aunt out if it." Malcolm's voice was cool. "In fact, if I were you, I'd avoid my aunt at all times."

"Is that a threat?"

"Take it as a warning." There was a rustling, then a dull thud. Inside the shower stall, Clare tensed. "Here." Malcolm's voice was decidedly warmer. "Take this, as well. It's yours."

"Are you kidding? What am I supposed to do with this? Throw a party?"

"Sell it. That neatly sealed bag is worth about ten thousand dollars on the open market. You could use ten thousand, couldn't you?"

"No way. If I got caught with this, I'd be looking at ten years playing girlfriend to some guy in Attica. Look, I really didn't get into this for the money."

Malcolm laughed.

"Well, not like that. Not for this. I didn't think anyone was going to get hurt. I was assured—"

"I know what you were told. And I know what you want. You think I didn't know?" His voice became caressing, persuasive. "Tell you what. You take this, as a surety. I'll set up a sale. You return it to me, I get the cash, and the cash goes to you. Then you can go off to Texas or Alaska or something and lie low until this business about Bill blows over."

"What's to keep you from calling the cops as soon as I leave this house and having me picked up? With this much, I'd be charged with felony dealing for sure."

Malcolm sighed. "Oh, for Chrissakes, use your head. If you were to get arrested, the first thing you'd do would be to roll on me. I'm not in any hurry to try to flush my entire stock down the toilet. It's not going to do me any good to dick you over. It's profitable for me to keep you happy. Just like it's profitable for you to keep your head down and your mouth shut. If you don't panic, we'll all get out of this with what we want."

"Except for Bill Ingraham."

Malcolm's voice was sharp. "Bill had a lifetime of getting what he wanted. Eventually, you have to roll off the bed and give someone else a turn. Here. Take it."

Clare strained to hear what was happening, but the horn and floating guitar line of "Lie in Our Graves" masked any sound quieter than a voice.

Eventually, the other man spoke again. "All right."

"Good. You going back to the party?"

"Are you kidding? I'm going to hide this thing under the seat of my car and drive slowly and carefully home. You?"

"I'm going to work the phones a bit and see if I can set up a sale. Ciao-ciao, man. You don't have to worry. I'm going to take care of you."

Clare thought that sounded like reason enough to worry right there. Then the realization struck her: Malcolm wasn't going back downstairs.

There wasn't any answering farewell, just a silence filled with quiet music. She pictured Malcolm tossing his jacket on the bed—on top of a suitcase stuffed with a gun and fat bags of heroin. Or maybe it wasn't heroin. She wasn't up on current trends in the drug market. She could feel a hysterical laugh waiting to bubble up from her chest, and she pressed both hands on her diaphragm and willed herself to stop.

"Hey, Joe. It's Mal. Look, man, I'm calling because you had suggested I get in touch with you when I was ready to move a little more product than previously."

He was getting on the phone and calling people who would be willing to spend ten thousand dollars for illegal drugs. She rubbed her lips hard, taking off what was left of her lipstick. Any guesses as to how he might deal with a woman who overheard his sales pitch? Any guesses as to what his customers might do?

CHAPTER TWENTY-FOUR

Time to bail out of this plane, Clare told herself. And with Malcolm settling in for an evening of telephone conversation and music, there was only one exit still open to her. She picked up her shoes and, holding them tightly against her stomach, slipped between the edge of the shower curtain and the cool tile wall, all the while thinking to herself, flat, flat, flat.

Several hooks slid along the curtain rod with a scrape that sounded to Clare like a Klaxon. Her breath hitched up in her throat and she forced herself to keep on moving, until she was standing next to the toilet in her stocking feet. She couldn't see out the crack in the door without getting right in front of it, but there was enough light spilling in from the bedroom to pick out all the details in the bath. The detail she was interested in was the window.

It was larger than the usual bathroom window, the same size as the two in the bedroom. Two stories up, looking out onto mountains, one wouldn't require much privacy, she guessed. Like one of the bedroom windows, its lower pane had been pulled up almost to the level of the middle sash. She pressed her fingers against the screen's releasing locks and slid it up as far as she could. It clicked into place on its runner with a noise that sounded as loud as a rifle shot.

Behind her, Malcolm was still chatting away and the Dave Matthews CD had looped around to the beginning and was jazzing along with "So Much to Say." She loved the *Crash* album, but she wondered if she would ever be able to listen to it again after tonight. She eased the latches into place in the uppermost notches and stuck her head out the window to scope out her escape route.

The good news was that Malcolm's suite overlooked a six-foot-square porch roof, an easy drop from the window if she were hanging from the bottom of the sill. The bad news was, the porch and its roof were attached to the kitchen. Over the jazzy beat of the Dave Matthews Band, she could hear the clang and clatter and chatter of kitchen staff engaged in a full-scale cleanup. Craning her neck to one side, she could see the outlines of several people clustered in conversation on the flagstone terrace surrounding the pool. All it would take would be someone glancing up at the wrong moment and she would look like a character from a Lawrence Block novel. She could see the title now: *The Burglar Who Thought She Was a Priest*.

Once she got down to the ground, the view from the pool would be cut off by a wide-planked wind fence that shielded swimmers and sunbathers from the sight of three large trash cans. How long would it take her to climb out of the window, drop, and slide off the porch roof? Thirty seconds? A minute?

She heard the *thump-thump* of footsteps down a pair of steps and then one of the caterers emerged from beneath the roof, striding to the nearest trash can with a white plastic bag swinging from his fist. He tossed it in and vanished back into the kitchen, never once looking up or about.

A quote from *Macbeth* bubbled up from the primordial English-lit ooze: "If it were done when 'tis done, then 'twere well it were done quickly . . ." She glanced at the sandals dangling from her hand. Bogatta Veneta. Italian leather. Bought back when she was flush with a captain's pay. Praying she would be able to find them again, she leaned out the window and tossed them as hard as she could past the light spilling from the kitchen, toward the gravel drive. She wiggled through the opening until she was sitting on the sill, then stood up, clutching the window's exterior frame. She awkwardly lowered herself to her knees and then, her hands digging into the sill, let her legs slip off the reassuring solidity of the wood and into space.

The edge of the windowsill dug into her abdomen as she slid farther and farther down. Something interrupted her descent for a moment, tugged at her, and then she felt a release as two silk-covered buttons popped off her jacket and pitter-pattered across the roof and into the darkness below. She dangled for a moment by her hands alone and then let go, dropping as limply as she could. She skidded off the side of the porch roof and tumbled to the ground with a blow that knocked the wind out of her.

Inside the kitchen, someone said, "What the hell was that?" Clare staggered upright and lurched backward, bouncing off a rubberized trash can.

A woman in a large white apron appeared in the kitchen doorway. "Hello?" she said to the night air in general. Then, as she spotted Clare tottering beside the trash cans, she said, "Excuse me? Can I help you?" The woman glanced doubtfully at Clare's bare feet and her jacket, which was gaping open over her midsection. Clare grabbed the edges and smiled cheerfully. "Great party!" she said, loosening her southern Virginia drawl to sound drunk. More drunk, she amended.

The caterer squinted at her. "Are you okay?" She looked back into the kitchen. "Look, why don't you come in and let me get you some coffee?"

Clare clutched the jacket more closely and squeezed her bare toes in the dirt she had recently rolled in. "No, thank you, ma'am. 'M just going out front. Waiting for my ride."

"You do have a ride." It was a statement, not a question.

"Yes, ma'am," Clare said, saluting for full effect. Her jacket swung open, revealing a great deal of skin.

The woman smiled at her uncertainly. "Okay, then. Good night."

Clare waved, crossed the kitchen yard, and headed toward the drive, walking straight until the woman retreated into the house. Then she cast about the edges of the gravel drive, trying to spot her sandals somewhere amid the grass and dirt and sweep of stones. She failed to turn up anything except a couple more mosquito bites. She let herself curse under her breath. There was no way she could afford to replace those babies on her priest's salary. She abandoned the search and headed for her car, parked at the other end of the house.

The top of her convertible was up because she had left her purse and her keys in the car when she had arrived. Even she wouldn't normally be so careless, but in a secluded mountain estate, she had yielded to the impulse not to have to keep track of her things while at the party. She got into the passenger seat and let herself sag against the vinyl, which felt warm and tacky against her skin. She rubbed the soles of her feet together and thought that she had even fewer things to keep track of now. She curled over, buried her face in her hands, and gave in to the shakes, her teeth chattering, throat whimpering, skin shivering. Then she felt better. She scrubbed at her face with her hands, remembering as she did so that she was wearing makeup.

She dug into her purse for the lighted compact her sister Grace had given her years ago and examined the damage. Her lipstick was long gone, her skin was blotchy, and her mascara and eye shadow were smeared. She popped open the glove compartment and retrieved one of the little wet foil-wrapped towels she kept there, a habit of her mother's that had stuck with Clare throughout the years. After she mopped off her face, she used the compact light to check out the rest of her appearance, which was even more disreputable-looking than she had imagined. Her elegant pantsuit was crumpled, the jacket gaping open where her buttons had come off, one leg stained with something dark and unidentifiable—though from the smell, she thought she must have picked it up when she rolled into the trash can.

She snapped the compact shut and closed her eyes. She didn't care if it was rude; she was not going back in to join the partygoers. She might not be sober enough to drive, but she sure wasn't drunk enough to appear looking like she had been out for a roll in the clover. She could hide away here in her car, and when the rest of the alcohol had worked its way out of her system, she would drive home. Then tomorrow, she would call Russ and tell him that—

Her eyes snapped open. Call Russ. Holy cow, he needed to know about Malcolm's little business venture. And that it sounded like Bill Ingraham's ex-lover knew a lot more about his death than what he had read about in the papers. She fumbled in her purse for her phone, letting her grandmother's voice—which was saying *No lady would ever call after ten o'clock at night*—wash away on a tide of exhaustion, relief, and the remnants of several kir royales.

As she pressed the send button, she had a flash of panic. What do I say if his wife answers? The phone rang. Once. Twice. She clicked it off, sagging back into her seat. Coward. Then she remembered. Friday. Dinner at his mother's. Maybe he was still there. She called information for the number and dialed it, hoping against hope that she wasn't about to wake Margy Van Alstyne, who might have retired early.

"Hello?"

Margy's voice sounded crisp. Clare closed her eyes in relief.

"Mrs. Van Alstyne? Margy? It's Clare Fergusson."

"Clare Fergusson. Well, I'll be. What can I do for you this hour of the night?"

You see? Her grandmother said. *Calling after ten is an imposition.* Clare repressed the urge to apologize and hang up. "I was just wondering . . . I needed to speak to Russ, and I recalled he said he was going to be at your house for the evening. Is he there?"

"Yes, he's here." Margy Van Alstyne's voice sounded as if only good manners kept her from asking why St. Alban's rector was calling her son at 10:30 on a Friday night.

"It's business," Clare assured her.

"Oh, it's none of my—never mind. Let me give him the phone. Here he is."

CHAPTER TWENTY-FIVE

R uss had been lying back in his mom's ancient La-Z-Boy recliner, watching Roger Clemens getting shelled by the Angels. He had stayed well past the time it took to replace a few boards on the porch and have dinner, enjoying the comforting familiarity of his mom's house, where no one ever redecorated and the walls had been the same color since she moved in a quarter of a century ago.

Clemens had given up five runs in the last two innings, and the Yankees were going down hard. Now Mel Stottlemyre was marching out toward the mound. "Give him the hook, already," Russ told the pitching coach. "Any relief pitcher could do better than that. My mother can do better than that."

Stottlemyre was talking to Clemens, who was evidently arguing. Now the catcher was coming out to the mound. "Oh, for God's sake, it's not the UN. Get him offa there."

His mother walked into the living room, holding the phone and eyeing him speculatively. She clamped her palm over the handset. "It's Clare Fergusson," she whispered. "Says it's a business call." She handed him the phone.

"Clare?" His mother stood there watching. He frowned and shooed her away. "What's up?" He glanced at the clock. "It's late."

"I'm sorry," she said. "Did I wake you up?"

"No, I'm not spending the night. I was just hanging out, watching the Yankees lose to Los Angeles. What's going on?"

"I'm at a party at Peggy Landry's house."

He listened for the usual background noises you could hear during a phone call in the middle of a party. Nothing.

"It's a pretty quiet party."

"I'm calling from my car. I can't go in."

"You can't go in. Clare, you're not making any sense." A thought struck him. "Have you been drinking?"

"Yes, but that's not why I—"

"You're not planning on driving that car anyplace, are you?"

"No. Well, not yet. I'm going to wait here until I'm fit to drive again."

He closed his eyes. Christ on a bicycle. "Okay," he said, enunciating clearly. "Get out of the car and give someone your keys. Then ask Peggy Landry to fix you up with a ride home."

"I told you, I can't go inside!" Her whisper sharpened. "Will you please listen to me?"

He clicked off the game. "Go ahead."

"I was in Malcolm's room tonight. Here. At Peggy's house."

"Who's Malcolm?"

"Her nephew. He used to be Bill Ingraham's boyfriend."

"His *boyfriend*? He got out of his chair. The import of this statement struck him. "And you were in his room? What the hell were you doing in his room?"

"I'm trying to tell you!"

He pushed up his glasses and pinched the bridge of his nose. "Go ahead."

"I got talking with someone at the party about Peggy's business, and about Malcolm, and I thought it would be a good idea to see if there was anything connecting him to Ingraham's death—in his room."

"How much had you had to drink at this point?"

"That doesn't matter! Listen. Malcolm knows something about Ingraham's death. I'm sure of it. And he's selling drugs!"

He walked past his mother, who was methodically folding and stuffing envelopes for a fund-raiser, listening to his every word. He opened the fridge and grabbed a soda. "Uh-huh."

"Don't patronize me. I know he's selling drugs because he was talking to someone in the room with him."

That brought him up short. "This guy was in the room at the same time you were?" His mom's head perked right up at that. He frowned at her.

"He and another man. The other guy was talking about Ingraham's death. At least I'm pretty sure he was. He was scared. And then Malcolm gave him something, some sort of drug."

He put the soda can down on the counter, unopened. "What did they do? Shoot up? Do you know what they were using?"

"No, not like that. Like a payment. Or a payoff. I didn't actually see any-thing. I was hiding in the bathroom."

He lifted his keys from a row of hooks next to the back door. "You were hiding in the bathroom."

"Yes. And then the other man left, the one who was worried, and Mal-colm started making phone calls to potential buyers. And to a friend named Poppy."

The priest he knew spoke in a clear, well-organized way, one thought flowing coherently into another. But this garbled story . . . He couldn't tell if she was drunk or delusional, or maybe had been hit on the head.

"He just stayed there on the phone, with the music going, and I needed to leave, because all I could think about was that I'd be in deep trouble if a drug lord found me in his shower stall while he was peddling his wares. Not to mention the way he was talking about how they were going to take care of the other man. So I climbed out of his bathroom window and—"

"You did what? Are you nuts?"

"It was the only way out. So I climbed out of his bathroom window, jumped onto a porch roof, and made it back to my car. I thought I had bet-ter call you, because you can get a warrant and search Malcolm's room. He keeps the stuff under his bed. Oh, and he has a gun, too."

He pocketed his keys. "And why is it you can't go back into the house?" His mom had given up pretending to do work and was staring with un-disguised interest at him.

"I threw away my sandals. And I lost two buttons on my top, and wiped off most of my makeup. I'm a complete mess."

It was the first time he had ever heard Clare say anything that indicated she had any awareness of how she looked at all. If her story hadn't been so completely bizarre, he'd have teased her about it. But she spoke with an ear-nest literalness that undoubtedly came out of a bottle but made her sound like a kid.

"Where are you right now?"

"In the passenger seat."

"No, I mean where is Peggy Landry's house?"

"Um, on the Old Lake George Road. You turn off at a place called Lucher's Corners."

"I know where that is. What's her house number?"

"I can't remember. Wait—" He heard the sound of papers flipping around. She came back on. "Okay, I got the directions she gave me. Number two thousand twelve."

"Okay, this is what we're going to do. You stay put in your car. I'm going to come get you and take you home."

"No! That's not why I called! You have to come and arrest him! I wouldn't have called for a ride. That would be imposing on you." She said "imposing on you" in the same tone of voice someone might use to say "sacrificing your firstborn child."

"I'll just stay here until I feel sober enough to drive safely. Do not come out here to give me a ride," Clare told him.

He wasn't going to waste time arguing with a woman under the influence. Not over the phone, with his mom hanging on every word. "I'll be there in about a half hour. Stay put." He turned the phone off and replaced it in its cradle.

"Trouble?"

He nodded. "She needs a ride. And she thinks she may have some information about this murder we're working on."

His mother's face changed from amused to worried. "Maybe you should call for backup."

He shook his head. "It's not like that, Mom. And Clare's a little under the influence. I don't want to embarrass her in front of anyone else. I'll take her to her house and then head home from there."

Margy got to her feet and wrapped her arms around him. He squeezed her hard and dropped a kiss on her springy white curls. "Don't worry, Mom. There aren't going to be any bad guys."

She tipped her head back to look him straight in the eye. "That's not the only sort of trouble out there."

◆ ◆ ◆

The Old Lake George road was familiar to him, part of the regular patrol route. When he had been in school—back around the Civil War, it felt like—the road had been mostly undeveloped, except for a few scraggly cabins inhabited by cranky loners. It had been, as its name suggested, a shortcut over the mountains toward Lake George, not a place anyone with a lick of sense would build on, back when the surrounding area was all devoted to dairy farming. Things started to change in the eighties, when a "pristine mountainside between a quaint Adirondack village"—he had seen the language in an ad his mother had sent him—and the old resort area of Lake George suddenly became a hot commodity. Overnight, neo-

Adirondack lodges that would have given Teddy Roosevelt nightmares had sprung up along the road, interspersed with fake Swiss chalets and Frank Lloyd Wright Fallingwater rip-offs. One of the latter, whose architect had insisted on flat roofs to "blend in with nature," had come to a spectacular end when a twenty-four-hour storm dumped three feet of snow on the area and the whole house collapsed in on itself.

He recognized Peggy Landry's house when he pulled into the long drive. She couldn't have owned it long—it had been purchased and expensively renovated by a dot-com millionaire from New York City just a few years ago. He remembered the guy because he was constantly calling in intruder alerts during his summer stays, until Mark Durkee went up and pointed out that the open-air kitchen he had installed at the end of the pool house was attracting a steady stream of black bears.

The drive was still full of cars, but it was easy enough to pick out Clare's god-awful Shelby Cobra. He pulled his truck into the nearest empty spot and got out. He glanced up at the facade of the house, three stories of vaguely rustic clapboarding rising up to a modern-cladded roof. He tried to picture Clare dropping out one of the windows, three sheets to the wind, and the image made him wince. An adrenaline addict, she had once described herself as. How she ever made it through a seminary and into the priesthood was a mystery to him.

He crunched over to her car. There was no sign of life until he bent down and peered into the shadowy interior. She had fallen asleep in the passenger seat. He knocked on the driver's door and opened it.

"I'm here," she said loudly, bolting upright.

"Take it easy. You're not asleep on duty." The light from the house reached the interior of the car dimly, but even in the shadows, he could see she hadn't exaggerated. She looked like she'd been dragged through the bushes backward.

"No, of course not, I was just—" She blinked several times. "Russ! What are you doing here? No, wait, I remember. Are you going to arrest Malcolm?"

He squinted past her into the tiny sports car. "I don't think I can fit inside this tin can. Why don't we get into my truck? We can talk there. Grab your purse and keys."

She nodded, and a moment later they were crossing the gravel drive to his pickup, Clare muttering quiet "Ouch" noises as she, barefooted, picked her way across the stones.

As soon as they were both inside, he fired up the ignition and shifted into gear.

"Hey! What are you doing?"

"Taking you home," he said, craning over his shoulder to see as he backed up. "Fasten your seat belt."

"You're supposed to be searching Malcolm's room! Didn't you hear anything I said on the phone?"

"Yep." He threw his pickup into first and headed down the drive to the road.

"You can't just drive away! There are illegal drugs in that house. And persons with knowledge of a murder!"

"You been watching *Law & Order* again, haven't you?" He grinned at her. "Listen. I'll give you a free tutorial on the way the criminal-justice system works in our country. I am a law-enforcement agent. Before I go into anyone's house and search it, I have to get permission from a judge, called a warrant. I convince the judge to issue me a warrant based on evidence I can show or information I can give that will persuade him that there's a reasonable chance I can find some evidence of a crime. Now, while it's true that there are some jurisdictions where an honest cop can get a warrant based on his say-so, here in Washington County I have to deal with Judge Ryswick. And Judge Ryswick likes solid evidence before issuing a warrant. Especially when he's asked to issue warrants against well-heeled businessmen. Judge Ryswick would be very unhappy with me if I woke him up and asked for a warrant to search Peggy Landry's home based on a drunken woman's statement that she overheard what she thinks was a drug deal while going to the bathroom. Although I admit that the fact you're a priest is good. The DA always likes to tell juries that priests and bishops don't normally witness crimes. To explain the scumball witnesses he has to put on the stand, you see?"

"I wasn't going to the bathroom! I was hiding there. And I'm not drunk. I only had four drinks. Or five. I'm just a tad . . . tipsy."

He laughed.

"Don't patronize me!"

"I'm practically old enough to be your father. That gives me the right to patronize you. Plus, I'm sober and you're not."

She clicked her seat-belt buckle into place. He gunned the truck and turned onto the Seven Mile Road as she opened her mouth several times, inhaling sharply, as if she were about to light into him but couldn't make up her mind where to start. Finally, she said, "You are not old enough to be my father."

"I'll be forty-nine in November."

"Well, there you are. My father is fifty-eight." She crossed her arms.

The fact that he was a lot closer to her father's age than to hers was not a comfortable thought. "What the hell were you thinking of, leaping out a window onto a porch roof? You could have broken both your legs."

"Believe me, it wasn't my first choice. I was planning—" She stopped and thought for a minute. "Actually, I have to confess that I didn't go into Malcolm's room with any plan for getting back out again. I wasn't thinking very far ahead."

"There's a surprise," he said under his breath.

She twisted in her seat. "Mal Wintour is selling drugs," she said. "He's got a stash in a suitcase under his bed. The man who was in the room with him said it must be worth a million." She jabbed her hands reflexively at her French twist and whatever had been holding it in place slid and a quarter of her hair tumbled down. "Darn it." She fumbled with a clip. "Just because I wasn't in the same room with them doesn't mean I couldn't hear them."

"Okay. I believe you thought you heard what you did. I'll even accept that you may be right that he is holding. I'm still not going to get anywhere based on your say-so."

"Russ—"

He held up a hand. "Let me finish. I'll put Mark on him, do some background checking, see if we can connect him to any known dealers or buyers."

"But it's more than that. I think he's connected to the murder."

"Which one?"

"What do you mean, which one? Bill Ingraham's, of course. Why? There hasn't been—has there been another murder?"

"Maybe. We found Chris Dessaint's body. He's the guy I told you about—the one McKinley fingered as the ringleader of those punks. Looks like he OD'd. Scheeler's doing an autopsy to see what he can find out."

"Wasn't he the one who was supposedly giving the others drugs and money?"

"That's him."

"It makes perfect sense!" She smacked her hands together. "Malcolm gave him drugs and money, and he did the dirty work. Mal said something to the other guy in his bedroom—'I know what you were told.' Doesn't that sound as if there was someone else involved?"

"Huh." He glanced away from the mountain road to look at her for a moment. "Did you hear the other guy's name?"

"No." She bit her lip and dropped her eyelids, as if she were concentrating intently on remembering. "He said, 'I didn't sign up for anything like this.' He told Mal he wasn't in it for the money, and Mal laughed at him. Then Mal gave him the . . . well, whatever it was and told him it was worth ten thousand dollars, and he—Malcolm, that is—would arrange a sale for the other guy. So he could take the money and leave the state. 'Until this business about Bill blows over'—that's what he said." She opened her eyes and looked at Russ. "What do you think? Do you have an idea of who it might be?"

He returned his attention to the road. "Dunno if it's an idea. A possibility, maybe." He tapped the steering wheel with two fingers. "According to Elliott McKinley, there was a third man involved in the beatings. Jason Colvin. No priors on him, although we know he used to hang in the fringes of our little local hate-mongering group. We've tracked him to his girlfriend's house, but the last time she saw him was Monday morning."

"The morning after Bill Ingraham was killed."

"Yep. Noble's checked his work, hangouts, family—no one's seen him since then. He's disappeared off the face of the earth. Since we found Dessaint, I've been wondering if he took a camping trip, too."

"What do you mean?"

"Dessaint. He was camped out in a remote location in the woods. If he hadn't died and attracted a flock of carrion birds, we wouldn't have found him on a bet."

Clare wrinkled her nose. "That's awful. And he died of an overdose? Accidentally?"

"Don't know. It's mighty convenient that the only person who knew who was passing out drugs and money in exchange for the assaults happened to OD a couple days after Ingraham's death."

"But if you think it might have been this Jason Colvin guy who was talking to Malcolm, then Chris Dessaint couldn't have been the only one to know." She brought one leg up and tucked her foot under her other leg. "If Malcolm Wintour's been pulling the strings, maybe he's trying to tie off all the loose ends. Maybe he adulterated whatever it was that he gave to

Dessaint. And now Jason Colvin's come to him. Maybe the package he gave to him wasn't a payoff. Maybe it was meant for personal use."

"If Colvin is a regular user, it wouldn't stretch the imagination to think he'd dip into the goods. Even if he did plan on selling most of it." He slowed the truck down as they approached a T-junction, then turned left and headed back into town. "The problem I have is seeing Malcolm Wintour as the bad guy. Why? What's in it for him? Even granted the spurned-lover scenario, this is way too complicated. People who are enraged that their lover left grab the nearest gun and blow the person away. They don't hire a bunch of guys and arrange incidents to cover their tracks. Besides, McKinley said the guy who was bankrolling them felt like they did about queers. Wanted to teach 'em a lesson. Wintour's gay. He's not going to beat up on his own kind."

"It's not a club with a secret handshake and vows of fraternal loyalty, Russ. Besides, from everything I've heard about Malcolm, the only person he feels loyalty to is himself. And maybe his aunt." She twisted in her seat again. "And that's another reason he may have done it. He's living with Peggy Landry, relying on her for his housing and his support."

"If he's been selling . . ."

She waved a hand impatiently. "Details. I'm going for the big picture."

"Oh."

"He's living with his aunt, the only other person to whom he's attached, by both self-interest and affection. He thinks she's likely to go under if the Algonquin Spa doesn't go through, which is what Bill Ingraham is considering. So he does away with Bill. Or arranges to have him—" She closed her mouth abruptly.

He knew without asking that she was remembering what Ingraham's body looked like the night she found him.

"The problem with that scenario," he said, hoping to distract her, "is that Emil Dvorak was attacked the same night that Ingraham was making his threat at the town meeting to close down the project."

She looked at him, her expression alert, indicating she'd returned to the present. "Sure, but chances are good that Ingraham had at least discussed the possibility with his other business partners. And if Peggy knew, Malcolm could have known. Or he might have talked about it with Malcolm himself before they broke up. Of course"—she flipped her hand over to indicate another possibility—"no one I've spoken with claims Malcolm is a genius of any kind, let alone a criminal one. His aunt described him as a sort of family project, and a man I was speaking with tonight said he couldn't find—he wasn't very smart."

"Well, see, that's something you would think of, because you're used to dealing with smart people. Believe me, most crimes are committed by idiots. That's why we usually catch them. It wouldn't take intellect for Wintour to set up a series of hits on his ex and the others, just meanness and a few bucks. From what McKinley told me, they had control over the people they targeted and how they did it. The only instruction they had from the lead guy was that there be no thieving. Which, I have to admit, was smart, because once stolen goods start reappearing on the market, we usually have a much better chance of tracking down the thieves."

"So you do think it could have been Malcolm." She looked pleased with herself. "Hah." She twisted toward him. "What are you going to do?"

He felt an unaccustomed warmth, centered in his chest and seeping outward, making his skin flush. It wasn't sexual arousal, or embarrassment—he couldn't identify the feeling.

"About what?"

"What are you going to do to be able to get a warrant to search Malcolm's room? Besides sending Officer Entwhistle out. I can't imagine he'll find much, since Malcolm hasn't been back in Millers Kill very long. He used to live with Bill in Baltimore. Hey, do you think the guys over at the Stuyvesant Inn might know more? Since he and Bill used to stay there together?"

It was pleasure, he realized. Simple pleasure at her genuine interest in him, in what he did, in what was important to him. A cold wave of guilt instantly washed over him. He was comparing Clare to his wife, which was completely unfair. Linda's lack of interest in his work was her way of protecting herself from fear and anxiety. Her interests and her way of thinking were very different from his, and he had known that when he married her. He had welcomed it, as a respite from all the crap he'd had to deal with day in and day out as an MP. She hadn't changed; he had. And the fact that Clare somehow seemed to . . . fit with who he was now should never, never reflect poorly on his wife, who was beautiful and funny and faithful. Not like him, who was driving around in his truck close to midnight, committing adultery in his heart.

"Russ? Yoo-hoo. Let me in. What are you thinking about?"

"Jimmy Carter," he said. He quirked his mouth in a half smile and glanced at her, but instead of the amusement or puzzlement he expected, she met his eyes with a look of such utter understanding that he had to shift in his seat from discomfort and chagrin.

She ducked her head and straightened in her seat as well, facing forward. She looked straight ahead as he slowed and turned onto Meersham Street, with its small, neat houses and evenly spaced trees. "What are you going to do?"

"About Malcolm?"

"Yes, about Malcolm."

Screw Malcolm, he wanted to say, but instead he forced his mind into the familiar and safe channels of investigation and deduction. "I'd like to have a talk with Peggy Landry about him. Nothing formal—just feel her out. What his relationship was to BWI Development, instead of just what it was to Ingraham. If he has any income she knows about, and where it's coming from. If she's noticed any behavior that might indicate drug use." He glanced at her for a second and then returned his attention to driving. "Do you think she'd talk to me about him? Willingly?"

"She seemed more exasperated with him than protective," Clare said. "She strikes me as the sort who would throw him out of the house if she knew he had illegal drugs there, for his own good. You know. Tough love. He seemed protective of her, though, in his conversation with the other guy."

He nodded. "I'll think of a good reason to drop in on her, then. I don't want to ask her to the station or make it seem like another round of questioning on what she knows about Ingraham."

"Help me get my car."

"What?"

"Tomorrow. It's still parked at her house. I'll need someone to drive me up there so I can retrieve it. If you take me, it will seem completely unrelated to the investigation. I can come up with something to ask her—a question about the wedding. Then you can get into a conversation with her."

"You're very sneaky, for a priest." He felt her shrug, rather than saw it.

"What can I say? I was a sneaky kid. Probably a sneaky officer. I was trained to fly under the radar."

He turned onto Elm Street, approaching the rectory the back way. Her house was the last one on the street, just before you reached the church on the corner. He turned into her drive and twisted the key in the ignition.

"Okay," he said into the silence once the engine had died. "I'll take you there. Do you need to have your car back at any particular time?"

She opened the passenger door and climbed out. "I have a wedding in the morning. I was going to do some grocery shopping in the afternoon, but I can always walk over to the IGA."

He popped his own door open and swung himself out. "I'll walk you up," he said.

"That's not necessary."

"When are you going to get an automatic floodlight so you can see if someone's in your yard after dark? They're butt-easy to install. 'Scuse my French. You could probably do it yourself."

Instead of heading up the drive toward her kitchen door, she walked across the lawn to the wide front porch. "I hate those things. They go off every time a squirrel walks across the lawn. I don't like lights coming on and waking me up."

She walked up the three steps, and he followed her. "Get some curtains," he said. Unlike his own heavily accessorized windows, Clare's didn't have a single valance, balloon shade, or drapery.

"There's an idea. You think maybe I could hire your wife to do them up for me?" The twist in her voice when she said "your wife" startled him. He stopped where he stood, one foot on the top step. "I'm sorry," she said. "I'm sorry. That was uncalled for."

He could smell roses heavy in the warm, humid air. He wondered if the church's flower committee worked on her garden, as well. He looked at Clare, who was standing between the steps and the double door, almost invisible in the dark because of her black clothing.

"Thanks for bringing me home," she said.

"I'll call you tomorrow about retrieving your car."

"Thanks." She didn't move. Neither did he. "You've walked me to the door. I'm safe. You can go now."

"You go in first. And lock the door behind you, for once."

There was a rustle as she crossed her arms. "Why can't you leave first?"

He took the last step up onto the porch. "You know why."

Her chin jerked up. Her face a pattern of pale and dark. She stood absolutely still, watching him. Measuring him. He didn't think he could move even if a car jumped the curb and came straight toward them. Then she was gone, a whirl, the swish of cloth, and the door clunked shut behind her. He heard the clack of the bolt turning.

He backed down the steps, watching the house, but no lights came on. He climbed into his seat, fired up the truck, and pulled away. He unrolled the window, hung his arm outside, and, half-seeing the stars, drove all the way home.

CHAPTER TWENTY-SIX

When Clare woke up Saturday morning, she lay in bed for a long time, not moving. She hadn't turned the fan on last night, and the air was thick and still, like another blanket weighing her down. From her open window came the drone of a lawn mower as someone got to their yard work early, before the heat and humidity became unbearable. She knew she should get up and get her run in early for the same reason. She lay on her back and studied the ceiling. There was a smear in the semigloss paint that looked like a bank of cumulus clouds. If she didn't get up now and run, she would be cutting it too close to the time of the Veerhoos-James nuptials. The bride-to-be had described it as a "brunch wedding," although no one would be eating before noon, since the service didn't begin until eleven o'clock. Clare had turned down the invitation to the reception, so she would be free after the photos in the church. She wouldn't want to run then, because it would be too hot. Or raining, from the feel of it. And she had to get her grocery shopping done and pick up her car.

The night before reassembled in her memory, the pieces clicking into place—the kir royales, Hugh Parteger, her raid on Malcolm's bedroom, the porch roof. What in God's name had she been thinking of? Then riding home with Russ—no, with Chief Van Alstyne. Her attempt at distancing him was so transparent, she sneered at herself as soon as she thought it.

She rolled over and buried her face in her pillow. She tried lying in that position until her mind went blank, but she couldn't breathe very well. If she didn't get up and strap on her running shoes right now, it wasn't going to happen. With a groan, she surrendered to the demands of life and climbed out of bed.

She had known several priests and seminarians who liked to use the early-morning hours for private prayer and contemplation. She got the same results from running. Rain or shine, hot or cold, at some point during her five-mile run, the worries and questions that swarmed around her head like blackflies always blew away and she could feel that simple, bell-clear connection to the world around her, the weather, the working of her body. Being in the moment, that was being with God. One of her seminarian friends told her she should have been a Buddhist. One of her army buddies had pointed out that her spiritual experience was more likely the result of endorphins kicking in than opening a channel to the divine. Clare didn't care. She would take whatever peace and certainty she could get. And run with it.

She was in a much more balanced state of mind a few hours later when she stood before the lower altar, facing Michael Veerhoos and Delia James. The bride and groom kept looking away from her and at each other, their expressions mirroring a kind of awed disbelief that they were doing this monumental thing. Clare looked at their family and friends during the prayers, at the wistful smiles and silent tears, at the way couples glanced at each other or took hands when she prayed, "Give them wisdom and devotion in the ordering of their common life, that each may be to the other a strength in need, a counselor in perplexity, a comfort in sorrow, and a companion in joy." The parents of the bride and the groom—each post-divorce, each with a new spouse—were all pride and teary tenderness. It never ceased to amaze her, the power of this act, that people who had been through the worst of marriage, its ruin and desolation, still beamed with happiness as another couple bound themselves together in hope and ignorance and courage.

The new Mr. and Mrs. Veerhoos still looked shell-shocked by delight during the photo session afterward. Clare had to be in a couple of obligatory shots, re-creating parts of the ceremony the photographer had missed during the actual event, and then she escaped to the sidelines. The photographer herded family members in and out of formation in front of the altar while his assistant darted back and forth, adjusting lights and reflective umbrellas. Clare accepted three damp, crumpled envelopes from the best man, addressed to "Priest," "Organist," and "Custodian." Mr. Hadley wouldn't like that last. He was proud of his title of sexton of St. Alban's. She heard him banging around in the supply closet as the picture taking wound down, and by the time she had ushered out the last guest, he had fired up the floor polisher and was already attacking the tiles in the center aisle. It was 12:15. Excellent time for a wedding without Communion.

Clare retreated to the sacristy to remove her vestments, then walked to her office, wishing she had had the foresight to bring shorts and a T-shirt from the rectory. The offices and meeting rooms didn't have the advantage of the church's stone walls, which were thick enough to repel cannon fire, so Clare was damp and sticky by the time she reached her desk. She flicked on the standing fan, which cheerfully began blowing hot air at her. She sank into her chair, intent on finishing the paperwork she would have to mail to the state's Department of Records.

Over the rush of her fan, she heard the floor polisher shut off. There was a pause, and then it started up again. She bent her head over the officiant's record. There was a rap on her doorjamb, and Russ stuck his head inside. "Hey," he said.

"Hi there."

He leaned against the door frame, not entering the office. "There's birdseed on the walkway in front of your church. I'm afraid I tracked some in." He lifted one foot and examined the deep tread of his hiking boot. A few minuscule pellets dropped to the floor with a faint *tic-tic.* The wind from the fan immediately blew them into the hallway.

"Did Mr. Hadley yell at you?"

"Not yell, exactly. He wasn't very happy, though."

She squared off the marriage papers and stood. "You're not in uniform."

He looked down at himself, as if surprised to see jeans and a polo shirt instead of brown poplin. "It's my weekend off, so I'm not officially on duty." He grinned at her, showing a bit of his eyeteeth. "You look like you are, though." He gestured toward her short-sleeved clerical blouse and black skirt.

"I'm finished up for now. Let me hit the rectory and change; then I'll be ready to get my car." She glanced at him before unnecessarily squaring off the documents again. "If you still want to take me."

"I told you I would, didn't I?"

"I could always get a ride from"—she drew a blank on any of her parishioners who might be headed out toward Peggy Landry's house—"someone."

"But you don't have to, because I'm taking you. Besides, you're supposed to smooth the way so I can question Ms. Landry about her nephew, remember?"

She wished she didn't. It was amazing how drink-induced ideas looked in the clear light of day. "Okay, then."

"I'm parked out back."

"I'll meet you there in five minutes."

"Bring some water. It's going to be easy to get dehydrated today."

She fled before she could drivel on with increasingly meaningless sentences. In the rectory, she threw on shorts and a sleeveless blouse, grateful to be shucked of her hot black uniform. She took a quick look at her hair in the bathroom mirror, but she had taken the time to braid it tightly against her scalp after her shower, so it was still neat and cool. She slipped on her sneakers, grabbed a bottle of Poland Spring from the fridge, and ran back to the small parking lot behind St. Alban's.

The seat in Russ's pickup stuck to the back of her thighs. He had both windows rolled down, but the wind that blew through the cab felt like exhaust from a dryer. "Don't you have any air conditioning in this thing?" she said.

"Oh, yeah." He patted the dashboard affectionately. "This is my baby. She comes fully loaded."

Clare looked at him pointedly and let her eyes drift toward the temperature controls. "What?" he said. "You want me to turn it on? We're only going thirty-five miles an hour. The breeze feels good."

"You have a speed limit for your AC? When does it kick in?"

"When I'm driving so fast that I can't hear the radio over the sound of the wind."

"What is it with you people and air conditioning? One of the greatest inventions of the twentieth century, and folks in the north country act as if it were some sort of leprous beggar. You know, something you occasionally have to put up with in public but not something you'd ever take home."

He stopped at a red light. Several shoppers staggered across the crosswalk, sucking iced coffees and clutching bags labeled ADIRONDACK GIFT SHOPPE. "I guess," he said slowly, "it's because air conditioning feels like an indulgence. An imported indulgence, like paying someone to detail your car, or installing an in-ground swimming pool." The light turned green and he drove on to a residential street. "Look there." He pointed to the back-yard of a house where several children were jumping into a round above-ground pool. "See? That's the sort of pool we have here. Not something that costs ten thousand dollars to install and only gets used three months out of the year."

"But an air conditioner only costs a few hundred bucks!"

"It's the principle of the thing."

She sat back in her seat, trying to ignore the way her shirt slid against her damp skin.

"Oh, all right. Wussy."

"I am not a wussy." They drove the rest of the way in silence, the thrum of the truck's air conditioning and the music from a country station taking the place of conversation.

When they pulled into the long driveway leading up to Peggy Landry's house, Clare's car was still where she had left it. There were several other vehicles pulled off to the edges of the gravel. "Houseguests," Clare said in response to Russ's dubious look at the vehicles. She climbed out of the cab as soon as he stopped the truck. "How do you want to do this?" she asked.

"How about you thank her and introduce me as the guy who brought you up here. Then I'll ask her if I can take a little of her time. I don't want to scare her off."

"Sounds like a plan."

Their brilliant plan hit a major roadblock when the door was opened by the bride-to-be, looking considerably less vivacious than she had the night before. "She's not here, Reverend Clare," Diana said after Clare asked for Peggy. "I don't know where she went to. Cary and I were still asleep."

From the foyer, Cary's great-uncle called out, "I talked to her before she left."

Clare leaned around Diana. "Hi, Mr. Wood. Did Peggy say where she went?"

"Got a phone call, she said. Had to go out to her construction site. Say, we're just about to sit down to lunch. Care to join us? Helen and I can show you the rest of our trip."

"I'm afraid we have to head back into town," Russ broke in. "Thanks for the info. You don't happen to know if Malcolm is here?"

Diana waved a hand. "He borrowed my car. God knows if I'll ever see it again." She pushed her hair away from her face. "Do you want to leave him a message?"

"No," Russ said. "No message. Thanks for your time. Sorry to bother you."

Russ and Clare retreated back to his pickup. "I don't like it," he said.

"I'm sure she gets called out to the construction site frequently."

He waved a hand. "The work site's been closed down since Monday. What would she be doing?"

"The office is still there."

He shook his head, squinting up at the dull glare of the sky. "If you heard what you thought you heard—"

"Please don't say 'if,'" she said.

"*If* you heard what you thought you heard, there's a scared co-conspirator out there who has already gone to Malcolm for help. He's gotten a Baggie of trouble for his time, worse than useless, because now he's carrying, and if he gets stopped while holding, he's in deep sh—trouble."

"You think he might try to shake down Peggy?"

"Maybe. Try to hit her up for money. Or try to hold her until Malcolm comes up with cash. I don't know; I'm just feeling my way here. But I don't like the feeling."

She dug her keys out of her pocket. "Let's go, then."

"Whoa. What is this 'we,' kemosabe?"

She crunched over the gravel to her car. "I am going to go to the Algonquin Spa construction site now to see if I can offer any aid or comfort to Peggy Landry. You can come along if you like."

"Clare, you have no business—"

She shut the door, partially blocking out his harangue. She cranked up the air conditioner as high as it would go and turned on the radio. She checked the rear window to make sure he was following. He was stomping across the ground, evidently talking to himself, or swearing. Clare readjusted the rearview mirror and reversed in a smart turn, kicking up gravel. She grinned. She didn't want anything to happen to Peggy, of course, but she was alive with the prospect of finally answering the questions surrounding Bill Ingraham's murder and Dr. Dvorak's and Todd's assaults.

She gunned the Shelby and sped down the drive. A quick glance in the mirror confirmed that Russ's truck was behind her. She envisioned herself triumphantly bearing the truth to the MacPhersons, and to Stephen and Ron. You don't have to be afraid because of who you are! she'd say. She pictured herself laying her cleverness before the vestry—the man responsible caught! And imagine if her role in uncovering Malcolm was recounted in the *Post-Star*. It could deliver a huge boost in attendance at a candlelight vigil. Maybe she could follow up with organized discussion groups at St. Alban's, involve the outreach commission. . . .

With plans cascading through her head, she went back through town on autopilot, just aware enough of her surroundings to avoid rear-ending a tanker trailer whose driver had stopped shy of the Route 117 bridge in order to back into a Stewart's convenience store. Waiting for a truck to turn would normally have had her drumming her fingers on the steering wheel and glancing at her watch, but at this point in her daydream, her activities and outreach had brought large numbers of new members into St. Alban's, and she smiled so beatifically at the overflowing pews that the startled truck driver smiled and waved back.

By the time she passed the Stuyvesant Inn, she was being feted by the vestry and acclaimed by the bishop for her fearless dedication to the truth. The little Cobra bounced and jounced up the road to the construction site, clouds of dust roiling up behind her for Russ's pickup to drive through.

As he had said, the site was closed to work. It would have been obvious even if there had been other vehicles alongside Peggy Landry's Volvo in the dirt parking area. The excavators and bulldozers rested in exactly the same positions they had been in when Clare visited five days before. The clear plastic tarpaulins on the pallets of brick and Sheetrock were dusted over with a gold-green layer of pollen, giving them the look of tomb relics.

She pulled in a few feet away from Peggy's sedan and got out. No piney mountain breezes today. The air was thick with humidity and smelled of the rich humus composting on the forest floor all around them. Russ had driven past Peggy's car and parked the truck farther away, angled sharply, its nose out. So he could pull out and onto the road without having to reverse and turn, she realized. Probably picks the corner seat on a bar, Clare thought, with his back to the wall and his eyes on the door. She leaned on the hood of her car, scuffing the toe of her sneaker through the talc-fine dirt.

Russ walked over. "Well, her car's here. Let's try the office."

But the office door was locked. "Now what?" Clare asked.

"I don't like this." Russ looked at the ground, which had been beaten into a formless wash of fine dirt by the constant pounding of feet and machinery. "We're never going to be able to track her here." He took his glasses off and polished them with the corner of his polo shirt, squinting at the woods surrounding the site.

"The only car around is hers," she said. "What if he's already met her and taken her away?"

"Her purse is still in her car," Russ replied. "If this guy you heard is really up against the wall, I doubt he'd leave behind her credit cards, cash, and ATM card."

"Oh. I didn't see that."

"Didn't look, did you?"

She ignored the amusement in his voice and pointed to the edge of the site. "There's a rough road back there. Just a couple of ruts between the trees, but if I were walking away from here"—she swept her arm around, encompassing the work zone, "I'd use it, instead of bushwhacking through these woods."

"Do you know where it goes?"

"The foreman took me around. If you head to the left, there's a helipad." He looked at her. "Yeah, I know; I thought it was pretty cool myself. In the other direction, it leads to the old quarry. It branches off there and follows the gorge farther up the mountain. The less attractive stuff is going to be up there—their power plant, their laundry, the garage, things like that."

"How far does it go?"

"I don't know. We didn't go there."

"Okay. Hang on a sec." Russ returned to his truck, bent the driver's seat forward, and pulled something from the back. He emerged with a standard-issue gun belt. He buckled it on and drew the gun, inspecting the ammunition clip before returning it to the holster. In his jeans and knit shirt, he looked almost like a tourist playacting at Frontier Town, but the heavy solidity of the belt and holster could never be mistaken for a toy.

"Is that really necessary?" she asked.

"I sure as hell hope not," he said. "But it's better to have it and not need it than the other way around." He paused in front of her. "I don't suppose I can convince you to get back into your car and go home."

She shook her head, her braid thumping against her neck.

"Wait for me here?"

She laughed.

"Yeah, I didn't think so." He headed for the nearest earthen ramp. She fell in beside him. "Stick close. If we see anything funny, get behind me and let me do the talking. Got it?"

"Sir, yes, sir."

"And don't 'sir' me. You were the captain. I was just a lowly warrant officer. And I had to work my way up to that from being a dumb grunt."

"We're civilians now. Who do you think outranks, the chief of police or the rector?"

"The chief of police does. I've got more years on the job and more people I have to worry about."

"Plus, you're older than I am. A lot older."

He shot her a look as they entered the forest track. Unlike the last time she had been here, there was no current of cool air running beneath the trees. The leaves around them hung limp in the humidity, and the smell of rotting vegetation was everywhere. "This way," she said, pointing toward the quarry.

They trudged through the green tunnel in silence. Clare's blouse clung to a damp patch at the small of her back. She waved away a mosquito that was attempting to land on her thigh. Russ slapped his forearm and flicked off a tiny corpse. They passed a tree-clinging vine dotted with starry white flowers that gave off a sickly-sweet smell. "Pretty," she observed.

He just grunted. "Do you know what it is?" she asked.

He shook his head. "Y'know, Ray Yardhaas was a lot more entertaining as a hiking companion than you are," she said.

"Be quiet," he replied. "If there's somebody in here with Peggy Landry, I don't want to give him advance notice we're coming."

"Oh. Sorry."

He waved her apology away. They reached the fork in the track she remembered from Monday. "Quarry," she said, pointing right.

He gestured with his head that they should go right. After a few yards, the forest canopy opened up and she could see the hazy sky, colorless and cloudless. He waved her behind him and walked toward the edge slowly. When he got within a few yards of the rocky outcrop that Clare and Ray had stood on to view the quarry, Russ dropped down on his belly and crawled forward. Clare did the same, the small rocks and scrub grass scraping her exposed skin.

"Anything?" she asked as she drew near to the edge.

He pushed back and clambered to his feet. "No." She stood up as well, gratefully brushing away the bits of rock embedded in her thighs. They looked over the smooth chunks of shale that marked the upper rim of the quarry. "What's that over there?" he asked, pointing to where the crevasse opened into the rear of the quarry. After several days without rain, the waterfall was a weak trickle down the rock face. "Is it part of the construction?"

"No, it's a natural gorge. Runs down from the mountain."

"Could they have hiked up there?"

"I don't think so. I met the state's geologist when I was here on Monday, and he described it as knifing down the mountain. I suppose someone could climb up the back wall of the quarry and get in, but I can't imagine this Colvin guy getting Peggy up there under duress. Look at it. That's a real toe-and-fingerhold climb for at least fifteen or twenty feet."

"Yeah." Russ squatted on his haunches and took a long, slow look at the quarry beneath them. "What about past those dump trucks? Where the forest takes up again?"

"I don't know. I guess if you headed downhill long enough, you'd eventually run into the road. I can't say I took a close look around when I was down there, but I sure didn't see anything that leapt out at me as a trail."

"I don't like it," he said. He stood up again, rubbing his hands on his jeans. "If she really is here on spa business, why the hell isn't she at the office? I don't see her as the type to take spontaneous hikes through the deep woods on a ninety-degree day."

"Not with a houseful of guests," she said.

"And if Colvin or someone was trying to lure her here, where did he take her? If you want to rob someone, you take the valuables and leave. If you want to kidnap someone, you take the person and leave. Except this guy, from the way you describe hearing him, sounded too chickenshit for an actual kidnapping. 'Scuse my French."

"Maybe he took her in his car and left the purse behind."

"In which case, we're back to square one." He twisted around, looking back into the woods. "What I worry about is that he might have met up with her here, tried to intimidate her into paying him off, and—"

"And then something went wrong," she said.

He looked at her. "There're lots of places to hide a body in these woods."

Despite the heat, she felt a prickle of gooseflesh along her arms. "Let's try the other trail, the one that heads up the mountain." Even as she made the suggestion, she knew that it was more an attempt to deny the awful possibility that Peggy was lying dead out there than a realistic hope that they might find her.

He shifted his weight. "Okay. We'll try it for a ways. But if we don't see anything, we're turning around and heading into town."

"Will you put together a search team?"

He nodded. "And get a dog up here."

CHAPTER TWENTY-SEVEN

The track up the mountain was harder. They walked side by side, silent once more, although Clare had stopped expecting they would find anyone lurking ahead. At least any one alive. Silence in the woods seemed to come naturally to Russ. She slogged along, one foot in front of the other feeling as if she were hiking with a wet Turkish towel draped around her, but his back and arms had a line of tension about them, and each step he took was deliberate He kept looking into the trees, left, right, scanning overhead.

They passed a dump site barely hacked out of the woods filled with cracked pallets and bags of rubbish. One of those golf carts Ray had mentioned to Clare lay tipped over on its side. Russ made her get behind him, then drew his gun from its holster before approaching the pile of trash. He peered into an open barrel before retreating back to the trail. He shook his head and motioned to Clare to keep walking as he reholstered his gun.

She didn't know if it was the quiet, or Russ's behavior, or the tangled thicket of underbrush, which reminded her of where she had found Ingraham's body, but she was getting seriously creeped out. When he paused at the sound of a woodpecker's knock and searched the trees, she hissed at him, "Why are you doing that?"

"What?" He turned to her. "Doing what?"

"Acting like we're about to come under fire. I ferried guys to the front during Desert Storm who were less tense than you are."

"I didn't know you were in the Gulf."

"Cut it out. You're making me more nervous than I already am."

"Sorry." A dried-up streambed cut across the trail, and they picked their way across the smooth stones. His eyes flicked across the trees.

"Do you really think that the guy who took Peggy is waiting to ambush us?" She kept her voice close to a whisper.

He shook his head. "No. I don't know. It's just . . ." He flipped his hands out. "The green. The heat. The humidity."

"I thought you liked to go into the woods. Don't you hunt?"

"That's in the fall. Not when everything's green." He looked again, left, right, up. "I like the fall. And the spring. Nothing good ever happened to me in green leaves." The trail twisted to the right, running parallel to a dense stand of hardwood. Clare could feel her calf muscles sigh with relief at the chance to travel on more level ground.

"Sometimes I have dreams," he said. "Red on green."

"Oh," she said, and then, after a moment, "Tell me about them."

He smiled at her, but his eyes were still far away. Lost in the green. "I would, but I'd have to have a bottle of whiskey while I was doing it, and then the folks at my AA meeting would be cheesed off at me."

There was a sound from up the trail. They both stopped. She heard it again, a beat, or a rustle. Hard to tell. Not a sound made by nature. He motioned her to the side of the trail and she pressed herself into the underbrush, hardly feeling the sharp twigs and tickling leaves, her heart pounding. She had a second to wonder if he was just going to stand there in the middle of the track, and another second to start to feel irritation along with fear, and then he faded into the shadows of the big trees on the opposite side of the trail. She peered through the tiny branches to where the rutted track turned uphill again and disappeared from view.

Peggy Landry walked around the bend. Clare looked at Russ, but he held up one finger. She waited. Peggy was a mess, her arms scratched, a sleeve half-torn off her camp shirt, a reddening mark across her temple and eye that looked as if it would bloom into a very bad bruise. She was walking quickly, watching her footing on the trail, but not running. Clare looked over at Russ again. He was still holding up a finger, looking well past Peggy to the bend in the trail, clearly waiting to see if she was being pursued. Clare held her breath and tried to ignore an itchy trickle of sweat on her chest. Peggy walked past their concealed positions. She was almost at the next turn of the track when Russ stepped out from the trees. "Ms. Landry," he said.

She screamed. Clare stumbled out of her hiding place. Peggy screamed again.

"Peggy!" Clare shouted. "It's me! Clare Fergusson!"

Russ threw his hands up into the air. "And Chief Van Alstyne."

Peggy staggered back, clutching her chest, and collapsed on the ground.

"Oh, my God!" They both ran toward Peggy, Clare reaching her first and skidding as she dropped down next to the older woman. "Peggy! Are you okay?"

Russ knelt on Peggy's other side. "Let me take a look at her," he said, brushing Clare's hands away. Peggy was hunched over, panting so fast that Clare was sure she would pass out from hyperventilation. Russ took Peggy's head between his hands and tilted her face toward him. Her eyes were wide and white-rimmed, like a spooked horse. "I don't think she's in shock," he said. He brushed her hair away from her temple. "This looks nasty, though." He looked at Clare. "Run your hands over her torso. Make sure she doesn't have any puncture wounds."

Clare did as he asked. "Nothing," she said.

"Peggy," Russ said slowly and clearly, "you need to calm down and tell us what happened. Was someone with you? Were you threatened? Did he injure you?"

"How . . . what . . ." Peggy gasped for air.

"We went to your house," Clare said. "Mr. Wood told us you had left for the construction site after getting a phone call." She glanced up at Russ, uncertain how much to say to the woman huddled between them.

"We had reason to believe you might be in danger from Jason Colvin." Russ said. "He's wanted for questioning in the Ingraham murder."

Peggy buried her face in her hands and rocked forward. "Please, Peggy, tell us what happened," Clare said.

Russ looked grim. "Ms. Landry, were you sexually assaulted?"

That seemed to reach her. She sat up straighter and pushed her hair out of her face. "No," she said. She covered her eyes with her hands again. "But I think he was trying to kill me."

"Who?" Clare could hear Russ trying to keep a tight rein on his voice.

"Leo Waxman."

Clare rocked back on her heels. "Leo Waxman?"

Russ spread his hands with a look of complete confusion on his face. "Who's he?"

"The state's geologist for the project. Remember I told you he showed me around the quarry when I was here Monday? That's him."

"What the hell does the geologist have to do with any of this?" Clare could empathize with the bafflement in Russ's voice.

"He called me," Peggy said. "He told me he had something very important to show me at the site. Something that could affect the project going forward. I met him at the spa area and he insisted on driving me way up here to show me something. He wouldn't say what." She hunched over again. "He took me as far as you can on this road, up to where it gets very close to the gorge. He—he demanded money from me. Told me Bill had promised him a job with BWI and a fat salary, and then Bill reneged. He was crazy. Furious." She looked up at them. "I think he may have murdered Bill." She closed her eyes. "I was terrified. He came at me. We fought. Somehow—I'm not sure how—he went over." Her voice thinned out into little more than a whisper. "Into the gorge. I didn't know what to do. So I started walking back. I didn't know what else to do."

Russ looked over her head to where the trail twisted out of sight. "How far from here?"

Peggy shook her head. "I'm not sure. I wasn't paying much attention. Everything seems sort of unreal. Like in a horrible dream."

"Peggy," Clare said. "Is he injured? Is he dead? Did you get a good look at him?"

She shook her head. "I don't know. He was near the stream, facedown, very still. I yelled, but he didn't move or answer. I was going to call for help when I got back to my car. He was just lying there. It's a deep gorge. My grandfather would never let us hike near it when we were kids."

"How come you didn't drive back down?" Russ said.

Peggy blinked. There was a pause, as if she was trying to remember her thoughts at the scene of the accident. "I can't drive a standard," she finally said. She looked up at them. "I'm sorry. I guess I should have tried."

Clare looked at Russ. "What do you think we should do?"

"I gotta go up and see. Will you take Ms. Landry back down to the cars?"

"Do you want me to call for help?"

He shook his head. "It'll have to be Mountain Rescue. I want to be able to tell them if it's a medical emergency or a body recovery. It can't be that far, and I can travel faster without her. I'll scope it out and get back to you as soon as possible." He hunkered down to get close to Peggy again. "Did he park on the trail? Did you wander far from the vehicle?"

"No. I mean, yes, he parked on the trail. We walked from there to the gorge. You can hear—there's still a bit of water running in the stream at the bottom. You can hear it."

He stood up, rubbing his hands on his jeans. "I'll meet you back there as soon as I can."

Clare nodded. She watched until he disappeared from view. Then she stood up. "Do you think you can get up?" she asked Peggy, extending her hand. Peggy took it and let Clare haul her into a standing position. "Are you sure you're not hurt anywhere? You're going to have a bad bruise around your eye."

Peggy touched her face lightly. "I'm not hurt. Other than this. I'm more shaken up than anything."

Clare squeezed her arm. "You have every right to be."

She led Peggy down the trail, murmuring assurances and encouragement, listening to her rattle on while keeping an ear cocked for the sound of Russ behind them. Peggy kept returning to Leo Waxman and how he was lying at the bottom of the gorge. "What if he's still alive? Will the Mountain Rescue be able to help him? Won't they take an awfully long time? What are his chances?"

"If that gorge is as steep as I think it is, yes, it'll take a long time to rescue him," Clare said. "They'll have to rappel men and equipment down, fix him on a board, and then carry him out the long way, through the quarry. Either that or figure out a way to lift him back up the wall of the gorge without hurting him more. I think you need to prepare yourself. Unless he was only stunned when you looked at him, the chances are good that he's not going to survive."

Peggy moaned. "Oh, God."

Clare looked ahead. They were getting closer to where the trail joined the rutted road leading from the quarry to the helipad. She recognized the rottingly sweet white-flowered vines running up the trees and—The force of her thought literally made her stop in her tracks. She whirled on Peggy. "I know how we can get him!"

"What?"

"Waxman. We don't have to wait for the Mountain Rescue team. I can get him out. With the BWI helicopter."

"What?" Peggy's second "What?" was closer to a screech than a question.

"BWI keeps a helicopter right here at the site. I've been in it. It has a first-aid pack and, more important, it's rigged with a cargo net and boom." She looked up, as if she could see through the leaf canopy to the skies overhead. "It's lousy flying weather, of course. The humidity will make it slow going, but there's no wind. Once I'm over the gorge, I can just hover there and let Russ bring Waxman up."

"You're joking." Peggy's expression reminded Clare that declaring oneself capable of aerial extractions was not something most people did with confidence.

"It's okay," she said. "I was a pilot in the army. I've logged thousands and thousands of hours in helicopters."

"You're not joking."

"Hurry up." Clare quickened her pace. "Let's get down to the site and get your cell phone. We can call ahead to the hospital and find out what to do for him. Then I can run back up to the helipad and do a preflight check." She frowned. "I hope Mr. Opperman didn't fly it back to Baltimore or anything."

They trotted along at a fast pace. Peggy looked drawn and ashy, and Clare felt a wash of guilt at pushing her after her ordeal. But no matter what Leo Waxman had done, he didn't deserve to die all alone at the bottom of a gorge. Not when she had within her the power to help.

She sighed with relief when they reached the turnoff to the spa site.

"Wait," Peggy said, clutching at Clare's arm. "Let me go get the phone. And maybe get a couple bottles of cold water from the office fridge?" She smiled weakly. "You go ahead and do what you have to with the helicopter. I'll join you there. It'll be quicker."

"You're right," Clare said. "Are you sure you'll be okay on your own?"

Peggy smiled, more forcefully this time. "I've made it this far, haven't. I?"

Clare threw her arms around the older woman and hugged her quickly. "You sure have. I'll see you in a few minutes." She jog-trotted the rest of the way to the helipad, arriving there slick with sweat and breathless.

The Bell was right where she had left it last, center stage on its tarmac square. She tried the door. Unlocked. Key still in the ignition. "Thank you, Lord," she said. She flicked the key switch on, grabbed the fuel pipette, which the previous pilot had left wedged in the off-side seat, and hopped out to check the fuel.

It wasn't full up, but there would be more than enough to get her safely to Glens Falls, or even Albany, if necessary. She drew down some fuel into the pipette and held it up to the colorless sky, looking for water or sediment that could spell a serious problem. It looked clean.

She climbed back into the cockpit and checked the buss and batt switches. She tapped the control panel. She knew she should test all the lights, since this was a new ship for her, but it wasn't absolutely necessary, and right now, time was of the essence. Reflexively, she did verify that the fire extinguisher behind the pilot's seat was full before clambering outside again to untie the Bell and do the exterior preflight check.

She had finished the right-side fuselage check, had untied the main rotor blade, and was closing up the tail rotor gearbox when she heard sounds coming from the track.

"Hey! Clare!" Russ emerged from the woods, closely followed by Peggy, who was carrying a large sailcloth L. L. Bean bag. Clare ducked under the tail boom to talk to them. Russ's shirt was clinging to his chest in damp patches and his hair was plastered to his scalp. Peggy reached into the bulging bag and handed him a bottle of water dripping with condensation. He unscrewed the top and dumped half the contents over his head, shaking his shaggy hair like a dog.

"Is he still alive?" Clare asked. Peggy pulled an identical bottle out of the bag and handed it to her.

Russ swigged most of the rest of his water and wiped his mouth with the back of his hand. "Yes. He didn't answer me when I called to him, but he shifted a bit. He's about twenty, twenty-five feet down. Ms. Landry says you have some cockamamy idea about using the helicopter to get him out?"

Clare swallowed a mouthful of the almost painfully cold water and turned back to the ship. "It's not a cockamamy idea." She moved to the left side of the fuselage to check the engine compartment and the transmission.

"The hell it's not. It's not that I doubt you can fly this monster, but how do you think you're going to rescue him?"

She looked up from the hydraulic servos. "I'm not going to do it alone. You're going to help me."

He held up his hands. "Whoa."

"The chopper is fitted out for cargo. I fly over to where Waxman is and hover. You get in the net, I lower you to the bottom of the crevasse, you get Waxman, and I pull you both up."

His face was set in a mask of denial. "That's insane."

"No it's not. I admit that I wouldn't want to try it on a gusty day, but it's perfectly calm. The winch can be controlled right from the cockpit. I can do it all without getting out of my seat." She secured the transmission cowling and climbed up to the top of the fuselage to check the hydraulic reservoir.

"What if something happens? What if you have a choice between leaving the cockpit and . . . and me falling?"

She looked up from where she was examining the main rotor system. He sounded almost panicky. "It has a four-axis autopilot, Russ. If you need me, I'll be there." She gestured toward the locked shed at the edge of the clearing. "I didn't see any headsets in the cabin, so I suspect they're in there. We'll have to break in, I'm afraid. But with those on, we'll be able to communicate with each other the whole time." She swung herself down and crouched under the ship's belly to check the landing gear.

Russ crouched down across from her. "I can't do this."

"Sure, you can."

"No. You don't understand. *I can't do this.*" He spoke each word slowly and distinctly.

The import of his words finally sank in. "Are you afraid? To fly?"

His jaw worked. "Helicopters," he said.

"You're afraid to fly in helicopters. You were in the army, for heaven's sake. You must have used helicopter transport before." She stood up on tiptoe to check the windscreens. He stood up as well, leaning across the Bell's pointed nose.

"I had a bad experience." His voice was barely louder than a rumble. He obviously didn't want Peggy to hear anything. "A very bad experience."

She slapped the windscreen. "Get over it."

"What?"

She backed away from the ship and strolled slowly around it, giving it a last once-over with her eyes, half her attention on looking for anything out of place, the other half on getting Russ to fall in with her plan. It wasn't the first time she had had to deal with a panicky crew member. "What happened? You took incoming fire? Lightning fried your electrical system?" She looked up at him. "It's not going to happen here and now. Here and now, a man may very well die if we don't get him up out of that gorge. So get over it."

He stopped dead. "I can't believe you. This isn't some sort of whim I just made up. This is real. You think I go around confessing to anyone how I feel? What kind of priest are you anyway?"

She swung around to face him. "I don't know, Russ. I guess I'm the kind who flies helicopters and speaks without thinking and screws up on a regular basis." She wiped her oily hands on her shorts, instantly converting them from good to trash. "But I'll tell you one thing," she said, stepping into his space, crowding him, hissing her words. "I'm not the sort who would let a man die because she's too chickenshit to climb into a machine!" She pointed to the shed, never breaking eye contact with him. "Now break into that shed and get me those headsets!"

He stepped back. She saw his Adam's apple bob up and down. He stared at her. "Ma'am," he said. "Yes, ma'am."

She marched behind him to the shed. Although the door was chained and padlocked, the shed itself was a flimsy affair, the sort you could buy prefab at a home and garden center. Russ circled the shed, ran his fingers assessingly over the chain, then headed straight for one of the two Plexiglas windows set into the side walls. He pushed against it and felt around the edges. "You care if this looks pretty or not?" he said.

"No."

"Okay. C'mere." He pulled her to him, turned her around, and wrapped his arms around her waist. "You're going to be the battering ram. Keep your feet about as wide apart as the window."

She didn't have a chance to respond, because with a grunt, he hoisted her off the ground, squeezing the breath out of her. She drew her legs up and braced her feet. He staggered back a few steps and then lumbered forward. Her sneakers struck the window with a jolt that made her legs buzz up to her knees, and the entire window, Plexiglas and frame, flew into the shed, crashing and clattering as it fell into a rack of shelves.

He set her on the sill and she slipped through into the oven-hot interior. It was pretty much what she had expected, shelving filled with tools, several small barrels of transmission and hydraulic fluid, rags in a plastic grocery bag. There was a metal cabinet set next to where the window had been, and she pried it open. Bingo: four headsets hanging on a dowel. She took two and passed them out to Russ, then turned to case out the shed more carefully, looking for something that might be helpful. The shelving was too heavy, the clipboards way too small; then she spotted two grimy lawn chairs, folded and tossed into the corner. They would do nicely. She grabbed them and stuffed them through the window.

"What are these for?" he asked.

"Waxman's going to need some sort of restraint before we move him," she said. She went back to the shelves, took the bag of rags, and thrust it out, as well. "You can stomp on the chairs to flatten them and tie him down to the webbing with these."

"The gunk on these rags will kill him, if the lift doesn't."

She glared through the window. "I'm open to suggestions, if you have a better idea." He lifted his hands and backed away. She turned back to the shed's interior. Now, all she needed to find was . . . Frowning, she went through the rest of the cabinet.

"No charts," she said half to herself.

"What?"

She pulled a paper towel from a roll in the cabinet and wiped the sweat off her face. "No charts. I didn't see any in the cockpit, and I was hoping they would be stored here. Opperman must have taken them with him."

"Is this something you need to fly?"

She almost said yes, then remembered to whom she was talking. "I just needed them for the radio frequencies. But it doesn't really matter. Whoever flew the ship the last time would have tuned the radio to the right approach control. Probably Albany. Maybe Boston. It'll be there." She upended a pail in front of the window space. "Help me out."

She levered herself over the edge, the shed wall shaking hard beneath her weight, and Russ grabbed her under her arms and dragged her out. She shook herself. "I wouldn't have believed it, but it actually feels cooler out here after that."

"You sure you don't need those charts?"

She looked up at him. "I'm sure."

"Did you turn on the radio to make sure?"

"We're in the mountains, Russ. I'm going to have to be at a couple thousand feet before I can get any signal." He looked pale again. She laid her hand on his arm. "Do you trust me?"

He nodded.

"Then you let me worry about the piloting. You're the dumb grunt, remember?"

He laughed, an explosive choked sound that was very close to the edge, but not going over. She scooped up the bag of oily rags, satisfied. "Let's get those helmets and go."

Peggy was backing out of the passenger-side cockpit door. "I put another two water bottles in," she said. "I thought you might need them."

"Thanks, Peggy." Clare kept her eyes on Russ as he tossed the lawn chairs through the cargo doorway and then clipped his headset over his ears. He adjusted the mike into the proper position. He may not have liked choppers, but he had certainly done this before.

"I didn't have a chance to tell you because"—Peggy tilted her head toward Russ, indicating his attempts to keep his problem under wraps hadn't been entirely successful—"but I phoned the Glens Falls Hospital while I was down in the office and told them what you were attempting. The triage nurse I spoke with said you should take him straight to Albany Medical Center."

Clare bit her lower lip. "Without stopping for any medical personnel first?"

"That's what she said."

Clare gestured at the sailcloth bag, which was drooping on the ground near the tail boom. "You didn't bring your phone with you, did you?"

Peggy spread her hands. "I forgot. I'm sorry. I don't know what's wrong with me. I'm having a hard time stringing two thoughts together."

"That's natural. Look, are you going to be okay to drive yourself?"

"I think I will be. I know the route so well from here that it's like the old gray mare returning to the barn."

"Okay. We'll let you know what's happening as soon as we get into Albany." Clare stuffed the bag of rags under her arm and placed the headset on her head, tilting the mike into position. "Better get back to the edge of the tarmac. Don't approach the ship once I've got the rotors going."

Peggy nodded, scooped up her bag, and retreated to the trailhead. Clare switched on the set-to-set transmitter. "Russ?" she said. He didn't respond. She glanced over to where he stood staring into the cargo area. She walked over, tapped him on one of the headphones, and switched him on. "Can you hear me?" she asked quietly.

"Yeah," he said.

She pointed up to the cargo boom jutting out over the open door. "That's what the net hangs from, obviously." She tossed the rags inside, jumped up into the cargo area, and found the manual control. She unlocked it and cranked the handle, letting the wide web strap clipped to the net spool through the boom until several feet of it lay on the tarmac at Russ's feet. She secured the control and squatted at the edge of the door. "Can you wrestle that in here?" she asked. He gathered up the pile of netting and tossed it through the doorway as Clare scrambled to get out of the way. She dragged the net toward the opposite side of the ship, pulled back the edges, and slid the folded lawn chairs and the plastic rag bag inside. She looked around for something to secure the stuff during the flight. Hanging from a grommet in the bright orange safety web were half a dozen short bungee cords.

"Perfect," she said, hooking the end of one through the D ring connecting the net to the boom strap. She hooked the other end through another grommet. It wasn't very shipshape, but the bungee cord held the boom strap off the floor and away from the cargo door, so that even if she should have to angle hard during the flight, the net wouldn't be able to slip though the door and out of Russ's reach.

She squatted at the edge of the door again. "Hop on up here," she said.

Russ backed against the door and levered himself up until he was sitting beside her. In the small cargo area, his head almost touched the roof. "Okay, I've secured the net back here," she said, thumbing toward the pile on the floor. "This is what we're going to do. When we reach Waxman, I'll hover overhead. You take off the bungee strap, drag the net over to the doorway, and get inside."

"Right." His tone was so flat, she couldn't tell if he was being sarcastic or was just scared.

"Once you're in the net, I'll use the cockpit control to pull the boom strap up tight. That'll swing you out the door. Then I'll lower the netting nice and easy until you're on the ground."

"Nice and easy."

She ducked her head. "You may take a couple of bumps when you reach the ground. I'll do everything I can to set you down smoothly."

He bent over and put his head between his knees. "Oh, God," he said. She thought it might be as authentic a prayer as she had ever heard.

"If anything happens, if you need me, I'll be right behind you. Look." She pointed to where one of the passenger seats rested against the partial bulkhead. "You'll sit there. You can see the pilot's seat right behind it. I can be up and over in a few seconds."

"I have to tell you that's not a big comfort right now."

"You ready?"

He nodded. He looked like a man going to his own execution, but he gave her a thumbs-up.

"Then let's fly."

CHAPTER TWENTY-EIGHT

Of course, it wasn't as simple as that. Russ had been there before. Pilots could never just get you on board and go. They had to stretch it out, playing with switches and revving up the engine until it sounded like it was going to explode, and all the time poor jackasses like him had to sit in a puddle of sweat and misery. His skin was itching and creeping, until he wanted to scratch it off, tear off the headphones that made his skull feel like a china cup in a vise, jump out of the chopper, and run far enough away that he would no longer hear the *thwap-thwap-thwap* noise that was the sound track to all his nightmares.

He was strapped into the left-side passenger seat, hands on knees, eyes forward. He fixed his field of vision on the hunter's orange of the safety web hanging between him and the cargo area. He tried not to look out the open cargo door, or out the window to his right, although that was damn hard, because the thing was as big as a minivan's windshield. He tried not to listen to the whine of the engine and the beat of the rotors, which, although muffled by his headphones, penetrated straight into the back of his neck.

Instead, he listened to the sounds of Clare getting ready for takeoff. She had the same habit as one of the helo jocks he had flown with in 'Nam. She was singing under her breath as she worked her controls.

"I don't know why I love you like I do, all the things you put me through," his headset sang. Jesus Christ, he thought, I think that's the same song. What do they do, give them a sound track in flight school?

"Take me to the river," his headset sang. "Drop me in the water." Over his head, the rotors powered up into a dull roar. Under his feet, the skids shifted. He braced his elbows on his knees and shut his eyes. Clare was making *ch-ch-ch* sounds between her teeth, accompanying her mental music.

"Here we go," she sang out. The floor lurched beneath him and then they rose slowly, slowly into the sky. Beyond the open cargo doors, the world sank out of view. He thought if he looked at the seat to his left, he would see his buddy Mac, his transistor radio blasting between his boots, his hands slapping out the rhythm of the song.

"I-I-I want to know, can you tell me?" his headphones sang.

Mac would have liked Clare. Except she was sixteen years older than he would ever get. And he, Russ, would look like an old man to Mac. How had he gotten to be so old when he still felt the same inside?

"I need your help here." Clare's voice cut through his reverie. "I don't know where the gorge is. I'm having a hard time sighting the road through all these trees."

He opened his eyes and looked out the window in the cabin door. Forget the minivan. This was a frickin' picture window. He shifted sideways in his seat and pressed his hands against the solid metal edges of the door to hold back the sensation of falling. "Um," he said, taking a deep breath. They were creeping along a dozen yards above the trees. "That's it, down there. The road. Keep heading in that direction and you'll be over the gorge." If he turned his head, he could look at the back of Clare's.

"There?" she asked, twisting and pointing at the window in the cockpit door.

"Shouldn't you keep your eyes on the instruments?"

"The army gives us special training on how to look out the window and fly at the same time."

He could tell she was having a good old time. He leaned forward and closed his eyes again. The rotors whined and the chopper tilted forward slightly as she brought it around and headed toward the crevasse.

"Okay, I've got it in sight," she said. "Russ—where are you?"

He sat up again. He could see the curve of her jaw beneath her helmet as she twisted back, craning to see him.

"Are you feeling airsick?" She sounded doubtful. As she should be, since the drive up the mountain road to the spa site had bounced him around a lot more than anything she had done.

"No."

"Okay. Can you unbuckle and shift seats? I want you to look out the other cabin window. It makes for a better search if you cover both sides."

"Okay." He didn't have the wherewithal to answer in anything more than single-word sentences. He unclipped and shifted to the ghostly Mac's seat. The geologist's description of the gorge knifing down the mountains was more clearly accurate from this height. The crevasse looked a lot narrower than it had when he'd peered over the edge. He thought of descending into that crack in the rock, wrapped in nothing but cargo netting. It'd be a miracle if he didn't end up a smear on the rock wall.

"See anything?"

"No."

"Are you doing okay?"

"Yes."

"I'm going to drop her down a bit." The chopper sank in a series of jerks, like an elevator on the fritz. He pressed his lips tightly together and braced his hands for another look out the window. Green leaves, everywhere green pulsing in the hazy sunlight, with a gray slash through the jungle, a scar in the earth.

Jesus, he thought. Get a grip. He forced himself to focus on the crevasse, picking out boulders and scrubby plants, the tobacco brown trickle that was all that remained of the brook at summer's height, the flash of metal—

"Wait! I think I see something."

The chopper stopped its forward motion and hovered, twisting slightly back and forth. He saw it again, a glint of metal on a lumpy bundle rolled against a small boulder. A backpack? He hadn't noticed one when he'd surveyed the accident scene the first time. "Can you go a little lower?"

Clare dropped the chopper another few yards. He let his eyes spiral out from the backpack, searching, searching. . . . He spotted the geologist's hiking boots first.

"I've got him."

"Where?"

"See where there's a clump of birch saplings growing low on the wall?"

"Yeah, okay."

"That's ten o'clock. Look at two o'clock."

There was a pause as she searched over the floor of the ravine. "Okay, I see him, too. I'm going to maneuver us so that the cargo door is above him. Good Lord, he's still. Are you sure he's not dead?"

"If he is, and I go through all this for nothing, I'm going to be seriously pissed off."

There was a sound in his headset that might have been a stifled laugh. The chopper dipped and swayed into position.

"Okay, you're on."

He rose from his seat and, crouching, crossed back to the left side of the chopper and pushed the webbing out of the way. The thing he noticed—and he wished he had noticed it when Clare was going through how all this was going to work—was that there was nothing beside the safety webbing and the bungee cord to hold on to while he got himself inside the net. And he was going to have to unclip the bungee cord anyway.

"Clare," he said.

"Yeah."

"There's nothing to hold on to."

"What do you mean?"

"Getting into the net. There's nothing I can hold on to."

"We went over this. You hold on to the edges of the net while you step inside."

"It's in front of an open door!"

There was a pause. Then she said in the patient voice of a kindergarten teacher explaining something to a new student, "I'm holding the ship dead even. There's nothing to cause you to lose your balance and fall."

"What if I trip?" He realized how whiny he sounded, but he couldn't help it.

"Russ." The teacher was gone; the officer was back. "Get into the net."

He took a deep breath. With his fingers clutching the safety webbing, he took the D ring in a death grip. Then he let go of the webbing and jerked the bungee cord out. It sprang back against the bulkhead with a metallic clang. He looked along the wide strap running from the ring in his fist, out the door, and up out of sight to the boom. One twitch of the helicopter and he would be dangling sixty feet above the gorge's rocky bottom. His palm was so sweaty, the D ring was already slipping in his grasp. He pawed the edges of the net open and tumbled inside with a tailbone-bruising jolt.

"I'm in," he said. The relief of it made him laugh.

"Are you okay?"

"Yeah. I just can't believe I'm doing this. It reminds me of the time I tried to trim one of the old trees in our yard with a chain saw."

"That sounds pretty normal to me."

"I was twenty feet up on a limb at the time. Without a safety harness."

"What happened?"

"I fell." He laughed again, this time with the realization that he now had to scoot over to the door so she could reel in the net and lift him out.

He tugged the folded lawn chairs half over his knees and kicked against the floor, pushing with his thighs. He and the netting skidded a foot. "It was just two years ago, and I remember thinking that at my age, it was the last really stupid thing I'd ever do. I'm glad to see that I still have it in me."

He kicked again and moved along another foot. The lawn chairs bumped into his head. The cargo door yawned open behind him like the gateway to the next world. His back was to it, deliberately, so he wouldn't have to see the tops of the trees shaking madly in the chopper's wash below. He kicked a third time, but his butt jammed up against a line of smooth-headed rivets sunk into the cargo floor. He shifted his weight and tried again. Nothing.

"What are you doing back there?"

"I'm just getting myself closer to the door. I'm hung up on some rivets."

"Don't bother," she said as he wiggled himself over the obstacle. Then just as she said, "I'm going to pull in the strap from there," he kicked out hard with his legs. There was a rush and a grinding sound and a scrape as his rear end went over the edge, and then he was falling and yelling until he came up hard with a jerk and a snap.

The lawn chairs slammed flat against his face as the cording of the net tightened around him, cutting into his skin. The helicopter tilted hard. He swung wide, away from and then toward the landing gear. Clare was snarling something into the earphones, but he couldn't make any sense of it. The jolt as the strap caught had cut him off mid-yell, and the spasms in his lungs and ribs made him cough violently. The downwash from the rotors made his eyes water. He fought to clear his face of green webbing and aluminum, shoving and twisting until the chairs were at his side instead of pressing against his nose and chest. The net swung in ever-decreasing arcs as the helicopter circled tightly, slowly tipping back into a stable position.

"I didn't ask you to jump out the door!" He heard that one. "Okay, I'm leveled out. I'm going to lower you now. For God's sake, don't try any more stunts."

"No," he wheezed.

There was a vibration along the strap. The net quivered and then began to descend. He glanced up, but the blur of rotors and the fat tadpole-shaped body of the chopper made him queasy, so he looked down instead. The bottom of the crevasse was rushing up at him, its boulders and shale suddenly a lot larger and more alarming than they had been from the air. He was between the trees, then below the lip of the gorge, then descending

between its narrow walls, every striation in the rock and every plant clinging to a minute cleft burning itself into his vision with a kind of hyper-
clarity. The part of his brain that wasn't numbed over marveled at Clare's
precision. He went down, down, down—and stopped with a jerk.

"Where are you?"

He squeezed his eyes shut, forcing his mind back into its normal channels. Opening them again, he peered at the ground, estimating his distance. "You done good," he said. "I'm maybe five feet above the stream."

"Okay. Get ready. Here we go."

The net jerked, jerked, jerked down, and then his butt was in the cold
water, sliding over slick round rocks. "I'm down, I'm down," he said.

"Okay, I'm letting it go," she said. The net collapsed all around him as
several yards of the wide strap ribboned over itself. He flailed out of the
wet netting and sloshed the two steps to dry ground. He reflexively patted
himself down to make sure everything was there and wiggled the bows of
his glasses where they were clamped to the side of his head by his headset.
He was intact. He glanced up and waved his arms. "I see you," she said.
"You're a couple yards downstream from Waxman. Can you see him?"

He picked his way upstream over loose stones. He could clearly see
Waxman's backpack resting against the cutaway curve where the sides of
the crevasse met the bottom. Then he spotted Waxman. He was sprawled
awkwardly near the stream, half-hidden by a boulder.

"I've got him." Russ crouched next to the unmoving form and placed
two fingers at the side of his neck. "He's got a pulse." He ran his hands
lightly over Waxman's body and head. "I'm pretty sure both his arms are
broken. His legs may be okay. God only knows about his spine." He looked
up to the chopper as if he could see Clare's face. "Even with the stuff we
brought, we're taking a risk by moving him."

"I could fly us to Glens Falls and alert the life-flight helicopter. That'll
tack on another hour and a half, two hours before he gets any treatment.
You're the man on the ground, Russ. Literally. It's your call."

He looked back down at Waxman. His face was pale despite his tan,
and a swollen purple bruise spread across his forehead and disappeared
into his hair. Russ pried open one eyelid, but Waxman remained unconscious, his pupil fixed and unresponsive.

"I don't think he's got that kind of time," he said finally. "Let me get
the stuff and I'll bind him up as tightly as I can." He picked his way back

to the net and hauled out the lawn chairs and bag of rags. Opening one chair, he leaned it against the boulder and jumped on it like a kid engaged in vandalism. The flimsy rivets snapped, and he had a floppy chaise longue. He wrenched off the U-shaped leg pieces and stomped them into relative flatness before jamming them through the webbing in two parallel lines. He held up his impromptu backboard and shook it. It still shifted more than he liked, but it would give Waxman a chance to get out of this without being paralyzed. He laid it on the ground next to the unconscious man and carefully rolled him into place on top of the aluminum poles, praying that he wasn't causing more unseen damage.

The rags needed to be knotted together before he could stretch them across Waxman's chest and tie them to the chair's webbing. Waxman's breathing was shallow and sparse, more like hiccups than actual breaths. Russ pulled his headphones off to listen for the telltale hiss of a punctured lung, but he didn't hear anything. He tied Waxman's shoulder, chest, and waist to the supports and stood up to tackle the other chair.

This one he smashed against the boulder until it broke apart into pieces. He took the aluminum poles, splinted them against Waxman's arms, and tied them in place with the remainder of the rags. Then he tore the plastic grocery bag in two and used it to tie Waxman's immobilized arms to the jury-rigged backboard. He stood up and surveyed his handiwork, wiping the sweat from his eyes. Waxman looked like a victim of backyard bondage gone awry. *If we don't kill this guy trying to save him, it'll be a miracle,* he thought.

"Okay, I'm going to load him in," Russ said. He picked up the top edges of the lawn chair contraption and dragged the injured man travois-style to the net. He unfolded the edges of the net and pulled it out of the water before wrestling Waxman into place at the center. He stood up, looked around the area one more time, then hefted the abandoned backpack onto his shoulder and rolled it into the net, next to its owner.

Russ stepped into the net, sat down tailor-style facing Waxman, and tugged the backboard onto his lap. It was awkward, but he figured he could give some added support with his crossed legs. "Clare," he said, "we're good to go."

"Great. Here we go." The boom strap began to rise out of its loose folds like a film running backward. He had thought he was prepared, but the jolt when the strap caught and yanked the netting off the ground still knocked the breath out of him. He threw his arms across Waxman's chest. The man's legs were forced upright by the press of the net until his knees fell forward and he spraddled like a roadkill frog. The backpack wedged itself against Russ's shins, its metal buckles biting into his jeans. The net spun so that he had to close his eyes against the stomach-churning whirl of the horizon.

Clare was hauling him in a lot faster than she had thrown him out. The net spun up and up, then stopped with a jerk that vibrated into his bones. He opened his eyes and looked up. The sausage-shaped boom was over-head, maybe three feet away, and above it, the blur of the rotors, their hard chop pulsing through his ears and into his brain. The cargo area gaped open a couple of feet away from where he and Waxman hung. He suddenly re-alized that Clare had never discussed this part of the plan.

"Clare!"

"Don't yell. I can hear you fine."

"How am I supposed to get back in?"

"You're not."

The chopper rose from where it had been hovering and ascended slowly, crossing the lip of the crevasse and leaving it behind.

"You can't just leave me hanging here!"

The voice over his headphones was soothing. "I'm heading back to the helipad. We'll be there in a minute. Then we can get you out of the net and get Waxman settled into the cargo area."

He closed his eyes and began counting to sixty out loud. He had reached thirty-one when her amused voice said, "Are you looking?"

"Are you kidding?"

"Go ahead. Open your eyes."

He did, and then shut them again with relief when he saw the helipad rising up to meet them. The *thwap-thwap-thwap* of the rotors reverberated from all around and the downwash threw a whirl of grit and dust into the air. Then there was a gentle rocking and they were down. A few seconds later, Clare appeared in the cargo doorway.

"Climbed over the seat," she said. "I don't like to leave the ship while the engine is on." She leaned to one side of the doorway, and the strap holding him and his load off the tarmac rolled out of the boom again, dropping him to the ground. He threw the netting off his shoulders and rose in a crouch, intently aware of the rotors still chopping overhead.

"How come it's still going?" he yelled.

She winced, poking at her headphones. He snapped his mike off and she did the same. "I want us back in the air ASAP. Tilt him up this way and I'll grab one end."

He wrapped his hands around the aluminum struts protruding above Waxman's shoulders and gave a heave. Clare knelt at the edge of the door and grabbed, pulling up and back. He worked his arms under Waxman's legs and together they slid the unconscious man into the cargo area. Russ tossed the backpack in beside Waxman.

"Are you coming or going?" she yelled.

He opened his hands, indicating he didn't understand the question.

"Are you flying with us to Albany? I'd like the help, but I'm not going to make you."

He stopped, his hand on the edge of the cargo door. He hadn't thought about just heading back to his truck and driving away. He could do that. It wasn't as if he could do anything more for Waxman than he already had. He could head back to the station, get the paperwork started on this incident, track down Peggy, and get her statement. He looked up at Clare, who was waiting for him to make up his mind. "I'm coming with you," he said and hauled himself up into the cargo area.

She didn't say anything, merely winched the net back up and yanked the cargo door shut, but he could see her smiling to herself. She fiddled with her headset and tapped one of his headphones. He switched his back on. "Help me move him closer over there," she said, gesturing past the safety web. She picked the web up and draped it over her back to keep it out of the way; then, hunched over, they half-dragged, half-lifted Waxman's still form into place within arm's reach of the passenger seats. She nodded, stepped into his seat, and climbed over the partial bulkhead into the oilot's chair. "Strap in and let's get going," she said.

His butt was barely in the seat when the chopper rose. This he remembered, too, the scramble to get off the ground, the wounded on the floor, the trees bending and shaking as the slicks rose out of the grass. Clare was at it again. "Fee-fee-fi-fi-fo-fo-fum, Lookin' mighty nice, now here she comes," his headphones sang. He rested his elbows on his knees and laughed. Mitch Ryder and the Detroit Wheels. All she had to do was throw in some Doors and she'd have the complete sound track to his youth. He looked at Waxman's pale face and was suddenly consumed with the urge for a cigarette, something he had given up in 1985.

Up they went. Up and up, angling slightly to the east as Clare sang

"Devil with a Blue Dress" into the headphones and the rotors thundered to her rhythm. "Wearing her perfume, Chanel Number Five, got to be the—what the heck?"

He sat up again and looked out the window, immediately wishing he hadn't. They were up. Way up. As high as an airplane. The mountaintops stretched out beneath them in rough and rounded shades of dark green and smoky blue. Clare had gone silent. In his experience, it was never good when a pilot went silent.

"What is it?"

She didn't answer him. He craned around. She was leaning over, working a control he couldn't see. "Clare, what is it?"

"The radio," she said. "I can't use it."

"What do you mean?"

"I mean that instead of leaving the last station on, whoever was flying this spun the dial. It's on dead air now. And that's not all." She reached over her head. "Look at this." She had a small black plastic cylinder in her hand. He took it from her. "That's the control knob. It came off in my hand. Take a look."

Inside the cylinder was a small hollow tube, meant to fasten tightly over whatever metal stud actually connected to the radio's workings. The tube was splintered apart, as if someone had jammed a screwdriver or awl into it.

He tried to ignore the sick feeling in his stomach. "What's this mean? Are we in trouble? Do we go back down?"

"It means I can't rely on the local air-control stations to lead me to Albany. I'll have to do it by sight. I'm going to bring her up a little higher so I can get my bearings. The visibility is lousy today because of the humidity."

She sounded very calm and authoritative, which didn't reassure him one bit. Pilots always sounded the most calm when they were in the deepest trouble. The chopper whined, but now the engine had a shrill note that made his back teeth ache.

"What's that? Is the engine supposed to sound like that?"

"It's having to work a little harder, that's all. The humid air means there's not as much lift under the rotors as there would be if it were cool and dry."

"How far up are we going?"

"Four thousand feet."

"Four thousand feet! I thought choppers only went five hundred, a thousand feet high."

She actually laughed. "We're only going to be about two thousand feet above the ground. Where we started from was almost two thousand feet above sea level to begin with. Okay, help me out here. I'm not very familiar with the geography around here. I see two fairly big rivers, a handful of smaller tributaries, a medium-sized lake. I don't know what I'm looking at."

As before, he braced his hands against the metal frame and looked out the window. He tried to pretend he was safely stowed away in a small airplane, but the laborious *chop-chop-chop* of the rotors made it impossible. "Which way are we pointing?"

"North."

"Okay." He took a breath. "The lake must be Lake Luzerne. The river to the west is the Sacandaga. It heads west, to the Great Sacandaga Lake. The river to the east has to be the Hudson."

"Are you sure? It looks kind of small."

"It is small this far north. It broadens out past West Point."

"And Albany is on the Hudson?"

He leaned back into his seat and closed his eyes. "It was the last time I was there."

"Okay. I've got my bearing on the compass. I'm going to take us back down to five hundred feet and head east."

He shoved the useless control knob into his pocket and tried to ignore the queasy sensation their descent was giving him. Clare was still silent. He wished she would start singing again. He looked at Waxman, whose face was damp and pale beneath his trendy goatee, and thought how young he was. And that even at that, the men he had seen dying on helicopter floors had been younger still. Boys. Waxman would have been an old man in 'Nam.

The chopper bumped abruptly, emitting a sound like a leaky cough. He lurched in his seat belt, reaching down to keep the unconscious geologist from sliding. Waxman's backpack rolled across the floor. Clare was talking to herself under her breath, something about airflow.

Waxman's backpack. Which had been lying several feet away from the man. He had been fighting with Peggy before he fell. How had his backpack gotten down there? He unbuckled his seat belt and started toward where the backpack rested against the orange cargo webbing.

That was when he heard the sound, the spluttering, coughing, choking sound that sounded like some great beast dying.

"What is it?" he asked. "Clare?"

"Fuel," she said, her voice tight. "Get into your seat and strap down."

He could feel the question howling behind his clenched teeth: What do you mean? Didn't you check it? He kept it there. Of course she'd checked it. She was snapping off words like items on a list in a subaudible whisper. He heard a brief roar, then another choke.

"Strap yourself in and get into the crash position!"

He dived for his seat and yanked the restraint across himself. The helicopter tilted abruptly, and his inner ear sloshed sickeningly out of balance. Through the windows, he saw nothing but colorless sky, but his stomach and head felt as if they were spinning down in a spiral. Another roar. They jerked up so violently, Waxman lifted off the floor a few inches at the apogee, then slammed back down. The machine seemed to wheeze. "Come on, come on," Clare was urging.

"Clare? How bad is this?"

"Bad." Her voice was short, clipped, professional. "Something's keeping the gas from getting to the engine." She hissed, then resumed speaking in the same matter-of-fact way. "I'm going to do something called an autorotation. I'm going to plunge the ship nose down while cutting power to the rotors. They'll spin on their own, giving us lift and slowing our descent. It'll be a controlled crash."

Thirty years on, and he was still going to die in a helicopter crash. Linda, his mom, and his sister flashed through his mind, but it was Mac he fixed on, Mac laughing and smoking and drumming out a rhythm on a helmet with his hands. God, he thought, just kill me quick. Don't hang me up and make me linger.

"Here we go," Clare said.

The floor under his feet tilted farther and farther. Waxman, still strapped tightly to his makeshift frame, slid toward the seats, ramming into Russ's feet. His backpack rolled and bounced against Russ's legs. The safety webbing flapped and the bungee cords clattered wildly against the window. They were balanced on the chopper's nose when the sound cut off just like that. The sudden silence was like the sound of the grave. Then he could hear his heart beating. He could hear the rotors overhead whistling and whirring. He could hear Clare praying. They were going down so fast, his body strained against the belt strapping him in.

He heard Clare saying, "Hold on hold onholdon . . ."

Then they hit.

CHAPTER TWENTY-NINE

Metal screamed. There was an impossibly loud noise as the rotors chopped into wood and dirt and stone and broke off. One knife-edged blade sliced through the tail boom, the machine eviscerating itself in its death throes. Another blade shattered into shrapnel, peppering the fuselage with a hailstorm of metallic fire. One heaved away into the dirt, still trying to do its job, and lifted and turned the body of the helicopter so that it rolled downhill once, twice, landing gear snapping off like fragile bird bones, pieces of steel sheeting peeling off like an orange rind.

A last shudder and creak. Clare, dangling from her harness, opened her eyes to find she was surprisingly still alive. Her first thought was Thank you, God. Her second was that more people die from explosion than impact when helicopters go down.

"Russ?"

There was a groan behind her. She let out the breath she hadn't realized she was holding. "We need to get out and away from the ship. Can you move?"

There was another groan.

"Russ!"

"Yeah," he said. "I think I'm going to need some help."

She braced her feet on the twisted pieces of metal, glass, and plastic that had been the front of the cockpit and unclipped her safety belt. She sagged, lost her balance, and fell heavily against the passenger-side door, which was buckled and stained with green and brown from the forest floor. She twisted around and looked over the partial bulkhead.

"Holy God in heaven," she said. The force of the impact had driven the tail boom into the cabin as they'd somersaulted downhill. The cargo area had imploded around the boom, the metal bunched like wet papier-mâché. The sawed-off end had come to rest less than a hand's width away from where Russ was hanging in his seat; it looked like a steel-mouthed shark waiting to slice into his chest.

"Okay," she said, hoping her voice didn't betray her terror. "Stay put."

"Don't worry," he said, then coughed.

"Can you see Waxman?"

"Yeah. He's on the floor underneath me. Well, now it's the floor. It used to be a big window."

"How's he look?"

"Not great."

She pressed up against the door on the pilot's side and pushed hard. It popped open like a hatch and just kept going, banging and clanging its way off the nose. She looked at the edge as she levered herself carefully through. The hinges had come clean off. She perched on the door frame and took her bearings. They had come to rest on a forested slope, wedged against several thick maples. The ship was resting on its right side, its nose angled forward. They had scraped a raw gash in the hillside when they'd landed, and the remains of what looked like several young pines were ground into the freshly exposed dirt.

She shivered in the muggy air. She felt cold, lightheaded, and so over-whelmed that she just wanted to lie down and wait for someone to take this disaster off her hands. But there wasn't anyone else. She pressed one spread-fingered hand over her eyes and breathed deeply. "God," she said, "hold me up. I can't do this on my own."

"Are you praying up there?" Russ's voice came up through the open doorway.

She got her feet under her and leaned over toward the cabin door. Its handle was battered and bent out of line. "Yes, I am," she said.

"Lemme tell you: Admitting you can't do something isn't very reassur-ing."

She gripped the handle and twisted. "Didn't say that," she said, yank-ing and tugging. "Said I can't do it by myself. Ooof!" Something inside the handle mechanism gave way and the door shot back several feet before jamming.

"Good girl."

She braced herself on hands and knees and examined the situation. The sheared-off tail section looked even worse from this angle. "Can you hold on to the edge of the door?"

He turned his head awkwardly. "I think so." He reached toward her and she took his hand, placing it near the upper edge of the frame, where he could stabilize himself.

"Great. This is what I want you to do. You're going to push against the roof with your other hand and against the floor with your feet. I'm going to unbuckle your seat belt. At that point, I'll pull this arm"—she touched the hand squeezing the door frame—"and you right yourself."

"I can't stand up. I'll be stepping on Waxman."

"See the seat below you? Put your feet on its side. Once you're upright, we'll see if we can slide you around this thing and pull you out. Ready?"

"Wait a minute!" She paused. He didn't say anything. Finally, he pushed his glasses to the bridge of his nose with his free hand and said, "Let's do it."

She watched as he stretched out as best he could and lodged himself between the ceiling and floor. She snaked her hand around the corner of his seat and found the buckle of the seat belt by touch. With a click, she freed him.

His knuckles went white. He lifted one leg and let it dangle down toward the second passenger seat. She couldn't see if his foot had connected with it yet, but she could see his arms and his other leg trembling with the effort of keeping himself from falling onto the ragged steel edge of the broken tail.

"Got it," he said.

"Careful."

"Oh yeah."

She moved so that she was straddling the frame of the cabin door, one sneakered foot on either side. She squatted deeply so that she could hold him with the strength of her thighs. "Give me your hand. I'll keep you upright."

He laughed hoarsely.

"Shut up and give me your hand," she said, irrationally cheered that he could still see a double entendre in what she said. He let go of the door frame and she caught him around the wrist, pulling slowly and steadily upward. She heard a smack as his other foot landed on the seat, and then his head and shoulders moved, coming upright, rotating in line.

"I feel," he said, almost whispering, "like a chicken on a rotisserie." Then his other arm was free, thrusting through the doorway, his hand feeling for something to hold on to.

"Are you all set?" she said.

"Yeah. I'm on my feet. You can let me go."

She released his wrist. The top of his head was level with the doorway, and the raw end of the tail section was now in front of his stomach. He thrust both arms out and banged his hands against the fuselage. Then he curled them over the edge behind his head. "If this thing wasn't in my way, I could probably get myself up with a backward flip," he said. "I have pretty good upper-body strength."

"If that thing wasn't in your way, you could get out a lot easier than that," she said. "As it is, you aren't going to be able to lever yourself up. I want you to lock your hands around my neck; then I'll pull you up."

"What, deadlifting? Forget it, darlin'. I must outweigh you by sixty or seventy pounds."

"I'll get you up, Russ." A thread of fear that he might be right made her voice sharp. "Trust me."

"I trusted you before I got into the damned chopper, and look where it got me." He squinted up at her and attempted a smile, which made his glasses slip farther down his nose. "Damn. Fix that, will you?" She set his glasses more firmly on his nose while swallowing back the softball-sized lump in her throat.

When she could speak without her voice cracking, she said, "I told you no incoming fire and no lightning. If you wanted no mechanical failures, you should have specified." She bent her head very close to his. "Put your arms around my neck."

To her surprise, he didn't argue further, just released one hand at a time and clasped them together behind her neck. She reached behind her head and flipped her braid out of the way. "Hold on."

"I will."

She settled her feet more firmly, took two fistfuls of his shirt, and straightened very slowly. Good Lord, he was heavy. She gritted her teeth and hissed out air as her thighs shook with the effort of bringing him out. She could feel him flexing his lower body to avoid the tail boom, but she couldn't see anything except the top of his head and his shirt, which was peeling off his torso. Damn! She jammed her hands under the shirt, below his armpits, and dug into his clammy flesh, pressing until she could feel the bones beneath his skin. Sweat was dripping into her eyes and tickling her chest. She grunted, lifting with her arms and legs now, her muscles trembling with the strain and the fear that he was right, that she wouldn't be able to lift him after all. Her legs, biceps, and shoulders were burning, and she was afraid she was going to let go, going to lose him.

Just then, he said, "I'm over the edge! Push me back a few inches."

She did as instructed, and suddenly he let go of her neck. The cessation of weight and pressure made her stumble forward, and he caught her around the waist. "Steady. Easy," he said. He was sitting on the edge of the door frame. He eased her away from the yawning cabin door, and she slid down the chopper's half-exposed belly. When her feet hit the dirt, her legs almost collapsed beneath her.

There was a moment of silence, broken only by their labored breathing; then he said, "Thanks."

She waved his gratitude away. She bent over and rubbed her lower back. Tomorrow, it would feel like she'd had her kidneys removed. She straightened. "We need to get Waxman out."

"Clare, he may be dead already."

"If he is, I want to know it. And if he isn't, we have to do what we can to get him out."

He sniffed in an exaggerated fashion. "Do you smell that? That's fuel. We need to get away from here as quickly . . ." His voice faded away under her steady gaze. "We should at least consider that we might help him more by hurrying to get help than by trying to hoist him out of there."

"And if something sparks and the fuel explodes?" She didn't bother to put much heat into her argument, because she had already won. She knew Russ, and there was no way he would leave a man to burn to death, even if it was a remote possibility. She clambered up to the doorway and peered inside again. "I think I can slide in here"—she pointed to the outside edge of the door—"and slip around the side of the tail boom. I'll go underneath it and have a look at him."

"Then what?"

She examined the boom. Except for the serrated edge that had been facing Russ, it looked relatively safe. The problem was its size. For a relatively slim woman, it wasn't much of a bar getting in and out: she could, as she'd said, slide around it. For a man strapped to a stabilizing board, it posed a significant challenge. She looked up at Russ. "Then I pray for inspiration to strike. Help me down?"

He grunted, but he took the same position she had just quit, feet braced on either side of the doorway, straddling the opening. She sat with her legs dangling into the cabin, her feet lightly brushing against the side of the tail boom. He reached toward her and they grasped each other's wrists. She edged off the door frame and let him take her weight, concentrating on getting around the boom with a minimal amount of bumping and banging. She didn't know how stable it was, and she could easily imagine it tipping and crashing onto Waxman's unmoving body, its razor-sharp edge piercing his flesh.

She was cheek-to-cheek with the tail boom when her foot connected with the solid angle between the floor and the bulkhead. "Okay, let me go," she said.

Russ released her wrists. She let herself fall backward, bumping hard against the floor but keeping her footing. She ducked beneath the boom and got her first look at Waxman.

He was lying facedown across the other cabin window, looking as if he had been placed over a hermetically sealed square of soil. Russ's home-made backboard and arm splints were still in place, and it was the aluminum supports she grabbed when she rolled him over onto his back. She winced. In addition to sporting the purple welt from his initial fall, his forehead was deeply gashed and bleeding freely. In some indefinable way, his nose looked off, and she suspected it was broken. She knew immediately that he was still alive, however, because he was whistling with each exhalation, as if someone were capping and uncapping a boiling teakettle.

"He's alive," she said, "but I'm afraid one of his lungs may be punctured."

"He is one hard-to-kill son of a bitch, isn't he? 'Scuse my French."

She crouched over the still form. She had brought the poor man to this place. How was she going to get him out of here? She considered the idea of wrestling him upright and shoving him over the tail boom until Russ could reach him. No, that wouldn't do. Maybe it wouldn't kill him, but the damage she could cause to his broken bones might leave him wishing he had died. The Day-Glo orange of the safety webbing caught her eye. The tail boom, spiking through the cargo area, had evidently sliced the webbing in two, scattering bungee cords in its wake. She wiped the sweat out of her eyes with the palm of her hand. She could use the webbing . . . the cords . . .

"I have an idea," she said.

"Let's hear it."

She edged her way to where the webbing sagged from its cleats and then began unfastening it. "I'm going to wrap him as tightly as I can in this cargo webbing. Then I'm going to lift him on top of the tail boom, back here where it's narrower. I'll push him forward until you and I can lift him through the door."

"What if the tail section falls down?"

"It may jar him, but after what he's already been through, it'll hardly be a bump. As long as neither of us is under it, we'll be fine." She kicked Waxman's backpack away from where it had come to rest near his legs and threw the webbing on the Plexiglas surface beneath him. She bunched half of it along his body, then lifted him onto the web, first by his immobilized shoulders, then his feet, then by kneeling and working her arms under his buttocks to get his midsection in line.

She was collecting all the bungee cords she could see, when she heard a thudding sound from above, as if Russ had abruptly stepped across part of the fuselage. "Get off of there," she yelled. "I don't know how sound that—"

"Holy shit!" His cry made her break off in midsentence. There was a hollow clang and then nothing.

"Russ? Russ?"

No reply. She returned to Waxman's side and knelt, lashing bungee cords through the webbing and onto his makeshift support. "Russ?" she called again. She stood and looked up at the rectangle of daylight visible from inside the cabin. She couldn't hear anything, which was more unnerving than any sound of breaking helicopter parts or unwelcome visitors. "Russ?" She glanced down at Waxman, who was swathed in aluminum spars and ragged orange webbing, looking like a rejected resuscitation dummy from some Coast Guard rescue-training exercise. She would have to leave him and climb out to find out what had happened to Russ.

She half-dragged, half-lifted Waxman to the rear of what was left of the cargo section, out of the way of the damaged tail section. When she was just about ready to lever herself up on the tail to see if it would hold her, she heard the banging sound of someone climbing across the helicopter. Russ appeared in the cabin doorway.

"Thank God," she said. "Where were you?"

"Putting out a fire. You need to get out of there *now*."

"A fire!"

"Something threw a spark into a bunch of old pine needles three or four yards from here. I stomped it dead, but there could be a dozen others all around this place that we won't see until they hit enough oxygen to bring 'em up. C'mon." He thrust his hand down toward her. "Now."

"We have to get Waxman out."

"Leave him! He's half-dead already. I'm not going to lose you trying to save somebody who's neck-deep in Ingraham's murder."

She set her hands atop the tail boom and heaved herself up. With an agonized squeal, it sank beneath her like a teeter-totter, its fulcrum the hole it had blown in the rear of the helicopter. She stood up on the rounded form, her feet gripping it through her sneakers. Her head was through the doorway.

"Good. Take my hand. We'll have you out of there in no time."

She held up her hands, but instead of clutching his wrist, she threaded her fingers through his. "I can't leave him behind." She looked into his eyes, willing him to understand her. "It was my idea to bring him out with the helicopter. I was at the controls when we went down." To her mortification, she felt her eyes begin to tear up. She squeezed them shut. "If we had done what you suggested, the Mountain Rescue people would already be on their way to get him out of the ravine." She opened her eyes again, blinking hard against unwanted emotion. "I can't leave him behind. I can't."

He let go of her hands, and for a moment she thought she had failed to persuade him. Then he took her face between his hands and rocked it back and forth. "What am I going to do with you?" he said.

It didn't seem like a question requiring an answer. He released her. "As quickly as possible," he said. "Every second counts."

She nodded and slid off the tail boom. "There's a fire extinguisher behind the pilot's seat," she called up.

"I'll get it," he said. She saw him reach through the pilot's door and yank the extinguisher free. Then he dropped over the edge of the cabin door, hitting the now-stabilized tail boom with a thud and sliding to the floor in her wake. He glanced around at the cabin wreckage. "Wait." He grabbed Waxman's backpack and hurtled it through the open doorway. "Okay, let's get him on top of this thing."

They each squatted at one end of the unconscious man, Clare at his head and Russ at his feet. "One, two, three," she said, and they lifted him onto the tail boom.

Russ looked at the raggedly wrapped form and shook his head. "Can you climb through the door by yourself?"

"Sure," she said.

"I'll hand you up the webbing and then climb out myself. Between the two of us, we can fish him out."

Clare climbed onto the tail boom and straddled Waxman's body. She crouched down and jumped, her abdomen hitting the edge of the doorway, forcing out a loud "Ooof!" but gaining her enough leverage to swing first one leg and then another up onto the door frame. Immediately, Russ thrust two handfuls of webbing at her. She grabbed them as he began hoisting himself. In a minute, he sat facing her across the opening. She pulled up more webbing, handing him the leading edge, and he leaned forward, drawing it to him until the webbing hung between their hands like a fishing net waiting to be cast.

"Okay?" she said. He nodded.

Gripping their catch, they each got to their feet, teetering on the edge of the frame for balance while bending down so as to not loose the webbing they were drawing taut.

"Ready?" he said.

"Let's do it."

She reached down, tangled her fingers in the webbing, and heaved, her biceps contracting into a hard bunch. Across the doorway, Russ did the same. She reached and pulled. He reached and pulled. Waxman rose from the depths.

" 'Follow me, and I will make you fishers of men,' " she quoted. She felt almost giddy, buoyed up by the conviction that at least here and now, she was where she was meant to be, doing what she was supposed to do.

Russ grunted. One more pull and the unconscious geologist was out of the cabin, hanging between them. Russ jerked his head toward the lower edge of the doorway. Awkwardly, they sidestepped until they could rest him on the helicopter's pitted skin. Russ sat down by Waxman's head and she followed suit.

"Lower him to the ground," Russ said. Leaning back, they eased him over the ship's belly onto the raw dirt. Clare followed, sliding down with a thump, which was echoed a moment later by Russ, fire extinguisher in hand. "Now," he said, "can we please get out of here?"

"Oh yes."

Russ shouldered Waxman's backpack and picked up the webbing above the man's head. Standing at Waxman's feet, Clare did the same. They shuffled awkwardly uphill with him, his legs bumping into Clare's shin and the aluminum struts poking into Russ's calves. Russ twisted back, as if he was going to say something to her, but his face went pale as he looked over her shoulder.

She turned to see, and her eyes immediately caught sight of a curl of flame and smoke scarcely bigger than if coming from a pipe bowl. It crackled through a pile of dried leaves beyond the remnants of the helicopter's tail.

"Double time," she said, her voice higher than usual.

Russ glanced at the fire extinguisher, which was still dangling from one hand, and threw it toward the helicopter. Lopsided, they sprinted up the hill, the geologist's body swinging and banging into their legs with bruising force, their free arms churning to counterbalance the load. Clare beat against the hill, attempting to keep pace with Russ's longer stride, trying not to slip as the almost-smooth soles of her sneakers skidded against the dirt and tufts of grass.

They reached the top and headed down the other side without pausing, dodging trees and saplings, picking up momentum until they were loping. Her arm and shoulder were burning and cramping with Waxman's weight. She staggered as the ground beneath her rose again and they lurched upward to another small summit.

"Stream," Russ gasped out, pointing with his free hand to a rock-bottomed brook below them. They plummeted down toward it, thrashing through thick ferns that obscured the forest floor. A rock rolled beneath her heel and she went down on her backside with bone-jarring force but kept her forward momentum so that she rolled up again and continued with only a break in stride.

They had just reached the stream when an enormous *whumpf* sent them sprawling on their bellies. It was like the hammer of God striking the forest, a sound so huge, it seemed a solid thing pressing them down. Clare could feel the air around them compress, causing pressure in her inner ears. Then came the rush of hot wind, blasting out through the forest, shaking leaves wildly and sending a torrent of birds squawking into the skies. Then the wind was gone, like a departed train, and she could hear a clattering, crackling, roaring noise from where they had left the helicopter and the pipe bowl's worth of smoke.

She rolled over and sat up. Russ pushed himself onto his knees. She looked at him, amazed, excited, and profoundly grateful to be sitting there, filthy, sweat-stained, aching in every muscle.

"We made it!" she said.

He dropped to his hands and knees and threw up.

CHAPTER THIRTY

R uss was conscious of two things: the sour taste in his mouth and the cold water pouring over his head and shoulders.

He heard a voice making sympathetic noises, felt the weight of the backpack being lifted off him, the straps tugging over his arms. His ribs ached, his knees were throbbing, and the slow wind rolling over him felt like waves of heat from a furnace grate. The fire. The explosion. The crash. Involuntarily, his stomach spasmed again, trying to wring out the last ounce of bile.

"Rinse your mouth with this." Clare bent over him, water brimming in her cupped hands. He slurped a mouthful, swished it around his mouth, and spit it out.

"More?" he managed to say. She reappeared with another handful of water. He gargled it into the back of his throat and spat again. She wiped the rest of the water on his face.

He sat back on his haunches. "Sorry."

She was all practicality. "Take off your shirt. I'll soak it in the stream. You'll feel better." Her matter-of-fact attitude helped him feel less embarrassed about tossing his lunch. He peeled off the stinking, sweat-soaked garment, and when she brought it back, he rubbed the sopping cloth over his face, neck, and hair before putting it on. It was shockingly cold for a moment, before his skin got accustomed to the clinging wet. The cool barrier against the heat attacking him everywhere helped him to breathe again. He sank back into the ferns. Clare sat beside him, cross-legged. She reached out and began stroking his forehead, pushing his wet hair back, her hand cool and firm. And her touch undid him, just undid him. He felt a knot in his chest loosen, and there he was, opened like a package. He closed his eyes.

"We were flying into the central highlands. It was hot, heavy VC activity in the area, and the artillery units were hammering the place night and day, laying down fire to clear out enough space for the slicks to land and for the squads to set up their perimeters. So we're in the chopper, me and my friend

Mac and a bunch of other guys and our lieutenant." He opened his eyes, looking into the green leaves above him. "We were kind of goofing, getting ourselves revved up, 'cause we figured we were dropping straight into a firefight. All of a sudden, we get hit. The helicopter starts to drop. The pilot's screaming, 'Jump! Jump!' and the chopper's bucking like a bronco and we're all hanging on for dear life. I could see out the door we weren't too far above the trees. The lieutenant yells, 'Come on,' and me and Mac stand up, but the other three guys are yelling that there was no fucking way they were going to jump into the fucking jungle. The pilot's still screaming, 'Jump, jump,' and I look at Mac and he kind of shrugs. The lieutenant sees it, and he slaps his pistol into my hand and yells, 'Go for it,' like he's got to stay with the other guys, maybe persuade them off. Like he had more than a minute anyway. So we jumped. Mac and me."

He glanced at Clare. She was sitting very still, not looking at him directly, looking just past him, as if the ferns were something she had never seen before. She nodded without taking her eyes off the ferns.

"I bounced down through some trees, and next thing I know, I'm on the ground. Right away, I knew I had broken both my legs. I'm looking around for Mac, when the whole sky lights up. The slick had crashed and exploded. And I could hear . . . there was so much noise, but I could hear guys screaming and screaming like animals trapped in a burning barn." He paused for a moment. "Then over the sound, I can hear Mac. Above me. He's kind of sobbing and moaning. And for a while, in the light from the fire, I could see what had happened to him." He shut his mouth for a moment. "I don't know how long it went on. When I remember it, it seems like an hour, but it couldn't have been. Mac hanging in the tree, going, 'Kill me, Christ, kill me,' and crying. And the noise from the chopper dying down, the fire burning out. And I knew . . . knew Charlie was closing in on us, and that as soon as the VC heard Mac, they would find us. So I . . . I took the lieutenant's gun and I . . . did what Mac wanted."

She took his hand in hers and squeezed hard.

"They came about a half hour after. They didn't find me, and no one else was alive, so they went away after awhile. I tried dragging myself a ways, but where could I go with two broken legs? So I gave up and laid there in the brush beneath the tree until this squad of marines came around and hauled my ass out."

Clare laid her other hand on top of his. "How long were you there?"

"Two days."

"Beneath the tree."

"Yeah." He looked at her directly for the first time. "Only three people have ever heard about this. And you're the third."

She rubbed his hand between hers.

"I didn't tell you so you'd feel sorry for me."

"I don't feel sorry for you. I—" She shut her eyes slowly and then opened them again. "I hurt. For what you had to go through. For the boy you were. For what you have to keep in your head."

They were both silent for a moment. He felt lighter somehow, as if he'd been lifting weights for a long time and then put them down and taken a cool shower. Tired out, but fresh at the same time.

"Thank you," she said.

"For what?"

"For being there. For going over and doing what you did. For being faithful to your country even when what your country asked of you was terrible and futile and confused. Thank you."

He started to laugh. "Only you, Clare. Only you."

He let go of her hand and stood up, his legs trembling and his sides aching. Clare rose in front of him, holding his glasses. He hadn't even realized they had come off.

He put them on and glanced up the last hill. No signs of fire. He recalled, from the weekly volunteer fire department's report, that the hazard was low to moderate. Still, it didn't mean they weren't in danger. He looked downstream. God. Right now, he felt as if he would collapse if he had to take one more step.

Clare touched his arm. Her hand was still wet. "Do you . . . Should I . . ." She pressed her lips together and shut her eyes for a moment. When she opened them, she said, "What do you need to do right now and how can I help you?"

He felt an ache, a tenderness so real, he thought he might see a bruise on his sternum if he looked beneath his soggy shirt. He knew if he wanted to, he could lie down in the ferns and have her bring him handfuls of water. Knew that if he sent her ahead to find help, she would do it. Knew if he said he couldn't go on, she'd make a travois for Waxman and drag him out of this forest. She didn't need him to be the leader, to make decisions, to stand in front. And because she didn't, he found he could take that one more step after all.

"Let's head downstream."

"Are you sure?"

He nodded. "If it doesn't take us anywhere, at least it'll be easier than hiking over these hills."

She looked at him carefully, as if measuring his ability against his words. Then she smiled. "Let's go."

Once more, he shouldered the backpack and took Waxman's head while she took his feet. As they walked, he kept an eye out for a branch they could sling through the webbing to carry it on their shoulders, but there were no sturdy eight-foot-long pieces of wood conveniently left about. Instead, there was a thick bank of ferns, and the occasional root or stone to avoid. The constant whack—although it was never regular enough to antici-pate—of the aluminum spars hitting him in the calves slowed him down.

The heat squeezed him like a hand wringing a sponge. His shirt didn't dry out, but warmed, until it seemed a solidified part of the humid air. Except for the gurgle of the stream and the *swish, swish* as they strode through the ferns, the woods were quiet. Even the usual insect droning was muted. He could feel the tension tightening inside him, the creeping fear that he was exposed, open to fire. He knew it was dumb, that there were no snipers lurking in the Adirondacks, that what he and Clare had to fear was a turned ankle or heat stroke, not a sudden shattering report through the leaves. That green and heat and wet didn't automatically add up to death.

Then as they rounded a bend in the stream that twisted behind a bluff of earth and pines, he saw three armed men in fatigues.

He dropped Waxman to the ground and drew his gun in the space be-tween one heartbeat and the next. Clare dived over Waxman as he crouched deep into a firing stance. "Drop your weapons," he roared.

The three men paused from where they had been toiling uphill and stared at him. They didn't toss down their weapons, just stood in a ragged line, curious, relaxed. One of them had his arms akimbo and another one wiped his forehead.

"Hey," the man with his hands on his hips said. "We're not—"

"Police!" Russ yelled. "Put your weapons down *now!*" He tightened his finger slightly and a round fell into the firing chamber with an audible snick.

"Holy crap," one of the men said. "That's a real gun." All three threw their weapons into the ferns. They glanced at one another and raised their hands. The man who had spoken before said, "If we're trespassing, we're sorry."

"We had the landowner's permission to be on the property," a man behind him said.

Russ lowered his gun and relaxed his stance. "Who the hell are you?"

They glanced at one another. "Um. We're from BancNorth," their apparent leader said. "We're part of a paintball team."

From the corner of his eye, he could see Clare clamber off Waxman's half-hidden form.

"Our base camp called us maybe twenty minutes ago. Someone had reported a small aircraft going down, near our position. We decided to check it out."

"They know where we are," the man behind him said. "They're sending in search and rescue teams and rangers right now." The rest remained unspoken: So if you kill us, you won't get away with it.

Russ was suddenly aware that he must look like an extra in *Deliverance*. He holstered his gun and stepped forward. "Please, put your hands down. Sorry I scared you. I'm Chief Van Alstyne, of the Millers Kill Police Department." He thumbed back toward Clare. "This is, um, the pilot of the aircraft you're looking for. We were transporting a badly injured man when our helicopter went down. We could use some help."

The three bankers looked at one another. He could see the excitement crackle between them as they realized they were on the scene of a real live emergency. "Sure," their leader said.

As they drew near, Russ could see their fatigues were streaked with dried paint. One of them had on an outfit so new, there were fold lines faintly visible on his shirt. They had the thickening waists and excellent teeth of successful forty-year-old businessmen. That he had mistaken them for soldiers was clear evidence that his in-country reflexes were running amok.

"Do you guys have a topo map I can use to figure out where we are?" he said.

"Yeah, but you may as well do it the easy way," said one, a pale man whose cheeks were blotchy red from the heat. He fished out something the size of a glasses case and handed it to Russ. "GPS. Hooks us up to the satellite system and tells us the exact coordinates of where we are. You can zoom in and out on the map here." He pointed to buttons along the edge of the device.

"You know," said their leader as Russ switched it on, "that's cheating."

"I'm not using it during the exercise," the pale man said. "It's just in case we get lost."

Russ looked at the blinking spot on the map and handed the thing to Clare. She glanced up at him. "This is the Five Mile Road," she said. "We're no more than a couple of miles away from the Stuyvesant Inn." She started to laugh. The paintball team looked at her.

"Can we use those walkie-talkies to get your base camp to relay a message for us?" Russ asked.

"You could, I guess," the leader said. "But it'd be a lot quicker using a phone." All three fished into their commodious pants pockets and held out cell phones.

Clare laughed even harder.

Russ made a few phone calls while she calmed down enough to cobble together a better way of carrying Waxman. He watched the guys from the paintball team search for sturdy branches long enough to serve as crossbars as he confirmed the Millers Kill Emergency Department would send an ambulance to the Stuyvesant Inn. As the men worked the poles through the webbing, Russ briefed Noble Entwhistle, who was holding down the fort at the station house, on the situation. By the time he had called the volunteer fire department and warned them about the fuel explosion, the three bankers and Clare had shouldered the crossbars like native bearers in an old movie, with Waxman swinging in the middle like a bagged tiger.

"Okay, let's go," Russ said, closing the cell phone and returning it to its owner. "If we follow this stream, it'll empty into a pasture just above the Stuyvesant Inn's land. We'll just need to follow the cow fence at that point. I'm thinking it'll be maybe a half-hour walk. The hospital's sending an ambulance to meet us there. Clare, let me take that for you."

She shook her head. "The best way to do this, since we've got an extra man, is to rotate."

"Okay, five minute's rotation." He glanced at the bankers, who quivered with suppressed excitement. "Fall in," he said. "March!" Clare cast him a sidelong look, but the other three sprang to it like retrievers on the scent.

By the time Russ had taken his turn lugging the unconscious geologist and then rotated out again, they were clearing the woods and entering the upper pasture. They lifted Waxman bodily over the barbed-wire fence and struck off down the fence line, their path impeded by nothing more than the occasional large rock or cow patty. Within ten minutes, Russ spotted the inn's mauve-and-turquoise exterior, and he realized he hadn't properly appreciated that beautiful paint job before.

The group crossed over the fence a second time and headed across the rolling meadow toward the inn. He heard a chorus of high-pitched, frantic barks as they approached, and he thought he might get down and kiss every one of those mop head–size dogs. And when Stephen Obrowski and Ron Handler appeared at the back door, waving and hallooing, it felt as good as seeing his own men greeting him from the squad room at the station house.

They lugged Waxman around to the front of the inn, where Karl and Annie, two of the regular Millers Kill EMS team, were waiting to drive him to the Glens Falls Hospital.

"What'n the blue blazes happened to him?" Karl asked while Annie checked his vitals.

"He fell off a cliff," Clare said.

"Then he crashed in a helicopter," Russ added.

"Sounds like a bad comedy sketch," the ambulance driver said. "You sure a marching band and a steamroller didn't go over him, too?"

Standing beneath the shade of the big maple, watching them pull away with Waxman, Russ was still shaking his head. "I can't believe that guy has survived to this point," he said to Clare. "Maybe there is something to this God thing of yours after all."

Up on the porch, the paintball-playing bankers were regaling Obrowski and Handler with the exciting tale of their adventures. The younger man was ushering them in through the double doors. "Chief, come on in," Obrowski said. "It's too hot to stay outside. We've got fresh lemonade."

Russ shook his head. "I've got a squad car coming for me," he said. "I'd better wait for it here."

"Reverend Fergusson?"

"I think I'll stay out here with the chief. You'd just have to burn any furniture I sit on anyway." She plucked at her clothes. "I would surely appreciate some of that lemonade, though."

"Coming right up."

She plodded up the porch steps and collapsed into one of the wicker chairs. Russ followed her, dropping the backpack to the floor before sitting down. Beyond the shady maples and the thin gray road, the valley rolled away in pastures and cornfields and distant farms, a crazy-quilt landscape stitched by rocky outcroppings, steep rises, and stony brooks. The valley shimmered in the heat, oddly one-dimensional under the colorless sky, and for a moment Russ felt that he was in a dream, that the wicker furniture and the wooden floor and the far-off farms would disappear with a shake of his shoulder and he would be back in the green leaves, looking for death over every nameless, numbered hill.

Obrowski brought out lemonade, a whole pitcher of it, and two blue glasses stacked with ice. He arranged them with a flourish on a round teak table midway between their chairs. "Unbelievable," he said, pouring their drinks. "Were you really flying the plane that went down, Reverend Fergusson?"

Clare accepted one of the glasses. "Helicopter," she said. She had a look in her eyes that made Russ think maybe she, too, was uncertain how much of this was real.

"Those bankers of yours are quite something. I've never thought much of the paintball crowd that shows up on the weekends around here. I remember once when Bill Ingraham went with his business partner. He told me it was the most pointless exercise he had ever undertaken in his life, and that included his draft-induction physical." He laughed. Russ took his glass from Obrowski and drained it so fast, all he was aware of was the slide of the cold and tart-tasting liquid over his tongue.

Obrowski looked at Russ, then at Clare, then back at Russ. "I'll leave you two to catch your breath, then, shall I?"

The screen door banged behind him and they were alone. He poured himself another glass of lemonade and drank it more slowly. Thinking about the whole incident with the helicopter made his stomach ache, and thinking about the whole thing with Clare made the rest of him ache. So he propped his feet on the backpack, looked at the slightly unreal scenery, and thought about Waxman. Waxman taking Peggy to the gorge and hitting her up for money. Threatening her, fighting with her, a lucky push or punch—lucky, because she wasn't a big woman and Waxman must outweigh her by quite a few pounds—and he goes over the edge.

With his backpack.

Christ.

"Clare," he said.

"Hmm?"

"Waxman's backpack was down in the ravine with him."

"Yeah, you told me."

He took his feet off the pack and bent forward. This was the reason his subconscious mind had ragged at him to keep the thing with them, from the ravine, to their wild ride, to their headlong flight through the forest.

"Why would his backpack be in the ravine with him? If you're extorting someone or fighting, would you be carrying your backpack?"

There was a pause. Her ice cubes clinked in her glass, another off-kilter piece of normality. "No," she said finally.

"It wasn't on him. It wasn't even near him." He unbuckled the flap and flipped it open. Inside, atop dirty T-shirts, plastic jars filled with algae-speckled water, and a dog-eared copy of *Topographical Maps of New York State,* was a plastic bag the size of a woman's clutch. It was full of white powder. He heard Clare breath in sharply.

The backpack, thrown into the ravine. Evidence to be found with the body. Except he and Clare had stumbled on the scene too soon.

"What was it you overheard Malcolm saying to his mystery visitor about Peggy?"

"He told him to stay away from his aunt."

One good hard shove into the gorge. Just enough evidence to link Waxman to Dessaint. He was tempted to give the powder a taste and verify that it was horse or coke, but he'd bet good money it was already cut with the same stuff that had killed the other man.

Stay away from his aunt. No kidding.

And they had met her coming down the trail. And offered to help her. And she had helped them. He remembered seeing her backing out of the cockpit door while he was pulling his headset on. He fished into his pants pocket, and sure enough, it was still there, the broken piece of plastic that had rendered the radio useless. All she would have needed was a screwdriver to jam into it. Easy to swipe one from the office and stick into that big bag of hers. Right there under the bottles of cold water. Evidently, Peggy Landry could think on her feet.

And she had been alone and unwatched with the chopper for what— ten minutes? While he and Clare were breaking into the shed.

"What do you think caused the crash?"

She kept staring at the white powder in the bag, then at the black plastic in his palm. "I'm not sure," she said. "Something with the fuel lines?" She looked at him for the first time. "I thought I must have rushed my preflight check. I thought I'd missed something."

He shook his head. "No. You did just right." He reached for her hand and pressed the splintered radio control into it. "Peggy Landry," he said.

"It can't be." She looked at the knob. "Helos are complicated creatures.

And that ship flew. For what—twenty minutes after we had left her? That sort of delayed . . ."

"Sabotage," he said, supplying the word.

"That would take a great deal of knowledge about the helo's systems. You'd need to be a mechanic. And you'd have to open the ship up, get into the engine or something. She couldn't have—" She stopped, frowning. She slid her fingers absently up and down her sweating glass. "Unless . . . All those water bottles." She turned to him. "She could have squirted water into one of the tanks. We were low on fuel, and I switched from the first tank to the second after we made our ascent to spot the Hudson." Her face, dirty and sweat-streaked, shone with revelation. "It would have been pretty much dumb luck, getting the second tank. If she'd put it in the first, we wouldn't have made it to the ravine."

"But you don't need to know much about any machine to know putting water into the gas tank is going to screw it up."

They looked at each other. He thought about Ingraham's bloody death and Dessaint's bloated corpse. He thought about Todd MacPherson and Emil Dvorak. People treated like disposable lighters. He thought about what might have happened if they had been a shade less lucky, if Clare had been slightly less skilled as a pilot, if the sparks had caught fire a few minutes earlier.

He stood up so abruptly, his wicker chair skidded back half a foot.

"What?"

He turned to the inn's door. "I'm getting out an APB on Landry and her nephew. And telling Kevin to get here now." She had tried to kill *Clare.* And had almost succeeded. "I don't want anyone else to make this collar. I want to be the one to strap that woman to the gurney."

CHAPTER THIRTY-ONE

R uss tried to get rid of Clare, of course. First, he wanted her to stay at the inn and accept Ron and Stephen's offer of a shower and a room to rest in. Then, when Officer Flynn arrived and drove them up to the construction site to reclaim their cars, he ordered her to go home, a direction he emphasized by driving past the rectory on his way to the Landry house and pointing his finger out his window at her driveway. When they got to the imposing modern house—Clare still dogging Russ's Ford 250—and discovered that Peggy, her laptop, and two suitcases were gone, she could see he was tempted to leave her there, with the nearly hysterical bride-to-be and the poor confused Woods. She crossed her arms and simply ignored everything he said that didn't involve her sticking around. His heart wasn't really in it anyway. Maybe there was something about throwing up on another person's shoes.

"I know why you're doing this," he said as he rifled through Peggy Landry's home office. He, Kevin, Noble Entwhistle, and a friendly cop introduced as Duane were searching the house. "You're an adrenaline junkie. I'm here to tell you that the only way to get over that is to live a life of quiet contemplation." He tossed several folders on the floor. "Here, make yourself useful." She sat on the Oriental rug and began paging through the documents. "Quiet contemplation," he went on. "Like the priesthood."

Officer Entwhistle stuck his head in the doorway. "Thought you'd like to know. We pulled a suitcase full of goodies from under the nephew's bed. Meth and ecstasy, and some heroin, too. We're leaving it in place until the lab guy can get here. It may be another hour."

"Speedy as always. Any indications where Wintour might have gone?"

"Nothing yet. We're still looking." Entwhistle glanced over at Clare, who sat cross-legged on the floor, and raised his eyebrows. "Helping out, Reverend Fergusson?"

"Yes, I am."

"I'll, uh, leave you two to it, then." He retreated down the hall.

"That's great," Russ said under his breath.

"What?" The folder held an endless correspondence between Landry Properties, Inc., and its insurance carrier, dating back several years. Even letting weekend warriors play paintball on your mountains was apparently a potential pitfall of litigation.

"Nothing," he said. "Just another misunderstanding."

"Huh," she said, trying to decipher the arcane agreement that had BWI paying a portion of Peggy's insurance on the land not leased for the spa. Statements for January, February, March . . . then something different in April.

"Russ. Come take a look at this." He knelt beside her. She laid the paper on the rug and they both bent over it. "If this says what I think it does, Peggy's share of the BWI insurance was canceled in April."

He pushed his glasses up the bridge of his nose. "Would that include that provision Opperman told me about? Where she gets paid out of insurance money if the project didn't go forward?"

"I'm guessing so." She flipped through another few pages. "Look at this. Her insurance company writes her that they've been refused payment because BWI's dropped her policy." She underlined the words with her fingernail. "Hugh Parteger," she glanced at him, "a financier I met at Peggy's party, he told me BWI was overloaded with debt and looking for cash."

"Her insurance situation wouldn't be that big a deal so long as the construction was going through," he said, sitting back on his heels. "But if she thought Ingraham was going to pull the plug on the project . . ."

"She'd be left with nothing except a hunk of cleared land and a reputation as someone who had a major deal drop through her fingers. She's spent years trying to make something of that property."

He nodded. "Could be she decided that if Bill Ingraham was out of the way, the spa could be built without him. Opperman said pretty much the same thing to me. With the design all in place, all Ingraham was doing at this point was acting as the lead contractor. Could be she thought she could safeguard her investment." He shook his shoulders. "Remind me to stay away from real estate speculation."

There was a screeching noise outside, and the sound of flying gravel. Someone shouted from the main floor.

"What the—" Russ was on his feet and pounding down the hall before Clare had a chance to get up. She followed him, two steps at a time, up the stairs to the main floor, guided by the shouts and slamming doors. The elderly Woods were huddled beside a grandfather clock in the foyer. "Which way?" Clare said.

Cyrus Wood pointed to the front door. She burst outside in time to see both the squad cars gunning down the sloping drive, wheels spinning, stones *rat-tat-tatting*. Russ was flinging open the door of his pickup. She put on a burst of speed and ran headlong into the truck, banging on the hood. "Let me in! Let me in!"

The passenger door unlocked with a sharp click and she fell into the seat, clutching at the oven-hot leather as Russ spun the vehicle around and slammed on the accelerator. She couldn't believe he had actually fallen for it and let her get in.

"What is it?"

"The nephew pulled right into the driveway. He saw our black-and-whites and backed out of there, but not before Kevin spotted him. Hang on."

They took the turn onto the road on two wheels. His hand twitched where the radio would be in his squad car. She could hear the sirens wailing, the sound shifting, growing higher and fainter as the lightweight cars drew farther and farther ahead of Russ's heavy truck.

"Will they be able to catch him?" she asked.

"Eventually." His focus was all on the road as he leaned into his accelerator.

"What if he drives through town like that? That fast?"

He didn't answer. He didn't have to. It was a stupid question. She could picture the tourists jaywalking across the streets, the kids biking. She squeezed her eyes shut and prayed the best she knew how, scarcely coherent, all her fear and belief laid out in the open. *Please, God. Please.*

The sirens cut off. Russ swore. The truck flew over the road, heading toward the intersection, lofting over bumps and jarring high and wide over asphalt patches filling last winter's potholes.

"Hang on!" The two black-and-whites were catercorner across the intersection, blocking a Volvo sedan that had, from the skid marks, spun around in the turn and nosed into a ditch thick with daylilies and Queen Anne's lace. Russ jammed down on the brake, throwing both of them forward until her shoulder belt caught and bit into her neck. The back end of the truck danced across the road but stopped safely in the breakdown lane. Great, she thought. Now I'll have matching bruises on both shoulders.

The uniformed officers spilled from their cars, taking protective stances behind their open doors. Russ opened his own door, drawing his weapon at the same time. *"Stay here,"* he said.

She nodded.

Officer Entwhistle was yelling at Malcolm Wintour to get out of the car with his hands showing. She couldn't see any movement inside the sedan. Lord, what if he was dead, too? The awful toll of human life and pain was already too high. And for what? To get a lousy piece of land developed. To make more money for a woman who already had more than anyone really needed.

Russ closed in on his men, staying low, his gun out in front of him. She saw him signal Noble Entwhistle, who ducked behind his own car and edged around toward the back of the Volvo, which was angled up so that the tires were barely touching the asphalt.

"Wintour," Russ bellowed. "We've got your aunt. We've got Waxman. We know everything. Get out of the car."

The door on the driver's side shuddered, opened a few inches, and then stuck fast in the side of the ditch. Clare rolled her window down. She had to hear what was going to happen. A hand emerged from the opening. "It wasn't my idea!" The thin, frightened voice she heard was not at all like the one she had heard from the bathroom. "She made me do it!"

"Get out of the goddamned car!"

"I can't!"

Russ looked at Noble Entwhistle and nodded. The uniformed officer crept closer to the Volvo's trunk as Russ sidled closer toward the driver's door. Clare wanted to scream, *Stay away from there, you idiot! He's got a gun!* But he knew Malcolm had a gun. He knew what he was doing. She forced her fingernails out of the palms of her hands.

She still couldn't see the interior of the car, but from where he stood, Russ must have had a bead directly on Malcolm. He stood there, gun pointed at the car, while Noble slid into the ditch and opened the back door. It wasn't until he had hauled Malcolm out, literally by the collar, that Clare realized she had been holding her breath.

They got him down on the ground and then Duane and Kevin came running. Clare could hear a rumble of male voices, but she couldn't make out anything. Russ squatted down and spoke directly to Malcolm. She wasn't sure, but it looked as if the younger man was crying. She looked away, not wanting to see any more, and so it wasn't until she heard the crunch of his hiking boots on the road grit that she realized Russ was coming back to the truck.

She glanced up. Noble was ushering Malcolm into the backseat of his cruiser, and as she watched, the red lights whirled atop the other police car and Kevin and Duane were off, headed toward town. She looked at Russ as he opened his door.

"He says his aunt didn't drive away, because he had her car." He got in, pinching the bridge of his nose. "He doesn't know where she's gone. The only people he knows she might get in touch with are his mother or her other sister. Both of whom live more than halfway across the state. She must have called a friend to come pick her up."

He crawled in behind the wheel and leaned back against the headrest. "We've got an APB out on her, but it's not going to do us a damn bit of good if we don't know what the hell car she's in. 'Scuse my French."

"Could she have rented a car?"

"That was my first thought. The nearest car-rental place is at the Fort Henry Ford dealership. I sent Duane and Kevin off to check it out."

Officer Entwhistle's car came to life. He pulled away from the side of the road and headed toward town, waving through the window at Russ.

"We need to get someone to secure that Volvo," Russ said, sounding weary. "We're so damned overextended at this point that I'm going to have to call the staties in. God, I hate that." He reached for his keys and started the truck. "We'd better get back to the house and start calling names in Peggy's Rolodex. Maybe we'll find a girlfriend who just happened to have plans to drive out of town today."

Clare's mind returned to the party the night before. Sitting in the window seat of the Landry house while the guests swirled around her. The expression of disbelief on Hugh Parteger's face. The smell of black currants and Thai chicken. Peggy saying, "John Opperman's flying to Baltimore tomorrow afternoon, and he won't be back until Tuesday."

"I know where she is."

He looked at her.

"No, really. I know where she is. John Opperman's supposed to fly out of town this afternoon. I bet she called him and asked to come along. I bet he'd pick her up, no questions asked."

He shoved his hand into his hair, spiking his sweat-stiff locks in every direction. "He would, wouldn't he? A little freebie business trip." He slammed the heel of his hand into his steering wheel. "Damn, that woman thinks fast on her feet. We're not going to find her with an APB because she's not going to be on the road. Or buying a ticket anywhere." He threw the truck into gear and pulled onto the road. "Do you know when Opperman's supposed to leave?"

"She just said he was leaving this afternoon. And that he was headed for Baltimore."

He heeled the truck hard to the left and stomped on the gas pedal. "If I take the back roads, I can be at the Glens Falls Airport in twenty minutes." He glanced at her for a split second. "I don't suppose you have your cell phone with you?"

"In my car. Sorry."

"Never mind. If they're still there, we can stop them before he takes off. And if they've left, they would have had to tell the airport-control people where they're going, right?"

"He would have to have filed a flight plan, yeah. And if he's flying on instruments, he'll be passed from one flight-control center to another. You'll be able to call ahead and have someone waiting for her at their destination." She grabbed the door handle as he took another hard turn onto an unmarked road. They jounced in and out of potholes as they flew through thickets of sumac and ancient overgrown apple orchards. "You know, I like to speed, but isn't this—"

"Hang on." He turned onto a one-lane bridge. Steel plates *ca-chunk-ca-chunk-ca-chunked* beneath the tires.

"Are you sure you know where you're going?"

He grinned at her. "Do you trust me?"

She groaned.

At one point, she was sure they'd passed under the Northway, but other than that, she had no bearing on where they were until they emerged from a tree-shaded road and saw the airport in front of them, its four runways stretched like a top-heavy X past a handful of hangars and a tiny tower. They drove through a gate marked EMPIRE EAST AVIATION.

"Where do you think he'd be?" Russ asked.

She glanced around as he slowed the truck to a crawl. There were twenty or twenty-five small planes at tie-downs and another two on the tarmac. As she watched, a Beech King took off from runway 12.

"Could that have been it?"

"No," she said, still scanning the area. "That's a single-engine. If he's actually using it for long-range transport, he's got to have a double-prop, maybe a jet, and I don't see any around here. Head for—whoa! There! Pull over, pull over."

She was scrambling out of her door before he turned the engine off. In front of the next hangar, past the tie-down area and ready to roll onto runway 1, was a Piper Cheyenne II, twin turboprop, six seats—the biggest plane she had seen so far. A skinny young man in greasy overalls was rolling back a fuel hose. Whoever was in the plane was in a big hurry—finishing the refueling only minutes before getting the go-ahead. She could hear Russ behind her, yelling, "Millers Kill PD. Stop that plane!"

Clare skidded to a halt in front of the fuel attendant's tubing spool. "Who owns this?" she said. He gawped at them. "Who owns this turbo-prop?" she demanded.

"Uh . . . uh . . ."

She snatched an order pad from the front pocket of his overalls.

"Hey!"

"Is this the order?" she asked, pointing to the top sheet.

"Yeah, but—"

She had already read the owner's name beneath the grimy fingerprints. She waved the pad at Russ. "It says BWI!"

She heard the engine turn over, the plane purr to life. Russ flashed his badge at the fuel attendant. "Police! There's a murder suspect on board that plane! Go tell whoever's in charge to shut it down!"

The kid's eyes bulged out of his bony face. He turned and fled toward the tower.

Russ sprinted the rest of the way to the plane and banged on the tail. "Stop! Stop!"

She caught at Russ's arm and dragged him away. "You idiot! If that plane turns, those props will slice you into julienned fries! Don't ever, ever get next to a plane with its props running!"

"There's no way the tower can stop him if he wants to take off, can it?" She shook her head.

"Then I have to do it." He ran wide around the Cheyenne's wing, drawing his gun. The plane slowly pivoted toward the runway. She saw the flaps moving as the pilot adjusted them before running up his engines.

Russ skidded to a halt a dozen feet from the Cheyenne's nose. He leveled his gun toward the cockpit. The self-sacrificing stupidity of it took her breath away. She didn't think one bullet, or even a full clip, would ground that plane, unless he could hit the pilot. And she knew he would never shoot Opperman just to stop Peggy Landry from escaping.

The plane's twin engines whined and it began to roll forward. Evidently, whoever was inside had realized the same thing Clare had. The plane changed its angle slightly, so that instead of the nose facing Russ, it was the right wing prop. Russ jogged sideways until he was dead-on the nose again, but this was a duel he couldn't win.

Stop the plane, stop the plane—Possibilities flipped through her mind as the Cheyenne rolled forward and Russ backed away ahead of it. He was shouting something about being under arrest, but she couldn't pay attention to his words as she cast about for something, anything to—Then she spotted the wheel chocks. Long wooden and rubber triangles, each hanging from a length of rope, flight equipment unchanged since Orville and Wilbur Wright flew at Kitty Hawk. There were two pairs resting next to an empty tie-down cleat on the tarmac.

She grabbed three by their rope handles and sprinted toward the back of the plane. She ducked low and scurried under the right wing. The plane was moving at a brisk pace now, and the trick was going to be to get the chock in front of the wheel without walking straight into the propeller, which was whirring five feet in front of her. She twirled the handle and tossed one, wishing fervently that she had spent more time playing horseshoes with her brothers. The chock hit the tarmac, bounced, and came to rest at a slant.

The right wheel hit it. The whole plane trembled. There was a pause; then the engines revved louder. The pilot was going to push it. And with only one wheel blocked, and that at an angle, he would be able to roll over the chock within a minute.

"What the hell are you doing?" Russ yelled.

The Cheyenne was pivoting again, this time against the obstruction. She had maybe ten seconds left before it was free—nine—she threw herself on the tarmac and rolled under the tail—eight—staggered to her feet and ducked under the left wing—seven—took the second wheel chock and jammed it under the left wheel.

The plane seemed to hiccup. Its engines screamed in complaint as the pilot revved them higher. She could see the chock in front of the right wheel skid as the plane's tire ground it out of the way. Her eyes went to the nose wheel—small, unpowered, there to hold up the plane on an even triangle of support. She stooped under the belly and ran, crouching so low, her knees were hitting her nose. The props roared, each less than two feet from her head. If the wheel got over the chock, the plane would turn and Russ would have to ship her home to her parents in Baggies. She flung herself on her belly and thrust the last chock beneath the nose wheel. Then she scrambled to her hands and knees, crawled forward a couple of yards, and lurched to her feet, well away from the spinning propellers.

For a moment, she could hear the voice of her survival school instructor. *You like to live on the edge, don't you, Fergusson?*

Sir, yes, sir.

Russ grabbed her arm and hauled her behind him. "Now, who's the idiot?" he hissed.

"It worked," she said. She stepped away from him so she could see the cockpit windows. The height and tilt of them made it impossible to make out any details about who was sitting there, but she knew he—or they—could see her. She gestured, using the universal language of flight crews: Three. Wheels. Stop.

Nothing. She and Russ stood there in front of the immobilized plane while the engines roared fruitlessly on. She had just enough time to wonder if the cockpit's side windows were sealed, or if they could open, and if so, whether someone would stick a gun out and start firing at them.

"Maybe we should—"

"Let's move to—"

The cabin door opened. It was Opperman, his face a mask.

"Turn off those engines and get down from there," Russ shouted. "I'm here to arrest Peggy Landry for attempted murder and conspiracy to commit murder."

"I'd love to oblige you, Chief," Opperman said. His eyes shifted toward something inside the plane. "Unfortunately, Peggy has taken possession of my gun and is quite determined to have me fly her out of here."

"Christ," Russ said under his breath. "This is why guns in the cockpit are such a bad idea." He raised his voice. "Peggy, what do you want?"

Opperman held one edge of the door frame and moved to one side. And there was Peggy, pressing a handgun into his side. She wasn't the cool, acerbic hostess Clare remembered from her party, nor the nearly hysterical victim from earlier today. This was a woman stripped to the bone. Her eyes were red-rimmed and teary, but not with remorse or self-pity. With rage. Peggy Landry looked ready to jump over the edge, not caring whom she took with her.

"Ms. Landry," Russ said, raising his voice to be heard over the thrum of the propellers, "put down the weapon and come with me. There's not any way you're going to get out of this."

"I might have said the same thing about you and the helicopter," she said. "I understood it wouldn't fly if the gas supply was compromised. But here you are." Her voice was firm, but the gun in her hand trembled.

"The helicopter went down. It was Clare's piloting that kept us alive."

Clare thought it was more likely dumb luck. However, she wasn't going to try to put her two cents in.

"Waxman?"

"He's still hanging on. You pushed him into that ravine, didn't you? Why?"

Opperman looked at Peggy, his expression pained. Clare couldn't tell if it was from the news of his helicopter's fate or Waxman's. From what she had seen of the man, she suspected the former.

"He thought he knew things he didn't. He was trying to blackmail me, the little weasel. He had discovered PCBs in the groundwater around the quarry pond on my land. He . . . was promised a job if he kept his mouth shut about it." Her eyes flicked down, as if to make sure the gun was still firmly against Opperman's waist. "He knew if the DEP found out, it would be the end of the project. He was threatening me! He threatened me!"

Opperman was shaking his head. "There's no PCB contamination." He spoke loudly enough for them all to hear. "Leo found contaminated water when he first came to the site, but the levels have been going down every time he tested. I was suspicious—I thought maybe he was setting us up. I hired a diver to check things out this past week. He found an empty chem-hazard container at the bottom of the quarry pond." He looked directly at Russ. "My guess is that Leo seeded the pond with sludge from the Allen Mill cleanup site, or those antidevelopment environmental extremists did."

"What?"

Clare's amazement was so strong, she could almost believe her thought rang out loud. But it was Peggy who spoke, clutching at the door frame and the gun with equal fervor.

"What the fuck do you mean, 'There's no PCB contamination'? I saw Waxman's test results. I know—if he—"

"I just found out myself," Opperman said. "I hadn't had the chance to tell you. I was going to talk to some people I know at the EPA on Monday and report the sabotage." He looked at Russ again. "Of course, I thought—we all thought—that if there was residual contamination from when the quarry was used for storage, we'd have to shutdown the project."

"Why the hell didn't you tell me any of this when I interviewed you Monday?" Russ's voice cracked with frustration.

"Why didn't you tell *me*?" Peggy added, jabbing Opperman in the ribs for emphasis.

He stiffened against the gun's prodding. "I told you—I just found out myself!" He looked at Russ. "And when you spoke to me, I thought Bill had been killed as a result of a sexual encounter gone wrong. How was I supposed to guess there was some connection to a confidential business situation?" Clare was amazed that, even held hostage, Opperman managed to play the autocrat. "Besides, I already suspected tampering from that tree-hugger group. And we certainly know where your sympathies lie, don't we?"

Clare could feel the tension radiating from Russ, but he ignored Opperman's jab. "Ms. Landry," he said, "did you order Bill Ingraham killed?"

"The son of a bitch was going to pull the plug on the project," Peggy protested. "He was going to fold up and go home because of the goddamned PCBs. . . ." For a moment, she looked lost. "I would have been left with nothing. With nothing!" She practically howled her words.

"Russ," Clare said in his ear.

"I know."

She had seen suicidal people before, people driven to the brink of utter hopelessness. That mad despair was in Peggy's eyes.

Evidently, Opperman saw it, too. "Peg," he said, almost too softly to be heard over the engines' roar. "Let's sit down and talk about this. I can help you. I know some of the best lawyers—"

"You!"

Now the madness turned outward.

"You! Always being so damn helpful! Always telling me everything's going to turn out all right! Well, it hasn't, has it? My life is ruined! And I swear to God yours will be, too!"

Opperman lunged at her, knocking her off her feet. They both disappeared into the plane's shadowed interior.

"Oh, Christ!" Russ launched himself at the lip of the door. A shot resounded. Clare flung her arms over her head and ducked, a useless, instinctual move. Just as Russ was heaving himself over the edge, Opperman crawled into view.

For an endless second, Clare waited for Peggy to follow, imagining her looming over the injured man in the doorway. Russ would never be able to get his weapon up in time. Peggy would gun them all down and eat the last bullet herself. And the only thing Clare could think of was the Act of Contrition from her eighth-grade confirmation class—"Oh, my God, I am heartily sorry for having offended Thee and I detest of all my sins"—and it wasn't even an Episcopal prayer.

Then Opperman clambered to his feet and reached down to help Russ into the plane. Russ disappeared for a moment and then returned. He looked at her, his face more grim than she had ever seen. And she realized Peggy Landry was never going to appear in that doorway, or any other, again.

CHAPTER THIRTY-TWO

W hen the farmhouse door opened, Clare thrust her flowers into Paul's hands. "Welcome home," she said.

He wrapped one meaty arm around her shoulders and hugged her close. "I'm glad to be here, believe me." He glanced over her shoulder. "Hello! I'm Paul Foubert."

"You said I should bring a date," Clare said, stepping aside to let the two men shake hands. "Paul, this is Hugh Parteger."

"Pleased to meet you," Hugh said, handing Paul a bottle of wine.

"Whoa. You're not from around here, are you?"

"You can tell," Hugh said, his face falling. "No matter how I work on the accent, people can always tell I'm Swedish." Paul laughed.

"Hugh is based in New York City, but he has ambitions to be a summer person in Saratoga," Clare explained. "He was up this weekend, so when he called me, I asked him along."

"Wonderful!" Paul said. "Stephen and Ron's inn was full up tonight, so they couldn't get away. Now it'll just be us and the Van Alstynes."

Clare kept her smile firmly in place. "I'm looking forward to meeting Mrs. Van Alstyne."

Paul looked at her oddly. "From the way she's been talking about you since she got here, I assumed you two had already met."

"Linda Van Alstyne was talking about me?" Her stomach lurched. Which was ridiculous. She had nothing to feel guilty about. Nothing.

Paul's face relaxed. "No, *Margy* Van Alstyne was talking about you." He turned to Hugh. "Chief Van Alstyne's mother. Dynamite woman. She took care of our dogs for us while I was with Emil in Albany." He gave them as much of a confidential glance as his broad, open face was capable of. "We invited her first, before the chief and his wife. I get the impression that the daughter-in-law doesn't show up at social events where the mother-in-law will be present."

305

Clare felt almost giddy with relief. "Speaking of the dogs, where are—" A chorus of happy dog noises cut off her sentence.

"The hairy beasts are out back, on the patio. We're taking advantage of the breeze. I decided to have dinner at 6:00 because Emil gets tired so early, but it'll work out perfectly with the weather. The thunderstorms should hold off for a few more hours. That gives us lots of time to eat, talk, and swill down this very nice merlot you've brought."

"Oh, Lord," Hugh said. "I hope mine isn't the only drink available. From what I've seen of the vicar, she'll polish it off before the hors d'oeuvres." He grinned at Clare, who elbowed him in the ribs.

Paul led them through the living room and dining room to a set of French doors open to the evening light. The dogs rushed them in a wiggling mass of silky hair and wet noses as they came out onto the flagstone patio. Clare scratched their heads and shoulders as they ecstatically butted against her linen shift.

"Go lie down, Bob." Paul tugged at the Bern's collar. "No, Gal. Down." The dogs retreated to a spot beneath a glass-topped iron table already set for dinner. "No," Paul warned. The dogs gave him a pitiful look and dragged themselves into banishment next to a low stone wall. "Hey, Emil. This is Clare and her friend Hugh Parteger."

With the help of a cane, Emil Dvorak rose from one of the teak benches that edged the patio. Clare took his outstretched hand.

"I'm happy to meet you," he said. He had a precise, almost European way of talking. His speech evidently hadn't been affected by his brain trauma. "Paul's told me so many wonderful things about you. Thank you for everything you've done."

She felt her cheeks go pink. "It wasn't anything." Where he grasped his cane, his knuckles were white. "Please, sit down." Beside the medical examiner, Russ had risen, as well. He nodded to her.

"Reverend Fergusson."

"Chief Van Alstyne." She tucked her hand behind Hugh's elbow and pulled him forward. "I'd like you to meet Hugh Parteger. Hugh, this is Russ Van Alstyne."

Russ was in his civvies, but as he shook hands with the Englishman, he managed to make jeans and a button-down shirt look like a uniform. "What brings you to Millers Kill?" he asked. It sounded like the beginning of an interrogation, rather than a social pleasantry.

As Hugh explained his presence in Russ's jurisdiction, Paul dragged over a pair of slouchy canvas chairs and offered two glasses of fruit-clotted sangria. "Mrs. Van Alstyne's using the little girls' room," he said, and, as if called by his words, Margy waltzed through the French doors.

"Clare!" She hugged her firmly. "And who is this Russ is talking to? Is this good-looking fellow your date?"

Clare introduced the two. Hugh looked relieved to have someone to speak with besides Russ, who, when Clare pressed one of the glasses of sangria into Hugh's hand, asked, "One of you is a designated driver tonight, right?"

They all sat down, ranged around Dr. Dvorak. Seven weeks after his near-fatal beating, Emil Dvorak looked frail and stitched together. His hair was a stubble of new growth around pink lines of scars, and the left side of his face wasn't quite symmetrical with the right—his eye didn't open as wide and his smile didn't reach as far. But as he told them stories about his hospital stay, he spoke clearly, displaying an acerbic humor that she liked right away.

The conversation turned to health care, with Margy Van Alstyne telling them the trials of life under Medicare, and Hugh weighing in on the British National Health system. Clare let the talk flow around her while she sipped her icy sangria. It wasn't until she accepted Paul's offer of a second glass that Russ spoke to her.

"You're not going to want to break into their bedroom and climb out the bathroom window if you have that, are you?"

She snorted. The other four looked at her with polite incomprehension. "Just . . . it's a long story," she said. "I was trying to find out more about Malcolm Wintour."

"I trust they're going to put him away for a long time," Hugh said.

"The victim's advocate interviewed me," Emil said. "She told me Wintour's going to plead guilty to possession and dealing but is trying to duck the murder charges."

Russ pinched the bridge of his nose. "The DA thinks she won't have much of a problem hanging Chris Dessaint's death on him, but conspiracy's difficult to prove, and we haven't been able to give her much evidence." He looked at Clare. "From what we can tell, Peggy was giving orders to her nephew, who, in turn, was giving orders to Chris Dessaint, who was bringing in Colvin and McKinley."

Clare's shoulders twitched. "It's like puppets playing puppets."

"Yeah. But there's not much of a paper trail, other than a few phone calls from Wintour's cell phone to Dessaint. And with Peggy and Dessaint both dead, there isn't much hope of ever getting all the details. I tell you what really bugs me." He leaned forward, resting his elbows on his knees. "We still don't know how Peggy hooked up with Chris Dessaint."

"I thought Malcolm was the one giving him orders," Clare said.

"He was. But Wintour didn't know him before. He claims his aunt fingered Dessaint, gave him his name and phone number." He made a noise of frustration. "You can imagine how hard it's going to be to get the conspiracy charge to stick." He glanced around at the others, as if recalling that he wasn't in a private conversation. "But to get back to Mr. Parteger's statement . . . You can rest assured that the three surviving stooges will be going away for a long, long time."

Emil smiled slightly. "You know, I don't really care. Nearly dying has a way of giving you perspective." He looked at his partner, the strained lines of his square face softening. "We all have only so much time. I don't want to waste what's left to me on things that aren't important."

Paul smiled back. "And that makes me think," he said. "Clare, how did your candlelight vigil go?"

"Huh? Oh, it was great. More people than I expected." Thanks to Todd MacPherson's new friends from the Adirondack Pride team, she said to herself. She had spent much of the evening dodging their attempts to interview her. She wanted to do the work she needed to do, but she wasn't interested in becoming their poster priest.

"What did your congregation think of it?"

"I think it boosted attendance the next Sunday. I actually had forty people in the pews." She decided not to mention that half of them had wanted a "little word" with her about her activism.

"Good," Paul said. He took his partner's hand and breathed deeply. "Because Emil and I would like to ask you to marry us."

Clare blinked.

"Well, I guess that calls for congratulations," Margy said stoutly. Hugh and Russ glanced at each other. Hugh cleared his throat.

"Yes, congrats and best wishes," he said.

Everyone looked at Clare. In the meadow beyond the overgrown lawn, cicadas were chirping their end-of-August call. The thick wineglass suddenly felt heavy in her hand. "New York State doesn't recognize same-sex marriages," she said, throwing out the first thing she could think of. "No ceremony is legally valid, no matter who officiates."

"We know," Paul said. "We can call it a commitment ceremony or a celebration of union. The important thing is, we want to stand up together and
make promises in front of our friends and family. We want to say we'll be
together until we die."

"The church I was raised in can't do this for us," Emil said. "But I
have . . . reconnected to the fact that my belief in God is part of my life. I
know that the Episcopal church is more liberal about these issues."

"The church is in conflict about these issues," Clare said, stressing the
word *conflict*. "Some dioceses allow commitment ceremonies, or at least
look the other way while individual priests perform them. But the bishop of
Albany—my bishop—is a traditionalist." Not wanting the bishop to come
across as some sort of hide-bound old crank, she added, "I mean, he's very
much in favor of civil rights for gays and for including them—you—in the
church community. Just . . . not . . ."

"Just not giving the stamp of approval to them actually living together,"
Russ said.

She shot him a look. He should talk, Mr. I'm Uncomfortable Around
Them. "Please try to understand," she said. "I don't have the authority to
decide policy on my own. I'm part of a hierarchy, under the direction of my
bishop, who's under the direction of the General Convention. It's not that
I'm against it, but I . . ."

They were all watching her dig her own grave. Paul looked as if she
had gotten up and kicked Bob and Gal. Emil's face was sinking into lines
of resignation. And Russ looked . . . disappointed in her.

You like to live on the edge, don't you, Fergusson?

Make whole that which is broken.

"But I have to live as I believe Christ leads me. If that doesn't sound too
pompous." She laid one hand on Paul's arm and one on Emil's. "Yes. Okay.
I will celebrate your union."

Dinner was a much more festive affair after that, although Clare had to
work at ignoring what might happen to her if—when—her bishop found
out what she had agreed to do.

Emil held up well throughout the meal and dessert, but by the time
Paul poured them coffee, his face was gray and strained. "Paul," he said,
"I'm afraid I've overdone it a bit. Could you . . ."

Russ pushed his chair back. "We ought to be going."

"No, no," Emil insisted. "I need a little help, but Paul would love to visit
some more."

"Do me a favor," Paul said, turning to Clare as he pulled Emil's chair away from the table and guided him to his feet. "Take the dogs for a turn around the meadow. They haven't had a chance to get much exercise since we've gotten home. I'll be down as soon as I've gotten Emil all set."

Russ glanced at Clare. "Sure," she said. She looked around the glass-topped table at Margy and Hugh.

"Not me," Margy said. "I'm going to sit here and digest that wonderful meal."

Hugh smiled apologetically at Clare. "Can you manage without me, Vicar? I hate to sound like a weed, but I've got allergies on top of allergies. My medication's holding them at bay, but if I go strolling through all that goldenrod, I'll turn into a giant inflated sinus. I won't bore you with the details. It would be too disgusting."

Clare laughed. "That's fine. You two save some coffee for us."

The men scraped their chairs away from the table as she stood, and, as if they had been eavesdropping, Gal and Bob bounded over. Russ and Clare both called their good-nights to Emil, who was making his way with difficulty through the French doors.

"After you," Russ said, sweeping his hand toward the edge of the patio. She stepped into the grass, the dogs dancing ahead. "So," he said. "This Hugh seems like a nice guy."

"Yeah."

"You been seeing much of him?" He fell into step beside her.

"We met at Peggy's party, that night I . . . the night you came to get me. He called me a few days later and asked if we could get together next time he was in Saratoga." She shrugged. "So here he is. It's our first time out together."

"Oh." He yanked a cluster of goldenrod off its stalk and flicked it, piece by piece, into the air. "You think this is going to go someplace?"

She looked him square in the face. "I thought," she said, speaking deliberately, "that it would be a good idea for me to start dating. It doesn't much matter with whom."

He looked down, brushing the goldenrod fuzz off his hands. They walked on in silence. The dogs flushed a red-winged blackbird off its perch on a maple sapling and leaped about wildly, trying to catch it. "I understand you visited Leo Waxman before he went into rehab," he said after awhile.

She welcomed the change of subject. "I felt like I had to apologize to him—for dropping him. You know the state's fired him for not reporting the PCB contamination in the quarry pool. Although I understand there are hardly any traces of it now." She tugged at a stem of Queen Anne's lace and snapped it off. "They've confirmed it was planted there?"

"That's what they tell me."

"Do you have any idea who did it?"

"I don't think we'll ever be able to tell." He shoved his hands in his pockets. "I know it wasn't my mother. If she had done it, she would have done it right, and stopped the project cold."

She laughed.

"He's going ahead with the construction. Did you know that?" he said.

"Who?"

"Opperman. He's renamed the business BWI/Opperman and hired some guy from out of state to act as the general. He bought the land outright, too. No more leasing."

"Peggy's sisters sold it to him?"

"I guess after everything that happened, they couldn't get rid of it fast enough."

"Huh. What do you want to bet he got the fire-sale rate?"

He laughed shortly. "He's one of those guys who can fall into a pile of manure and come up with a fistful of diamonds."

She paused. The sun had dropped below the mountains while they had been eating, and the gathering thunderheads were underlined by the dull red glow of the sunset's echo. The dogs, nosing into a woodchuck hole, were making snuffling noises. She breathed in the smell of the long, ripe grass. "It's beautiful out here."

"Yeah."

"I feel so bad for her." He didn't ask her to whom she was referring. "It was like she was poisoned by the contamination in the water. And it spread all around her, like a sickness. Everyone lost. No one won."

"Opperman did."

She swished the stalk of Queen Anne's lace through the tall grass. "Yeah, well, like you said." She paused. "He did win, didn't he?" She looked up at Russ. "He's got total control now—of the business, the land, the project."

Russ nodded.

"What you said about not knowing how Peggy knew Chris Dessaint?"

"Yeah?"

"Aren't there any connections between his life and hers?"

"Not that we can see. He worked at Shape Industries, which had no connection to her real estate and development business, he moved in completely different social circles, and, according to witnesses, he didn't use drugs. Wintour hasn't confessed, but Dr. Scheeler thinks Dessaint was knocked out by a blow to the head and then injected with an overdose of heroin. The only way in which he and she intersect is that he was one of those hard-core paintball players. But even if he did use her land once in awhile, she only dealt with the league organizers. Just made arrangements over the phone. She never laid eyes on the players."

She closed her eyes. A refreshing breeze sprang up, the leading edge of the front carrying the storm over the mountains. She shivered, and her arms goosefleshed. She opened her eyes. Looked at Russ.

"Opperman played paintball."

He looked as if she had slapped him.

"Remember? Stephen Obrowski said so. Opperman stayed in the area lots of weekends. He played paintball."

"Jesus," he said. "Jesus, you're right."

They stared at each other. It was a horrible feeling, like opening up a nice, neatly wrapped package to find something dead and rotting inside.

Russ strode off, his head bowed. She skip-hopped to keep up with him. "Opperman," he said. The dogs bounded beside them. "He could have seeded the pond himself before that poor sucker Waxman tested it."

"The night of the town meeting, Ingraham said something about them being involved once before on a project that had PCB contamination. He said they were still involved with the cleanup."

"So Opperman has access to some of that sludge. Waxman tests it, comes up with an off-the-chart level, and runs to Opperman, who offers him a job to keep him quiet. Then he makes sure Peggy knows. Maybe he even drops rumors around town." He stopped abruptly, causing Clare to stumble to a halt. "But there really is contamination in the groundwater. That little bit in the quarry pool couldn't have caused that."

She caught at his arm. "Don't you see? Leo Waxman was right. Even though he thought he was lying, he was right. The PCBs are coming from the Allen Mill cleanup."

Russ spun on his heel and struck off in another direction. "Peggy thinks she's about to be screwed out of her deal. Opperman—what? He whispers in her ear? Makes suggestions? If it was just the two of them, he wouldn't back away from the project? They could split the profits two ways instead of three?"

"And then he points her to Chris Dessaint, who has already proven his mettle by beating up some unlucky soul outside a Lake George bar."

"She does the rest. She thinks fast; we saw that. He must have known how smart she was."

"Not smart enough to know she was being manipulated."

He turned to her and clutched her upper arms. "She got rid of his partner for him. And then he got rid of her. In self-defense."

The speculation, the whole idea, gave her a sour feeling in her stomach. "Puppets playing puppets," she said. "And over them all, one puppet master." She shuddered. "God, it's vile. And she turned to him in the end. Like an abused woman running back to the man who beats her."

"Where else did she have to go? Maybe she thought he could protect her. After all, there was no warrant out for his arrest."

Russ was still holding Clare by the arms. "And now?" she asked.

He leaned forward until his forehead was touching hers. "And now nothing." His voice was flat. "This is all just you and me talking. I can't think of a shred of evidence to back up anything we've said. And even if we could prove he knew Dessaint, what's he guilty of? Giving away someone's phone number?"

She broke away from his grip. "No! That's wrong." She walked away, as if movement could bring about a different result. She wrapped her arms around herself. "He can't play with people's lives and then take his toys home, the winner. He can't. It's not . . . right."

"I do law enforcement, not good works. That's your field. Isn't ultimate justice supposed to rest with God anyway?"

"Stop it! Don't say it like that. Like it's a bad joke on us."

He moved toward her, the grass swishing around his legs. "I'm sorry."

"It's wrong."

"I know it is."

They were silent for a moment. Bob thumped into her legs and she bent down to scratch between his shoulders. "I don't believe that God allows bad things to happen, that He can choose thumbs-up or thumbs-down for us." She straightened and looked at Russ. "But sometimes it's very hard to resist asking Him, 'Why are you doing this?'"

His hands moved as if he wanted to hug her, but he stopped himself. "Come on. Let's take the dogs as far as the cow fence before we go back."

They walked through the fading light, the long grass rustling around them. Over the mountains, the sky was the color of bruised flesh. The

Berns coursed ahead, black-and-white flashes amid the grayed gold and darkening green. The fence, rusty barbed wire and weathered posts, stopped them. They stood side by side, looking at the mountains and the sky. They did not touch.

He took his glasses off and polished them on his shirtfront. "Remember when you were getting me out of the helicopter? You told me to hold on tight?" He replaced his glasses and looked back to the high horizon. "I'm still holding on." He glanced down at his hand. "I don't know how to let go."

"Holding on . . ." She bit her lip. Cleared her throat. "Doesn't do you much good when the person you're holding is falling, too."

Gal bumped the side of her knee. She reached down to scratch her head. Bob barked once, twice. She turned and looked back along the way they had walked. The house seemed a long way off from this perspective.

"We better head back," he said. "There's a storm coming."

"Yes," she said. "I know there is."

1. Should Clare be attempting to convince her congregation of her views on morality, or should she reflect their views?

2. When Clare assures Russ he isn't homophobic by pointing out that he has a gay friend, Russ says, "I never had to think about that." Is Russ homophobic? Do you think anyone else is, or are there simply different degrees of acceptance?

3. Millers Kill is in an economic slump—so much so that many citizens are willing to risk cancer for the certainty of jobs. Are they practical or reckless? Is this decision comparable to real-life decisions we, and people we know, have made?

4. Russ has valid fears about traveling by helicopter, based on his Vietnam experience. But he still gets into a helicopter. Why do you think he does so?

5. Is Leo Waxman a villain or a dupe? Why?

6. Do you think the falling helicopter—and the way Clare and Russ rescue each other—is a metaphor for their relationship? How so?

7. Weddings are a theme that runs through the novel—Diana and Cary, Trish and Kurt, Paul and Emil's desire to wed, Russ and Linda. What different aspects of marriage do you see in the story? Do you agree with Clare's assertion that "Divorce was like an animal gnawing its leg off to escape a trap before it dies. It should only be considered as the very last resort." Do you think Clare believes her own words?

8. *A Fountain Filled with Blood* features several particularly brutal assaults and murders. However, actual violence is never shown. Does this play down the severity of the crimes or increase it?

9. When arguing whether to reveal the connection between the assault victims, Clare implies the community will rally to protect its own. Russ, on the other hand, points out that in a small town, everyone thinks they "know" who is gay, leaving potential victims vulnerable. Which one of them is right? Is there a difference between being close-knit and insular? If small-town gossip can be deadly, who else in Millers Kill is in danger?

A
Reading
Group
Guide

St. Martin's
Griffin

10. At the time *A Fountain Filled with Blood* was written, same-sex marriage was still unavailable in New York. Would Emil Dvorak's and Paul Foubert's relationship be different if the book were written today? Does their relationship in the novel—partners, but unable to be legally recognized—parallel Russ and Clare's relationship?

11. At the very end of the book, Russ says, "There's a storm coming." What do you think will happen between Russ and Clare, and Russ and his wife? What do you want to happen?

12. The grim events of *A Fountain Filled with Blood* are interspersed with some levity: Margy Van Alstyne's protest and arrest and Clare's interactions with dashing financier Hugh Parteger. Do you like humor alongside the more serious moments of the mystery? Is it appropriate?

13. In interviews, the author has said she created Margy Van Alstyne to reflect the active, community-centered older women she knew. Do you know a Margy Van Alstyne? Is her activism realistic for a woman in her seventies? What do you think of her relationship with her son?

A Reading Group Guide

For more reading group suggestions,
visit www.readinggroupgold.com

St. Martin's
Griffin

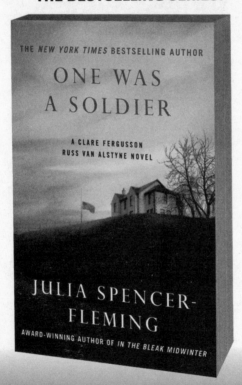